The Same Sides of a Coin

By

Dominic Wong

First edition October 2022

Book design by Karen Lloyd
Author photography by Owen Vachell

ISBN: 9798355493080
www.DominicWongBooks.co.uk

For Ollie and Milo
Two boys finding their place in the world.

The Same Sides of a Coin

Imagine a world where healed people helped hurt people heal and become strong.

James Cavitt

Part One

Rachel

Half of Rachel's tanned face rested on soft white sand. A few, coarse grains tickled the inside of her nose as she breathed in. Calm waves lapped quietly in the near distance. Sunlight danced painfully into her soft brown eyes, causing her to squint and blink. She turned her head, as much as she could, to look up at the bright light. Palm tree fronds breezed in the gentle wind, like fingers waving, scattering the sun's rays. Their trunks appeared to bend towards her, bowing heavy, green coconut-clustered heads at her. Or perhaps leaning over to take a closer look.

The humidity was high, even for this time in the morning, laying over her like an uncomfortable blanket. Sand stuck to her cheek, lodged inside her ear and speckled her light brown hair. It covered her peeling shoulders and legs, dusting the pretty red dress with the printed yellow butterflies which was being pushed up her dimpled thighs.

The events from the previous night still echoed around her head. As she angrily kicked her legs, she could smell the musty odours of the fire in the air. Or perhaps it was the ash lining her nostrils or rising from the fabric of the dress. In front of her was the makeshift camp, where they sat every evening watching the sunset over the horizon. In a parallel universe, she would be sunbathing in this paradise, letting the rays soak into her skin. Her stomach would be full of fresh, tropical fruit and a handsome man would be by her side.

Just like yesterday.

A dream come true for a backpacker trying to find themselves. All she wanted to do was heal from her scars and escape from her past. To figure out what her future could be. And in the meantime not cause any more trouble.

But here she was. A handkerchief shoved in her mouth.

Punishment for her stupidity.

Again.

It was all her fault, of course. She was the reason she was in this predicament. All she wanted to do was to move on. The sadness. The emptiness. Erase the pain and start again. The vicar had said it was His test. Was this really what He had in store for her? Even after what He had already put her through: the trauma, the heartache, the loss. It was such a burden for such a young woman. Twenty-one years old and she was already damaged – physically and mentally.

Now, the plastic ties cut into her wrists. Her shoulders were aching from her arms being forced behind her back.

The vicar's face came into her mind – blue eyes, balding head, hair escaping from his ears. He had such a kind face and always seemed to find the right words. Something about perseverance and being mature and complete. It was all part of His plan: her journey to greatness. She'd left on a whim to get away from it all. That was a few months ago. Here she was in the middle of nowhere, lying pinned down on a beach, her fate out of her control. Maybe this was another of His tests she needed to pass.

Her body relaxed into surrender.
Let's get this over with and move on. Like everything else.
Another scar to heal.
Then Nathan acted as if sensing her change.
Tears cascaded from her eyes onto the sand and a sob rose into her throat. She swallowed it, not wanting a sound to escape her lips.
Nathan looked up.
Strength grew with every word.
Here it was.
At last.
God's Will.

Chapter One

A noise behind the jungle canopy took everyone's attention. A buzzing sound grew louder. Hidden birds amongst the foliage chattered and squawked. The tops of the trees started to violently shiver and dance.

Beyond the greenery, a dirty yellow helicopter rose high into the sky. A red line ran around its base, interrupted by a jagged red line, imitating a heartbeat. Dust kicked up. It banked heavily to the side and disappeared. The trees stilled and the heat descended. Tourists dressed in brightly coloured sarongs turned their faces back to the path and trudged onwards.

"Well, that's the most exciting thing that's happened today," Rachel said out loud to no one in particular. Footsteps behind her suddenly stopped. It was the petite American girl with straggly blonde hair and dark roots, not much younger than her. Maddison was her name. Their paths had crossed several times through her travels. Always surrounded by a gaggle of boys, twirling her hair and giggling at their stories. Nobody paid much attention to Rachel.

"What do you mean?" Maddison said, screwing up her face in disbelief. Rachel felt her stomach drop.

"I mean," Rachel said, with a hint of nervousness. "This is all well and good. But it's a bit boring and…"

"Boring?"

Her shrill voice transported Rachel to a high-school movie where the cheerleader was about to start a fight with the dweeb. "This is one of *the* hidden treasures in Cambodia – in the World even. I mean it's a UNESCO World Heritage Site!"

Rachel gazed around at the dilapidated temple, undergrowth and leaves. As far as she could see thick, leafy vines snaked their way up into the dark green canopy like they were engulfing the ancient sandstone carvings and structures to keep it a secret away from prying eyes.

If she'd seen one, she'd seen them all. Rachel exaggerated a stifled laugh.

"I bet you hadn't even heard of UNESCO before you'd picked up your gap-year guidebook."

"Bite me, fatty," she said and huffed past, almost nudging Rachel's shoulder on the tight path. "Fucking cry baby," she spat as she went.

"What?"

Maddison spun around; her face contorted with disgust.

"Rach-y cry-baby," she sing-songed. "It's what we all call you."

Rachel involuntarily stepped backwards, her foot crunching on twigs and leaves.

"Whaddaya mean 'All?'"

The American moved towards her. Rachel could see light freckles over the bridge of her nose. Her heart was smashing against her ribs.

"Every time. Wherever you are, you cry. What is *that* about? Homesickness? Scared? No one want to be your friend? You hardly speak to anyone. You just hang around us like a bad smell. Always on the same bus. The same tour. The same café. Jesus, we've tried to get rid of you. Your vibe, man, it sucks." The girl threw her arms up in the air, making Rachel flinch. "We thought we'd lost you at the Bon Om Touk when you started bawling at that beggar – the one with the baby with no legs. But no, there you were at the next hostel."

Rachel suddenly felt lightheaded. She was aware of water cascading down her spine and pooling in the small of her back.

"What are you talking about?" she scoffed, her ears feeling like they were in a sauna.

"You're clearly not enjoying yourself *and* you're ruining it for the rest of us," Maddison spat. "Why are you even here?"

With a hand on her hip, she looked Rachel up and down and shook her head. Rachel pulled her sarong tighter around her waist and shoulders, unable to find words to reply.

"Just go home and lose some weight," Madison sneered, spun around, and ran along the path until she disappeared into the darkness of the trees.

"Bitch!" Rachel shouted, sticking her middle finger up through clenched fists.

Her body felt like collapsing in on itself as she stood alone amongst the leaves and thick stems, a kaleidoscope of greens and browns all around her.

It was true though. She did cry a lot. Sometimes spontaneously, sometimes triggered by something she'd seen, jolting her memory back home. That was okay though, wasn't it? *It's all part of life's experience*, Rachel kept telling herself. All part of the journey. *God's Will*.

Maddison was right. She wasn't enjoying it. Maybe she should go home. The colours were becoming less vibrant; the food no longer appealed; the vistas became boring. 'Traveller's fatigue', a German girl who never stopped talking said to her one evening over a steaming plate of noodles. She pictured the American girl, her pink sarong dancing around golden, tanned legs and incredibly tight shorts. An orange and blue pashmina draped loosely over her shoulders and torso, attempting to hide a tiny vest-top hugging her slim waist.

No love handles on her, she thought. No lumps, bumps, or scars. A magnet for her fellow, horny backpackers. She couldn't compete with that.

Rachel looked around and stretched her back. The sun was high and the heat was bearable. The tips of three temples jutted up behind the canopy into a vibrant blue cloudless sky.

No.

To go back now meant she would never return. She would slip onto the conveyor belt of normality. Besides, a nagging feeling kept rising in her chest that wouldn't go away. The feeling that she was traversing a well-worn road. Crappy hostels and bed & breakfasts (all with WIFI and English-translated menus) filled with middle-class youngsters pretending to be slumming it on a budget when safety, money and a consulate were never far away. Most of them had smartphones anyway. Even on the remotest of beaches or on a mountain top temple, a message alert would break the ethereal atmosphere.

A sanitised adventure.

It was far too safe. If she was to heal, she needed to get away from these clowns for a start and get her mojo back. This adventure wasn't her. Even though she was only a couple of years older than these teenagers, she *felt* so much older than them. Choose a different route. Her route, away from the well-trodden backpacking path. Forget who she was and define who she'll be. To set her place in the world. To find herself. Whatever that entailed.

She didn't want to be like them because she wasn't one of them. There was no way she'd be wearing a crop top like Maddison any time soon, not with her stretch marks. Yes, she was more mature – not in age but in life's experience.

The death of her baby was always going to age her quicker than them.

Chapter Two

Rachel huffed as she folded her arms in frustration in the plain white office. Her black blazer and pencil-striped skirt tightened around her. Fluorescent lights starkly illuminated a white table and grey filing cabinets. Her black leggings started to feel itchy against her pale skin.

"I ain't got no attitude," she spat at the man in the open-topped shirt and blazer. "It's you that's got the attitude."

Her new boss rolled his eyes, keeping silent.

"Look, you're making this job boring. I got a 2:1. I'm better than arranging your diary and filing crap."

"Everyone has to start somewhere Rachel," he sighed as if talking to a child. "You're straight out of university, you need some experience under your belt."

"By making cups of tea?"

The man shrugged his shoulders. "It's how it works. You start at the bottom and work your wa-"

"Spare me the corporate bullshit."

He took a breath in and shuffled some papers on his desk. "Good luck, Rachel, whatever you do," he said and pointed to the door.

"Screw you," she said, insolently raising her middle finger and stomping out of the room.

She made a point of slamming the door behind her. Faces in the open-plan office looked up, then wordlessly back to their screens. An awkward silence descended as she grabbed her coat and bag and strode out into the cold London air.

She was fuming. What she needed were validation and flattery. She sent a WhatsApp message to her friend's group.

'Sacked from job. Who's up for a night out? 7 p.m., in town. I wanna get wasted', she typed.

Her phone immediately pinged with supportive messages. They consoled her, telling her to stuff that job anyway, something better was around the corner.

That night, she downed the Vodkas and Red Bulls on the two-for-one offers without a care, trying to get rid of the negative vibes running around in her head. She was sure she'd had a kebab and chips to make her feel better and some guy had come on to her at the end of the night. And she must have agreed to go back to his place because she could still hear her friends cackling and laughing, telling her to be careful 'the dirty stop out'. His face was sketchy in detail, but she could definitely recall him slobbering over her mouth, down her body and between her legs.

The next morning, she snuck out whilst he lay curled up with the duvet wrapped around him, his head obscured by a pillow sticking to his face. The bright morning sunlight made her squint as her head throbbed. She turned a corner, threw up the kebab and hailed a passing black taxi. She closed her eyes and hoped the swaying motion inside her head would soon disappear.

When she missed her period the next month she cried alone in her flat, violently hitting her stomach and willing time to reverse.

How could she be so stupid?

When the test came back positive, her friends had rallied around her, telling her it would be all right, offering to go to the clinic to get rid of it – they'd be there every step of the way. Of course, her mum had told her she had to keep it. Her dad the same. It was 'God's Will' and He had chosen Rachel. They weren't even angry. She'd made a half-hearted attempt to find the guy but couldn't remember where he lived or what he looked like, least of all his name. Her phone buzzed constantly from friends asking if she was okay and giving advice. It was all so overwhelming and confusing and so much to think about – whether to keep it or get an abortion. Even that word made her feel sick.

One afternoon, her parents surprised her when they brought along their vicar to her flat. How dare they! What could she do? Turn him away? As the short man she had seen so often in the pulpit reverently cross the threshold, her fists balled and she shot daggers through the air at her mum. Noticing her narrowed eyes, her dad escorted his wife out as soon as the kettle was on.

Rachel had her hands on the kitchen surface, her face red and twisted.

"I understand", he said tentatively. "It's not a situation you'd thought you'd be in. But here we are. God often has a plan for us. Of bigger and better things. You need to trust His instincts."

His soft voice was calming and neutral, his eyes as blue as the sky.

She looked up to the ceiling, tears forming and threatening to spill.

"But I can't be a mum. I'm too young."

"I've met a lot of mums younger than you," he said, helping himself to the chocolate biscuits Rachel's mum had opened. "And they are wonderful mothers. Plus, your mum and dad are so supportive." He looked around the open-plan kitchen and living room, a London flat her parents had bought her as a graduation present.

"But a baby? I'd be a single mum. People would talk. Look at me diff –"

"And I would say, let them. You can't control what people think or do. That's on them. That has nothing to do with you."

"I couldn't take it. I mean my friends, they would –"

"Again," he interrupted, his voice firm but gentle. "Your friends will rally around you. The good ones will support you."

Rachel sniffed.

"I put a post on Insta and the first reply I had was 'Miss Piggy's having a piglet'."

The vicar sighed and shook his head.

"A bit of advice. Delete social media from your life. It does more harm than good. As I said, the good ones will support you."

"You know, when I found out I was pregnant – I won't lie – I loved the attention. All my friends messaging me and mum and dad fussing. But then, you know, I got a baby growing inside me. Like a real human."

"It's a miraculous thing."

"But a child? I just can't see how I could raise a —"

"People do," he said, his forehead crinkling. "They figure it out. There is always help available." He motioned his eyes up to the ceiling. "I'm not saying, whatever you decide, is going to be easy. Whether you keep the baby or not, that's a choice only you can make. But know this: life contains both dark *and* light. There will be love around you."

"I'm not sure about that. Mum'll probably disown me," she said, looking down.

"Now, that's not true, is it?" he said, lowering his face to make eye contact. "Whatever happens, your parents will be there to hug and support you. That is something you can be one hundred percent sure about. I've known them for a long time. Longer even than you." He chuckled and stood up. "Your parents will always be there for you, no matter what. And so will He."

Rachel's mind raced through a million different possibilities. It was so confusing.

"I don't know what to do," she said.

The vicar placed his hand on top of her hand.

"You'll know," he said with knowing eyes. "God will guide you."

The next few weeks were a whirlwind of activity, mainly on the part of her mum and dad who found a new lease of life in their forthcoming grandchild. Nappies started to fill her flat, bottles, sterilisers, little outfits, and packages from Auntie Barbara with knitted booties, tops and hats. Her dad took her to road-test buggies, making a checklist of the pros and cons of various models.

How does this one feel love, do you think you could manage that?

And then him cuddling her as she sobbed in the middle of the car seat aisle.

Her dad fussed over putting a crib together for a whole afternoon and unveiled it with great pomp and pride. He had even hung a mobile from the ceiling; airplanes, cars and trucks softly chasing each other in a circle to a tinny soundtrack.

With so much going on, her indecision had chosen for her; soon it became too late for an abortion.

God's Will.

Her belly was growing and stretch marks were appearing. Her clothes – young people's clothes – started to be too small for her and her breasts became sore. *A normal girl my age wouldn't have to deal with this,* she said to herself whilst looking in the mirror. Tears would burst out at any given moment: in the make-up aisle in the supermarket, in a café with her friends as they recounted the previous evening's debauchery or scrolling through other people's perfect lives on Insta. Even her daily viewings of Home and Away slouched on the sofa made her an emotional wreck.

But mostly she cried when she was alone in her home, looking at the empty crib, the tiny pairs of socks waiting to be filled or the jars of baby formula lining her cupboard. The Bank of Mum and Dad had eased money worries, but she knew it wasn't going to last.

Like the baby, at some point, she would have to stand on her own two feet.

It was a Saturday night. Her mum had just left after an afternoon of cooking, faffing and tidying up. Rachel's phone was pinging from WhatsApp messages of friends arranging a night out while she was sitting on a rocking chair rubbing her belly, her ankles sore, her back throbbing. She shut down her phone. Saturday nights were going to be very different. Boys and girls names were swirling around her head after her mum started throwing out names of relatives and her friends' granddaughters.

'Matthew, that's a solid boy's name,' her mum would say. 'Your great-grandfather was a Matthew. Or what about Jacob? That's trendy these days. Vicki's girl had a Jacob. Of course, you can't beat Daniel or Joshua. Or Noah. If it's a girl Mary is a goodun' but a tad old-fashioned these days….'

One of her friends had sent a book full of lists of names. Rachel had started to flick through it, but the names and meanings were just so overwhelming. She put it down thinking she would open it nearer the time. Never mind growing the baby and then looking after it, the name it would have forever was such a responsibility.

Another package had arrived from Auntie Barbara, full to the brim with knitted socks, bobble hats and cardigans in a variety of different colours. Rachel laid the items out on her lap, smiling inwardly at the kind gesture and the thought of her baby in them, taking photos and sending them back.

She peeled down her maternity trousers, exposing her round tummy and balanced a blue hat on the top, a pink cardigan around her belly button and put two white socks on her forefingers, making them dance on her thighs, imagining what it would be like – just the two of them in on a Saturday night. She reached over to a stack of bottles on a side table, slid the top off and pretended to feed the baby, pushing the plastic teat against her skin between the hat and the cardy. For a moment, she sat there cooing and ahhing in her fictionalised world, knowing that the reality would come soon enough. She imagined waking up, looking over and seeing the baby sleeping peacefully in its cot, its tiny hands moving by itself, its first steps and first words. She thought about taking it to school, watching it toddle off into the classroom and sitting down next to a new friend. She dreamed of having chats with it and discussing their day, their hopes and their futures.

It.

He. She.

A girl would be nice.

She pictured her mum and dad's face when they first met their granddaughter, beaming so proudly and wanting to show her off to their friends and family.

The blue bobble hat fell off her belly and Rachel came back to the present, her place empty, the air still. A little kick made her instinctively rub the spot, a smile spread on her lips. Maybe it wouldn't be so bad after all.

Her and her little baby in the world together.

Chapter Three

Behind her, coming through the undergrowth, Rachel heard a guide lead a tour group.

"Angkor Wat became a Buddhist temple by the end of the 12th century but was originally dedicated to the Hindu god Vishnu. It's significance...."

She moved forward along the stony path into the jungle where Madison had disappeared. It was there that she decided to try travelling alone for a while. Really alone. No one else to share decisions, take charge of her destiny or bail her out if she struggled with the language or for bitches like Madison to slag her off if she got upset. No more latching on to others or joining groups. Let fate decide what happened to her.

God's Will.

The largest religious monument in the world was as good a place as any to start her newfound direction. The Thai border was only a couple of hours away and there were loads of buses to Bangkok. She closed her eyes and took a deep breath, allowing herself to smile a little. It would be amazing. She imagined herself traversing the huge country without help, finding out that her own company was enough. Standing on her own two feet. No one judging her. What if she became happy? What if she found someone?

Amongst the sightseeing trips, the food, the long journeys and the hostels, Rachel's travels were littered with stories of ordinary travellers doing extraordinary things. Tales went around of people setting up a yoga practice on a far-out beach or becoming hermits at the top of isolated mountains or converting to Buddhism and taking a vow of celibacy. How many of those stories were myths, exaggerations, or truths she didn't have a clue, but the mysticism of such things propelled a hidden desire to go and find them. Maybe even become enlightened herself and find something worthwhile to do. Like building a school or digging a well. Along her travels, she listened intently to these stories of travellers who had left the western world which made her tummy fizz with excitement.

Sometimes a name would crop up twice, or a familiar story slightly altered. Some would say it was a woman, others would say it was a man. Chinese whispers would embellish a well-worn story to the point of ridiculousness. Still, they were fascinating, charming and desirable for the wistful traveller in search of adventure.

What if *she* became a legendary story that other backpackers spoke about?

As the sun beat down on her, a smile crept on her lips.

But it quickly disappeared.

A knot formed in her stomach. Blood drained from her face.

What if she got robbed? What if she hated it? What if she got into trouble? What if she couldn't be understood? So many what-ifs.

But.

But.

She pushed those thoughts to the back of her mind. There were going to be bumps along the way. She would have to embrace them. And she was sure He would guide her.

Getting to Bangkok was a doddle. The nine-hour bus journey from Angor Wat ended at the Khao San Road: a tragedy of tacky shops, bars, dirty hostels and the smell of weed. As Rachel disembarked from the cool air-conditioning, a swarm of local hawkers surrounded the door, enveloping her as the heat did, chattering in broken English for bargain hotels and free drinks (*"cheaper than Tescos!"*).

Bangkok was a bustling, dirty metropolis: noisy, hectic and big. Maybe it was the heavy, hot air but the countryside called out to her. She needed to get out. Minutes from getting off the bus, she was squashed in a tuk-tuk, weaving in and out of traffic, the air rushing across her face. Her heart was beating fast, and she was breathless with fear.

Or was it exhilaration?

She grinned like an inane child as she enjoyed the moment, holding on for dear life as the little three-wheeler came startling close to lorries, scooters and cars.

The tuk-tuk flew away in a haze of dust after Rachel had clambered out at the bus station. A line of backpackers was queuing to get on to a double-decker coach, ready for the twelve-hour journey to Phuket. She'd no desire to go to another backpacker haven so she looked at the departure board and spotted "Trang". She checked her map and saw it was in the middle of Thailand, surrounded by a national park. It looked a long way, but she was in no hurry. On the bus, she could see more of the country. The ageing coach smelt of fried food and sweat, the floor sticky. Locals and students with plastic bags tied at the top and children with dirty clothes filled the seats. There were no Westerners that she could see.

Perfect.

An ancient-looking woman smiled a toothy grin at her as she squeezed into an empty seat by the window. Her eyes were wide as the bus lurched through the city, beeping and honking its way through the impossible traffic. The grey and browns of the city turned to the greens and blues of the countryside. Eventually, the rocking of the bus and the stifling heat made her eyes droop. By dusk, she was fast asleep.

A disturbance from the seat behind woke her from her slumber. The bus had stopped. There was movement and rustling and people were standing in the aisle, delving into their bags, and stretching their backs from the uncomfortable seats. The front door of the bus was open and people were wandering out into the pitch black. A Thai teenager, no older than 18, smiled at her confused face.

"We stop for bathroom."

"Oh" she replied, rubbing her eyes.

"Twenty minute," he countered, holding up two fingers.

"Thanks" was all she mustered as she unfurled herself from the seat. She stuffed essentials and valuables from her backpack that was squeezed overhead into her daypack – money, passport, toiletries – and moved down the gangway. Out of the other side of the bus, she spotted a couple of concrete shacks lit up – one with plastic chairs and tables outside and the other with crisp packets and bottles of cola in front. Stepping from the air-conditioned bus, the humid air hit her. The hairs on her skin stood to attention. Despite it being night, the heat opened her pores and she felt sweat flood from her skin. Like a moth, she followed the others to the bright lights shining in the darkness.

The air inside the shop was ice-cold, and goosebumps immediately rose on her skin. She took a few dusty snacks from the shelves, bumping into a couple of other passengers in the tight aisles. Whilst she paid, she asked the weathered attendant where the toilet was, saying the word slow and loud: *toil - et*. He pointed to the back of the shop as he handed back her change and took the items off the next person in line. Rachel scooped up her snacks and headed to the back of the shop. There was no sign of a doorway amongst the rows of packaged bread and buns. She asked a Thai woman browsing the sweets if she knew where the toilet was, and she pointed to the back wall, arching her arm to signal it was on the other side, then pinched her nose and gave a 'yuck' expression. She sighed to the woman, used to unsanitary holes-in-the-ground by now.

Outside, the wide vegetation swallowed the unnatural light. A dimmed bulb hung outside two concrete cubicles with a corrugated tin roof that served as toilets. Pushing one of the two doors, a shriek accompanied the creaking hinges and Rachel mumbled an apology to the woman inside. She tried the second door and the soft light illuminated all sorts of horrible sights and smells.

From behind the block came a rustling and moaning. A small Thai woman stumbled out of the undergrowth, momentarily shocking Rachel. She smiled a wide grin and held up her hands in apology.

It's better in there, she nodded to the trees, *than in there,* she seemed to imply as she glanced to the cubicles with a wink. Rachel looked over at the cubicles and nodded back, theatrically rolling her eyes. She ventured into the trees, nervously dropped her light cotton trousers and squatted, keeping a beady eye alert for anyone approaching. A bug landed on her shin and she attempted to brush it away whilst keeping her balance. Then, high above, a squawking noise made her jump and urine splashed onto her trousers around her ankles. Even in the dark, she could see a wet patch growing.

Embarrassing.

She cursed loudly and the squawking bird responded with a cacophony of noise, encouraging its neighbours to join in. A rustle deeper in the jungle pricked her ears. She was half squatting and half turning when a ruckus by the shops caught her attention. The bus's engine started up and shouts cut through the air.

The bus must be getting ready to leave.

Panicking, Rachel abruptly stood up, hitting her head on a thick branch. She grabbed her scalp where the pain cut and stumbled forward. The material around her ankles tightened and she fell where she'd peed. Her hand instinctively shot out to regain balance and she grimaced in pain as a thorn dug its way into her palm. She tried to examine her hand, but the dim light made it impossible to see. She struggled to pull up her underwear and trousers in the tight space, brushing off dirt and leaves that had stuck to her damp skin. On her haunches, she slunk crab-like out of the undergrowth whilst putting her arm above her head to protect it. Emerging into the clearing, she inspected her palm in the light from the toilet cubicles. A thorn only a centimetre long was wedged into the muscle beneath her thumb. She pinched her skin to try and get it out. At the same time, she could hear the unmistakable sound of tyres on gravel as her bus moved on to hard asphalt. With her heart in her throat, she sprinted after the bus, screaming, yelling and waving her arms to get its attention. The bus replied by extinguishing its yellow flashing indicator, a cloud of smoke following it into the pitch black. Her backpack and clothes disappeared. She swore loudly after it, a panic rising in her body. She let out an ear-piercing scream, then a silence came down. Crickets filled the void. A fly landed on her neck as tears filled her eyes.

A calm came over her. A realisation of fate.

At least she had what she wanted.

She was all alone in the middle of Thailand.

Chapter Four

It was a typical English spring day with candyfloss clouds against a light blue sky. Bright yellow daffodils stood in clumps amongst green grass and a trace of pine wafted in the chilly air. Rachel sat on the park bench, pulling her wool jacket tighter around her neck. Her belly was the size of a small football and she found she needed to sit down more often, taking the weight off her swelling ankles.

In a playground opposite, a toddler was being thrust on a swing by a bored mum, scrolling through her phone with one arm whilst the other mechanically pushed the child when it returned. Another small girl in a yellow duffle coat sat alone on one end of a seesaw, busying herself with a posy of grass and daisies. A doll with straw-yellow hair stuck out of her pocket. A buggy stood sentry at the gate along with a pink scooter, stickers attached to its metal pole. Rachel observed the scene whilst nonchalantly stroking the black coat over the top of her growing bump. Unable to explain it, she just knew that a little girl was growing inside her. A feeling. She pictured herself coming along to this park, standing by the swing, pushing a giggling, screaming girl as she pretended to push higher and faster, then scooping her out and brushing their noses together.

A couple of squirrels drew her attention, scampering in the tall grass next to the bench before running up a tree and freezing, looking down for any threats. Along the path, a slim woman pushed her buggy confidently in front of her at a brisk pace, her long bleached blonde hair bouncing in rhythm to her strides, wisps flying behind her. Her make-up was impeccable, making her cheeks glow and her striking eyes stand out. Her clothes were trendy and well-fitting, black tights riding up to a black-and-white checked mini skirt, a long, open coat flapped behind her, and a pastel red top complemented the look. Only a spot of dark liquid on her top spoiled the look of faultlessness. She swung her buggy around when she approached the bench, peered inside and gave a satisfied smile. As she ran her fingers through her hair, she looked over at Rachel and gave a small smile.

"How long to go?" she asked, pointing at Rachel's bump.

"Oh, um," Rachel spluttered. Usually, people asked how far gone she was. She did a rough calculation. "Three months left," she said with a grimace.

"Ah, lovely. Well, enjoy the peace and quiet whilst you can." She peered back inside her pram. "All quiet on the Western Front," she said to herself and continued to prune her hair.

"How old is ….?" she enquired, trailing off not knowing which article to use.

"*She*'s four months. Her name's Natalie," came the reply. "Do you know what you're having?"

"No. Waiting for the surprise."

"Oh," came a stiff retort. "I decided to find out. There are enough 'surprises' on the day, trust me! Plus, you can sort stuff out you know. It's so much more practical." Rachel stayed silent, contemplating what 'surprises' might happen on the day.

"Oh, I mean, it's totally your choice of course," she backtracked as if she saw Rachel's face contort. "I didn't mean to… you know."

Rachel looked up at the woman. She looked so perfect, so in control of everything. Her hair was clean and straight, her clothes smart and coordinated. It wasn't a picture she imagined she would look like four months in. She could have been the nanny.

"It's fine. I haven't thought about the 'day' yet," Rachel said, looking her up and down. She inched closer to the woman.

"What's it like? You know, really like?" she pointed to the bump and made a motion with both her hands toward the ground. "I mean, I know it's going to hurt, but …" The woman smiled back at her; a perfect row of white teeth glistened back at her. A whiff of perfume tickled Rachel's nose.

"Oh, it's wonderful. It really is. Knowing that a baby, your baby, is being born from you. At the time, during the birth, you can't think of anything else but the pain. I'm not going to lie; it hurts like hell. But afterwards… the only way I can describe it is that nothing else matters in the world. It's like everything disappears except you and that baby. You don't think of anything – family, friends, work, bills. I just felt a massive relief that it was over and this little, um, creature, was on my chest and I was its protector." She looked distantly into the space in front, her head cocked to the side, remembering the time she just described.

"Really?" Rachel said, in awe. "Did it really feel like that?"

"Yes. Well, that's what I remember. It was the happiest, most fulfilling time. Everyone talks about the pain, like in the ante-natal classes because that's what everyone's afraid of. Is that what you are afraid of?"

"Yes. I haven't been to any birthing classes though."

The woman flicked her head around sharply, her blonde hair spraying out and then resting in its place.

"Oh, you must. It's an eye-opener and you get to meet women who are at the same stages as you, share your experiences you know? I tell you, most of the things that I was worried about, they were having the same worries." She reached into her mouth and plucked out a wrinkled ball of gum with her thumb and forefinger, tore a small corner of tissue that she'd got from her pocket and wrapped it up.

"And what about, you know, after it came out? Did it latch okay, what was it like when you brought it home?"

"She," the woman corrected. "Yeah, I've been lucky. I haven't had many problems. The other girls in my group have had problems with breastfeeding, and Natty has been sleeping okay– not through the night but bearable."

The woman appeared to take having a baby in her stride, like completing a project at work or buying a car. How did she seem so calm and collected with a four-month-old? Rachel was sure she was going to be a wreck.

"But you know you just got to keep going. The one thing you got to remember," she raised her forefinger and pointed it to the sky as she turned to face Rachel full on, adjusting her bum on the park bench. "If I can just give you one piece of advice?"

She looked at Rachel expecting an answer. Rachel nodded enthusiastically.

"You've got to adjust *your* life to the baby. The baby doesn't know what's going on, what time bedtime is or when she should wake up, or when she should be eating. So many parents think that the baby should just blend into their life, their schedule. Nah. You can't expect the baby to sleep when you want to sleep or eat when you want it to eat. Not yet. I can't believe that some of my mum friends do the controlled crying. You know about that?"

Rachel nodded, thinking it was a reasonable way to get babies to sleep through the night. She couldn't bear to be up at stupid o'clock, probably when her friends were getting home from the nightclubs.

"It's a baby, they need attention, and comfort and, you know, cuddles. When she feels safe, then she will relax and get into a routine."

Rachel's mum had been talking about routines for a while.

The woman peered back inside the pram, reached in and fiddled with the blanket. They both sat in silence for a while, letting their thoughts envelop them. The woman turned her head slightly and dipped her eyes to Rachel's hands. A concerned look etched across her face.

"Do you have a support network? You know people around you to help?"

"Yeah, my mum and dad," Rachel replied indifferently. "They've been great."

"Yeah, but anyone else?"

"My mates said they are going to help. They've been good too."

The woman let out a sigh and looked at Rachel straight on, twisting her body.

"And the dad?"

No one had ever asked her so directly before, especially a stranger. Most had tried to avoid the question.

Rachel shrugged her shoulders and let them fall heavily.

"One-night stand. Don't know who he is. I seriously can't remember much of that night."

The woman reached over and confidently put her hands over Rachel's.

"Me too," she replied with a pained smile.

Rachel glanced up. The woman nodded ruefully.

"Seriously? But you look so, so, with it!" she said, a bit too loudly. "I mean, you look so…."

"Thanks. I'll take that as a compliment." She lifted her left hand and spread her fingers out, proving there was no ring. She used the same hand to flick her hair as she put it back on her lap.

"Yeah," she nodded, "My mum and dad help too. Well, my stepdad. He's been an angel. Never had kids of his own and is bloody brilliant with her. I live with them so it's a big help. Which means I can look after myself a bit too." Rachel's shock didn't elude her face. This woman who looked so confident, perfect and together was in the same boat as her. A weird sense of relief flooded her. She immediately felt a kinship with the stranger – could she be a new friend?

"Did you, erm, try to find him?" Rachel asked, tentatively.

"To be honest, no. I'd been through a bit of a rough time at work. Well, with a work colleague. And went off the rails a bit. In my work, champagne and lines are the norm and I kinda got pressured by a friend of mine. I woke up one morning and he'd gone. Couldn't remember much of the night before except that I knew *stuff* had happened. And you?"

"Yeah, similar. Except I left his place and didn't know where the hell I was, jumped in a cab and fell asleep." Rachel looked up at her, noticing her eyes were unfocused. "Mum and dad were pretty convincing. For me to have it. I think every day whether it was the right choice."

"And it will be the right choice," the woman replied looking right back into Rachel's eyes, patting her hand. "I promise you. Look, let's swap numbers. Us single mums have to stick together, right?"

The words 'Single Mum' still shocked Rachel. She'd said it to herself over and over and was sure those were the words other people were saying but had never heard anyone say it out loud to her.

"Yes, yes that would be great. Thank you."

"Of course! No problem," she said as she pulled out her phone from her pocket, flicked up and fiddled with the apps.

"As I said, we've got to stick together, okay..." she trailed off, hoping for Rachel to fill in the blank.

"Oh. Rachel."

"Okay Rach, what's your number?"

Rachel gave out her number as she reached in her bag for her phone, opened it up and brought up the Contacts app. The phone rang and vibrated in her hand.

"That's me."

She cancelled the call and brought up the row of numbers in the address book.

"Sorry, what's your name," Rachel asked.

"Oh, yeah sorry. It's Jessica," she replied. "But everyone calls me Jess."

Chapter Five

As Rachel watched the red lights of the bus disappear around a corner, the bright lights of the shop and the café shone like a beacon in the darkness. A Thai woman wiping down tables with a ragged dishcloth had her eyes on her. Rachel walked slowly back, willing the tears to stay where they were.

What was she going to do? How would she get her rucksack back?

The café owner stood up straight as she approached.

"Missed bus huh? You not first," she sighed. "You sleep in café 100 Baht."

"Um, what time is the next bus?" Rachel said pointing to her wrist.

"To Malaysia? Tomorrow."

"No, no – to Trang."

"Oh Trang? Not far. Walk maybe 8 hours. Drive one hour. Bus tomorrow, maybe eleven. Quicker to walk. Or sleep in café 100 Baht." Rachel considered it for a split second before tears started to flow. She felt lost, in the middle of nowhere, with her backpack on its way to Trang without her. The humid air suffocated her.

"It okay, no cry," the café owner said with a frown on her face. She got a red plastic chair and motioned her to sit. "No money?"

"A little, my bag..." she sniffed, using her hands to draw a large bag, "is on the bus."

"Tsk. No cry little girl," the woman said as she reached up and put both her hands around Rachel's cheeks. They were warm and hard. She gently lowered her face so that their eyes met. Squeezing slightly harder than Rachel expected, the older woman's dark brown eyes penetrated hers like she was looking directly at her soul. After what seemed like an abnormal amount of time, she finally let go.

"Okay, wait."

She hollered in the direction of the shop and the bushes and trees behind the shacks bustled to life, squawking and rustling like a giant had been roused from its sleep. The man who had served her came out, rubbing his hands on his already grubby jeans. The woman shouted at the man in Thai, pointing to Rachel and to the distance where the bus had gone. The man rattled something back and walked back into the shop.

"It okay, little girl. You come home with us. Not far," she said in a kind, motherly voice. She probably wasn't that old, mid-thirties perhaps, but her chaffed hands and deep wrinkles told a life of toil and hardship. Running a café in the sticks must do that to you. Rachel jumped up. "Oh no, no. I sleep in café. It's okay. No trouble."

"Tsk. No trouble," the woman repeated with a wide smile. "No trouble. Hard floor in café. Not nice. Come." She gently took Rachel's hand and lifted her from the plastic chair.

"No pay. But you. Chair. Here," she said as she stacked the chair Rachel had been sitting on. She pointed to the others.

"You, help. Quicker!"

Rachel willingly obliged as the woman continued to wipe the tables, keeping one eye on her as they cleaned up for the night. Rachel worked quickly and moved the stacked chairs under the corrugated tin roof. She heard the shop door shut and watched the man lock up with a single key. The man must have been about the same age as the woman, his dirty misshapen clothes making him seem older. He had several plastic carrier bags tied up at the top which he gathered and walked out towards the road.

"Come. We go."

"No trouble?" Rachel said.

"No trouble little girl" she replied with a half-smile. As they caught up with the man, Rachel reached out to the plastic bags.

"Please," she said. "I help." The man grinned and gave half the bags to Rachel with a nod. The three of them walked in a line down the rudimentary road. As they left the lights of the shops, her eyes adjusted to the dark and could just make out where the tree line finished and the sky started. Crickets chirped on either side of them in the black, occasionally a rustle sounded deep in the undergrowth of the trees surrounding them. Rachel kept looking around, expecting something to jump out. Stars shone brightly, providing the only illumination for the trio. The man and the woman mechanically walked on, seemingly unaware of the noises. The woman looked over to Rachel and glanced up and down.

"Where from? America?"

"No, England," she responded, glad of the distraction.

"HAHA!" blurted the man, shattering the quiet, "DAVID BECKHAM!", and he swept his right foot out as if taking a shot on goal, his carrier bags jiggled with the motion.

"Erm, where are we?" Rachel enquired.

"Nearby Bo Hin," the woman answered, swivelling her head behind her to motion where the village sat. That name sounded vaguely familiar. She'd heard it before, maybe even written it in her diary of foreigners' tales – some guy took a vow of silence or something. If they were about an hour from Trang, it meant she was further south than Phuket and close to the sea. Somewhere in the middle of Thailand's long body.

"Sea?" Rachel said, pointing in no particular direction and moving her arm in a wave motion.

"Sea," the man replied, pointing directly in front of them with the hand used to carry the plastic bags. "Not far. Pretty. Sun…" and he slowly lowered his arm indicting the setting sun.

They reached a dirt track going off to the left after walking for what seemed like an hour. The loose gravel slid under their feet, more so for the man who had been dragging his worn-out plimsolls the whole time. Clouds had covered the stars. It was so dark Rachel couldn't see where the road ended. A palm tree branch occasionally tickled her cheek as she went down the dusty road. She could just make out the outline of pineapple-like trunks in the darkness. The air had a chill to it as the heat and humidity evaporated with the night. Eventually, she saw the shadow of a dwelling in the distance. A satellite dish balanced on a ribbed-shaped roof. As she got closer, she saw a small golden shrine standing guard in front of the building. The man laid down his bags on the porch of the house. As he reached into his pocket, he turned his head slightly and motioned Rachel to put down her bags. A nervousness crept into her. Every instinct told her to trust these two people – local business owners, maternal instincts, friendliness to a stranger. But she couldn't help looking around, for help or a way out. Just in case.

The man opened the door and the woman encouraged Rachel inside.

"Come. Please."

A click illuminated a solitary bulb in the middle of an almost-bare room. In its centre was a weathered rug, flanked by a sofa which had seen better days and a table with a plastic covering and two plastic chairs, identical to the ones she just stacked at the café. On the wall, beneath a framed picture of Buddha, was a shrine to the great man himself. Perched on a thin cupboard sat a golden statue with two incense sticks on either side of him. A bowl of white, cooked rice sat as an offering in front of his large belly.

"Please," the woman motioned. "Sleep." She bowed her head and swept her arms towards the back of the house, to a room on the left, where a solitary single mattress lay on a rusty frame against the far wall beneath a window with no pane.

"Sleep," the woman ordered and ushered her inside.

"Oh. Thank you. Thank you." Rachel replied. The woman responded by clasping her hands together in prayer and bowed her head, her thumbs touching her nose. She reached up and touched Rachel's forehead above and between her eyes.

"Sleep," she nodded with the kindest eyes Rachel had ever seen.

Chapter Six

Jess had been part of Rachel's life for two weeks now, but it felt like they had been friends forever – hanging out and messaging each other. Jess'd been so welcoming, like two sisters sharing an unequivocal bond brought together by the coincidence of being young single mums.

The first time Jess invited her to her home she was so nervous, like meeting a boyfriend's mum and dad for the first time, that she brought a bunch of flowers with her. An older man opened the door, his large round belly underneath a white vest, and a well-worn pair of tracksuit bottoms completed the look. He looked at her and then down to the flowers.

"You know the last time Jess brought a girl here all sorts of crazy things happ –"

"Jim!" Jess' voice shouted from within. "Leave her alone! Come in."

Jim moved his back to the wall allowing Rachel to enter. She had to turn so she was face-to-face with him as she inched past. Their bellies brushed each other as his eyes didn't waver from hers. She felt he was judging her. What had Jess said?

"Mine's due in three months too," he chortled. She could feel his eyes on the back of her head as she walked toward Jess.

"Hold on love," he called after her. "That won't do, no, no, no."

Rachel stood still and she could hear Jim paddle up to her. He stroked her hair, allowing bunches of it through his fingers.

"When was the last time you had this blow-dried?"

Jess appeared around a door frame.

"Oh jeez, sorry Rach. He's a hairdresser. Leave it off Jim!" she said with a hint of warmth.

"Come on love, take a seat, let me sort it out," Jim said, escorting her to the kitchen. He grabbed a chair, spun it around, motioned Rachel to sit and left the room.

"He is a REALLY good hairdresser," Jess said, taking the flowers from her hand, "Enjoy it!"

She turned and switched the kettle on. At that moment a bubbly middle-aged woman blustered into the kitchen.

"Oh, there you are Rach! Jess has told us all about you," she said, a huge smile across her face. "Call me Jules. So good that she's found someone, you know, in the same situation." She pulled a chair out and sat down, took her hand, and faced Rachel full on. She had the same eyes as Jess – bright and twinkly – and a short bob with a centre parting. Her cheeks were as high as Jess'.

"How are you coping love?"

"Um, I'm okay thanks. My mum and dad have been great," she answered looking up at Jess for confidence.

"Oh, that's brilliant. Thank goodness for mums and dads eh, Jess?!"

"Yes mum," Jess grinned back. Jim flurried back into the kitchen, a blue plastic cover in his hands and a small black bag and a hairdryer in the other.

"Oh Jim, she's just got through the door!"

Jim fussed around with Rachel whilst Jules interrogated her, asking where she was from and how she was preparing for the baby and how her mum and dad must be over-the-moon becoming grandparents.

"Do you know the sex?" Jules said.

Rachel shook her head.

"Oh good. Yes, it's always nice to have a surprise. Jess wanted to find out. I think it's better to wait. Kids these days are so impatient! What about names? Any thoughts yet?"

Rachel's mouth gaped open. The excitement from Jess' mum was palpable, like an aunt who'd known her since a baby. Jess put mugs of steaming tea in front of them just as a cry came from another room. Everyone froze until another cry broke the silence. Jess sighed, set the mugs down and went to the other room.

"She's doing so well, you know," Jules said in a whisper. "She puts on a brave face, but I know when she's, erm, emotional. Doesn't like for us to see it." She looked up at Jim and they gave a knowing nod to each other.

"I was your age when I had her you know. Barely out of school. Us young mums need to stick together. Okay? If you ever need anything, love, anything, you know you'll always be welcome here," and she reached over and clasped Rachel's hand. She squeezed a thank you through her lips as her brow furrowed, willing her tears to stay inside at the friendliness these kind people were giving to a perfect stranger.

As if she could read her mind, Jules stood up and indicated Rachel to stand, flapping her hands. She swathed her with a motherly hug.

"Oi, I'm busy here," Jim retorted. Jules cupped Rachel's face in her hands and locked eyes. Her hands were warm and soft.

"*Anything* love, just ask," she said as she wiped away a tear which was threatening to escape from Rachel's eye.

Jess came back with a sniffly Natalie balanced on her hip.

"Almost done Rach," Jim said as he moved his head around the back of her.

"Oh, lovely Jim!" Jules responded.

"Yeah, looks great Rach. Best looking mum in this place!"

"Thank you so much, it's so kind of you."

"No problem at all Rach," Jim stood back with a flourish. "I'll go and get a mirror. Stay here love," he said as he disappeared out of the room. The three women looked at the baby bouncing up and down on Jess' knee. She had the same blue eyes and cleft chin as her mum, but her hair was jet black and short. Rachel tried to imagine what the baby inside her would look like – would it have her eyes or the eyes of the stranger she slept with? Would it be tall or short, fat or thin, dark or light hair, curly or straight? She tried to think back, through the fog of that night as to what he looked like, anything. Jim thrust a mirror in front of her which jolted her from her thoughts.

"Ta-da," Jim announced. Rachel looked back at herself, a young woman with brown hair set in a side parting, the ends reached just above her shoulders. It framed her face which made it look like her eyes glowed. She'd never liked her chubby cheeks, but they at least matched her broad shoulders.

"Oh, very Julia Roberts!" Jules said, clapping.

"Do you like it?" Jim asked, running his fingers through her hair, looking into the mirror Rachel was holding.

"I love it Jim, thank you," she replied, swinging her head so the hair rustled and settled. "I really do."

"You look a million pounds, Rach," Jess said. "And Natty loves it too, don't ya, Natty?" As Jess forced her hands to clap, the baby pulled a strained face.

"Uh-oh," said Jim. "Looks like Natty is getting busy." Jess lifted her and smelt the back of her nappy.

"Yep! Come on Rach, let me show you how it's done. Jim, clear up this mess," she said with a wink.

"Oh no, please, leave it, let me do it," said Rachel.

"Won't hear it, Rach. Not in your condition anyway," he retorted. "Next time, eh?"

"Pinkie promise," she replied and followed Jess and the smell to the nursery.

Rachel sat with her back against the dusty pink wallpaper, her legs outstretched. The blind was pulled, giving a soft hue to the room. A shaft of light illuminated the side of Jess' face as she looked down at Natty against her breast, her nappy changed. Stillness surrounded them. Just a faint suckling and a gentle creak of the rocking chair stole the silence.

"Jess, why did your stepdad say the last time you brought a girl home, it went crazy?" Rachel said, barely above a whisper.

"Oh, well, it seems a lifetime ago," replied Jess distantly.

"I don't want to pry, or bring up bad memories, so it's okay, you know, if you don't want to say."

"No, it's fine. I haven't spoken to anyone about it really. It was a traumatic time. I worked with a girl called Lucy who's transexual. Everyone knew, you could tell. Well, some people couldn't tell but to me, it was obvious the first time I met her. Even Jim thought it, or so he said when it all came out. We got on quite well." Pain appeared to spread across Jess' face.

"Anyway, she was really shy. Had a lot of confidence issues, as you can imagine. Long story short, she meets this random guy and OMG she was smitten by him, even though she'd only known him, literally, a few hours. Love at first sight kind of thing. He says exactly the right things, is a proper gentleman, pays for everything, has the same dreams as her, makes her feel like she's the only person in the whole world blah blah blah. He's American and she LOVES America."

Rachel interjected. "Didn't he realise that... you know...?"

"No, he didn't know at all. I guess they say love is blind. It really was. In court, he said he started having weird memories of bullies at his school —"

"In court?" Rachel interrupted a bit too loudly. They both looked at Natty who continued feeding as if nothing had happened.

"Oh yes, it gets better. I'll come to that. So..." she was on a roll, telling the story, her eyes flickering back and forth trying to remember the details. "So, she misses a date with him and doesn't have his number. There was no way of contacting him and she'd only met him once. But the next day, he turns up at our office, looking for her. Tells her that he's been searching all the offices in Covent Garden. She lapped it up. The romance of it all; a man trying to find his lost beau. To be honest, so did I. From what she was telling me, he was this amazingly perfect guy that was smitten by her."

"Flipping hell, he does sound like the perfect guy," Rachel said, rubbing her belly. She thought back to the man that put her in this predicament. Did *he* even remember her or was she just a notch on his bedpost?

"Exactly Rach. *Exactly*. He was perfect. *Too* perfect. And here's the crazy part. He's a frigging stalker. He's not American at all, some wideboy, loaded City trader who got his kicks from being his victim's perfect date, beds them and gets rid of them." Rachel gasped.

"Yeah, I know," Jess said, seeing Rachel's reaction. "Does all this research first, dresses up as their perfect man, even changes his hairstyle. He says all the right things, like *exactly* the right things, to turn them on. He didn't go searching all the offices. He knew exactly where she worked. And lived."

"You. Are. Kidding. Me."

"I know. I felt like that too. It took me a long time to get over it."

"Flipping hell Jess, what did she do?" she said wide-eyed.

"Well, she found a letter in his bag that was addressed to someone in Ealing. Which was strange cos he was on holiday from America. Stupidly, she went to the address to figure it out. Some over-friendly neighbour let her in and in the spare room were rows of files with all his other victims. Like loads of them. He came back and found her, knocked her unconscious and tied her up."

"Oh my god," Rachel said, crossing herself. She noticed Jess's eyebrows raise in surprise.

"This is where it gets even crazier." Jess' eyes lit up as the conclusion beckoned. "When Lucy found all the box files and the photos, she figured out she used to know him! When the penny dropped and he wasn't this American guy, but some English twat in disguise, she realised she used to go to school with him! That's why they reckoned he started having all the nightmares of bullies cos somewhere in his subconsciousness he must have recognised her. Or him. Of course, he didn't know cos *he* was a *she* now and didn't see it. So, because his masculinity had taken a beating, he decided to give *her* a beating. The neighbour heard the screams, and the police came."

Rachel crossed herself again. "What happened to him?"

"Well, he lawyered up with his rich banker money." Jess screwed up her face. "So unfair. He pleaded guilty, convinced the judge he was full of remorse and said he would never do it again. They only found one other woman, but she was unreliable, and he'd burnt all the files, all the evidence. The lawyer was bloody good. That's what money buys you. First offence so got a suspended sentence and a bunch of community service. Suspended! No wonder women don't feel bloody safe walking the streets these days." Jess paused, taking a deep breath, visibly shaken.

"What happened to Lucy?"

"She went completely back in her shell, wouldn't say anything to anyone. Left the company when it all finished. That's the last I've heard from her. I did try but kept getting blanked." She dabbed the corner of her eye with Natty's muslin, not realising the make-up was already smudged.

"Poor girl. After everything she went through, she had to go through that too. I guess it shows that her transformation was a success. If this guy genuinely fancied her."

"Yeah, that's right because Nathan, that's the name of the guy, said in court he was totally smitten by her, how she was unlike any of the other women he dated. By the way, he always said he 'dated' them, never stalked them."

Jess shuddered like a chill had gone through her spine.

"Jeez," was all Rachel could say.

"He said he was about to come clean to Lucy and admit it cos he was SO in love with her, how she made him feel like nothing he ever felt before." She pretended to put two fingers down her throat. "Load of tosh if you ask me."

Rachel looked into the middle distance, comprehending what Jess had just said. Would she ever know if someone was doing the same to her? Was the father of her baby stalking her now? The thought made goosebumps on her skin.

"Do you know what happened to him? The guy, Nathan."

"Not really. I heard he scarpered out of the country after doing his community service at a foodbank. In court, he looked broken. Not that I could care." She sniffed as she flicked her hair back. "And that was the last I heard of him. Best thing for him to get out of the country in my view. If I ever see him again…"

"What a wanker."

"Yeah, wanker," Jess echoed, smiling at the insult.

A silence filled the room.

"Here, take a look." She whipped out her phone, found an article from the local newspaper and handed the device to Rachel. The headline read: LOCAL STALKER GIVEN 120 HOURS COMMUNITY SERVICE. Underneath was a photo of a suited man walking through a street with an older man carrying a briefcase.

"Nathaniel Clyne, yeah that's his name," Jess said to herself. "Nathan."

Rachel looked at the photo. He was attractive with dark hair, spiked at the front, hunched shoulders and a slim waist, exaggerated by the tailored suit he was wearing. He was looking directly at the camera, mid-walk, his face full with a five o'clock shadow.

He wasn't bad looking, was the first thought that flashed through her mind, *she could see why women would fall for him*. Then she felt repulsed for thinking such a thing.

"Anyway, that's in the past and you are the future," Jess said pointing at Rachel's belly. "If you're a boy, we don't want you growing up to be a wanker like him."

Chapter Seven

A cockerel crowed millimetres from Rachel's head. She opened an eye and the bird peered down at her from its perch in the window's void. Its red wattle flapped as he tilted its head at her. She sat bolt upright and shoed it away. It squawked as it half-flapped and half-fell to the outside ground. Looking out of the empty window, squat palm trees stretched out in uniform lines. Above them, whispery clouds littered a light blue sky. The heat was starting to rise.

Rachel got up and slowly opened the door. The silence of the house amplified the creaking hinge. She looked into the room she'd entered the previous evening. Everything was as she remembered – the golden buddha, the scratchy-looking sofa. All except the man and the woman who were fast asleep on the weathered rug in the middle of the room. A light blanket covered the woman. The man was lying on his back, his hands on his stomach, his eyes closed and lost in a dream. She turned around and saw a basic, small kitchen compromising of a gas stove, a small cupboard, a couple of pans and a bucket. Broken tiles made the floor look like a complicated jigsaw. An ancient television covered in dust sat in the corner. An empty window on the far side drew in light and beyond it laid a covered well and more squat palm trees. The only way out was through the room with the sleeping couple.

She went back into her room and slowly closed the door. Had they given her their only bed? To a stranger? And welcomed her into their home, knowing they would have a night on a hard floor? She felt an overwhelming sense of guilt, gratitude and privilege. She heard a door click and she looked outside the window. The woman wandered around the corner and Rachel quietly said 'hello.' The woman clasped her hands together in prayer, beamed and came up to the window.

"Sleep good?" she asked, giving a thumbs-up.

"Yes," Rachel nodded, also giving a thumbs-up.

"Toilet," she replied, pointing along the dust surrounding the house and into the bushes.

"Okay," Rachel responded, not knowing what would be out there. She felt the top of her head where she'd banged it the last time she went for a rural wee. The woman turned to go.

"Oh. And thank you," she called after her, putting her hands into a prayer. The woman turned and came back and gripped her hands over Rachel's through the pane-less window. She shook her hands and forced the tips of her fingers to Rachel's forehead and back onto hers. Then she patted Rachel on the cheek, murmuring something in Thai.

When Rachel returned from the bushes, the woman had laid out a blanket on the dusty forecourt. The man was already sitting cross-legged peeling a banana. They greeted each other with their palms pressed together. Spread on top of the blanket was a breakfast of boiled eggs, cut-up watermelon and bananas. They invited her to join them. It was the sweetest tasting fruit she'd encountered on her travels.

The man and woman were conversing in Thai, gesturing wildly with their hands, whilst hens pecked about in the shade of low palm trees. The woman sighed and looked up to the skies. She gesticulated to Rachel the despair of the man next to her, and Rachel shrugged her shoulders with an exasperated sigh and with a smile on her face. She pointed at herself and made a walking motion with her fingers and then a circle.

"I. Go. For. A. Walk."

The woman responded with a thumbs up and a babble. The man sternly said "Bus. 11 o'clock" and he pointed outwards past the palm trees in what must be the general direction of the shops.

"Sea. There," and pointed along the dirt track.

"Okay," Rachel said and signalled with a thumbs up and then clasped her hands together in prayer and bowed her head with a "thank you."

As she walked along the side of the pot-holed road, she sucked in the warming air and spread out her arms. Alone and in the middle of nowhere. Hospitality from friendly locals.

This was it!

Helmetless scooter drivers beeped their horns as they whizzed by in the opposite direction. Pastel-coloured bungalows, shrines and curious barking dogs punctuated the road as she ambled along. Women selling a variety of fruit and vegetables laid out on blue plastic tarpaulin would call out to her as she passed, hoping for some custom. She detected the scent of salt in the air as the sky started to open and she could see the tops of jagged, craggy cliffs ahead. Dwellings were becoming more frequent. Tree trunks on the side of the road became thinner and the area became less dense. She could see further into the bush, lots of bricks, stones and rubbish were strewn along the ground. Occasionally she would see a derelict shack in the middle of the woods, a pile of rubble with a fallen rusted corrugated roof, vines and branches snaking around and through it. A line of smartly dressed uniformed children, standing to attention in front of a long low building, stared at her as she passed. She attempted a wave and a gaggle of girls at the back giggled amongst themselves. Chickens grew in numbers, randomly searching for scraps in the dirt. She noticed more rubbish littering the side of the road, creeping into the woods. At one point she was sure she saw a boat amongst the trees, vines trying to keep it a secret as the forest devoured it. A truck carrying goats hurtled around a corner, beeping as it went. Its cargo bleated as the dust rose in its wake.

She cautiously rounded the corner and the sea opened in front of her. As if drawn to the water like a magnet, she stepped over a low metal barrier and negotiated a few scattered rocks down onto a narrow white sandy beach. She slipped off her trainers and socks and dipped her toes into the water. Its coolness spread between her toes as her feet melted into the soft, caramel-coloured sand. Fishing boats chugged in opposite directions in front of towering islands of rock topped with rainforest. The calm, flat sea seemed to dance as the sunlight hit the water. The only sound was the lapping of the small waves against her ankles. She walked along the shore to an outcrop of grey rocks, found a dry patch and sat down, taking the weight of her daypack off her shoulders. She allowed the sun to warm her skin as her feet gently paddled the water. A few inquisitive fish moseyed around the rocks, hoping for crumbs of food. It was exactly what she'd envisioned when the idea of travelling first entered her mind. A million miles from home and a paradise setting. She let the moment surround her. She didn't even care what time it was, or about catching the bus. Or even where she might sleep that night. Whatever will be will be.

God's Will.

She gathered her things to explore more, hoping to find a clothes shop or something to replenish her lost supplies. The road she'd come along bent inland so instead of walking along the beach, she decided to follow it around. Thin trees stretched into the distance, newly built bungalows dotted the road, a golden shrine placed in front of each one. As she walked, she noticed a build-up of debris, strewn amongst the forest and the side of the road; discarded planks of red, white and blue painted wood protruded through the green of the trees. A battered house interrupted the denseness of the foliage – branches and trunks twisting through its windows and roof. Discarded faded green fishing nets punctuated the natural landscape. There was an air of sadness. They would have been someone's belongings some time ago.

Bare-footed men, blood dripping from their hands, trudged through the streets trailing fishing nets and baskets of small fish. They all gravitated to an opening, almost like a square, with a few scant trees in its centre providing shade for more fruit sellers and someone selling plastic tubs. A shack sat on one edge of the square: the village shop. On the opposite side, a wide, brick building loomed over the village. The tallest structure Rachel had seen for miles. A school perhaps, or even a Church, it looked out of place amongst the crumbling buildings and tarpaulin. A stone wall encased it, affording only a view of the top and rear, with what looked like a clock tower protruding into the sky and casting a shadow on the village square.

Squealing shouts and giggles of children on the other side of the wall pierced the air. Intrigued, Rachel crossed the square and followed the wall around, hoping to find an entrance. She turned a corner and was met with a view of the sea. Behind her, the wall facing the coast had collapsed, causing a big V-shaped hole to appear. Bricks and rubble stood at its base, framing a view of the courtyard and the large, imposing building behind it. Inside, children were running, hopping and limping around a level concrete area where a single basketball hoop stood. Dozens of children moved around, shouting for a ball, giggling and laughing at each other.

Some had one arm, others had one leg. One boy had a thick scar down the length of his bare back. Another boy was sitting in a wheelchair, using his arms to frantically move across the court to get the ball, two naked stubs where his legs should be. She heard a low, deep shout, giving commands.

In English.

It was a man. A tanned, white man, ran onto the court, a joyful smile on his face. He lifted the child in the wheelchair up as he caught the ball. In one swoop, he gave the ball to the boy, raised him over his head and the boy dunked it into the netless hoop. The other kids erupted and high-fived each other. The man instructed everyone to go inside, and the kids obliged. As if sensing someone was looking at him, he glanced quickly over at the hole in the wall, where Rachel stood in the middle of the V. She averted her eyes, guilty at spying where she shouldn't be.

"Hi there," he shouted as he jogged towards her. He was almost six feet tall with a close-cropped haircut, jagged around the edges like he had done it himself. A small tuft of hair extended up at the front. He looked like he hadn't shaved in a fortnight. Tanned, strong arms swung from a dirty white sleeveless t-shirt with a darkened V-shape of sweat on his chest. He looked maybe early-thirties – certainly not a standard backpacker that she'd encountered along her journey – but had a cheeky, boyish charm. He climbed up the rubble towards her in filthy unbranded plimsolls, shoelaces untied.

"How you doing?" he said confidently, looking Rachel in the eye, stretching out his hand, sweat prickling his forehead. She thought she recognised him, but couldn't place where: the broad shoulders, the five o'clock shadow, a spiked quiff. He was older than her but that didn't matter. He was gorgeous. Or maybe it was his confidence shining through, the setting of a westerner playing with disadvantaged kids in a damaged-yet-impressive building. Had she found one of the fabled travellers that so many backpackers had spoken about? Goosebumps prickled her skin. She suddenly noticed the heat on her face.

"I'm Rachel," she said, feeling her cheeks blush, excitement coursing through her body.

"Welcome to Bo Hin," he said with a huge smile, dimples appearing on his cheeks, grabbing her hand. "I'm Nathan."

Chapter Eight

Rachel's waters broke as she was waddling down the high street. Officially, and according to her plan, there were still two weeks to go. She'd been in Boots, mulling around the jars of baby foods, nappies, medicines for under six-month-olds, little cotton buds and nipple creams, dummies, wipes and gentle shampoo, seeing if there was anything she had missed. As she scanned the aisles, she pictured each product nestled tidily in her home. She remembered the little plastic bath that her dad had proudly removed from a shopping bag, placing it in the bathtub with multi-coloured bath toys in a drawer string bag – a smiling shark, an amused octopus and a happy-go-lucky wind-up turtle. Her dad had 'tested' the turtle by turning the little white cog and setting it free in the sink; the turtle went mad going around and around in circles. A boyish smile spread across his face as he poked it to keep it swimming and avoid the edges. She warmly rubbed her stomach, smiling at other mums-to-be and peering into buggies, picturing herself with her own little baby.

When she was outside Starbucks, she felt a trickle of water run down her leg, and then a gush. Luckily, an old woman rushed to her aide and held her hand, cooing and reassuring, as she puffed her cheeks in controlled breaths. Her mum and dad pulled up in the car moments later, as if they had been waiting around the corner for the phone call.

Dad sped to the hospital, mum in the back, patting her hand and repeating her mantra.

Breathe. Breathe.

Arriving at the hospital, Rachel was whisked away to be attached with wires to beeping monitors. The overwhelming surges within her body caused her to scream out at her mum, to call Jess to come.

Not enough time, love, the baby's coming. Breathe. Breathe.

When the contractions subsided, quiet enveloped the room, except for the gentle pulsing of the machines and the rasps coming from Rachel's mouth.

Breathe. Breathe.

She felt the pain coming again, like a fire burning into her and she screamed out for drugs. Her mum patted her hand as Rachel's grip threatened to crack her bones. As the pain receded again, she burst out in tears, begging her mum for it to stop, how sorry she was and she really didn't want it. Especially if it hurt *this* much.

Get rid of it!

Her mum's eyes watered but her face was unwavering. She hummed a prayer and her eyes kept darting up at the ceiling, muttering under her breath. The midwives busied themselves around the couple like they weren't there, casually checking notes and scribbling things down, leaving the room for what felt like a very long time. It was as if they were out doing their weekly shop, humming a jolly tune and saying things like 'baby comes when baby ready!' in a chirruping voice when they came back. Her screams had turned to grunts as she was coached by the most cheerful of midwives.

"You are doing great Rachel!!" she cooed, examining her, feeling around her bump and watching the monitors. "You are doing fabulous too Mum." Rachel's mum gave a shy smile, still patting her hand and saying *breathe* over and over.

Her dad put his head around the corner and retreated just as quickly when he saw the scene, extending his hand around the corner of the door frame, a carrier bag of food and drink dangling.

"Christine, love. Food."

Her mum grabbed it and peered inside, tutting at the contents.

"Can you eat anything darling?" she said. "Dad's got some crisps and …"

"Ah, ah ah," interrupted the midwife. "No food allowed. Just in case."

"Just in case of what?" Rachel huffed through gritted teeth.

"In the very unlikely event something happens and we need to give you an anaesthetic. Doctor's orders. Don't worry, there will be plenty of time for food later." She beamed and skipped out of the room.

A silence came over the room as both contemplated a different scenario.

"Ah, not to worry, love. I'll keep it safe for –"

Rachel grimaced again as a contraction started, a wave of cramp in her tummy. She stifled a yell and her mum slid the plastic bag under her chair, keeping a grip on Rachel's hand.

Contractions intensified and came closer together. A heaviness grew on her backside, making lying uncomfortable.

The minutes turned to hours.

"Isn't there something you can do for her?" her mum would ask the midwife at increasing regular intervals. "She's exhausted."

"The cervix is fully dilatated so too late for anything. Keep her breathing and use the gas and air."

Christine took the nurse by the arm and lead her firmly outside of the room. Rachel strained to hear.

"Baby comes when baby's ready," she heard the midwife say in a firm tone. "These things take time. It is for Him to decide." Rachel pictured the cross on her mum's necklace – an heirloom passed down. Would it get passed to her, and then the baby? She hoped so. She heard her mum's voice, muffled and indistinct.

"Look, I'll see if the obstetrician is free. Just to check. I won't be long," came the voice, softened.

"Thank you, I'd appreciate that," was the reply as Christine came back into the room, fingering the necklace.

"Is everything okay?" Rachel asked, registering a look of worry on her mum's crumpled forehead.

"Yes love," she replied, forcing a smile and pulling her cardy together at the front. Rachel noticed how thin she suddenly looked. "Keep breathing darling, nearly there."

Moments later the nurse returned with a man in a clean, white coat. He quickly introduced himself, his bushy eyebrows dancing as he spoke and felt around the top and sides of her bump. Rachel's skin juddered at the coldness of his hands. He mumbled something to the midwife who busied herself at a metallic station. After he examined her, constantly keeping his heavy dark eyes on the beeping machines, he looked up at

Rachel, then to her mum, then back again. His eyebrows were almost touching each other.

"Ahem," he began. "The baby has turned, and I think his head might have got a bit stuck. The heart rate seems to be deteriorating." He glanced over at the midwife. "We are going to try to turn the baby's head. Nothing to worry about." His tone was business-like, cold like his hands. Rachel exchanged glances with her mum as she felt another contraction begin.

"We want to try a ventouse delivery," he said. "It means we put a little suction cup on the baby's head. That should solve it. Are you happy for us to go ahead?"

Rachel grimaced as she felt another tightening around her stomach.

"Get it out."

Her mum was about to say something when her fingers were squashed together as Rachel grunted through her teeth.

The midwife returned wearing long blue gloves, a plastic apron and a facemask. She said something to the doctor, which Rachel couldn't decipher through the fabric. The doctor nodded back as the pain intensified and Rachel let out a guttural scream.

"Try to think of happy things love," her mum said, trying to draw attention away from the harried activity happening around her. "The lovely nursery your dad has done. He's done a super job, hasn't he? Those colours – he chose them. He's dead proud of you Rach."

Rachel breathed as the pain subsided. She noticed her mum's eyes flicking to and from the doctor.

"Is everything all right mum?"

Her eyes darted back to Rachel, focusing.

"Oh, and Auntie Barbara has been so busy and helpful. I don't know where she gets her knitting skills from. It certainly wasn't passed to me! And we'll be here, your dad and I, to help. Jess, she seems lovely, doesn't she?"

A quiet descended over the room.

"Something's wrong," Rachel said, nonchalantly. "I can feel it."

She said it so casually that both the midwife and the doctor looked up in surprise. Still holding Rachel's hand, her mum stood up and stared at the doctor waiting for a reply. The doctor nodded his head, keeping an eye on the monitors whilst the midwife fiddled with the dials and urgently moved the transducer over Rachel's tummy.

It was as if they were searching for something. An eternity seemed to go by.

The doctor moved his head like he had given up waiting.

"The baby's heartbeat is decreasing behind the contractions. The head isn't moving. We may need to do a c-section," he said quickly.

A gasp came from Rachel's mum, instinctively reaching up to the cross on her necklace.

He checked his watch. "We have two choices both of which require us to head to the operating theatre. Firstly, we try forceps, for the baby to come out of the birth canal." He was still in business mode like he was in a boardroom giving a presentation.

"If that doesn't work, we will be in the right place to perform an emergency c-section. Either way, you will need an epidural. I'll go now to organise the OR whilst the midwife here will explain the pros and cons. We'll need a signed consent."

He snapped off his surgical gloves and darted out of the room. The midwife came over and patted them both on the arm.

"It's okay! This happens all the time," she said cheerfully through darkened eyes.

A rush of activity followed as the pain intensified. A pen and a form were shoved under Rachel's nose as they forced a squiggle out of her.

"Just a tiny, sharp scratch coming," the midwife said as a cannula was inserted and clear liquid pumped in. The relief was immediate, and she opened and closed her eyes, the feeling of pain rising and falling, her lids heavy with exhaustion.

An alarm suddenly woke her. It was like an ambulance that was parked right next to her bed – screeching, urgent, grating. A rush of activity was happening around her. She tried to force her eyes open. Through the slits, she could only make out a blur of people moving around, people in white coats, figures in blue overalls. She heard snatches of words.

"Emergency"

"Falling under 100 bpm"

"Category one!"

"Let's move!"

She didn't know what they meant or referred to. Plus, she felt nauseous. And when did her mum start wearing blue? The pain had subsided. Was this a dream? She felt movement. Light danced over her closed eyelids. Her mum's voice was urgent like being scolded as a child. When the movement stopped, she tried to open her eyes again, but a bright fluorescent light forced them to shut. Something was covering her mouth; a cool mist made her mouth dry. She could hear noises: metal on metal, strange voices, plastic being stretched, beeping machines, footsteps of millions of different people, her skin being prodded. Her eyelids felt so heavy and she couldn't be bothered to even try to open them.

In the distance, she saw a baby with bright blue eyes looking at her, reaching out with chubby arms, beckoning her for a cuddle.

They were her eyes.

She felt pulling and pressure against her stomach. Urgent voices, her hand being squeezed tighter.

The vicar's face appeared hovering above her, the outline of his body fuzzy, sweeping up the baby and gathering it in a fatherly hug, gently cradling its head on his arm, gazing into its eyes. On its feet were little blue knitted booties, the ones Auntie Barbara had sent. The vicar floated higher as he rose to the ground, his bright eyes lost in the baby's face not seeing or hearing Rachel's cries.

Come back.

She felt her hand being squeezed again. There was no pain now except in the uncomfortableness of her fingers being crushed together. She heard urgent voices again. She half-opened her eyes, looking across the room, plastic straps tightening around the back of her head, holding a mask to her face. Her mum was standing, straining her neck, her lips moving in small motions like she was muttering. Rachel turned her head and saw the back of a white medical coat, a head bowed down, hands pumping at a white, floppy doll speckled with red, and other people running around. She could see the doll's feet and tiny, tiny toes at the end of a bloodied plump leg, its body above the knee hidden behind the white coat of the doctor.

She closed her eyes again and the baby appeared, floating above her, within touching distance. It smiled a sweet smile, opened its mouth and playfully gargled. It was naked and Rachel could see that it was a girl. She extended her chubby little arms to Rachel's face, but she couldn't quite reach as she drifted away. The baby tried to speak, each time crinkling her little forehead in frustration.

Gargle!

It gibbered the word over and over, getting louder.

Confused, Rachel strained to hear.

Are you saying something? Come back, come back here gorgeous.

Gargle, the baby babbled, a confused look on its face as it moved further from Rachel's outstretched arms.

What are you saying?

Garg-le, the baby burbled urgently, her head cocked to one side, trying to make itself understood.

Garg-le.

As it ascended beyond Rachel's reach and into the white light, Rachel realised what the baby was saying, and she understood what was happening in the room.

To her.

The images of baby clothes, cots, buggies and nappies slowly evaporated. Her friends' happy faces faded away. Rain started to fall in the playground against an empty swing.

God's Will, the baby was trying to say.

It was God's Will.

Chapter Nine

Nathan motioned his head across the empty courtyard.

"Would you like to come in? It's lunchtime. You can join us if you like," he said. Rachel glanced over his shoulder, remembering the disabled kids. She pictured the legless toddler being cradled by her mother at the boat festival, the look of despair and sorrow in her eyes.

"No. No, I can't" she said, taking a step backwards.

"Come on, it's fine," he encouraged as if reading her mind. "They won't bite."

"No, seriously, it's okay," she said, turning her shoulders.

"Please. Don't worry. I was the same as you. The first time I saw some of those kids with their legs and arms missing I was nervous too. But once you get to know them, they are just kids. Kids with a bit of misfortune."

"Yeah, maybe," Rachel replied touching her tummy, looking beyond Nathan through the hole in the wall. "It's not that, I just…."

"Just what? Come on," he insisted. "Looks like you've been travelling for a while," he said looking her up and down. "This will be an experience you'll never forget. Trust me." That was something that Rachel definitely wanted. Not just another tourist hotspot.

"Are you sure it's okay, just turn up and eat?"

"Oh yeah, they'll love it. Just you see."

She took a deep breath and grabbed hold of Nathan's outstretched hand as he led her over the rubble into the empty courtyard.

She could hear the noise before she entered the hall where tens of kids were chattering, eating and scraping their plates and cups along rows of heavy, plastic tables. The walls were covered with brightly coloured pictures, pieces of lined paper scribbled with Thai and English writing and official-looking typed timetables and letters. As they walked through the doorway, the room filled with a quiet hush. All the kids stared at the stranger. A small man hurried up to them, his flip-flops slapping against his heels, a broad toothless smile across his face. He grabbed Rachel's hand with two hands and shook them.

"Welcome, welcome!" he said in a thick Thai accent, bowing his head several times. A few of the children murmured to each other without taking their eyes off her.

"My name Anurak," he said slowly and carefully, trying to get his English right, putting one hand on his chest.

"My name is Rachel," she replied. All at once, as if being led by a conductor, the children chorused, 'Good afternoon, Miss Rachel.'

Rachel looked up stunned at the angelic sounds bouncing off the walls. All eyes were on her. A girl's voice at the back shouted out, "Mr Nathan girlfriend!" and the children all giggled. Blushing, Rachel looked at Nathan who rolled his eyes as if expected from the delinquents in his charge. Anurak let her hand go and motioned her over to a table.

"Please. Our honour."

He shooed a few children along the bench to make room for the three of them. He squeezed down next to her as Nathan sat opposite. A humped lady put a bowl of rice in front of them, smiling at Rachel, one tooth sticking through her gums.

"Thank you," Rachel said, putting her hands together in prayer. The lady responded in kind, backing away with her hands together, bowing as she went. The girl sitting next to Rachel covered her mouth as she giggled at her neighbour. She looked at her and gave a tentative smile and a small, embarrassed wave. The girl responded by snickering back to her friend, whispering something in Thai.

Rachel looked down at her bowl of rice and went to grab cutlery to eat it. She looked down the table and saw all the children eating with their hands, all eyes still locked on her, waiting for her move. She glanced over to Nathan who mimed a scooping motion with his hand.

"Why you here in Bo Hin?" Anurak asked, drawing her attention. The question sounded accusatory in his staccato accent.

"Um, the bus left me," she said quietly.

"HA-HA!" thundered Anurak slapping his hand down on the table, his shoulders shuddering making his whole body quiver. "You miss bus! Ha Ha! What is wrong with English? Haha! No time!" he said, pointing at his naked wrist.

He continued to chuckle as Nathan grinned at Rachel. He shrugged and his cheeks went pink.

"You too?" she mouthed. Nathan nodded, bashfully. A warm, safe feeling washed over her.

God's Will.

"Khun Pai help you?" Anurak asked. Rachel glanced at Nathan.

"Did the owners of the shop and café put you up?" he explained.

"Yeah. How did you know?"

"Very nice people," Anurak said, nodding his approval and shovelling a handful of rice into his mouth.

"Mr and Mrs Pai are very good friends of the orphanage," Nathan continued. "They bring food and toys for the kids. As you've seen they don't have much, they rely on the bus to Trang and Malaysia. They work long hours, walk everywhere, but still have time for the children. We make the kids write to them and we give them the letters when they come."

Rachel looked around the room at all the children chattering with each other, now focused on their food and their friends.

An orphanage.

Some had an arm missing, some were in old, rusted wheelchairs, and a few had the tell-tale look of Down's Syndrome. Not only did they have physical deformities, but they had no family either.

Nathan kept his eyes on her as she scanned the room.

"They're happy kids, you know," he said as if he was trying to read her mind. Rachel looked back at him, perplexed. Despite the smiles, they all appeared to have something *wrong* with them. How could they be happy?

"I know, it might not seem like it on the outside, but they're happy on the inside. Trust me," he smiled sweetly at her.

"This is the only orphanage for miles, so all the unwanted kids come here."

A group of girls on the other side of the hall giggled into their hands.

"Most are too young to know their parents or the circumstances, so they fit in here. They don't know any different really. Except for the older kids when they realise, you know, that others are different to them..." he trailed off looking at the kids. He straightened his back and sunk his hand into his rice and piled a handful into his mouth, bits of grain sticking to his fingers. Rachel copied him, unsure as her skin touched the wet rice. The girls giggled again as if waiting for her to do it. She cautiously raised her hand, screwing up her face for dramatic effect and stuck her tongue out to taste the rice. Then she quickly guzzled it, smearing it over her lips and cheeks, crossing her eyes showing her face dotted with white grains. The girls burst into laughter at the sight, one hand covering their mouths, the other pointing at the mess. She turned to Nathan, then to Anurak who both laughed along with the children.

Soon, all the kids were laughing as one.

The chatter receded as the novelty of the new stranger wore off. Rachel watched Nathan eating his rice with his hands. There was something quite familiar about him. He raised his eyes, feeling as if he was being watched.

"What?" he asked confused. "Have I got something on my face?"

"Nothing, no. It's weird but it feels like I've seen you before." The colour drained from his face. His eyes flickered as if mentally scanning through pictures whilst trying to see if he recognised her.

"Hmm, I don't know. Maybe I've got one of those faces," he contorted his face into a goofy look, drawing giggles from the girls opposite.

"Yeah maybe. Where are you from?"

"Reading."

"Hmm. I grew up in North London."

"Oh well, not that then." Without a word, he got up, scooped both his and Rachel's bowl up, joined a line of children putting theirs on trolleys and then followed them to a large trough to wash their hands. Rachel sat watching the scene as they all dispersed out of the hall, not quite knowing what to do. Nathan and Anurak chatted privately to each other, both looking at Rachel as she sat in the middle of all the movement and noise. Anurak nodded his head and Nathan came striding over.

"Come on you, let's go. I've got the afternoon off!"

Rachel followed him out of the hall, down the corridor with more drawings and writings on the wall and across the courtyard to the V-shaped hole in the wall. The sun was high in the sky and the heavy humidity caused her skin to prickle with sweat. They climbed over the rubble, Nathan offering his hand to help Rachel over the loose debris. They walked through the clearing of bamboo shoots onto soft white sand, the sea looking inviting in the bright blue sky. He flipped off his plimsolls and took off his vest, exposing a slim, tanned and muscular midriff, and set off for the water's edge, leaving Rachel to slip her pumps off. She followed him into the sea just as he sank his head under the water, a few metres offshore. He bobbed back up, flicking his head so that water sprayed.

"Come on in, the water's lovely!"

Rachel turned up her trouser legs and paddled up to her knees – she had no intention of stripping off like him. Nathan swam to meet her, stood up, hands on hips looking out to the horizon, water dripping over him.

"Not bad for a lunch break, is it?" he said, surveying the calm sea. Rachel looked out, breathing in, and letting the cool water lap over her knees. She felt an urge to say something, to respond to what he said in the dining hall, which was hanging in the air. A nagging feeling of familiarity.

"What's your last name?" she said. He sucked in the air, his shoulders rising.

"What does it matter?"

"I'm sure I know you from somewhere."

He glanced over to her, studying her face again for recognition. Drawing a blank, he sighed.

"You do know there aren't any more buses today?" he said, gazing back out to the horizon.

"Oh jeez, no I haven't even thought about it! Shit! What am I going to do?"

She turned to go, causing a splash as her legs tried to fight against the water. Such was the fluke of meeting Nathan, seeing the orphanage and standing in the sea she'd forgotten about what came next. A panic came over her. "I need to find a hostel or something."

"Calm down, it's okay," Nathan called after her. "You can stay with me." Rachel looked back with a frown.

"No, it's fine," she called back as she turned for the beach. "I'll find a hostel." She could hear Nathan struggling to catch up with her through the water, splashing against the small waves.

"Don't be silly, there isn't a hostel here. Look, come and have a look at my place and you can decide. It's not what you think," he said, raising his hands. Rachel looked at him, a half-naked man pleading at her, water around his ankles, a green-blue sea stretching far beyond him. He looked defenceless and vulnerable standing there in his trunks. She tried to read his face, but there was nothing. She sighed and shrugged her shoulders.

God's Will.

"Okay, great," he responded as he paddled out of the water. "It's nothing much and you'll probably run a mile anyway." He pulled on his vest over his wet body and picked up his plimsolls, carrying them with one hand. He motioned her to follow so she picked up her trainers and they walked along the sand, skirting the water's edge.

"What do you do there?" Rachel said, swatting away a fly threatening to land on her arm. "At the orphanage."

"Anything, play with the kids, help tidy up, teach them a bit of English."

"That's cool," she replied. "For you to do that."

"Yeah, they give me food in return so that works for me."

"So, you don't get paid? What do you do for money?"

"Course I don't get paid, it's an orphanage! I don't need much money here. I've got enough to live on and, well look at this place, what do you need to spend money on? Just a few supplies."

They moved up the beach away from the water and into sparse trees. The ground became littered with rough grass poking up through the sand and fallen leaves from the palm trees dotted around. Two butterflies chased each other, darting at impossible angles, before resting on a bamboo leaf. Amongst the foliage, Rachel could make out a hut, camouflaged in the browns and greens. A simple square structure with a triangle wooden roof with four pillars holding it up. A few slats made a wall which came up to Rachel's shins. There were no windows or doors, just open to the elements.

"Home sweet home," Nathan said cheerfully as he ducked his head under the beam supporting the roof. Inside a multi-coloured hammock hung from the beams diagonally across the entire space. A few plastic bags were the only other belongings. Rachel surveyed the space from outside, amazed, whilst Nathan squatted in a corner, searching through one of the bags. He turned around to her.

"Pretty basic, isn't it?" he said. "Watch your head." Rachel gingerly lowered her head under the beam and joined Nathan in his home as he returned to his bag. She looked around, astounded by the lack of comforts.

"But," she began. Nathan glanced around. "Wh… where…," she stammered, struggling to find the words or what to say, so taken aback by the simplicity.

"Oh, you can have the hammock, it's okay I've got a pillow in here somewhere. I'll sleep outside." He moved to another bag and searched through it.

"I mean, like, where do you shower?!"

He stood up and pointed out to the sea.

"That's the biggest bathtub in the world out there," he smiled. "And all my food is taken care of at the orphanage. And if you want to know about the bathroom facilities. Well…" he glanced back over to the sea.

"Eww!" she grimaced. He just nodded back. "Are you serious?"

"Yeah, why not? Natural flushing system. It's a drop in the ocean. Literally." Rachel looked back at him in disgust.

"If you want to you can go in the orphanage. But trust me, the toilets are *not* very nice in there." Rachel looked back at the hammock and the ground, slats of wood roughly making up a floor.

"And you're going to sleep outside?"

"Yeah," he said, stretching his back. "On the sand. It's cool. I've done it before."

"Is it... is it safe?" Rachel asked, frowning.

"Safer than in a hut with no windows or doors? Yeah, it's pretty safe in these parts. It's the spiders you've got to watch out for." Rachel's eyes widened as she looked into the crevasses of the roof.

"Only joking," he said, a broad grin covering his face, a cheeky smile, and a hint of a dimple on his cheek.

That evening Nathan lit a fire on the beach and roasted huge peppers, tomatoes and bananas that he had in one of his many plastic bags. The fire danced in the twilight as the sun set over the horizon in front of them. They talked until thousands of stars twinkled in the sky; about their travels and the places they'd been to, the people they had met along the way and the stories they'd heard. Before coming to Thailand Nathan had been in Bali on an eco-project, planting coral in the seas. That was three months ago. Around the same time, Rachel had been mourning her baby. A different world.

When the embers of the fire died down, Nathan led Rachel to the hammock over the rough palm leaves and twigs.

"You want to lie diagonally," Nathan said matter-of-factly. "Otherwise, you'll get a bad back from sleeping like a banana." Rachel eyed him suspiciously. "Trust me. I learned the hard way. See you in the morning. Weather will be glorious."

Nathan ducked out of the hut and Rachel watched him over the slats as he half-buried himself in the sand on the beach under an overhanging frond. The crickets sang their songs, appearing to get louder as the night wore on. Mosquitos buzzed, strange, distant birds called out in the dark, and a soft breeze rustled the leaves overhead. Rachel breathed deeply, her eyes heavy at the events of the day.

She absentmindedly stroked her stomach under her t-shirt and fingered the stretch marks and the scar, still tender to the touch. Her mind wandered to lunch in the orphanage. Unwanted kids or kids that seemed to have no future. Was that her child? Was she just a kid with no future? Is that why He took her baby? What was His plan for her - to be alone? Lost? She'd tried so hard not to be alone, attaching herself to Jess and tagging along with anyone on her travels that would speak to her.

Jess.

She pictured her new friend – her blonde straight hair, her confidence at being a single mum. Maybe it was all meant to be. He must have put all these pieces of a jigsaw together for a reason: Losing her job, going out on the tiles, getting pregnant, meeting Jess, losing the baby, a horrible girl that pushed her into action, a bus conveniently leaving her behind, an isolated hut in the middle of nowhere. This kind stranger. Keeping her hands on her stomach, she allowed herself to relax, listening to the crickets and the waves of the sea. Peace and tranquillity were all around her.

He must have a plan for her, and this was it.

She was in paradise, in a hammock, moments from a calm blue sea. She dozed in and out of sleep as her body started to shut down for the night. The intensifying sound of crickets and the odd call of a bird lulled her to sleep.

A snap of a branch nearby sent a shock through her body; an alien sound amongst the cacophony that she'd quickly gotten used to. She tried to sit up, but the hammock made it difficult, the fabric wrapped itself around her as she struggled to move. The darkness made it difficult to see out of the side of the hut. On one side, through the trees, it was pitch black. Over to the sea, the sky was lighter, stars twinkling brightly.

What time was it?

She laid back down, thinking her imagination was playing tricks on her. She could feel the cool breeze coming off the ocean.

SNAP!

Her eyes jolted wide open. She covered herself with the material of the hammock, lowering her head, trying to hide. She heard light footsteps, which got heavier as they appeared to get nearer and stopped. She heard heavy breathing and through the crack of the fabric, a flashlight danced across the inside of the hut casting deep shadows.

It stopped at her head.

She closed her eyes and pretended to sleep. There was a huff, a man's grunt. Then the footsteps receded into the trees.

She took a deep breath and realised her heart was beating loudly. The crickets were continuing their song as if nothing had happened, the waves continued their pilgrimage to the beach and the wind rustled the leaves. A mosquito landed on her head and she squashed it dead.

She sunk into the hammock and tried to force herself to sleep.

Chapter Ten

The small room was drenched in unnatural light. White clinical walls made Rachel squint as she slowly opened her eyes, her head fuzzy. She made out the shape of her dad – large and squidgy – leaning against the wall, hands in his pockets, his head slumped forward. A checked white and red shirt hung outside of his trousers.

She blinked to try to focus.

Senses started to come back to her: the tang of disinfectant, the cold air on her arms, plastic on her wrist. She could feel a wrinkled hand tightly holding hers. Her mum was sitting in a chair next to her bed, her head bowed down, much like her dad. Streaks creviced her cheeks. Rachel groaned as she tried to sit. Pain seared across her midriff. A figure came into view, partially blocking the fluorescent light, straight blonde hair framing a blurred face. She felt her other hand being squeezed. Rachel couldn't make out the features but knew it was Jess. A shuffling of feet pulled her attention back to the other side of the bed. The shape of her dad stood behind her mum, a hand on her shoulder.

"Oh Rachel."

Rachel flopped her head so her cheek rested against the pillow.

"I know mum, I know what happened," she said softly, sparing her saying the words.

A pause. A glance between eyes.

"I'm so sorry," a female voice said, trying to sound strong. Arms wrapped around her neck and she smelt Jess' perfume, her soft skin against her cheeks.

"We'll get through this together Rach, okay?" she said, pulling back.

"I'm fine. Really." Rachel sniffed; her eyes stung. She tried to sit up again but the sharp pain around her middle made it impossible. She instinctively grasped her stomach, a flabby piece of skin replacing the bigger one that had been growing over the few months.

There was no kicking sensation now.

"Take it easy, love," the deep voice of her dad said, as her mum gently pushed her shoulders down. "You've had major surgery." A hum of a monitor beeped nearby, cutting through the silence, no one knowing what to say. Rachel looked blankly at the ceiling, her back aching.

"It was a girl, wasn't it? she whispered to the ceiling.

Her mum nodded slowly. A long silence followed as they all contemplated the word.

"Charlotte," Rachel said, causing everyone to look at her. She turned her head at her mum. "If it was a girl, I was going to call her Charlotte. Little Lottie." She tried to picture the features of the baby that appeared in her vision.

The chair squeaked as her mum shifted in her seat.

"We'll have a funeral for her," Christine said.

Rachel pictured a small wooden box containing a person she'd got to know so well but never met. Tears silently flowed down the two other women in the room. Her dad turned to face the wall, his hand rising to his eye.

"When can I go home?" Rachel said, her face burning.

"Not for a few days, love," her mum said. "You need to heal from the surgery. Don't worry, you'll be out in no time. And we're allowed to stay with you."

Rachel lifted her head slightly and looked around the room. Somewhere new and different. A desk with an old-style TV on it and an occupied chair were the only pieces of furniture.

"You can't sleep in that chair mum. Go home and get some rest."

"Not a chance love. I'm staying here whether you like it or not. Your dad and I are going to take it in turns. Don't worry about us, concentrate on you."

"I'm fine mum. Seriously. You can't sleep in that chair; you'll do your back in. I just want to go home. Forget about all of this." She waved her hand in the air.

Jess looked up at the couple.

"Rach," Jess said softly. "You can't be alone after…" her eyes shifted down her body and quickly back up.

Rachel stared up at the ceiling. Her hands felt under the sheet again, over the surgical pad and along her sides, down to her legs. Slowly, she edged them over the paper pants she was wearing and then the insides of her thighs. Her skin was tender to the touch. Her body felt different, transformed.

All for nothing.

She looked over to her mum, still holding her hand, mouthing a prayer.

"This is real, isn't it? Not some kind of shitty joke you're playing on me."

"No love," she replied, her bottom lip trembling. "It's real. I'm so sorry." She leaned over and kissed her on the cheek. "You don't need to do this on your own you know. Me and dad are here. And Jess. She's been here as soon as you came out of theatre." Jess stepped over and grabbed her hand. "I'm sorry too, Rach."

"You all need to stop saying you're sorry. Okay? It's not your fault. It's mine."

"No love," her dad said sternly. "It's nobody's fault. It just happened."

"Of course, it's my fault. My stupid fault she got in there and my fault I went ahead with it. It's my stupid body that caused her to get stuck. Probably won't be able to have another one either." Her voice faltered as it raised in volume.

"Love, you can't blame yourself. It's one of those things. It's really rare," her mum said softly, reassuringly, squeezing her hand again. "We're all here for you. Everyone sends their love." Rachel snapped both her hands up and let out a frustrated sigh. She could feel the judgement of her friends and family: A failure.

"Can you stop being so bloody nice to me?" she shouted, startling them all. "I've lost a baby. I never even met it. I'll move on. My body, my baby. It's no big deal." She crossed her arms over her chest. "It's no big deal," she repeated loudly, covering her face with her palms. "I only lost my bloody baby!"

She sobbed through her fingers, tears wetting her hands.

Instantly and as one, all three in the room threw their arms over her shaking body, letting her wails fill the room.

Chapter Eleven

The sound of splashing water in the distance woke Rachel. The air was warm. It took her a moment to realise where she was: lying in a hammock, a gentle breeze coming through the windowless hut stroking her nose. The splashing continued and she strained to sit in the loose fabric but managed to swing her legs down. Her feet landed on smooth wooden slats; grains of sand tickled her skin. As she stood, she stretched her arms upwards, her fingertips brushing the roof.

A dark-haired head bobbed up and down on the waves. It rose to reveal the shape of a slim man. He cupped his hands and scooped water up and out of the sea, letting it fall over his head and body. She crept out of the hut barefooted and allowed the sand to mould around her toes, looking out to the horizon. He turned, aware of someone looking at him, the water at waist height. When he spotted her, he gave a cheerful wave and strode to the beach.

"Morning! Beautiful day for it!"

"Yeah, it's amazing," she called out, looking around at the scenery, tightening a pashmina around her upper body.

"Sleep alright? That hammock gets a bit of getting used to but once you do, you'll never go back."

"I'm a bit stiff but it was all right," she said rubbing the arch of her back. "I slept okay, I kept hearing noises in the night."

"Yeah, that's part of the adventure I suppose," he grinned. "Being out here, you are part of nature. I love it."

"I did hear something. No idea what time it was. A twig snapped or something and I heard some pretty heavy breathing, just outside the hut."

"Maybe it was boar. Some wild ones roam around here sometimes."

"No, there was a flashlight. It scanned the hut."

Nathan considered it for a moment. He shrugged it off.

"I'll leave you to have a bath," pointing his thumb out to the sea. "And then I need to go to work. You are welcome to come of course."

"Yeah, that would be fab, thanks."

"I'll lend you my towel," he called over his shoulder as he brushed past her, their skin faintly touching each other, causing Rachel's pulse to quicken.

Rachel let the warm water wash over her as she got deeper into the sea. She dipped her head under and let the cool water surround her, her skin tingling with salt. It felt like she was in a warm swimming pool, similar to the ones she had played in when she was little, lying on her back and kicking her legs, trying to get the droplets as high as possible before they came crashing down. Spreading her arms out she floated, looking up at the cloudless blue sky.

Out of the corner of her eye, she spotted some movement on the beach. Nathan was standing with his hands on his hips, naked from the waist up, a towel wrapped around his legs, talking to a man in a dark blue shirt with darker patches on the sleeves. It looked like he was wearing some kind of hat which made his head flat, but it was difficult to tell from where she was – heat haze was making the sand blur and the sun's reflection from little waves made her squint. The man was throwing his arms around and gesturing out to sea. In turn, Nathan then threw his arms about, gesticulating angrily. With a jerking movement, he reached out almost striking the man's face but stopped just short. The man cowered, taking a step back, putting his hands on a bulky belt. Nathan immediately put his hands up as if in surrender.

In apology.

Angry words petered out over the water. Nathan threw his arms up and stomped to his hut. It seemed odd to Rachel – Nathan came across as a calm, laid-back kind of guy.

He's got a bit of a tantrum in him.

He disappeared for a moment. The figure put his hands on his hips and swung around, looking out toward Rachel. Staring, as if into her eyes. Nathan reappeared with something in his hand. When he gave it to the man, he pocketed it quickly, looking around. As he did, he must have said something because Nathan recoiled. The shirted man turned and disappeared amongst the trees. With his head hung low, Nathan trudged into the hut.

"What was that about?" Rachel asked as she walked out of the water, covering her front with her arms. Nathan handed her a towel and crouched in the shade of a tree, an assortment of bananas and nuts laid out in front of him. She quickly wrapped herself in the thick fabric.

"Oh, nothing," he replied, despondently. "Just the local fuzz collecting their bribe."

"Bribe?" she repeated. "What do you mean?"

"Welcome to Thailand," he said sarcastically. "Sometimes you need to grease the wheels if you want to live like a nomad." He nodded towards the hut. "Think of it like a tax. For me to live here. Well, the tax just doubled. Here, have some almonds."

"Because of me?" she replied. "I'll pay you back, it's no problem."

"It's fine. It's pennies. Just the principle of it." He shook his head and motioned for Rachel to eat something. "And his attitude." His lips turned to a sneer as he peeled a banana. "Just the way, you know, he wins. Gets away with it."

"Is there nothing you can do? Go over his head?"

"Ha! They're all at it here. But let's not let him get us off to a bad start hey? Come on, make yourself decent and let's go." As Rachel got changed, he flung his banana peel far out into the trees and slipped on his plimsolls.

"Do I need to bring anything?"

He swivelled around as she stepped out of the hut. He eyed her up and down.

"Nah," he said with a wink. "Just your beautiful self," and they turned to go, following the water's edge to the imposing brick building.

Chapter Twelve

The few days in the solitary hospital room felt like months. Her dad kept flicking through the channels on the TV when each programme ended, ambling in and out of the room with hot drinks. The nurses were the only thing that disrupted the monotony, fussing over her vitals now and then. Sometimes she struggled to sit up as the scars and the stitches in her stomach stretched.

In her sleep, she would toss and turn, wincing in pain, before feeling the gentle patting of her arm and a shush-shushing from her mum. Her breasts would leak, reminding her of her body producing food for her non-existent baby. Occasionally, she would wake up confused.

"Is Lottie okay?

"Lottie didn't make it, love," her mum would respond, crinkling her forehead, and rubbing her eyes.

"Oh yeah." And then she would turn and go back to sleep.

She thought she'd convinced herself that it probably wasn't the best thing to see her baby. Mum and dad were right: it would be too traumatic. If she met Lottie, then maybe she would become real, rather than this abstract *thing* that everyone keeps talking about.

Out of sight, out of mind is what mum kept saying to her through her teenage years. *As long as you behave inside….*

Jess brought flowers every afternoon, but they reminded Rachel of a life that had been plucked from their safety, taken from its food source, and left to wilt and die. Still, she smiled and said thanks when she put them in the vase on the desk. She sometimes bought chocolate too, and some magazines, which her mum would put uneaten and unread in the waiting room when she left.

Rachel was glad that Jess didn't bring Natalie to visit. She would have to see her at some point, but not yet. Not in the hospital. A woman had visited every day, dressed in a smart suit and high heels, holding a notepad and taking notes as she repeatedly asked how she was feeling, how she was coping. The shame of having to talk to her, to go over the fact that she'd killed her baby. Her mum and dad were asked to leave the room whenever she came, and Rachel willed the time to go so they would come back. Even though they hardly spoke to each other, except for the odd sharp word from her mum.

"John! Stop fussing!"

But she liked being fussed over.

And having someone in the room with her.

Three days later Rachel left the hospital room, putting one foot gingerly in front of the other, her mum and dad holding either side of her. The car journey home wasn't the one she envisaged she would be having when she was panting and grimacing on the way in. She kept glancing at the empty space next to her on the back seat, where the baby carrier should have been. She looked out of the window expecting things to have changed. Shops, people, signs. Even the leaves of the trees. But everything was exactly as it had been. Life carried on.

No big drama.

The only thing that had changed was her.

The car pulled up outside her home and a neighbour's curtain twitched. Their door opened and an elderly woman with light grey styled hair came stumbling out, a huge, big smile etched on her face. She ran up to the car and peered in.

"Congratulations darling! What is it? A boy, a girl? Congratulations Grandma!"

Her smile froze and her face dropped when the faces weren't returning the same smile and there was no carrycot in the car. Rachel's mum shook her head and pursed her lips as if to say *don't*.

"Oh no," she spluttered softly. Rachel was escorted in through the front door by her dad hearing the neighbour's panicky voice fade "if you need anything, Christine, just ask…"

Inside, the kettle was put on and Rachel was forced to sit.

"I just need to go to the loo," she said.

"I'll help you," her mum replied, taking her by the arm.

"I can do it!" Rachel snapped back. Her dad raised his eyebrows then shrugged his shoulders. She carefully stood up, the pain returning to her midriff, and slowly made her way to the stairs, gripping hold of the banister and pulling herself up, one step at a time. Halfway she had to stop and rest. She looked down and her mum was at the bottom watching her.

"I'm okay," she shouted down and sat on the steps, pushing herself up backwards one step at a time. Whilst resting on the top step, she saw the open door of the nursery. With effort, she walked over to it, her hand soothing her back attempting to ease the pain. Peering in, she saw the empty crib and the mobile hanging listlessly above it. She padded over to the changing table and ran her hand over the nappies piled high, opening one up and laying it out flat. Next, she picked up the blue talcum powder bottle and squirted the contents onto the nappy, the dust going everywhere.

"There, there," she whispered.

She did the sticky straps up and tilted her head, smiling at an imaginary baby inside the empty nappy. She bent down, the pain in her stomach coursing through her, and kissed the top of the changing mat.

"There you go, little one," she said. "All clean and tidy."

She lifted the nappy and placed it gently in the crib, covered it with a knitted blanket, reached up and twisted the motor on the mobile. A tinny melody filled the room. Her head cocked, she looked down at the blanket, a satisfied smile crept onto her face and she softly sang the words in time to the tune from the mobile.

"I hear babies cry... I watch them grow..." Her voice started to crack.

"... They'll learn much more. Than I'll ever know..." She struggled to keep in time with the music.

"... And I think to myself..." Before she could say the next line, she burst out crying, sobbing loudly. Out of nowhere, her mum's arms swathed her, shushing her, and rocking her like a baby. The mobile slowed its tune as the tears streamed out, unable to stop.

***

Rachel sat alone in her flat for the first time in nearly three weeks. Flowers sat wilted in vases, the fridge was full of food from friends and family and unopened sympathy cards filled the bin. Now, in the silence, she could hear the ticking of a clock. She lay on the sofa, swinging her feet and staring up at the ceiling, thoughts swilling in her mind. What would it have been like the first time she would have been alone with Lottie? All the help gone and on her own.

She plumped a cushion and imagined it as Lottie, lying next to her on the sofa, her mouth opening and closing like a fish, her arms and legs moving independently. She pretended the baby was trying to grab her fingers and giggling whilst she tickled her tummy.

I made you.

She leaned over to kiss her head, her lips touching the rough fabric of the cushion. Surprised, she raised her head and realised the illusion. Her brow furrowed, she picked it up and slammed it back down on the sofa. She pounded the cushion again and again until she heard cries. She put it in the crook of her arm, apologising over and over.

"You must be hungry," she whispered aloud and carefully laid the cushion back on the sofa, pulling a blanket over it. She got up slowly and tiptoed to the kitchen. Whilst the kettle was boiling, she reached for a bottle and a canister of formula and carefully measured the powder into the little plastic spoon. Levelling off the top, she poured it into the bottle, filled it up with the hot water, replaced the cap and gave it a good shake. The water was scalding so she ran it under the cold tap and placed it on the counter. Feeling a pang of hunger herself, she popped two slices of bread into the toaster. She didn't have much time as Lottie would be getting grumpy, so she twisted the timer up to quicken the browning time. She walked over to the fridge and took out a tub of margarine and a jar of jam. Setting it on the counter she picked up the bottle and went into the living room, popping off the lid as she went. She sat down and was glad to have the weight off her feet. The bottle was still too hot to give Lottie, so she placed it on the floor. As she did, she noticed a putrid smell and looked down at the cushion.

"Have you done a stinky-winky young lady?" she said in a baby voice. "Have you done a stinky-winky?"

She picked up the cushion, cradling it in the crook of her arm and stood up, wincing again at the pain. The smell was getting stronger.

"Okay, okay, I'm on it. I can smell it," she cooed.

She made her way up slowly to the nursery, the stink replacing the urgency of the pain, and gently laid the cushion on the changing table.

A piercing alarm sounded from the kitchen.

"Don't cry Lottie, mummy's here," she shouted over the noise, stroking the top of the cushion. "Please stop crying."

The alarm continued and Rachel got more agitated. She raised her voice at the cushion.

"I'm sorting it, Lottie. Don't cry. I'm doing it."

She flustered for a nappy and the wipes and squeezed the talcum powder bottle. Dust filled the air and covered the table. The alarm appeared to be growing in volume.

"STOP CRYING LOTTIE, I'M DOING IT!"

Tears began to stream as she panicked trying to open the nappy with one hand whilst putting her palm over the cushion with the other, holding it down. The alarm continued to ring, reaching a crescendo.

"WILL YOU STOP BLOODY CRYING!"

She screamed at the cushion as the sticky straps wouldn't fit over it to do up.

"STOP IT! STOP IT!"

The ringing carried on.

"STOP IT!" She grabbed the cushion and flung it against the wall, making a soft thud before dropping to the floor. Rachel put her hands over her ears and sunk to the floor, curling up as much as her stomach would allow, screaming, willing the baby to stop crying.

Suddenly the noise stopped.

Silence.

A pipping noise broke the calm.

Pip-pip.

Rachel looked across the floor, seeing the cushion on its edge resting against the wall.

Pip-pip.

"I'm coming Lottie," she sobbed, crawling across the floor.

Pip-pip.

She cradled the cushion, apologising.

Shushing.

Pip-pip.

Apologising more.

Silence.

The pipping had stopped.

"That's right. Go to sleep honey."

Rachel leant against the wall, tears running down her face, rocking the cushion back and forth in her arms, shushing her.

"It's okay, it's okay, darling. Mummy's here, mummy's here."

***

In a daze, she heard her name being called out, each time more urgently.

"Oh my god, RACHEL! John, she's up here!"

She heard heavy footsteps race into the room. Rachel's mum crouched down and propped her up, putting her arm around her for support. Her dad towered over them, a full bottle of formula hanging from his fingers, looking down at the two women, one holding tightly to a cushion. He surveyed the room, talcum powder everywhere and an empty nappy in the crib, half-covered by Auntie Barbara's knitted blanket. A wet wipe laid limply on the changing table.

"It's okay, love, I'm here for you."

Rachel looked up at her mum and across to the bottle.

"I'm sorry mum," she sobbed.

"It's alright, everything will be okay."

Early morning sunlight filtered through the window.

"Look, I think it would be better if you came and stayed with us for a while, hmm," she said. "Just for a few weeks. It would be good to have some female company. So, you can get back on your feet. Let us look after you, huh?" Rachel nodded, sniffing. She reached around her mum's neck and squeezed her tightly.

"I'm so sorry."

"You've got nothing to be sorry for, love. Okay?"

Her mum pulled back and looked at the tear-filled eyes, the unconditional bond between mother and child – the same bond that Rachel thought she would be having right now.

In this room.

With her own little one.

Chapter Thirteen

Over the next two weeks, Rachel fell into a routine. Thoughts of catching a bus to an unknown place faded from her mind. She was in paradise. And she was enjoying it with a handsome, compassionate man who seemed to like her for who she was. Every morning she would wake up, have a swim, and walk along the beach to the orphanage with Nathan. The girls would run up and hug her around her waist, squealing and fighting to be the closest and have the longest cuddles. They would gravitate to her like a magnet at lunch when she sat with Anurak and Nathan, and when she needed to go to the hole-in-the-ground the girls would follow and wait outside.

The Pied Piper of Bo Hin, Nathan would tease.

Every few days, around three o'clock Mrs Pai, the shop owner, would come into the administration block, bringing parcels of food for the kids and gossip for the ladies. One day she brought Rachel a pretty red dress with yellow butterflies on it.

"So... Mr Nathan...?" she would say with a wink every time, eliciting howls of laughter from the other women in the office, which in turn led to a crescendo of kissing noises.

Not that anything had happened between the two of them.

Despite what Rachel took to be flirting, never amounted to anything. One evening, as they sat outside the hut in front of a campfire, bottles of Chang beer flowing, they accidentally brushed shoulders from belly laughing, tears rolling down their faces. The laughter subsided into an awkward silence, their faces inches from each other. It could have been the perfect romantic moment. Instead, the mood changed, and Nathan made his excuses and buried himself in the sand for the night.

Weirdly, Jess' face had popped into her mind at that exact moment.

"Come on you, let's go and get some supplies," Nathan said one afternoon as their shift finished. They sauntered along the dusty path next to the tall brick wall, the sun weakening but the air still warm. A stiff breeze rustled the tops of the trees.

They turned into the square and headed into a shack. As they paid for their supplies, a white patrol car pulled up, red and blue lights extinguished on its roof. The door swung open and a uniformed man stepped out.

Up close it was more of a grey colour than the blue Rachel thought when she was in the sea. The shapes that she made out were badges; one being the red, white and blue-striped Thai flag, the others being shields and crests that indicated police. The flat head she saw from the sea was a beret pulled down tightly, adorned with a silver badge over a red insignia, sitting at an angle. Beneath the hat was a round, chubby face – at odds with the thin faces of the villagers – small dark eyes and a bristly short moustache above his top lip. It reminded her of a metal brush her dad would use to scrap the front drive of weeds. He couldn't have been more than thirty, but the crisp uniform made him look older. As he strutted towards the shop, a large belt with handcuffs and a truncheon jostled.

He paused in front of Rachel and slowly looked her up and down, a sneer appearing on his face. She instinctively wrapped her arms around her waist. Old men in the square stopped and watched. The policeman put his hands on his hips and tucked his thumbs under his belt.

"Come on, let's go," Nathan said, grabbing her wrist, not taking his eyes off the policeman.

"Who is that?" she said as they rounded the tall wall.

"Ah, just the local fuzz. Nothing to worry about."

"The one you gave money to."

Nathan shot her a look.

"Like I said. Nothing to worry about. Let's get the fire going huh? Can you get some wood?"

Every evening Nathan would start a fire on the beach outside the hut. Sometimes they would swim in the sea, other times they would sit and watch the flames, dance and chat. Every time they would crack open a Chang beer and talk long after the sun had set about what had happened that day – the kids at the orphanage, the jokes and the gossip. They rarely spoke about the future or their pasts, their lives away from the beach. The only time Nathan creaked open the door of his past was when they were talking about the progress of Junta, a nine-year-old girl with Down syndrome. Nathan had taken quite a shine to her. They would sit together at the front of the class, staring intently at the teacher whilst Junta tried to copy all the words. Nathan said her mental age was about four and when Rachel asked how he knew, he indifferently said his sister used to have Downs.

"Used to?" Rachel asked, surprised.

"She died," was his curt response. "Hey, did I tell you about how the Pais met? Anurak told me. It's amazing. You wouldn't guess it looking at their little café and shop on the main road."

"Well, now you have to tell me," Rachel said, feeling like she was flirting. She opened a Chang and passed it over.

"When they were kids, they were living in neighbouring villages. Didn't know each other. Going along with their lives all nicely, nicely. Then the Tsunami happened."

He prodded the fire with a twig.

"Along with tens of other scared kids and adults, they were forced together. All this land here, where we are sitting, was devasted. People said the sea just disappeared. Most of them ran inland in panic, some climbed trees and many clambered over each other to get through the single door of the monastery, as it was then. The Pais were the lucky ones. They were only twelve when it happened.

"When the thunder of the water died down and they went outside, they said the first thing they saw was the sea through the hole in the outside wall: all calm and idyllic like nothing had happened. Only debris and rubbish littered the ground, the courtyard covered in a layer of water - bits of wood, fishing nets, fish flapping about and a body lying face down in the corner.

Rachel shook her head in disbelief.

"Well, when they stepped through the hole, they saw an image that would never leave them again: where once was lush rainforest, there was nothing. Just chaos. Inland, they saw an upside-down fishing boat in the far distance. A roof of a house - the walls and windows detached – had been tilted on its side. Trees were lying, bent, snapped, or uprooted. And there were loads of fish amongst the debris – fish they had never seen before. All sorts of weird shapes and sizes.

"Anyway, the Pais went to where their homes had been but found nothing. Their homes were gone. And so were their mums and dads. They didn't know what to do, so went back to the monastery. Mr Pai says that was the day he turned from a boy into a man."

"Bloody hell," Rachel said to herself.

"Tell me about it. I mean what were you doing when you were twelve?"

"Ha! Probably causing my parents grief."

"Exactly. A different world. So, yeah. The monastery turned into a refuge for survivors. Eventually, aid agencies reached them with food and medicine, blankets and clothes, but more importantly, said Mrs Pai, hope. The mood changed. There were smiles and optimism. Then the agencies left, carrying on down the coast, trying to find more survivors to give out supplies and hope."

"A happy ending?" Rachel smiled.

"Not sure I'd call it happy. But yeah." Rachel's cheeks flushed. "Obviously they were orphans now. They never saw their mums or dads, sisters, brothers or friends again."

Rachel cringed at her crass comment.

"Eventually they married. They had this unbreakable bond between them. They helped in the rebuilding and replanting of the area, painfully slow over the next few years. The village decided to keep the hole in the wall as a memorial and reminder of the power of the sea, and the vulnerability of the building which saved them."

"I guess it's no surprise then that Mr and Mrs Pais had the kindness to shelter a lost stranger," Rachel said. "Even sleeping on the floor of their own home, giving up their only bed."

"Yep. I suppose their scars are covered but the memories are still raw."

Crickets interrupted the silence as Nathan's eyes met Rachel's. The sun had dipped well below the horizon and only the glowing embers of the fire danced in each other's eyes.

"And what about you?" Rachel said softly.

"What about me?"

"How did you end up here?"

"Same as you."

"What do you mean?" Rachel's eyes narrowed.

"Mrs Pai offered me the floor of the café. 100 Baht."

Rachel's laugh boomed across the beach and the sea. Birds chattered in the trees at the sudden noise.

"My story is for another day," he smiled as he got up and tidied away the bottles.

Rachel climbed into her hammock. The material now caressed her back. Nathan nestled under the trees, burrowing with his shoulders and legs into a sandy cocoon. There was no hint of a peck on the cheek, no awkward do-you-want-to-come-back-to-mine. Just two people turning in for the night.

It was perfection, she thought. *Nothing could ruin it.*

Could it?

Chapter Fourteen

The sitting room was back to normal. No knitted blankets, cuddly toys or baby formula anymore. The spare room had its single bed back and a white desk, replacing the broken crib and ripped newborn clothes. The only memories of it being a nursery were strips of teddy bear wallpaper scribbled over with black marker pen and the damaged ceiling where the mobile once hung. Whilst Rachel was curled up asleep on the sofa, her mum and dad had spent a whole afternoon tidying the kitchen of broken glass and crockery, spilt formula powder and splinters of plastic from shattered bowls, two-handled cups and bottles. It had taken Rachel some effort with a hammer to crack that hard plastic. The electric sterilizer wasn't salvageable to sell or take to one of the many charity shops on the high street.

Sometimes she would hear her parents discussing her life.

"We've got to get Edward round now," Christine said, in a whisper. "She's tone-deaf to advice and she won't go to the support groups. You happy now?"

"Yeah, yeah," her dad said, impatiently. "We got to try and let Rach make her mind up. We can't go forcing anything on her."

"For God's sake John, she needs help. I'm calling him now."

"Alright, but ease him into it."

"Do you think I'm stupid?" she spat back.

"No love, of course not."

On instruction from Christine, the vicar crept into Rachel's room. The curtains were drawn, muting the bright lighting trying to come into the room. As he entered, a warmth seemed to descend on the room. He sat on the very edge of the bed where Rachel was lying, curled up, squeezing a pillow.

"Hello again, Rachel. It's been a while."

He received no reaction.

"I know you probably don't want to hear from me," he said earnestly and without judgement in a hushed voice. "But your parents thought it might be a good thing to talk. And I'm a good listener."

Rachel raised her head from the pillow, her eyes blurry, and saw his domed head and the fuzzy outline of his stubble.

"Aren't you going to say you're sorry?" she said. It didn't mean to come out sarcastically.

"Would that help?"

"No, it wouldn't."

"Then I won't. You know, I can't imagine what you are going through. The excitement of the last few months, your body changing, everyone fussing around you. The mental preparation. It's a miraculous time." With effort, Rachel sat up against the headboard. "People don't know what to say, how to respond. 'I'm sorry' is an easy thing to say. But it's said with love."

"I know," she sniffed. "But how am *I* supposed to respond?"

"There is no rule book. You've been through something so traumatic. Life-changing. No mother, no one, knows how to respond to losing a child. We all cope in our own way and that's okay."

"Are mum and dad angry I trashed the house?"

"No of course not. They are concerned. We all are. We want to help you get through it. And that begins with talking." She sighed and pulled the pillow tighter.

"You're good you know?"

"What do you mean?"

"I mean, your sermons. I like them. Well, some of them."

The vicar chuckled. "I'll take that as a compliment. From someone as young as you, too" His smile warmed Rachel. The creases around his eyes framed gentle, forgiving eyes.

"Some of the things you said made sense to me. Even before all of this. But I have questions." Her eyes glanced down to her lap. A silence ensued. The vicar waited for Rachel to speak first. Instead, she buried her face in the pillow and sobbed. He allowed her to finish not saying a thing, to compose herself and lower the pillow.

"Why me?" she wept. "You said that God is so great and loving, so why did He put that baby in me when I didn't even want it? Why did He put me through it all only to rip it away? If I am to believe in something which is 'all-seeing' and 'all-loving', why has He done this to me?"

The vicar stayed silent, allowing the tension to lower. He didn't want to get into a fight. After a minute, he cleared his throat.

"'Consider it pure joy, my brothers and sisters, whenever you face trials of many kinds, because you know that the testing of your faith produces perseverance. Let perseverance finish its work so that you may be mature and complete, not lacking anything.' James Chapter 1," he said, looking pleased with himself. "What this means is that God has bigger plans for you. He chose you for a reason. It's His Will, *God's Will*. We don't know what that is yet. But you must get through His test to understand the bigger picture He has for you."

"That sounds like bullshit to me."

The vicar chuckled again. He rubbed his eyes. "Okay, how about this one: 'the flower that blooms in adversity is the most rare and beautiful of all'," he said slowly, looking at the curtains.

"That's a nice one. Which chapter is that from?"

"Mulan," he said with a smile. "The Disney film."

The ends of Rachel's mouth curled up.

"Look, I'm not saying this is going to be easy. It's not. It's going to take a long time to overcome this. The important thing is that you have caring and loving people around you. There are two sitting downstairs right now, one looking at you, and I'm sure you have some lovely friends and family who would do anything for you. When you are ready, the flower will blossom and you will know. This is a step on your journey to greatness. I agree it's a challenging step, but strength and love will get you through."

The vicar allowed the silence to fill the room again whilst Rachel contemplated the words.

"You know, mum and dad thought I shouldn't see the baby. I don't even know what she looked like. Charlotte. That's the name I chose. Little Lottie."

Edward glanced up, the creases of his neck stretching to reveal an Adam's Apple.

"'I am no bird; and no net ensnares me: I am a free human being with an independent will which I now exert to leave you'," he said, looking pleased with himself

"What?"

"Charlotte. You know, the eldest of the Bronte sisters."

"Um, no."

"Oh. Jane Eyre?"

There was no response.

His cheeks flushed red, and he fiddled with his fingers.

"I don't know if that decision was the right one or the wrong one. I mean seeing the baby. I can imagine it can be traumatic for some. For others, it might be helpful. I don't know but whatever decision they made was to protect you. Grief is a process, not a thing you study for or tick off your list. The funeral will help."

"I'm not sure I can go through with it. Seeing a tiny little coffin, knowing my Lottie is in there. You must have done them before, what's it like?"

"Yes," he said. "It can be comforting. Not only saying goodbye but also grieving what hasn't happened. The hopes, the dreams, the projection of the future. That needs processing."

"But she was never born. I never even met her."

"But she was real. You felt her. You prepared for her, both physically and mentally. And emotionally. It's important to understand that grief is complex. Don't think of the funeral as closure. See it as a step in the healing process. I know it's not going to be as simple as that but it's a step. The funeral is a chance to speak to God and for God to speak to you. People will want to come and pay their respects. To you. The love of God and the people closest to you at that moment can help to heal." Rachel considered it, squeezing the pillow again. She looked up to the ceiling, tears welling up in her eyes.

"What if," she began. "I mean, I think it was a mistake. I think I should have gone to see her. I should have held her. I grew her. I killed her. I should have said sorry."

"Rachel," he said softly, reaching out a hand and placing it on her shoulder. "You did no such thing. There is nothing you or the doctors could have done. This is not your fault."

"But what if I'd told the midwife earlier that something was wrong? I felt it. I should have shouted at them, but I was too damn nice. I just listened to their advice when I knew something bad was happening. I could have saved her." The tears rolled down her cheeks and dropped onto the pillow. The vicar shifted closer and moved his hand so his arm could wrap around her shoulders. She sobbed into his chest.

"If I hadn't been so bloody stubborn and moved to my side rather than insisting on pushing on my back, maybe she wouldn't have got stuck. The umbilical cord would have fallen, away from her shoulders."

"Rachel, listen to me," he said, perhaps too forcefully. She pulled away from his chest. "It wasn't your fault; it isn't your fault and it will never be your fault. You must believe that. If you want to blame someone, blame Him. Because I know in my heart, He has a purpose for you. And this test is to make you strong. 'For I consider that the sufferings of this present time are not worth comparing with the glory that is to be revealed to us'."

Rachel blinked hard. "I think I prefer the flower quote." The vicar gave a sweet chuckle and removed his arm.

"Do you understand? Really understand? This is your journey to greatness."

She nodded. "Thank you."

"Your mum said that a cuppa tea was in the works," he said with a smile, standing up. "You are not going to heal overnight so be kind to yourself. This doesn't have to define who you are but will make you who you will be."

"Thank you."

"You are more than welcome Rachel. Any time."

He looked back over his shoulder, a worried look on his face as he closed the door.

***

Standing in the drizzly rain, she hadn't even noticed the grim shopfront on the high street before, sandwiched between the bakery and the chemist. But there it was, with two little black tombstones and a couple of white urns serving as window dressing. Her mum and dad were inside paying for the coffin, and she needed some air. She walked a few steps to get away and leaned against the window frame of a travel agent. A raindrop plopped on her phone as she dialled Jess' number, looking disinterestedly through the window. A digital screen scrolled through picturesque images of beaches, mountains and rivers whilst she waited for her to pick up. Jess had been a star, being there for her in a way that her mum and dad couldn't. The vicar had said some comforting things but sometimes she just wanted to shout and scream and get it off her chest. And Jess had let her. Let her get her anger out, let her spill out all the permutations of what ifs, what-would-have-happened and it's-not-fair. But she was also conscious that it was one-sided, and she didn't want to burden her with all her problems, depression and negativity. She had been so good with suppressing stories of Natalie, how cute she was and what she was doing.

"Am I a bad friend?" she'd asked.

"Don't be silly," was the stern reply.

But she needed a life too, Rachel thought, one away from a grieving mother constantly calling and messaging her. Nevertheless, Jess answered with a chirp. She could hear Natalie crying in the background.

"Hi, sorry. Is this a bad time?"

"No, no of course not babe. Anything for you. What's up?"

"Just been to the funeral parlour. I've chosen the coffin."

"Oh, Rach I'm so sorry, I completely forgot. You okay?"

The baby's cry became more intense, and she could hear clattering at the end of the phone.

"No, it's okay. It's fine. Sorry, sounds like I caught you at a bad time."

"Rubbish. You can call me anytime." She heard more rattling and crying. She pictured her in the kitchen, the phone wedged between the cheek and shoulder.

"I just wondered if you fancied a coffee. I'm on the high street."

"Yeah, sure babe. Um, can you give me 15?"

"Yeah, yeah of course." She stared at the screen in the travel agent's window, offers flashing up to far-flung places. "I want to run an idea past you."

Chapter Fifteen

Nathan and Rachel had left the orphanage when the last class had ended, opting to have dinner at the Pai's roadside café. Apparently, the daily bus from Bangkok hadn't stopped as usual which meant the tills were empty, so Nathan had suggested they helped them out. As they returned to the square and rounded the corner of the dusty road, they knew something was wrong. The villagers were all standing, tense and alert, staring at three policemen sitting under a tree on green plastic chairs. All eyes were focused on the foreigners as they came into view. The leader looked to his side at his lackey and chuckled, his shaking shoulders obvious as Nathan and Rachel approached the gathering. He stood, pushed his hand onto his knee to aid him in getting up and rested a coke bottle on the standard-issue belt, which bulged with handcuffs, a radio and a knife.

"Ah, Mr Nathan," he called out as the couple tried to walk past them. Nathan raised his hand in greeting and kept walking. Rachel stuttered behind.

"Er, Mr Nathan!" he sing-songed. "We talk." Nathan sighed, looked at Rachel and changed his course.

"It time, Mr Nathan," he grinned, his feet inching slightly apart giving a domineering stance. Nathan stood opposite the policeman, towering a good few inches above him. His sleeve-less vest, cheap shorts and dirty plimsolls looked comical mirrored against the unformed official.

"I don't have any more money," he said, his palms facing out.

"You lie," the policeman said, looking bored.

"No. No money. I don't earn money from the orphanage. I work for free." He rubbed his fingers and then wagged a finger.

"No money, no stay." He turned to his lackeys who smirked in solidarity.

Rachel took a step forward, hands on hips.

"Why do we have to pay to be here?" she said, raising her voice and stretching her back. All three policemen glanced over to Rachel without moving their heads. The villagers instinctively took a step back.

"We cause no trouble," Nathan interrupted, putting his hand on her shoulder, but she shrugged it off.

"No trouble," the policeman repeated, rubbing his fingers together as the other two policemen stood up behind him. "Money, no trouble."

"No money!" Rachel said, wagging her finger.

"Then you go," he said calmly, pointing his finger down the road.

"Why?" Rachel said, raising her voice, causing the villagers to cower. The policeman's eyes narrowed.

"Lady," he said, in barely a whisper. His hand moved to his belt. The other still clutched the coke bottle. "You bin here on beach for 4 weeks…." He paused and pulled a notepad from his top pocket, deliberately and slowly turned each page until he found the one he was looking for. He made a show of mentally counting on his fingers.

"You bin here on beach 32 days. Beach no hotel. It illegal to sleep on beach." His lips parted as his small mouth widened to a grin, revealing big gaps between his teeth.

"You must pay if you want stay."

"If it's illegal, then why are we paying?"

"You pay, I don't arrest. Simple."

"That sounds like a bribe to me." The policeman's smile faded and his eyes darkened. Nathan interjected, trying to calm Rachel down.

"It's okay, she doesn't understand. I'll pay. Tomorrow." The policeman took a small step forward and craned his neck, so his nose almost touched hers.

"You understand big girl. You understand." Rachel's hand balled into a fist by her side. His eyes flicked down her body. She felt a familiar energy course through her. He turned his shoulders whilst his eyes kept locked on hers. Rachel swallowed, standing defiantly, her heart pumping against her ribs. He looked over to Nathan.

"Tomorrow. You pay." The policemen swaggered away from the group, got into the police car and drove off, leaving a trail of dust in their wake. Rachel breathed a sigh of relief. Nathan bowed his head. The villagers chatted animatedly to each other, gesturing and pointing at Rachel.

"You need to be careful Rachel," Nathan said. "He's right you know. We can't sleep on the beach."

"If it's illegal, he can prove it. It's all guff, so he can get his bribe."

"Rachel, have you heard of the things that westerners get done for in Thailand? Drugs, drink, anything! They throw you in jail and make it very difficult to get out. We're on their turf out here. Their terms."

"Drugs? We're hardly doing drugs, Nathan! All we're doing is sleeping on a beach. And we're volunteering in their orphanage. For free!"

"I know I know," Nathan said, raising his palms. He sat down on the dirt and motioned her to sit next to him.

"That's Officer Mee Noi. Well, I don't know if he is an officer but it's what Anurak calls him. He's a nasty piece of work. I was the same as you when he first wanted money. I couldn't believe it. Refused to pay of course but Anurak was insistent. Better to keep the peace."

"It's so unfair," Rachel said, looking down, moving her feet amongst the dirt.

"Yeah, well, life's not fair, is it? Look at those kids in the orphanage. It's not fair they were abandoned or born without limbs or got disabilities. They make do."

"Doesn't mean it's right. Doesn't mean we can roll over and let him do what he wants."

"You need to understand the context a bit. He's a powerful person here. The badge says a lot. People here fear him. He's been here a long time and people know what he's capable of. Anurak hasn't said anything specific but the way he speaks…. He's not someone to mess with. Just toe the line."

"Well, I don't want to do that."

"Look I agree with you. I've been here a long time. Yeah, I've paid him and he's used to it."

"I haven't paid him," Rachel interjected. "He's not used to me." Nathan turned his head and looked at her.

"True," he sighed and leant back on his hands. "Come on, let's go."

They stood and they made their way back along the coastal road that Rachel had come from, through the dust track and past the Pai's house. A scooter tooted them as they came to the junction. Anurak pulled up alongside them.

"Hey," he said sternly, his eyebrows furled on a helmetless head. "Why you argue with Mee Noi?"

News travelled fast in the village. Nathan and Rachel looked at each other. It was Rachel that spoke.

"He was asking for money. To sleep on the beach!" Anurak shrugged his shoulders.

"You careful, he dangerous. Meet at Khun Pai. Now!"

When they reached the café, Anurak was talking animatedly with the husband and wife. As they got nearer, Rachel could see that they had worry etched over their faces.

"Mee Noi bad man," Anurak said as they approached. "Many trouble."

"That doesn't mean he can get away with what he likes," Rachel said. Anurak fluttered his hands up and down, beckoning her to stop.

"Yes, yes. Young girl. Very innocent. Want to change world." He turned to the Pais and spoke in fast Thai. They both rolled their eyes, muttering in Thai.

"Mee Noi make trouble for villagers. Very powerful man. Very important. Badge he wears very important. He has boss who is best friends with Chief of Police. In Bangkok."

Rachel drew breath, about to say something. An urge came over her: to fight and to stand up for them. She'd been so welcomed by everyone in the village – from the Pais to Anurak, the children and of course Nathan. The villagers had been so sweet. She'd had enough of fate and letting Him dictate things. Yet, her voice stayed firmly in her throat. The Pais were conversing quickly with Anurak. It sounded like an argument.

"Okay, okay," he seemed to concede. He paused as if trying to find the right English word.

"Mr Pai say I should tell you. Mrs Pai warn not." Anurak glanced at the two Thais. Khun Pai nodded his head, giving his approval.

"Mee Noi. He lost parents during Tsunami. He 14 years old. Baby really. He hide when wave hit and survived. Miracle. Men found him under wood. Took to monastery. He walking around village every day looking for parents. Crying. Every day he look but no find. Nothing. No house, no furniture, no toys. He also lost sister and brother."

"Mee Noi has a brother?" Nathan said, looking up suddenly.

"Yes yes. Long time ago dead," Anurak said impatiently. "But he look every day for family. Khun Pai help. They try feed him, find clothes for him but he no want. Every day for six month he walk around, looking under wood and rubbish. Six month." Anurak raised his two hands and spread out three fingers on each as if to reinforce the time.

"Villagers started to clean up. Western people come help. Remove rubbish and plant trees. Build road. He not stop looking. He angry at westerners for taking rubbish away. When trucks – any trucks – leave with rubbish he try to stop. He think maybe family are in truck. White men push him away to leave. He child, they not care. He not happy. Scream at them. One time he put knife in tyre." Rachel looked over at Nathan, her eyebrows raised in surprise. Anurak noticed.

"You cannot imagine disaster of Tsunami. Everything destroyed. No family. No house. Nothing. I come in 2007. Still nothing. Some trees start growing. Monastery only. Nothing else."

Rachel swallowed, trying to put herself in the situation.

"Khun Pai try help every day. Look with him. They say he speak no word. Mee Noi stay in monastery for long time. But get angry. Very angry. You know this age? Very confusing for boy growing up. Fight with other children. Throw food on floor. I come and try help. In Bangkok I spend many years with orphans before I come here. I see bad signs and try help. But he no want help. Very difficult child. Much trauma. Khun Pai, they together and help each other. Mee Noi no let anyone in." He pointed his finger to his head.

"He get more angry and fight more. We put him on own, no speak to children. Make trouble. He leave. Walk away with nothing. No take clothes. We hear no for many years. Maybe ten years. Khun Pai marry, make home, make business." He waved his hand around in the air. He smiled over to them and put his hand on the wife's hand.

"Then he come back." His face darkened. "He come back policeman. Drive big car. Badge on chest. He find Khun Pai and make trouble. He find other villagers and make trouble. Say he in charge. He boss now. Everyone sad. Everyone try hard to build village back and he make trouble. They say, he like, er, how you say: middle of coconut. Inside coconut is brown. White people drink from brown coconut. It make Thai sick," he stuck out his tongue mimicking being sick. "Green coconut better."

"We say 'a bad egg'," Nathan interrupted.

"Aha, yes! Very good words. He never make trouble with me. He never visit orphanage. Five year, maybe six year now. Never put foot in. No trouble for me but I hear trouble for villagers. And Khun Pai." He pointed to the couple who looked solemn. They knew the narrative of the story. Anurak sighed and shook his head. "Very difficult." Rachel took a deep breath.

"Why is he so angry with the Pais?"

Anurak shrugged his shoulders in exhaustion.

"I not know." He turned to the Pais and said something in rapid Thai. They both shrugged their shoulders in unison. The wife spoke back to Anurak, quietly and thoughtfully.

"Maybe he jealous they find love. No fair they find love in hardship."

Rachel and Nathan looked at each other.

"Look. I get the past. I understand why he's like that," Rachel started. "But it's still not right that he can get away with it. Someone needs to stand up to him." Anurak gave a weary sign, like he had heard it all before, and turned to the Pais translating in Thai. They both shook their heads in unison. Khun Pai spoke in English:

"Young girl. He dangerous. No trouble."

"You can't live your lives like this!" Rachel cried out, shocking them all. "You can't let him get away with it!"

Khun Pai looked directly at Nathan, then flicked his eyes to Rachel.

"Only money. Money no important. Give Mee Noi money, no trouble. Life good. Friends important."

"Rachel, these guys have been through a lot. Maybe we take their advice?"

"It's just not right. All they've done is help him and he throws it in their face." Rachel's tone was getting irritated, her heartbeat increasing.

"Their decision Rachel, not yours."

"But surely there's something we can do?"

"Well…." Nathan wanted to say something but trailed off. Everyone looked at him, expectedly. He looked at the three Thai people each in their eyes.

"Mee Noi has a brother?"

"Yes yes," Anurak repeated. "He dead. Why you so interested?"

"What was his name?" he replied slowly. Anurak spoke to the Pais in Thai. They both answered in unison: "Somchai."

Nathan suddenly went pale.

At that moment, they heard a vehicle rumbling in the distance, taking their attention to the road. The sound was different to the other scooters that had trundled past them. It was a car, a clean silver BMW with the same badge on its side as Officer Mee Noi's shirt and a strip of red, blue and white lights atop its roof. The nearside window was wound down and an arm lent casually out of it. The car slowed as it passed the five people, all in a huddle outside Khun Pai's roadside café like they were plotting something. Mee Noi strained his neck at them as he drove slowly past. His eyes narrowed as he looked at the group. The car crawled so slowly that it was like it was going to stop. Rachel quickly held her arm aloft, her hand a fist, and she raised her middle finger at the passing car, defiance in her eyes.

Mee Noi grinned in response, his mouth opening, his white-gapped teeth revealing themselves as his top lip curled upwards. He turned to face the road and sped off; a trail of dust followed into the distance.

Rachel saw the other four turn to her in horror.

Chapter Sixteen

Jess was still struggling to get Natalie out of the buggy when Rachel excitedly blurted out her idea to buy a backpack and see the world, words tripping over themselves to get out.

"I don't think it's a good idea," Jess said pointedly. "I mean, just not yet. Everything's still raw, you know?"

Rachel shrunk into herself.

"Look, why don't I get us a drink and we can chat it over?" she said whilst balancing Natalie on her hip. "Here, take Natty."

Jess handed her over and Rachel pulled her to her chest. Natalie shot out her hands, poked her in the eye and tried to push her stubby finger up her nose.

"Natty!" she cried, pushing the baby's hands away. She felt like an idiot for telling Jess the way she just had. So selfish. She bounced Natty on her knee, looking over at the line of people. Normally Jess looked a picture of perfection but standing in the queue she looked dishevelled; her hair messy and wavy, a dirty teal top exposing a white bra strap. Even at a distance she could see dark bags under her eyes, usually covered in perfect make-up. Rachel felt a wave of guilt. Since the day she met her, she'd been consumed by her pregnancy. Jess seemed to have a perfect set-up, coping and doing all right. Perhaps because she was older than her, she felt Jess could handle life better. She couldn't remember a time she asked how she was. And when the birth happened Jess dropped everything. Even today, Jess had come at the drop of a hat and here she was telling her that she was going to bugger off.

She came back with a tray with two mugs on it and placed them down on the table. She fell into the armchair opposite and let out a big sigh. A tired sigh. Rachel noticed she had stains down her trousers.

"I'm sorry Jess. I didn't mean to throw that on you."

"It was a bit of a shock. I mean, the funeral is in a few days and you've just picked out the coffin. I wasn't expecting you to say you were going to gallivant around the world!"

"Yeah, I know. Maybe I got a bit excited. The first time in a while. I just thought I could run away. Be the person I used to be before... you know." Natalie was trying to fit her fist in her mouth, dribble dripping down. Jess sat up and reached into her bag, found a muslin and wiped Natalie's hand and mouth.

"Yeah, I get that," she responded matter-of-factly. "I just think you should think about it. Wait until after the funeral, see how you feel then? Besides, I'll miss you." The words stuck in the air. Rachel's heart expanded. Jess lent over and took a sip of her coffee, looking over the rim of the cup at Natalie playing nicely on Rachel's bobbing knee.

"And so will Natty, won't cha Nat, eh?"

Rachel looked over Natty's shoulder at Jess.

She hadn't noticed but Jess appeared to have aged over the last few weeks. Maybe it was because of the baby or maybe because she wasn't wearing her usual make-up. Whatever it was, she looked tired.

"How are you getting on Jess?" Rachel said. Jess raised her eyes inquisitively, her brow furrowed ever so slightly. It caused Rachel to question whether it was the shock at being asked something about her or if she was being snapped back from a different world.

"Oh, um, I'm okay," she said, shaking her head.

"No. Really."

"Well, Natty's not sleeping too well, and she's on the move constantly. Like you have to keep three eyes on her all the time otherwise then she'll be in the cupboards pulling things out and trying to eat them. I can't complain though, mum and Jim have been awesome."

"You can, you know," Rachel said, wrapping her arms around Natty and pulling her into her chest. "Complain."

"Yeah, I know. Thanks. But you've got enough on your plate without worrying about my things. They are small-fry compared to... well." She let the sentence hang. "By the way, my mum keeps telling me to remind you if you ever want to talk. She's been through the same.... With my brother...."

"I can handle it. And say thanks to your mum. Jess, you've been amazing. A true friend and I seriously doubt I could have got this far without you. I want to be there for you too."

"Not by flying to the opposite side of the world," she said, too quickly and spitefully. Rachel leant back on her armchair, which gave the cue for Natty to try and wriggle off her knee. Jess scooped her up and tried to contain her by squeezing her arms together which made her more determined to squirm free to explore. She gave out a desperate cry. Jess fished in her bag, pulled out a packet and gave her a single stick of yellow crisp. Natty squealed in delight and shoved it in her little mouth, still gripping it tightly in her fist. Rachel swallowed again.

"Well, it wouldn't be forever. Anyway, you're right, it's not the right time."

"No, I'm sorry. Maybe I'm a bit jealous you know. You can do whatever you want, no ties. Whilst I'm stuck with her." A blob of yellow goo dropped down on her knee as if to prove a point.

"Jealous? Oh, Jess, I'm the envious one. Look at you. You've got a perfect, cutie baby. You've got a great set-up. You're frigging beautiful. I'm the fat friend no one fancies. I've got a saggy tummy, messed up insides, no job and probably years of therapy to come."

"Er, hello? Single mum," she frowned, pointing at herself. "It's not a perfect set-up. I'm still living at home with this crazy one, not sleeping cos of this crazy one and stink of shit and puke cos of this crazy one. Jesus, the amount of washing this one needs. Life's not a bed of roses for me Rach. Oh, and I do have a saggy tummy by the way. And probably years of therapy too." A silence hung between the two. Natty stared at Rachel, fist still in her mouth.

"The grass is always greener huh?" Rachel said eventually.

"Yeah, damn right," she huffed, visibly angry. "Look, I wasn't going to say anything but just before you called I found a lump on my breast."

"Oh Jess." Her voice trailed off.

"Yeah. Well, I had one before. That was a false alarm. And Natty was being grumpy and annoying, and then you called and I rushed out cos I thought you were having a breakdown or something. Maybe something in the funeral parlour triggered you so I just threw stuff in the buggy and then you said you were going to leave. It was quite a lot to take in." A silence hung in the air again. Rachel felt a pang of guilt.

"Do... do you want me to come and get it checked out with you?" she said softly, apologetically.

"Thanks, but I'll go by myself. Last time it was nothing and you've got enough to worry about." Rachel leant over and placed a hand on her knee.

"I've got nothing to worry about and it's fine. I don't mind."

"Alright, let me think about it. I'll give it a week and see if there's any change first."

"Deal," Rachel said, picking up her coffee and leaning back in the chair.

"So, how are you feeling about the funeral?"

"I just want it over with. Mum is fussing over all the details. I'm just going to let her get on with it and go along with whatever she says. Maybe that's why I'm thinking of after. What am I going to do next? I feel like the funeral is a full stop – even though the vicar said it's just a step in the grieving process."

"Are you still speaking to him?!"

"Yeah, he's been really good actually. He's got a quote for everything. Not just bible quotes either. I've been going to his church every day and talking. It's really helping."

"Every day?" she replied, crinkling her nose.

"Yeah, well mum suggested it and I thought why not. It's so peaceful there, I can hear my thoughts. And I don't have offers of cups of tea thrown at me every two seconds."

"There's the green grass again. Would love to have tea made for me all the time."

"Yeah okay, point taken. I know I've got to move on. I can't mope around forever and I don't fancy a job yet."

"I know, but you've got time. You can think about what you want to do. No hasty decisions, eh?"

"Yeah, I know." Natty started to get agitated on Jess' knee, the crisp crumpled into a messy gloop in her palm.

"Look, I think I better go. She needs a nap." Jess stood up and tried to put Natty in the pram. The determined baby fought against it, arching her back to avoid being strapped in. Jess used her hand to force her tummy down, which it eventually did and quickly did up the straps. As Natty began to cry out, Jess pulled a dummy out of her bag. As soon as it went in, Natty sucked hard and her eyes immediately drooped. Jess let out a sigh. She looked exhausted.

"The next time I see you, it'll probably be next week. In the church?"

"Yeah, thanks Jess. And seriously, let me know if you want me to come to the docs."

She nodded and manoeuvred the pram through the maze of tables and chairs sticking out. Rachel watched as she strode purposefully past the large window along the street, her blonde hair flowing behind.

She sat back and took in the café, bustling with mums with babies, older people eating cake and young types working on laptops. She didn't fancy going back to her house. It was better to be alone with people here than alone at home. She wrapped her arms around herself like she was cuddling herself. The vicar entered her mind, and then her mum and dad, and then all the baby things that she had destroyed. She felt guilt and then sorrow for smashing all the things her parents had bought her. And then they had picked up all the pieces. They had been wonderful to her and she'd just bashed them away, angry at their interfering. And Jess. She had so many things on her plate and yet she dropped everything to be with her. She was struggling too. Guilt came back. Why did she deserve these people who were so kind to her when she treated them like crap? An image of a black coffin popped quickly into her mind. She imagined the baby being lowered into it, her Charlotte, and the lid being closed on top, the light being extinguished.

For the first time, she thought about the funeral, the church, the invited people filling the pews, and the food and drink after. It wasn't a bloody party. What was expected of her? Should she be seen crying in the corner or a look of confidence and holding it all together? No way would she say a eulogy or anything – everyone staring at her. How could she say something about someone she had never met? It all became overwhelming all of a sudden. Maybe it would be easier if she just disappeared, like her baby. Then people wouldn't have to worry about her. Jess' reaction to her travelling had made her feel silly. Like a stupid little girl. A stupid little fat girl.

She got up and left the café. Dark clouds loomed overhead and sounds came into a sharp focus: A beeping horn, a distant siren, the shout of a workman.

With her head down she hurried along the street. She walked and walked, going nowhere in particular, letting her instincts lead her, dragging her feet along the concrete. Eventually, her legs became heavy, and her calves burnt. She sat on the edge of the kerb. Then tears started. She looked up at the thick and menacing clouds and screamed.

"GIVE ME A SIGN THEN, HUH! IF YOU'VE GOT SOMETHING BIGGER FOR ME WHAT THE HELL IS IT? WHY ARE YOU MAKING ME GO THROUGH THIS?"

A flutter of birds crossed the sky in response. She reached her hands into the air and closed her fists, trying to grip something, anything, and drag it down.

"CALL YOURSELF A LOVING GOD? GET DOWN HERE! AM I NOT WORTHY ENOUGH FOR YOU? YOU DON'T THINK I'M GOOD ENOUGH TO BE A MOTHER? GET DOWN HERE AND WE'LL SORT IT OUT!"

An air of silence was her only answer. She got up and trudged further along, reaching a bridge over a busy road.

She looked over the side. Cars, lorries, vans and motorbikes flashed underneath, speeding past her, ignoring her presence.

What do I need to do to prove that I am good enough for Him?

She had been through the whole pregnancy, embraced it, and was ready for it. And then He took it away, leaving a huge void.

What if I wasn't meant to exist, she contemplated looking down at the tarmac below. *What's the worst that can happen? They'll get over it. Have a funeral. They'll find closure. Just like I'm supposed to have.*

She leaned over the edge, the weight of her head making her judder. The vicar's face popped into her head, tutting this time and shaking his head, concern in his eyes. The wind picked up, her hair blowing aimlessly.

"WHO AM I?" she screamed at the passing traffic. "I COULDN'T EVEN BRING A CHILD INTO THE WORLD. THAT'S WHAT WOMEN ARE SUPPOSED TO DO!"

The imaginary vicar reached out a hand, attempting to cradle her cheek but it dissipated into thin air. Blood rushed to her head and she felt hard steel pushing against her knee. Her arms straightened as her feet left the ground.

Out of nowhere, she felt a strong tug around her waist pulling her backwards, her hands slipping from the cold metal rail as the vicar's face evaporated.

"It's okay, it's okay," said a deep male voice behind her. "It's okay. You're safe. It's okay." Her knees buckled beneath her, and she let herself fall into the stranger's arms as they crashed to the ground. She was unable to stop the tears cascading from her eyes.

Chapter Seventeen

After she had flipped Mee Noi (the policeman of all people!) the finger outside Khun Pai's café Nathan had bubbled with rage. Khun Pai had prayed. Anurak had sighed.

"We wait," was all Anurak had said calmly. "See what he do now."

Nathan pulled Rachel along the dirt road by the wrist, his fingernails puncturing her skin, dragging her like a naughty teenager. She cried out for him to stop, trying to defiantly put her heels in the ground. When they had got far enough away, Nathan laid into her, shouting, stomping and yelling, his face a crimson red. The anger in his eyes was frightening like he was losing control.

Like he wanted to hit her.

Birds clattered and flapped in the undergrowth, adding to the chaotic atmosphere. He walked off, trying to calm down.

"At least I'm doing something!" Rachel called after him. He spun around.

"What? By insulting him?" he screamed, his eyes fiery, frightening her. Alone in the middle of nowhere, only the birds would hear her scream. For some reason, Jess's face popped into her head again.

"By standing up to him," she answered back, her heart beating through her skin.

"You think swearing at him is standing up to him? This isn't school Rachel. Flicking a finger at a policeman is not the same as spitting in a teacher's tea. And he's a dangerous man! You don't know what he is capable of!"

"Do you? Do you know what he is capable of?" she shouted back at him, her voice quivering. Nathan began to say something then swallowed his words. He looked confused.

"No, actually. I don't," he said, regaining some composure. "Only what the villagers say." The colour left his cheeks. The vein on his forehead disappeared.

"So, he's just a bogeyman then. All bark and no bite," she huffed. Nathan looked at her from the corner of his eyes, his head deep in thought, shoulders slouched forward. He looked ashamed.

That look. I've seen it before. In a different world.

"The villagers, they said…" he trailed off. Rachel stood tall.

"Yeah, maybe he says things. The badge can be a powerful weapon. Makes you think of things that don't exist. You said it yourself. Westerners getting done for drugs and drink. Does it actually happen or is it just stories? I heard plenty of stories when I was travelling."

He looked up. His cheeks were back to his normal tanned self. Again, a hint of recognition shot into Rachel's mind. She remembered Jess showing her a news article on her phone, a dark-haired guy in a suit.

Nathan crouched by the side of the road on his haunches, putting his elbows on his bent knees. He was deep in thought.

"Do you think someone can change?" he said faintly.

"Pardon?" Rachel said, squatting next to him.

"Like really change. From being a bad person to good."

"Perhaps. Given the right conditions. What do you mean?"

"Mee Noi. Do you think he could be a good man?"

"Yeah, I do. But feeding him the same toxic things all the time won't help him."

Nathan just nodded, looking into the trees.

"You know, I got angry once. It changed my life," he said to the trees.

Rachel sat down in the dirt. This was the first time Nathan had offered a glimpse into his past.

"And look at you now. You've turned good. You're volunteering at an orphanage for Christ's sake."

"Yeah, but I don't want that person to come back again," Nathan said, still talking to the trees.

"It won't if you don't feed it. If the conditions are right. You just need the motivation. I guess that comes down to love."

She nonchalantly drew a circle in the dirt with her finger, looking at Nathan through the corner of her eye.

"I felt it just then. When we were just arguing," Nathan said, turning to her.

"It was just a fight. Our first one." He turned and looked at her, the corners of his mouth turning upwards. "Look, our blood pressure went up. All sorts of fantasies came into our minds about what he might do. Guess we have to see if he actually does anything. Let's not worry about what *might* happen."

"You know, you've got a mature head on your young shoulders," he said.

She beamed at the compliment.

"Do you ever find it strange how things come together? Like you being here and me missing the bus. Two people from England in the middle of nowhere in Thailand?"

"You mean like fate?"

"Yeah, something like that."

"*Of all the gin joints, in all the towns, in all the world, she walks into mine,*" he said in a flawless American accent.

Rachel jolted upright.

"What?" she said a worried look on her face.

"Casablanca," he replied confused. Rachel stood up and towered over him. He sat hunched looking up at her, looking scared.

Guilty.

Details dropped into her head one after the other like dominos. The image of Jess. The news article. The photo on the phone. The scary red mist. Pretending to be American. The deception. The name Nathan. Things she didn't even think she'd had stored. Her face went white.

Surely not.

Fate? God's Will?

Without thinking she blurted out: "You're Nathan Clyne, aren't you? The stalker."

The colour from his face drained. He almost lost his balance and had to shoot an arm out to stop himself from crashing to the ground. He regained his composure and straightened his back, standing up. He searched her eyes, trying to comprehend who she was. Rachel could tell he was going through his memory bank, trying to place her. Her heart was racing. Fear shot through her. *Had she awakened the bad in him?* He shook his head.

"No, I don't know what you're talking about. That's not me."

"Jess said to tell you. 'You're a wanker'," Rachel exclaimed, trying to convince him that she was right. His knees seemed to go as he stumbled again, his face going whiter still.

"You know Lucy?"

"I know Jess."

"Jess," he repeated, his face contorted trying to figure it out.

"She told me all about you. How you grassed-up your mate to lower your sentence." Nathan's face relaxed as recognition took hold.

"Ah, okay. Jess. The blonde woman."

"Yeah, she's my friend." Nathan turned slowly, looking into the trees. He put his hands on his hips. An uncomfortable silence grew between them, only the gentle breeze in the trees disturbed the tranquillity.

"So. A coincidence then? You just happened to miss the bus in the middle of Thailand, walk past the orphanage and see me. And now what? You know my name, my past and expect to, what? Expect me to beg for your forgiveness?"

"Well no. Yes! No!" Rachel shook her head at the confusion. "I mean, yes, it's a coincidence. A bloody weird one. Whatever you just said about all the gin joints in the world. I never set out to look for you. Look, I knew Jess when I, um, well never mind about that, and we became friends and she told me this story, well, *your* story and showed me a photo of you in the newspaper. I'm in the middle of, well I don't know where I am to be honest, and there you are. I didn't figure it out until just then. Well, you looked just like the man in the photo but here you are in shorts and a t-shirt, not in a suit." She caught herself looking down at his exposed arms. His eyes followed them as he twisted around to watch her, saying nothing.

"All the pieces just fitted together. It was luck. Maybe it's a sign," she continued, words spilling out. "God's bloody Will."

"Yeah, lucky me," he said, looking back at the trees. "And do you? You know, want me to beg? Beg for your forgiveness? Tell you how sorry I am and how I wish I'd never done it? Cos I am you know. Sorry. I've done my time. If you must know, I'm a shadow of what I used to be. By the way, I'm not looking for excuses or bloody pity. It's the truth. I've changed. If I could turn back time I would. I'm sorry." The word drifted between them as a small breeze rustled the leaves of the bamboo trees. Rachel realised how warm it had gotten. A fly bothered her as it landed on her arm.

"We've all got a past, haven't we? Guess that's why we're here. You know, I'm no spring chicken," she said. He shot a look back and held her eye for a moment, his eyebrow raised.

"Are you fishing for a compliment?"

Rachel blushed, not meaning that at all.

He chuckled to himself, folding his arms over his chest. "Cos if you are, I'm not giving you one."

"No! No, I'm bloody not," and ran her hand through her hair. Despite what she knew about him, he was a charmer, she'd give him that. He relaxed like the world had been lifted from his shoulders. Like he didn't have the pressure of keeping his history to himself like a dirty secret.

"Okay, so you know my past," he whispered to the trees. "I know you think you know me." There was no anger or spite in his tone like a teacher would talk to a child. "But I've changed. I'm a different person. Matured. The kids, they've taught me. Jasmine, she taught me. This is my present, right here right now. I am who I am."

He swung around, fixing his gaze on Rachel.

"And you finding me won't make a blind bit of difference. You can drag up my past if you want, but I'm okay with it. I've paid my debt, both to society and to myself. I've moved on. You can chastise me, you can hate me, you can make your judgements on me, and that's okay. I'm at peace with my past. Who I was. I've chilled out. And now I want to live in peace with who I am now. And if you don't believe me, I don't care. You can get on the next bus to Trang."

A silence hung in the air. Rachel didn't know what to say. Could a bad man change into a good? It depended on the conditions, the circumstances. The motivation.

Nathan started to walk along the road. Rachel followed a few steps behind, thinking of her past, and who she wanted to be now. Not labelled as a failed mother or a fat, rich girl. She jogged to catch up with him. The top of the orphanage loomed above the trees.

"What you said back then," she said, causing him to turn. "I understand what you said. I don't know you, and you don't know me. I didn't purposely come to find you and out you. Whatever you did, you did. You have to live with that and I promise you I won't judge you. I mean, look at this place, look at *that* place" she pointed up at the grey stone building ahead. "And you're here helping those kids out. You're stripped to your real self. No fancy suits or fast cars to hide in. I guess it was a bit of a shock. For both of us."

"Yeah, I think so," he replied, following her eyes to the orphanage.

"I suppose we are all running away from something," she said to herself.

Nathan stopped.

"And what are you running away from Rachel?" he asked, softly and sincerely. She didn't answer, the memories flooded back. She stopped and turned her back to Nathan. Her palms gravitated to her stomach as a tear escaped. Nathan stayed still, letting her have her moment.

A scooter beeped and she jumped. She wiped the side of her eyes with the back of her hand and continued walking. Nathan followed a few paces behind. She cut through the trees where the sea opened up, slipped off her shoes and padded across the warm sand. Her skin prickled as her feet sunk into the cool water. Nathan stood behind her, the water lapping against his ankles. It was as if the sea was nudging their pasts back to them.

Sweat pooled and ran down her back in the humid air as she let her mind wander. Was this really God's Will? Did he mean to put Nathan in her path?

A criminal. Yet a repented one. Could she trust him?

If she hadn't known his past, he would be just another nice man on her travels. If she was to have described this Nathan to Jess, there would be no way she would equate him to the old Nathan. Maybe he had atoned. Maybe people can change for the better. So what if he had had an unsavoury past? So had she. She'd gotten pregnant, could barely remember the guy who did it and carried on with the pregnancy anyway and killed the baby. What was she thinking? That she could raise a child by herself? Nathan was someone who had turned something bad into something good. Perhaps he was her saviour. Perhaps he would help her on her journey to figure out who she was. To help her heal. The questions rolled around in her head. Perhaps this was the place for that to happen. She looked out to the emerald sea.

Look at this. It's paradise.

And if he could help her, why *couldn't* she let these feelings she has for him grow?

She felt a hand on her shoulder.

"It's okay," Nathan said. "You can tell me."

Rachel sniffed and looked around at him.

"Okay, but first: Who the hell is Jasmine?"

Nathan blushed.

"She's not important right now."

He stood next to her, slid his fingers into her palm and they silently watched the sun set whilst the water danced around their ankles.

***

"Rachel. Wake up, wake up!" The voice was urgent.

"Rachel!" Nathan was leaning over her, his hands on her shoulders, making the hammock swing and shake unnaturally. It was still dark. The light of the moon made eerie shadows.

"What time is it?" she said, trying to get her bearings.

"It doesn't matter," he replied. "Somethings happening."

She tried to sit up, but the hammock's material made it difficult.

"What, what's happening?"

"I don't know. Get your shoes on." She swung her legs around and rubbed her eyes.

"Nathan, what's going on?"

"Listen," he said and put his finger to his lips.

The air was still. Unusually still. Neither a cricket nor a bird made a sound. An unnatural feeling engulfed them. In silence they let their ears and eyes adjust. Suddenly, they heard shouts in the far distance.

"See," he said, turning sharply. The details of his face were hidden in the dark, even though he was close. She could just make out the outline of his body. He was naked from the waist up, just sports shorts covering the rest. He strained to hear through the forest for more sounds.

"It's too quiet. There're no animal sounds. I can hear shouts but I don't know where they are coming from. Let's go."

Rachel quickly put on the nearest thing to her – the red dress Mrs Pai bought her.

"You don't think," she said, her voice quivering. "You don't think it's a Tsunami, do you?"

"I don't know Rach, I don't know." His voice was scared. That was the first time, in over a month, he had called her Rach.

"Nathan, you're scaring me."

As if he hadn't heard her, he led her out of the hut and into the darkness of the trees. She fumbled for his hand, caught it, and squeezed it tightly. They staggered through the trees, his hand in front of his head protecting them from low branches. They tripped over roots. Leaves brushed their faces. Shouts echoed in the distance, increasing in volume. Nathan changed course towards the commotion, not letting go of Rachel's hand. The shouts suddenly disappeared and they stood together, utterly still, straining to hear in complete silence.

In the jungle, even the moonlight didn't reach them. The canopy concealed the stars. The insects had ceased their nightly songs. They heard a snap of a twig which made Rachel scream out.

"Jesus Rach, you scared the life out of me," he said putting his hand over his chest. "Shush." He strained his neck, moving his head around to listen.

"Over there," he said suddenly and pulled Rachel with him. Voices were getting louder, followed by wails. Nathan moved faster, almost dragging Rachel along, her feet getting caught in roots and mud. She wasn't sure how far they had gone. They moved towards the voices, more shouts and screams. A crackle. A hot, musty smell filled the air.

"What is that?" Rachel panted out as she tried to keep up.

"I don't know but it doesn't sound, or smell, good."

Through the trees, they could see a fierce orange glow. Shapes danced in front of it, merging with the thin tree trunks. They could feel the heat before they reached the clearing. As they spilt out of the forest, a few faces turned to look at them, tears and worry stamped over their faces. They saw a woman beating the ground, a man trying to comfort her as she wailed into the night sky. The villagers stood and watched, helpless as the giant inferno engulfed a roadside shop and its neighbouring café. Anurak sidled up to them as they took in the sight and reached up to put an arm around Nathan's shoulders.

"What's going on?" she asked, bewilderment in her voice. Anurak clicked his tongue.

"Fire," he said, stating the obvious. He nodded down to the two figures wailing and comforting. "Khun Pai business. Gone." She looked down and up, trying to comprehend the situation.

"Where is the fire engine?" she shouted. "Why aren't they trying to put it out? Call for the fire service." Anurak looked solemnly at her, the weary look he gave her not 12 hours ago.

"No fire service. Many miles. No point."

He gazed back at the blaze, the worst of it over. The steel outline of the structure started to appear as the flames tried to find their next victim. Like a zombie, Nathan crossed the road to the Pais, releasing Rachel's hand and causing Anurak's arm to flop down. He knelt and put his arm around the woman wailing and crying in the dirt. She pushed him away.

The light of the fire was fading, and darkness was coming down. Rachel heard crickets in the distance, and a bird fluttered on a treetop somewhere. Headlights caused her to look to the right, her eyes squinting at the sudden bright white lights. A silver BMW came into view, on top the red, white and blue lights were extinguished.

An arm was swinging listlessly out of the window on her side of the road, dangling in front of the police badge, the Thai script above and below it. The car slowed as it passed Rachel, blocking the grieving figures on the ground. The arm rose, a fist on the end. Behind it, a grin beamed back at Rachel, thin lips curling up causing the short hairs of the moustache to bristle outwards. As the car almost came to a stop, the middle finger extended.

Chapter Eighteen

Rachel woke with a start. Everything was the way it had been when her mum and dad had left her, except a blanket now sagged off her body, half on the floor and it was dark. The familiarity of her flat warmed her, yet it felt empty.

Soulless.

She wiped the sleep from her eye and got up. She went to the kitchen and filled a glass with tap water. Tupperware boxes were stacked on the kitchen top. She opened the fridge and the light blinded her. Squinting, she saw glass casserole dishes half-empty with lasagne and desserts and cartons of juice leftover from Lottie's funeral. She lifted the tinfoil gently from a plate and scooped some cake crumbs and cream onto her finger, popping it into her mouth. A light flashed on the kitchen surface, illuminating the room.

A text message.

Glancing up at the digital clock on the wall – 23:12 – her brow furrowed, wondering who would be texting her at that time. She fired up the phone. Jess. She smiled as she opened the app to read the message.

Hey babe, how you doing? Hope you are in bed, but just on the off chance… [yawning emoji].

Rachel quickly typed, her fingers dancing over the keypad.

Just woke up. Probably knew you were going to text [smiling emoji]

She stared at the phone, waiting to see if she replied. A text popped up.

[laughing tears emoji] I'm up doing the dream feed. Boring. How you feeling?

[shocked emoji] I'm doing okay. Mum and dad were great, as usual. You okay?

[thumbs up] They are great. I thought the funeral went well. You did great.

[kiss emoji] Thanks, Jess. It was pretty much what I expected TBH. *The coffin though. So small. [sad face emoji]*

[sad face crying emoji] Lottie's in a better place now. I'm glad you got to say goodbye.

Rachel stared into space, running her finger up and down her glass. She put it down and typed:

Yeah. Better up there than down here. [halo emoji] Thanks for coming. I'm rubbish at saying things out loud, so maybe best on text [laughing emoji] but I really appreciate everything you've done for me. You've been there. And I haven't been there for you.

Rachel stared at the screen, rereading the message over.

[heart bursting emoji] Don't be silly babe. And thanks. Ditto BTW.

She imagined Jess sitting on her nursing chair in her room, Natty at an angle, her eyes closed, head resting on the arm that she was texting on, her other hand holding the bottle in.

[Kiss emoji] Well, now the funeral's over, I can think about "moving on" [upside down head emoji] Maybe I should disappear for a while. Find myself.

[sighing emoji] Seriously Rach, take your time. It's not a race. Let your body heal first. If you are going to be running around the world at least be in a good shape. Anyway, I am NOT having this discussion in the middle of the night, on a text message [eye rolling emoji]

Rachel sighed. Jess was right. Wrong time, wrong place. Her brain seemed to be empty of all other thoughts apart from beaches, palm trees and golden sands. She went into the living room and pulled out a handful of glossy brochures she'd ordered. An aerial photo of lush green rainforest next to the blue-green sea was on the cover of the first one, a sliver of sand separating the two textures, a bird's eye view of a white boat sitting in the sea. Her phone lit up.

Rach, you there?

Rachel placed the brochures on the sofa, sat down next to them and typed.

Yeah, sorry. You're right (again) [laughing emoji] Let's chat tomorrow about it [winking emoji]

RACH! Once you get something in your head, that's it is it?! [sighing emoji] Go to sleep babe. I need to go, Natty's finished her bottle [kiss emoji]

Rachel typed fast.

Okay babe, sleep tight [kiss emoji]

She watched the screen for a while, seeing if the conversation had ended or if Jess was going to message again. The screen stayed blank, so she picked up the brochures. Straining in the dull light she flicked through the pages. Images of temples, maps, idyllic beaches, shiny jumbo jets, impressive skyscrapers and giant Buddhas flashed before her. She laid down on the sofa and pulled the blanket over her. Her eyes felt heavy as she thumbed through the next and the next, eventually throwing them on the floor and closing her eyes. If this really was God's Will, then He would have put the travel agent in her path and made her follow her impulse to go in. Maybe he wanted to show her His beauty, the beauty of the world. Jess' text message came into her mind.

Once you get something in your head, that's it is it?!

Confidence surged through her. Or was it excitement? A prickle in her belly that wasn't something growing inside. Whatever it was, it was something that Rachel hadn't felt in a long time. Maybe even ever. This was for her. The only responsibility laid on her was her own. Out in the real world, away from the safety net of mum and dad. They'd be devastated. Like Jess, they'd protest that it was so soon. The funeral had only just finished. Was it still the same day? Rachel lent on her elbows to see the kitchen clock. 23:58. Moving on. That's what the vicar said. She had survived His tests which made her strong. She was mature and complete. God will show her the way and she would let Him.

He wouldn't put her in harm's way again, surely?

At the bridge, that had been rock bottom. Only one way from there and that was up. The decision was made. Jess, mum, dad, her friends, and her aunts and uncles wouldn't agree but she felt empowered. They had been a crutch, a well-needed one, but she couldn't rely on them for the rest of her life. And surely, they would be glad to see her move on. Leave the past behind and be a young woman again. They'd get over it. And it wasn't forever. A few months. Perhaps a year. Yeah, that's how she'd break it to them. She'd be back within a year – world-wise and tanned. People do it all the time. Kids, people younger than her.

What could possibly go wrong?

Chapter Nineteen

By daybreak, there were just dying red embers where the shop and the café used to be. Burnt metal girders stuck out at odd angles. Some of the villagers had gone over and stamped on some of the dying flames to put them out. In front, Khun Pai sat in the dirt calming his sobbing wife. Nathan sat next to them, crossed-legged, watching. Anurak had been comforting Rachel from witnessing the policeman flick her the finger, watching the fire die down with his arm over her shoulders, her arm around his waist.

Before he left to go back to the orphanage, he approached the sobbing woman and muttered something to her, his hands in prayer as he knelt before her. When most of the villagers had left, Khun Pai and Nathan helped the poor woman to her feet. Rachel went over and tried to hug her. The woman responded angrily, shouting and gesturing at her. Khun Pai led her away with his arm around her shoulder. He looked back at Nathan and nodded his head in thanks, his face etched in sadness and hopelessness.

"Let's leave them. She blames you."

"Blames me?" she shouted in surprise. Quietly she repeated herself. "Blames me, why? I didn't do it!"

"Shit, I shouldn't have said anything," he said, rubbing his face. He ran his hand through his hair. "Because you provoked the policeman."

Her stomach dropped and it felt like the colour left her cheeks.

"Rachel!" Nathan cried as he reached out to catch her as her knees buckled.

"They think it's my fault," she said out loud, burying her face in her hands and falling onto her knees. "They think it's my fault. It *is* my fault. Oh Christ."

She put her head in her hands and covered her face. "I'm so stupid. What an absolute idiot. What was I thinking?" She started to hit herself on her legs, her stomach, and her head. Nathan grabbed her arms and held them tightly.

"Look, it's been a long night huh? Let's go back, and get some rest. I'm sure it will be better in the morning." He looked up, noticing the morning was already upon them. He reached under Rachel's arms to help her. She stood, faltering like a newborn deer. Rachel stumbled along the road.

"I need to apologise."

"Leave it, Rachel," he said, holding her back. "Let's leave it for tonight huh? Let them grieve." She looked up at Nathan, the word coursing through her entire body.

"Grieve?" she repeated, her mind elsewhere. "What have they got to grieve about? No one died!"

Nathan shushed her rising voice, turning her into the trees they had emerged from. When they were far enough away, he turned to her.

"Yes," he whispered urgently. "Grieve. Their business has just gone up in smoke. They've worked a bloody lifetime for that. And they blame you. You provoked Mee Noi. We said he was dangerous and now you've got proof of what he can do. As it stands, they have nothing. They give everything, they are completely selfless. They've gone through enough don't you think?"

"Oh, so you think it's my fault too, do you? Blame me when you let that arsehole walk all over you and the villagers. He's bloody corrupt and taking them all for a ride. Including you. And you are happy to let that happen?"

"No, but it's not my place to."

"Not your place? Why not? I can't just sit back and watch like you."

"Change the world? Is that what you want? Is that why you're here? Is that why you left your nice middle-class existence to meet poor people to make their lives different? Well, here's the news, maybe they don't want to change. Having stability, a routine, normality, is maybe what they want after the Tsun…" he let the words trail off as he faced the trees. He allowed himself to take a few breaths, perhaps to calm himself down.

"Just because it's normal doesn't mean it's right," Rachel said. "The status quo is not okay if people are oppressed. And that policeman is oppressing them." Nathan turned to Rachel, his hands on his hips.

"It's not our battle to fight," he said, his mouth tightening. "We're guests here." He turned and carried on through the palm trees. The light was getting stronger, the air rapidly getting warmer. Rachel hurried to catch up with him.

"So, if you see wrong being done, you are happy to sit back and watch it happen." Rachel stepped in front of him, blocking his path. He lifted his head and looked distantly into her eyes.

"No," he whispered, his eyes seemed a million miles away.

"And you," she said poking his chest with her finger. "Sat back and watched it happen. You fuelled it! Let that bastard do whatever he wanted."

Nathan looked down at the indent where her finger had been. "And *you* blame *me?*"

A tear dropped down his face.

"Oh, look at me," she mocked, dancing about. "Helping kids with no arms and legs. Sleeping on a beach watching the sunset. Going about and not bothering anyone. My past is so sad. Stalking women and beating them up. You ran away little boy. And now you're hiding. Hiding from responsibility."

Nathan started to walk, brushing past Rachel with his shoulder, his eyes filled with water.

"Wait, I haven't finished yet."

Nathan spun around, anger rising in his face, his jaw clenched.

"Yes, you have! Yes, you have!" he shouted. "I may not have done anything, but I kept the peace. You came and lit the fire."

"The fire was already lit," she screamed back. "That fire has been burning for a long time Nathan."

"You haven't been here for five minutes and you think you know everything. This place has a history. Of sadness and trauma. Of devastation. You can't come here and wave a magic wand and make it all better."

"We've all got a history. We've all got a past of 'sadness and trauma'. Maybe that's why we're all here. In this spot. Maybe, just maybe, we *can* be the magic wand to make it all disappear."

"Oh yeah," Nathan shouted. "What's your past? What's your sadness? You're a little rich girl on a gap year. All I wanted was to give the Pais some space. Allow them to grieve!" He turned and stomped away. Rachel ran after him, grabbing him by the elbow.

"Grief? You think I don't know anything about grief?"

Her face was red. Her top lip curled up, bearing her teeth. She grabbed her t-shirt and lifted it, revealing dark stretch marks in the morning light. She lifted her loose skin.

"Look." Nathan's eyes didn't move. She roughly grabbed his chin, forcing it down. "Look! You don't think I know about grief? Look, see this? Stretch marks. See this scar. It's from a caesarean." Nathan stared at her belly, distraught and confused.

"Yeah, I had a stillbirth. The baby got stuck and died inside me. They had to cut me open to get her out."

His eyes widened.

"I'm sorry," he said, barely audible, not keeping his eyes from her flesh. She pulled her top down.

"God, I wished people would stop saying 'I'm sorry'."

"Why didn't you say anything?"

"Why should I? We don't talk about the past. I thought that's what you wanted. That's why you don't talk about anything back home. I assumed that was the deal. We just talk about the now." Nathan frowned.

"I didn't intend that. I never meant that" he said confused. "I don't know where you got that impression." Rachel softened; her heartbeat slowed. She strode through the trees, zigzagging past the thin trunks. He followed a few paces behind.

"Wait," he called. Rachel stopped in her tracks and waited for him to reach her.

"Who is Lottie?" he asked. She spun quickly around.

"How do you know about Lottie?"

"You say her name in your sleep. Quite often. I thought it might be your mum, or sister, or friend or something. It's your baby's name isn't it."

Tears spilt out of Rachel's eyes. Nathan reached out and put his arms around her neck and let her bury her head in his shoulder blade. He held her as she sobbed. She pulled back, her eyes puffy.

"At least everything's out in the open now. I guess we *are* both running away from something then," he said, and she spluttered an embarrassed laugh.

"Yeah, we're both messed up," she said, wiping her eyes with the back of her hand. "I just wanted to do something good. I didn't think about my actions. The consequences. I rarely do." Nathan cupped her face in his hands.

"That's nonsense. I've been trying to hide my past. I'm ashamed. But you don't need to be ashamed. You've been through something both incredible and incredibly sad. I can't imagine the emotions you've been through. Still going through! And you're still here and you're still trying to be the best version of you. It takes a lifetime of learning to do that. You weren't to know what was going to happen. We didn't know what Mee Noi would do and I'm pretty certain no one would have predicted the outcome of what happened to Lottie. Besides, you did do something good. You found me and made me happy."

Rachel's eyes widened.

"I…. I make you happy?"

"Yeah. You do," he said, stroking her hair.

Rachel leant in and kissed him on the lips. Everything seemed to melt away – her thoughts, her feelings, her inhibitions. She pushed her head into his as he responded – fiery and intense. He wound his arms around her waist and tightly pulled her in. They held each other as the birds started to chirp and the crickets sang their songs. She pulled back and wiped the remnants of tears from her eyes. Dirt and sand speckled his face.

They giggled like schoolchildren and embraced, alone in the middle of a forest.

For the first time, Rachel understood how life fitted together. How her journey was interwoven with adventures and tests, highs and lows, love and pain. And that's what makes life rich and interesting. As she heard the leaves rustling above her, she thought about the individuals that had been on her journey. Like a train where people got on and off at different periods of her life which shaped the direction she would go. Some would stay on the train for a long time; others would jump off. Some would influence the direction, some made it go faster. She thought about those that she wanted to stay on, perhaps nurture those relationships more and get rid of toxic ones which slowed her down.

She felt light. A smile creased across her face.

"Happy?" Nathan said as if sensing her smile.

"Yes. It feels like nothing can stop me now. We need to find that prick."

Chapter Twenty

Cathy Pacific flight CX252 took off from Heathrow on time. Rachel peered out of the window. The drop in air pressure and the increasing height made her feel woozy. Or perhaps it was the anxiety of being alone. As the plane banked left, the houses below got smaller and denser, trains snaked their way through the crowded metropolis and spots of green interrupted the grey. She pictured Jess and her mum and dad down there somewhere.

As expected, they hadn't taken her decision to travel too kindly. In hindsight maybe she should have eased them into it, rather than blurting it out, mind made up. She had gone to see the vicar and he had let out a long, deep sigh. When she had quoted the words he had said back to him, he had looked shocked and fidgeted with his fingers. That's what she liked about him – he didn't go on the defensive like her dad had done or shrieked out like mum. Her mum thought Jess had suggested it and Rachel had to calm her down. She hadn't the heart to put the vicar in the thick of it. Anyway, it was her idea, all hers. The vicar had just nudged her. This was her chance to heal, think things through, and have some head space.

But you're not well, her mum had protested, her dad nodding in agreement.

In a compromise, she agreed to continue taking the pills the doctor had given her after the bridge episode. Their ears were deaf to the 'I'll-be-back-within-a-year' argument too, pulling out the 'you've-got-plenty-of-time' response. Rachel wasn't sure how much 'time' she had before mum would be sitting her down, saying perhaps it's time to get a job. Get her mind busy with something else. The more Rachel thought about it, the more she convinced herself it was the right thing to do. Give her some space away from the same four walls. See the world. Get enlightenment. Perspective.

Whilst researching visas and routes, she stumbled upon the Banana Pancake Trail – a backpacker's route through Asia. The choices of flights were overwhelming, with the different destinations, airlines and stopovers, so in the end, she just chose the cheapest direct flight, which happened to be the one she was on right now.

Hong Kong.

Then she would head south, taking advice from fellow travellers, going with the flow. Who knows, she may end up in Australia.

For now, down below, the green became more prevalent as the grey houses disappeared, only congregating in small clumps, roads leading in and out of them. The engines quietened and a ding sounded above. Whispery clouds flew past. As the plane climbed higher, she peered upwards out of the oval window. Thick, white clouds covered her view as the plane sliced through them, before giving way to a bright piercing blue. Laid out before her was a carpet of jaggery clouds, like mountains made of cotton wool. It was ethereally beautiful. The sun seemingly sat on them in the distance. As the plane banked to the right, the sun disappeared, and she was treated to a window full of blue. The full spectrum from light to dark.

Wow. This is what heaven looks like then.

The vicar's face popped into her head. She nodded to herself.

Okay, I get it. He is showing me my path. I am meant to be here, to see the beauty of the world around us. I've gone through hell but I'm on this plane now, seeing His work.

She turned her head and looked at the seatback in front of her, her ears starting to get bunged up. She thought back to the events of the past few months: her boring job and getting fired, getting pregnant by who-knows-who, preparing for the baby, meeting Jess, the frantic time at the hospital, her mum and dad comforting her, the smashed glass, talking to the vicar, looking over the bridge, the brochures, the little black coffin sitting at the altar, the email confirmation of her flight. Maybe this was where she was meant to be, up above the clouds and going on an adventure.

Not with a baby.

The pregnancy was a mistake. She was sure of it. It was never supposed to happen. It was a glitch in the matrix. He had put her on the right path again. The vicar was right, the trauma and the heartbreak were only to make her stronger. She'd overcome it. Now was when her life began, and she was ready for it. Ready to be herself, her true self. Not a single mum. Not a victim.

It was God's Will.

She couldn't wait to see what He had in store for her.

Chapter Twenty-One

They meandered through the trees holding hands. The air was getting sticky with humidity and their palms were sliding against each other. They kept readjusting to get a grip, not wanting to let go, not wanting to lose their newfound connection.

Rachel's mind was whirring, contemplating the night's events. A mix of emotions cascaded through her: guilt and sorrow for the fire, anger for the policeman, relief that both their pasts were out in the open, holding hands with a man she felt a kinship with. Eventually, they came to the wall of the orphanage, the cries and giggles of the children within. Nathan turned to Rachel.

"Day off?"

"Yeah, probably not a good time. I'm sure Anurak will understand."

They turned and walked away along the beach, back to their hut.

Suddenly, Nathan froze on the spot. Rachel stared back at him.

"You alright?" she said, her eyebrows furrowed. He let go of her hand and sprinted away. By the remnants of the fire pit, Mee Noi was standing in front of a pile of splintered wood, pieces of planks lying strewn across the sand and grass. One of his lackeys was holding a sledgehammer. Rachel's feet sank into the sand as she moved like she was running in mud.

A broad grin spread across the policeman's face when he saw the couple survey the scene. Plastic bags littered the sand, the contents spilling out – their supplies open for the world to see: toothpaste, razors, underwear, bottles of water. The lackey moved and stood behind Mee Noi, hands on hips. Hearing his flunky behind him, Mee Noi deliberately put his hands to his belt and moved it up an inch or two. A long baton swung slightly into view behind his thigh.

"Mr Nathan," he slurred, his beady eyes squinting. "Mr Nathan, 'tomorrow' is today." His flunky laughed out loudly, giggling like a schoolboy.

"Time for money," he said. His voice and face turned serious; his hand slipped down to the trunk of the baton.

"No," came the reply from behind Nathan. Strong but with a hint of a quiver.

"Ah, the big girl," Mee Noi said, slowly straggling towards her, trying to keep in a straight line. He put his face right up to hers, and the bristles of his moustache twitched. Rachel could smell the strong odour of beer.

"Maybe _you_ have my money?"

He turned his head to Nathan and raised a stubby finger at him. "Mr Nathan, say he no money. We look." He pulled the baton out from its holder and used it to point to the debris. Then he moved it under her chin and gently lifted her head. In a flash, Nathan was next to her, pushing the baton away.

"Don't you touch her," he spat, raising his voice. In an instant, the other policeman was behind him, grabbing his wrist and pulling it sharply behind his back. In one swift movement, the policeman jabbed his arm upwards causing him to bend over and grabbed the wrist of his other hand. Nathan yelped in pain.

"Tsk, tsk, tsk," Mee Noi said, shaking his head. He sidestepped to Nathan and put the baton under his chin.

"I take money from her. No money? Maybe I get rent another way?"

He glanced over to Rachel, making a show of looking up and down her body. Nathan tried to wriggle free from the iron grip behind him. Mee Noi spoke in Thai to the other policeman, glancing down at a tree by the splintered wood. A nod and a plastic tie was fastened around Nathan's wrists. He swore as the plastic ripped tightly, piercing his skin. As the policeman heaved him to the tree, Mee Noi smashed his baton against Nathan's knee. He cried out in pain as his leg collapsed underneath him. Huffing, the policeman dragged him backwards, whipped out another plastic tie and wrapped it around the tree and through Nathan's tied wrists.

"Stop!" Rachel screamed. "You can't do that!" She lurched for Mee Noi, arms raised, aiming for his head. He jerked up his hands in defence, cowering and shielding him from her flailing arms. As she lunged, he grabbed her wrist. Before she knew it her arm was behind her back and she could feel his heavy breath against her neck. He pushed his groin against her bum.

"Mmm, a fighting girl."

"Don't you fucking touch her!" Nathan shouted from the base of the tree. Birds fluttered into the sky at the sharp words. Mee Noi said something in quick Thai and the other policeman took a handkerchief out of his back pocket, screwed it up and pushed it into Nathan's mouth. The muted screams failed to come out of his mouth, his eyes bulged red.

Rachel sank to her knees, her eyes locking into Nathan's. Determination was on her face. Mee Noi roughly pulled her back up as the other policeman joined them. Satisfied the situation was under control, he slowly reached into his pocket and pulled out a plastic tie. Rachel grimaced as it cut into her skin, her shoulders aching from the pressure of her arms behind her. She felt a shove between her blades and fell forward, face-down in the sand. Nathan emitted a stifled scream but it hardly registered, even to Rachel's ears. Mee Noi grabbed her hair and forcefully turned her so she faced Nathan. Their eyes locked together, terror on their faces. The policeman beckoned to his underling in Thai, who disappeared amongst the palm trees then a moment later came back holding two bottles of Chang. He passed one to Mee Noi who cracked it open and took a slug. He exhaled slowly, shaking his head. The other bottle fizzed open, followed by a noisy slurp. Mee Noi looked up at Nathan and tutted.

"Look what you make me do," he said. "*You* make trouble. *I* make trouble." The other policeman eyed Rachel, licking his lips.

"You no pay, what do I do?" He took a long swig from his bottle and threw it at Nathan, hitting his bended knee.

"No mon-ey" he sing-songed. "No prob-lem."

He shoved Rachel over and put his knees on either side of her left leg and bent over her to run his fingers through her hair. She froze. Nathan struggled against the tree, trying again to scream through the handkerchief. The other policeman laughed at him, threw his head back and drained the last drops of his beer. He too chucked his empty bottle at Nathan, missing by a metre. Mee Noi chuckled.

"Oh, Mr Nathan, you like the big girl huh?"

With his eyes fixed on Nathan, he traced a finger down her naked shoulder and arm. She jerked her body, attempting to push him away, and he laughed at her response. The other policeman laughed too. Then in a flash, Mee Noi grabbed a handful of hair and pulled it back. She screamed in pain. His face turned into a lecherous sneer. Nathan's feet scraped along the dirt, trying to run towards them. Mee Noi reached into his back pocket and pulled a dirty blue handkerchief from his pocket and shoved it roughly into her mouth. He sat up and faced Nathan, eyeball to eyeball, reached down and put his hands on her buttocks. Nathan's eyes expanded. Rachel squirmed, trying to get away, her attempted screams muffled in the cloth in her mouth. Slowly and deliberately, he rubbed his hands up and down Rachel's bum on top of the fabric of her red dress, his eyes not leaving Nathan's. The printed little yellow butterflies crumpled together as he did. Rachel tried to shake her body.

"No money?" he catcalled. "No problem."

He slowly pulled up the dress revealing her dimpled thighs. She kicked out but his weight was too much for her. Rachel rested her face on the sand, her sobs becoming even more muffled. Her body relaxed into surrender.

God's Will.

She heard a smack of lips and imagined him moistening them over his bristly moustache. Slowly, he put his fingers under the sides of her cotton knickers. Nathan was shaking his head violently from side to side, screaming through the handkerchief. His face reddened and the vein on his forehead bulged.

She closed her eyes and said a prayer.

Then Mee Noi froze.

Everything went quiet.

She shot a look at Nathan.

Head slouched forward. Slumped. Not a muscle moved.

A bird shrieked in the distance.

His head hung limply on his shoulders, his arms and legs slackened. Mee Noi shifted. The other policeman cautiously stood up. A sigh of relief washed over her as she felt Mee Noi's weight leave her legs. Both policemen edged slowly over to Nathan. The officer lifted his head which fell heavily back. He pulled the cloth out of Nathan's mouth and discarded it on the sand. Nathan opened his eyes, slowly, and raised his head. Mee Noi's eyes narrowed, realising the trick he had fallen for. He slapped Nathan with an open hand across his cheek.

"Oh Mr Nathan. You in very much trouble." Mee Noi turned his back, facing Rachel. She closed her eyes in surrender.

"Somchai," Nathan said loudly. Mee Noi turned his head slowly. "He's alive." The policeman turned back and chuckled, kneeling between Rachel's legs.

"Your brother, Somchai. He's alive." The words came out croakily. Mee Noi glanced at the slumped figure at the bottom of the tree.

"What you say?

"I said, Somchai, your brother, he's alive. I've met him." Strength grew in each word. Mee Noi stood up; Rachel sighed in relief again.

"You know nothing. You hear story from Khun Pai. Means nothing." He turned back to Rachel.

"I can prove it," Nathan said matter-of-factly. "Why do you think I am here? He told me about this place. His home. I came to find it. I fell in love with it." He blinked hard, trying to dislodge a bead of sweat threatening to drop into his eye. Mee Noi glanced at him.

"You lie. He dead. If he alive, why not come back."

"He thought everyone was dead. You. His parents. His sister. YOUR sister" At the sound of this word, tears filled Mee Noi's eyes. He sniffed them back, shaking his head.

"Lie. Khun Pai tell you my history, you lie for your friend." He spat at Rachel; the phlegm landed in the sand.

"I can prove it. I'll show you a photo." Mee Noi's eyes widened.

"Photo?"

"Yeah, a photo. Of me and him together. Untie me and I'll show you."

Mee Noi chewed on his lip.

"Haha, you very good Mr Nathan. I don't believe."

"Okay, carry on. But wouldn't you like to know?" He nodded towards Rachel and rested his head against the tree. Her eyes tightened, not believing what she was hearing. Was he bluffing? Mee Noi shifted on his feet, glanced at his flunky, and scratched his head. He stepped over to Nathan and squatted in front of him.

"How you know he my brother? Why you say now? Not before? Hmm, why not tell me brother alive. Why not say?"

"Because you are a bad man. I'm not going to tell you nice things if you are bad." Mee Noi considered this.

"But you give me money."

"A bribe." The policeman recoiled at the word, like a distaste in his mouth. "It was only yesterday that I realised. When we were outside the café, Khun Pai said you had a brother called Somchai. You look kinda similar, but you are so different. He's a lovely man. Wouldn't harm a fly. But you." Nathan's face twisted in disgust. "Why should I help you?"

The policeman harrumphed.

"Somchai told me about this place. What happened here. He described it to me. The monastery but he wasn't sure if it survived. It intrigued me. Imagine if it still stood! He told me when the Tsunami hit, he was carried away. Rescuers found him three miles away and he was put into a shelter. He was told that Bo Hin was destroyed. Completely flattened. TV images showed whole areas of Thailand had disappeared underwater. So, he believed it. He told me about his brother and sister. How they *must* be dead; they couldn't have survived it. Eventually, he moved to Bali, where I met him. A few months ago." Mee Noi's face was stiff in concentration, trying to understand the story and the rapid English.

Mee Noi clicked his tongue, shaking his head. A grin grew on his face.

"Haha, good story. You lie," his face turned serious.

"I'll prove it to you. Untie me." Nathan said quickly. Mee Noi glanced down at him and shook his head.

"How you know he my brother?"

"Because he looks like you. Not exactly but when Khun Pai said you had a brother called Somchai, I put two and two together. I mean, his belly is a bit smaller than yours..." Mee Noi chuckled to himself.

"Okay, Mr Nathan. Nice story. This is fun. I let you prove it. Show me evidence." He motioned to the other policeman to untie him, who pulled a penknife from his belt and sawed at the plastic.

"But if you lie..." he said, fingering his baton.

Nathan rubbed his wrists and got to his feet. He stood up straight and towered over Mee Noi. He looked down at Rachel and walked purposefully into the woods. She really hoped this wasn't a bluff, or Nathan had a solid plan. If not, it would be even worse. Rachel strained her neck to watch. The other policeman shadowed a few paces behind, a hand on his belt.

A few metres into the undergrowth, Nathan sank to his knees and started removing loose sand, soil and fallen leaves. He pulled a small backpack from the earth, shook it, walked back to the clearing and squatted down on his hunches in front of Rachel's eyes. He zipped the bag open and rummaged through its contents. Mee Noi instinctively wrapped his fingers around the base of the thick stick. At the same time, the other policeman started undoing the straps of a weapon.

"Slowly," Mee Noi warned. Nathan slowly pulled out a phone from the bag. Balanced between his fingers he showed it to the policemen, turning it to show it wasn't anything dangerous. The two policemen relaxed. So did Rachel. Nathan turned the phone on and the screen glowed. Everyone stared at it as it booted up. Time appeared to stand still before Nathan could busy himself with the screen. Rachel heard the faint lapping of the waves in the distance, then: *Ding, ding, ding, ding, ding.* The phone trilled with multiple messages coming through. Nathan glanced up and shrugged his shoulders.

"Popular guy," he said bashfully. Mee Noi grunted and edged closer, trying to see the front of the screen. Nathan pulled the phone to his chest, hiding it from view.

"First, untie her," he said, glancing down at Rachel. Mee Noi didn't budge.

"No. Evidence first." Nathan sighed. He scrolled, then tapped, then expanded the screen and then turned it to Mee Noi, whose eyes immediately filled with water. He reached out to the phone and cradled it in his palm, looking deeply into the screen. The photo was of Nathan with three other people, with his arm around the smaller of the figures, sandwiched between what looked like a split pyramid, a volcano behind them.

"Who are these people," he said, waving his hand over the picture.

"The tall man with the long hair, that's Pierre. Next to him is Jasmine, then me and Somchai."

"Another!" he demanded and gave the phone back to Nathan. He scrolled through the pictures until he found another.

"This is him on the boat." He passed it to Mee Noi who involuntarily choked, stumbling backwards. He reached out and leaned his outstretched arm against a tree trunk, taking it all in.

"We can call him if you like." Mee Noi bent over and rubbed the back of his neck. He looked up, his face wet with sweat and tears, his eyes wide. "But first you untie her."

He threw his arm out to Rachel and muttered something under his breath in Thai. The other policeman obeyed and untied her. She threw the handkerchief from her mouth in disgust. Mee Noi sat down at the base of the tree.

"Okay, we call him."

Nathan didn't move.

"You have phone?" he made the sign of a telephone with his hand. Mee Noi looked at him then at his phone.

"International calls very expensive," Nathan shrugged with a grin. Mee Noi leaned to his side and pulled out a brand-new Samsung Galaxy, entered the password and passed it over. Nathan took it and copied a phone number over. Rachel got up and walked over, rubbing her wrists. The phone started ringing and he pushed the 'speaker' button so everyone could hear. A woman answered the phone.

"Hello?"

"Jasmine? Jasmine! It's Nathan!"

Everyone moved away from the phone as a high-pitched squeal came from the device.

"NATHAN! NATHAN!" she repeated in excitement. "Where are you? I've been trying to reach you for ages. Oh god, I miss you so much. We need to talk!" Nathan went red as he glanced sheepishly at Rachel, who raised her eyebrows and crossed her arms.

"Oh Nathan, it's so good to hear your voice," she continued, not letting him answer. "Oh wait." Her voice faded as she turned from the phone.

"PIERRE, PIERRE, COME HERE QUICK! IT'S NATHAN!" The foursome heard running steps from inside the phone.

"Nathan? Is that you?" a thick French accent came through the phone. "Where *are* you, my man?!"

"I'm in Thailand. In Bo Hin." Mee Noi motioned with his hands to hurry on the conversation, not interested in chitchat.

"Whoop, Thailand! How exciting," came the female voice. "When are you coming back, I want to see you! I need to see you. We need to talk about everything!" Nathan's face reddened again as he felt Rachel's eyes burn into him. He interrupted her.

"Listen I haven't got much time. Is Sommy there?"

Mee Noi edged closer.

"Sommy? No, he's gone to the market." Mee Noi's shoulders sagged.

"He'll be back in a couple of hours. Why what's going on?"

"I've found his brother…" Mee Noi snatched his phone back.

"We call in two hours," he said curtly into the receiver.

"Yes of course," came back the husky French voice. "What is happening, what's going on?"

Mee Noi pressed the red 'end call' button on his phone. Nathan looked up in surprise.

"We wait two hours," Mee Noi said sternly, raising two fingers. He sauntered over to the shade of the tree and slumped down, resting his arms on his bent legs, his eyes glazed over, his mind a million miles away.

Rachel stood with her hands on her hips, her eyebrow cocked, glowering at Nathan.

"What?" he said, looking quizzically at her. She impatiently tapped her foot.

"So," she said back with an air of frustration. "Now do you want to tell me who the hell Jasmine is?"

Part Two

Jasmine

What is love? I pondered, gazing out into the emerald sea. Surely, I should know the answer to that question after forty-five years on this planet. But I'd screwed up so much of my life I didn't have time for that word. I picked up a small, speckled pebble embedded in the impossibly soft, white sand and threw it out into the ocean, watched it arc and then plop into the water.

The sun was high and the sky cloudless. I felt a hand move around my back, before resting on my bony hip. My skin was dark – not dirt this time but tanned. I never knew Indian skin could *glow*. The fresh fruit and sea swimming helped. Even my black hair was healthy. I never cared for it much – it was low down on my priorities. Now, it was tied into a loose plait, shining. When I was on the plane, squeezed into the tiny bathroom somewhere over Nepal, I noticed a few wisps of grey. Those were now hidden underneath a white straw hat. Its wide rim pushed against my head as he moved closer to me.

He kissed my shoulder. Then he stroked his fingertips down my arm, over the track marks punctuating my veins before interlocking his fingers within mine.

If anyone was watching this – us – they would say it was perfection. Two people canoodling in a honeymoon destination. Of course, nothing is ever perfect. There are the mosquitoes for a start. And my history. Could he really love me after knowing everything? He even knew my future.

The ticking timebomb inside me.

He said it didn't matter. He had said, the past is the past. The future is unwritten. What's important is who you are now.

Bloody hippy.

It couldn't be love. Affection maybe. Definitely not lust. A fondness. Men were always fond of me. Or should that be an opportunity to take advantage? An opportunity to exploit my vulnerabilities. A weakness that they would prey on and I would blindly lap up. I'd fallen for it so many times you'd think I would have learnt my lesson by now.

Perhaps it was trust. Did love equal trust?

This felt different somehow. Real. I wasn't on edge. My senses had relaxed. I could trust him. Or was that my imagination running wild? The holiday romance of the palm trees and Bali's golden sandy beaches, a million miles from London and the life I left behind. Following a stranger halfway across the world, escaping the cold of the park benches, the food handouts and the fireworks of my father.

Nearly 170 days sober now.

Wow, six months. That bit was real.

Everything happened so quickly. It was like I was floating in a whirlwind. Pushed and pulled in different directions, finally landing here on this picture-postcard beach.

After that: calm, like the flat sea after a storm.

I just got on with my new life. Planting coral polyps in the sea, growing our own reef in this patch of ocean. The tranquillity and the stability. The routine of tending to our sea garden. Watching it grow and thrive.

No dramas. Just being.

Time flies when you are in the stars and don't bother to look down at the gutter.

And just when you think everything has settled down the telephone rings.

Chapter One

A dark-skinned, young man stood out amongst the Indonesians hawking at arrivals. His Asian eyes grew wide when he spotted us.

"Mr Nathan! Ms Jasmine!"

He bounded over to us, arms extended as if ready to embrace us. He was shorter than both of us, easily, by a foot.

"My name Somchai," he said in a heavy accent. "But Mr Pierre, he call me Sommy."

He had a lean body and a crew-cut haircut, the length of which was similar to the bristly moustache on his top lip. His broad smile and humble eyes exuded warmth. His cheeks still had the freshness of a young man, not much older than Nathan but a good deal younger than me. He wore grimy jeans, open sandals and a dirty white t-shirt that had a faded sunset landscape of a tropical sunset. Above, in pale blue letters, read 'Bali is Paradise'.

He shook our hands, ever so softly, and picked up our rucksacks and threw them on his back, ushering Nathan and me out of the airport, past the hawkers all vying for taxi fares and tours. He placed my backpack in the boot of a rickety old Mercedes, peeled paint revealing rust around the tyre rims, and squeezed it next to a white cooler box. Beeping and honking his way through the bustle of the airport traffic, the car eventually purred through lush tropical rainforest and beside the blue-green ocean. The sea was hypnotic and I couldn't help but stare out at the expanse. It was humid and I hadn't realized how much I was sweating, my clothes sticking to my skin. Nathan leaned forward, revealing a sliver of damp sneaking towards the back of his jeans from his cotton shirt.

"How long have you been working with Pierre?" called out Nathan, trying to make his voice heard over the rushing wind.

"Two years," replied Sommy, putting two fingers up, shouting back over his shoulder. "He is good man. He respects me and local Balinese. Not many westerners do that. He is doing

a little bit good for Bali, more than these stupid drunk tourists."
He waved his hand in the air again. "A little bit, but a little bit
better than nothing ha? And here you two. A little bit bigger!
Even for a few days, it means we make faster progress,
inshallah." Our eyes met in the rear-view mirror. His callused
hands on the steering wheel and scarred skin told me he had
some stories in him. Nathan would like him immensely, I could
tell.

A thud came from the front of the car. Our heads flew
forward as Sommy hit the brakes. He jumped out of the car and
ran to the front. His hand covered his mouth as he looked
down, his eyes wide. A crowd of people quickly gathered
around. One man put his hand on Sommy's shoulder, muttering
something to him. Nathan and I slid out of the back seat,
curious as to what had happened. We held our breath as we
looked at what the others were seeing.

A skinny brown dog lay lifeless on the asphalt. I noticed
a fly land on its open eye, and it didn't flinch. Another settled on
its fur. Sommy's eyes were red as he squatted down and carefully
scooped it up. The dog's legs hung over his outstretched arms
and a blob of saliva dripped from its mouth. He laid it down on
the side of the road between two shacks and gently pushed its
eyelids shut. The crowd started to disperse. He stood there for a
few seconds and then raised clasped hands to his forehead.
Then he turned, wiped his hands on his jeans and climbed back
into the car. Nathan's mouth was agape, just staring down at the
animal. Our shoulders twisted to the car, but our eyes didn't –
couldn't – leave the dog.

"Very sad," Sommy sniffed as he put the car in gear as
we eventually climbed in. "But that is life. Sometimes you are
car. Sometimes dog."

Nobody said another word for the rest of the journey.

After a couple of hours of near-perfect roads,
meandering between two towering volcanos amongst lush green
trees, the right side of the car again opened to a vast expanse of
blue/green sea. My thoughts went between the beautiful scenery
and the death we had just witnessed. The dog's vacant eyes
reminded me of my father in his last few days. We turned along

a single dirt track road, the old car rocking sideways as the smooth road made way to pot-holes and mud. It bent around almost like a hairpin to reveal two single-story shacks sheltered by the wide fronds of several banana trees. Beyond them, pure white sand led to the dark sapphire sea sitting underneath a dazzling blue sky. Sommy swung the car around in an arc, so my door was next to the only entrance of the building. When the engine cut, as if on cue, its door swung open.

A well-built man with long curly hair brushing his shoulders filled the frame, his thick arms aloft as if in triumph, wearing frayed, faded denim shorts, flip-flops and a dirty vest top. Even from the car, I could spot wisps of grey at his temple. The hairs below his shins were stuck to his golden-brown skin as if he had just been for a paddle. A burnt-out hippy was the first description to cross my mind. His dark sunglasses, wrapped around his eyes, jolted up as his mouth made a huge grin.

"'Ello, bonjour mes amis!!!" he shouted in delight, swaggering out onto the threshold. "A hundred thousand welcomes my English friends. I could weep and I could laugh. I am light and heavy. Welcome to Bali! Or to be more precise: Tulamben!"

His thick French accent was smooth like chocolate. He reached out immediately as my door creaked open and pulled me to my feet. His sunglasses fell to the ground revealing piercing green eyes framed by deep creases on either side.

"Good afternoon to you, beautiful lady!" he cried theatrically as he kissed my hand. "May a curse reach to the very root of anyone's heart who isn't happy to see you! You must be Jasmine!" and gave me a tight bear hug, his huge arms wrapped around me like a snake to its prey. A mixture of salt and coconut filled my nostrils. I couldn't help but smile at the man.

He ran around the back of the car as Nathan extended his arm out to shake his hand.

"Please," he guffawed spreading his arms out. "A friend is waiting behind a stranger's face, to paraphrase a beautiful lady," he said as he ignored the hand and embraced him tightly, almost fatherly, like a long-lost friend.

"I'm guessing you are Nathan! Haha! Welcome my British friends. Come, come. I have some iced tea ready." He ushered us into the house whilst Sommy busied himself with our luggage.

"Thank you for having us, Pierre. I'm delighted to meet you. I can't wait to see what you do and to help, of course."

"Tsk. So formal are the British!" He winked at me. Pierre's French accent was thick and unmistakable. "Oui. All in good time Nathan. First, let's get your things and get a drink, no? Sommy!"

Pierre glanced over to Sommy and cocked his head ever so slightly. The infectious energy and enthusiasm that had welcomed us disappeared. Whilst looking at Sommy, Pierre thrust an iced tumbler into our hands and then left us. The walls were painted the same pastel blue on the inside as the outside and a worn guitar was propped up in a corner. A blue electric light buzzed above it. A few bits of tourist tat sat on top of a small bookshelf in the corner. Nathan wandered over and tilted his head to read the spines of the dog-eared books. Through the solitary window, I noticed Pierre's thick arm draped across Sommy's shoulders, his head bowed down. It was like a father speaking to a son. He was whispering into his ear, then rubbed the crook of his neck and patted him on the back. As he turned, I quickly moved, feigning interest in a plastic Taj Mahal.

"A drink!" Pierre called out, as he burst through the door. "Are you hungry? Sommy does the best coconut fritters. He prepared some earlier. You must eat!"

Pierre led us into another room with a small wooden table with two wooden chairs before dancing out. A gas stove, a few worn pans and items of dry food stood in a corner on a couple of DIY shelves. Sand covered the floor. A smoking firepit with a frying pan dangling above it, held aloft by a metal tripod, stood outside, centred in the doorframe like a theatre prop. Sommy sauntered into view, pouring white liquid into the pan. Two hammocks swayed on the other side of the room as if a ghostly visitor was asleep in them.

Pierre came back in holding a huge wet, silver fish in the crook of his arm. Its eyes dead like the dogs'.

"This is for dinner!" he cried, handing it over to Sommy who tentatively accepted it. "I caught it just before you arrived."

We tucked into the coconut fritters drinking fruity iced tea. Sommy was watching us intently as we bit into the moist, oily pancake. I rolled my eyes back in delight. His smile stretched so wide with pride, like a kid who had been praised for painting a nice picture. He turned and went out a door, a spring in his step, holding the fish like a baby.

"So...." I started, curiosity getting the better of me. "What exactly do you do here?"

Pierre looked over at Nathan, his eyebrows raised.

"You really didn't tell her?!" He was overcome with excitement, a schoolboy knowing a secret. Nathan shook his head, a wry smile on his face. "Haha! You only met a few months ago! I didn't believe you! That's crazy. 'A surprise is the greatest gift which life can grant us.'" He reached over and slapped Nathan on the knee.

"Only if it's a nice surprise," I warned. "An unwanted surprise is just a problem."

"Ha! So true Jasmine. But you still came all this way, and you have no idea what you will do. Your future dictated by this man."

I swallowed.

"If I'd known, I would have taken you to the area with all the garbage. That would have been a horrible surprise. All the trash that tourists make must go somewhere. Hundreds of thousands of tons of plastic goes into the sea. Down in Kuta, it is awful. Every December time the beaches become terrible. It's because the rains and the west winds push the garbage onto the beach and the locals must sweep it up. We go to help. The price of tourism. But Bali needs tourists to survive, you understand? Especially after..." He motioned a giant wave with his hand and arm.

"So, you're a bit of an eco-warrior then?" I said. Pierre chuckled to himself, glancing at Sommy out of the corner of his eye.

"I suppose you can say those words if you like. They are nice. I am trying to do my little bit to help. You see, there are hardly any fish left. Fish in the ocean here have reduced dramatically in the last few years. The phrase, I think you say, 'there is plenty of fish in the sea'? Ha! Not anymore. Many Balinese relied on fish. Now, their catches are small."

"So, what are you doing about it?" I asked. Pierre rubbed his hands.

"In Indonesia, the grouper fish, once the lifeblood of these seas, are almost gone." He had a fire in his eyes. "I'm trying to bring them back."

"Wow," I said, raising my eyebrows.

"Exactly," Pierre cried, shocking everyone. "Exactly Jasmine! And tomorrow, my new friends here will help me build my coral reef and bring the grouper back! Many hands make light work." Pierre knocked back the rest of his drink and slapped both his hands on his knees. "Viva Bali!" he exclaimed in utter delight.

It was hard not to be carried away by Pierre's infectious enthusiasm. But I had learned not to take people at face value, that there was always something hidden behind someone's smile. An ulterior motive perhaps or distrust that they were out to get you, take advantage in some way. The way Pierre rubbed his hands, or a quick look at Sommy, I couldn't help but think there was something else to him.

Something that didn't ring true.

The years I spent sleeping on the streets had taught me that.

Chapter Two

I walked into the church, unsure of what to say or do. It was familiar – the high wooden eaves, the musty smell, the cold, damp air. I had been here many times before when it provided shelter from the cold and rain. Usually, there would be rows of camp beds, uniformly laid out in a grid. I would be ushered to one, shivering and wet, clutching plastic bags or, if I was lucky, a rucksack. On most occasions my head would be fuzzy, coming down from a hit or a session, so I would be looking around to see if I recognised anyone that I could score off or might have a stash of beer or cider, or even better a strong spirit.

I looked around the huge nave, filled high with blue and green crates on metal shelves, full of colourful packets and tins. Towering over the raised pulpit, a tall Christmas tree adorned with red and gold tinsel and baubles, the same decorations year after year. Stacked in piles around the edge of the hall were pallets of crisps, toilet roll, rice and pasta. Above them, depictions of gods and biblical scenes looked down: so many times I had been here yet I had never noticed those stained-glass windows. Maybe it was because it was daytime now and the sun lit them from behind.

And I was sober.

102 days and counting. Milling around were smartly dressed people, each sporting a yellow high-vis bib; none of the torn, scruffy, stinking clothes that would usually greet me. A middle-aged woman, not much younger than me, sauntered up, sporting a red Santa's hat.

"You here for the foodbank?" she said, not in the most welcoming of manner. At least she didn't look me up and down with disgust.

"Down the hall and to the right." She handed me a clipboard and walked away down the central aisle.

In a cold room to the side of the church, a few people were standing around, trying not to look at each other. I nodded a hello to the one brave soul who attempted eye contact. We stood in awkward silence, pretending to be engrossed in the papers on the clipboard. I heard hurried footsteps echoing on the flagstones outside, and then a young, round man with a patchy beard breezed in wearing a Santa's hat and holding a clipboard.

"Hi everyone. Sorry! Been a bit manic this morning," he chirped. Everyone looked up, relieved that someone would be taking charge.

"I'm Paul. I'm the guy running this gig. Firstly, thank you. Thank you for volunteering." He dramatically put his hand over his heart, like he was acting on a stage, and bowed his head. "Your help is greatly appreciated.

"Secondly, and booooring, paperwork. Health and safety I'm afraid." He put his hand over his mouth, pretending to yawn. "Bend your knees and keep your back straight when lifting heavy boxes yadda, yadda, yadda. I'll let you read them at your leisure." He was trying to be our friend, one of us.

"Thirdly," he raised his three middle fingers into the air. "Please keep your mobile phones on silent. We want to keep a professional atmosphere when we are here, and to give our clients our full attention." Immediately, everyone raced to pull their phones out of their pockets to check. All except two. Me (because I knew my phone was off because I didn't have any credit on it), and a slight man standing at the back, behind the circle of people, with a black cap pulled down over his eyes and his hands in front of his crotch clutching the clipboard, his shoulders slouched forward. Shy and embarrassed was my first impression of him. Maybe even ashamed. I got the feeling he had to be here, rather than wanting to be.

"They are allowed three vouchers in six months," Paul continued. "This is so they don't rely on us all the time. The foodbank is an emergency support so they can focus on getting back on their feet."

I noticed everyone nodding. It was clear these people hadn't relied on handouts before. It was interesting to see this from the other side of the fence. Those food parcels were lifelines. I had begged for another voucher before, only to be told I'd had my three in six months. Even though I could see stacks of food behind them, the computer had said 'no'.

"Don't look so worried," he grinned. "We'll buddy you up with someone to show you the ropes. So, who would like to do the warehouse?" The man in the black cap shot his hand up whilst everyone else shifted about.

"Okay, well, how about you and, er, Damon?"

A young man with a tattooed head raised his hand.

"You too in the warehouse," he said. "And you, you and you to collection" that included me. He organised the others in the same way. We tentatively moved to our groups, nodding a silent hello to our new workmates.

"Right. Let's get your name badges sorted." Paul handed Damon a lanyard with his name on it and he popped it over his shorn head.

"Maggie?" An older woman, well, older than me, put her hand up and received her lanyard. She was wearing a pink floral dress and had her grey hair in bunches. We all listened carefully for our names to be called, each raising their hand like the previous one.

"And finally. Jasmine?" I raised my hand and popped the lanyard over my head.

"Right, has everyone got... oh!" The man in the black cap stood awkwardly at the back.

"Oh right. Ahem, sorry. Don't worry, we'll get you a lanyard. What's your name?" Paul said looking down at his clipboard.

"Nathan," he replied quietly, self-consciously stepping forward. "It might be under Nathaniel Clyne?"

"Oh yes! Nathan Clyne. Yes, I only got the email a few minutes ago so I didn't have time to print one out for you. I'll sort that for you later." Nathan stepped back, hoping to find a shadow. I watched him out of the corner of my eye, shrunken and subdued.

I wondered what his story was.

Chapter Three

Nathan shook me awake early the next morning. Dawn's ethereal light made his features all fuzzy.

"Jasmine," he said, urgently. My eyes focused. I put my hand on my back, stiff from laying in the hammock. I had tossed and turned for what seemed like hours when we went to bed, the jetlag keeping me awake.

"God, that hammock is uncomfortable," I said as I swung my legs around and my feet touched the floor. Sand. I could get used to that feeling. All the floors were covered in sand.

"You've got to come and see this! Come, quickly." He used his finger in a come-hither sign as he raced to the door, a wry smile on his lips.

"What is it?" I moaned. "What time is it?"

"I have no idea, before sunrise. Hurry." I pulled on the t-shirt that was resting on the end of the hammock, the one I had worn on the flight yesterday.

Standing on the beach were Pierre and Sommy, their backs to us, hands on hips. The whole sea in front of them was rippling, mini-waves chaotically churning the water. I spotted a fin. Then my eyes adjusted. Hundreds and hundreds of dolphins were breaking the surface, making an arch as their smooth bodies came briefly out of the water. One after the other, for what seemed like miles. Perfectly framed against a light blue and orange dawn sky. It was so hypnotic it felt as though everything else dissolved into nothing.

"Magical, isn't it?" Pierre said, breaking the tranquillity. He guided us to the water's edge as our eyes were transfixed by the scene in front of us. "A good morning in Bali. I organised this, especially for you." I turned my head slightly to him and caught his mischievous smile etched onto his face, fully looking at me, the orange sunrise reflected in his eye. I pushed his arm in jest. "Well thank you, how long did it take you to train them?!"

The sky lightened quickly and soon the sun peeped up over the horizon as the parade continued, thousands of dolphins in a blissful union of leaping and swimming in pilgrimage. It was one of those moments which will be forever in my memory. I put my arm around Nathan's shoulders and he turned his head to me. He smiled and put his arm around my waist. We watched in silence; time left to a different dimension. A world and a lifetime away from what I had back home.

When the last of the dolphins had disappeared into the depths, we found a table set full of cut fruit and boiled eggs back at the hut. Pierre was already sitting at the head of the table helping himself to melon and bananas.

"Come, come guys. Please eat. This morning we'll visit the reef to see what we have done so far. After lunch, we will make some coral and put it into the sea." He stuffed a pink slice of melon into his mouth, the juice rolling down his chin.

"How much have you done already?" Nathan said, pulling out a white plastic chair.

"Hmmm, well, I'm not sure. I guess it covers over three hectares, but it's not in rows, one after the other." Pierre drew imaginary lines on the table, like spokes on a bicycle wheel. "It's more like tentacles, reaching outwards. That way we can grow the reach. The corals will fill in between."

Pierre licked his fingers, scrapped his chair backwards and picked up a piece of pineapple from the centre of the table and popped it in his mouth. "Sommy!" he called, juice leaping from his mouth. "Let's get the boat ready and the snorkel equipment. Go and get changed, meet you on the beach."

I took my bikini into a small square room which served as a bathroom. A hole-in-the-ground and a square basin on the floor, a hose jutting out above. I'd been in worse. When I came out, Nathan was standing in bright yellow swimming trunks and a sleeveless vest top. I noticed his eyes quickly flick up and down my body. I wondered what went through his mind.

As we walked to the beach, a pile of white coolers, identical to the one that was in the back of the car that picked us up from the airport, took my attention. Four stacked up in a pile, four deep. They seemed out of place, but I couldn't think why.

Sommy stood thigh-deep in the water, bent over the side of a wide canoe with wooden stabilisers on both sides. Pierre offered a hand to each of us as we clambered on board, sitting single file facing forwards as Sommy pushed us off. The occasional splash of the paddle at the back of the boat rocked us forward. In the near distance, red flags were protruding from the water, one every few metres. I noticed more and more flags darting off in different directions.

"The red flags show where we have put the coral domes," Pierre informed us. "I have written on each flag the date we dropped them. It's a record of what we have done. As you can see, they go off in different directions." He raised his hand again and spread his fingers out. "Okay, Sommy, let's stop here." He reached out and grabbed a flag. "19th July 2017. Yes, the first one. History started here! Let's get your snorkel on and go for a swim, yes?"

I grabbed the snorkel and goggles that were being passed down and before I had a chance to get it on, I heard a big splash followed by the boat rocking. Pierre bobbed up, motioning us to get in. I gasped as the cool water went up my body as I sunk in. I squealed a girly squeal, the sound echoed through the snorkel. Treading water, I dipped my face to see what was underneath.

Coral.

Beautiful coral with tiny tentacles reaching out into the sea. Deep greens and faded blues, greys and browns, turquoises and dull reds. Corals clumped together like a floral bouquet – I could just make out the occasional white paint of unnatural domes hidden by the flourishing alien-looking plants. A few interested fish were swimming in between the structures, darting in and out, no more than a couple of inches long. A colourful fish, larger than the others, swam nonchalantly past, like a guard on patrol, making sure the littluns were behaving.

A small movement caught my eye – a black stone appeared to move on its own accord, a puff of sand rising and settling next to it. The coral stretched out into the distance. It was impossible to tell how far as the view faded quickly in the distance. I saw Nathan's yellow trunks a few feet from me, flapping from his kicking legs. His eyes were wide open through the mask. I swam over to him and gave him a thumbs-up. He responded with an 'OK' signal. I broke the surface and pulled my snorkel out. Pierre was right behind me. Sommy was grinning from the boat. He hadn't jumped in.

"Nice, huh?" he called, raising his thumbs.

"Amazing," I called back. That was the laziest adjective that sprang to mind.

Three heads bobbed up and down on the water's surface.

"Beautiful, right?" said Pierre. "And to think, a few years ago this was like an underwater desert. We created this."

"You've done a great job," gasped Nathan as he kicked his feet. The sun danced off his wet, brown hair.

"Have you noticed the domes? It's what started it all. You can hardly see them now the coral has grown so much. Swim along the main channel of coral. You will see. There are lots of cuttlefish today. I saw a few parrotfish. Let me show you." He pulled his goggles back on and forced the snorkel back into his mouth. A spit of water came out of the top as he blew any remnants of water. We followed suit and dove back under. Nathan and Pierre were out in front as I followed directly behind.

The Frenchman occasionally pointed to something on the seabed; a fish here and a fish there. Sometimes he dived right down to the bottom kicking his legs furiously to reach the bottom. From his pocket, he pulled out secateurs and clipped a piece of coral from the domes. He placed it into a net bag attached to his shorts and swam back to the surface where Sommy was waiting. He passed the coral to Sommy before swimming back towards us.

"Can you see the white domes?" he chirped.

"I saw some white, definitely not coral," I responded, gasping as the water splashed into my mouth. "But they are hard to see."

"That's it. It means the corals are growing healthily. The domes provide shelter underneath for the baby fish and a structure for the coral to grow. You may have seen some growth away from the domes. This is the best news; they are growing and populating. Hopefully, soon this whole area will be covered again." He gasped for breath as his legs kicked beneath him. "Okay, let's go to the boat and go home. Then we get to work!"

Pierre grabbed hold of the side of the boat and leapt back into it. Nathan and I swam up to the side and the two men offered their hands for help, feet astride as far as they could on the narrow boat to help steady the swaying. Nevertheless, the boat rocked violently as we both scrambled on board and into the wooden slat of a seat. Nathan sat at the front, me behind him, breathless from the kicking and swimming, the salt of the sea prickling my skin. Droplets cascaded from his hair down the spine of his back. I turned back and saw a white plastic bucket in between Pierre's legs, water splashing over the sides. He was inspecting the contents, putting his hand deep into the bucket. Occasionally he would pull out a bit of coral, lift it to the sun and twist it slightly in the air, before placing it back. He was joyfully humming to himself, the sun on his face, without a care in the world. His long hair was wet with water dripping down its length onto his bronzed shoulders, the sun glistening off his bare torso. He glanced up at me suddenly, realising I was watching him. He gave me a cheeky wink, his mouth wide in a grin.

Then his eyes darted over my shoulder. I spun around just as Nathan was turning away.

It made my skin crawl.

Chapter Four

Paul introduced me to a rotund man wearing a collared blue shirt and blue jeans, sitting in front of a pile of empty food crates. A red Santa's hat stood askew on his balding head. Age had not been kind to his belly which extended from below his chest and out over the rim of his trousers. The fabric of his shirt stretched against the skin. It reminded me of my dad's protruding belly when he sat in his armchair spittle flying as he shouted angry words. Except this man didn't have a fat belt sitting menacingly beneath the sag.

"Alright?" he said, in a voice higher than his body suggested.

"Yeah, alright," I replied with a smile. Paul beamed.

"Great! Mike, can you show Jasmine the ropes please?"

"Of course, with pleasure," he said as Paul danced off. Mike nodded after him.

"He's a good man Paul. A true Christian. Heart of bloody gold. Are you with the church?"

"What do you mean?" I said absentmindedly, watching to see if Paul was going to speak to Nathan as Mike offered me a chair next to his.

"Do you come here often? For the services I mean."

"Oh no. No." I shook my head. "No, I'm not a Christian."

"Muslim then? Hindi?" I looked back at him, realising he was making a judgement of me. A wrong one. I responded sternly back.

"No. Atheist." I wondered if I had offended him as he raised his eyebrows.

"Oh," he said in reply, looking downbeat.

Movement caught my eye which gave me a chance to feign interest in something else. It was Nathan. His black cap bowed down following a young woman with a ponytail and those tight legging things that seemed to be popular at the moment. He shuffled awkwardly behind her as they passed crates of food, her pointing at each item as they went.

Other volunteers were milling about the room, waiting for the clients to arrive. I noticed there were two types of people: do-gooders and users. The do-gooders walked around with their noses an inch higher in the air, with coordinated, clean, expensive-looking clothes, trying to look scruffy. The users, people like me who had been on the other side of the table, wore mixed-matched clothes with shoddy haircuts, looking dishevelled and rough because that was what we were used to. Even if they tried to be like the other side with decent clothes and a proper haircut, the big tell-tale was their skin. The do-gooder's skin shone, through a better diet or moisturiser, or both. The users had pockmarked skin, rashes and an unhealthy glow. That was something you couldn't hide.

This is what made Nathan sit in the 'do-gooder' camp, despite him trying to dress down and his haggard appearance. The bags under his eyes suggested he'd either not slept for weeks or had been shooting up. Not in a corner of a dirty bedsit but in some swanky apartment somewhere. His plain t-shirt and baseball cap were scuffed and dirtied blue Nike trainers looked like they had never been through the wash. He had a close-cut haircut which he probably did himself and a five o'clock shadow. But his skin looked fresh. I could tell a mile off. Mike, on the other hand, was definitely in the do-gooder camp: freshly pressed buttoned-down top and sparkly clean jeans that looked ironed, and clean, healthy skin.

"So, what do you do then, when you're not here?" His leg was bouncing up and down.

"I'm a ballet dancer. Well, I teach now," I said, noticing him raise his eyebrows in surprise.

"Really? Wow, you don't see many...." He cut himself off. "You've definitely got the body for it." It was my turn to raise my eyebrows. "I mean, I mean, you're very *svelte*." He looked down at my sitting body. I consciously crossed my legs. "That is impressive. Have you been in anything?"

"I was at the RBS for a while. That's the Royal Ballet School." I added condescendingly. "I studied there for a while. It was brutal though. I didn't last long." He nodded his head attempting to empathise. I bit my lip as I missed out the bigger part of the story. I didn't want to give Mike the full one. "So, I turned to jazz, a bit of tap and some street. That was the in-thing, so I tried that out, but I kept going back to ballet. And here I am." My potted history sounded pretty respectable. It was the bits in-between which weren't.

"Well done you," he said, his turn to be condescending. "That is very noble. Is there much demand for ballet around here?"

"Yeah, little girls mainly. Pushy parents with lots of money. This area is ripe for it." He just nodded back in thought.

"Married?" he asked. God, he wouldn't stop with the personal questions.

"No. Boyfriend."

"Ah! Is he *the one*?"

"We'll see," I said picturing Chris in my head, along with all the other boyfriends I thought were The One, only for them to use me as a punching bag.

A clattering took our attention away. A crate of tins had fallen and Nathan was standing next to them, his face bright red under his black cap. He crouched down and started picking them up. A couple of other volunteers and I rushed over to help, putting them all back in the crate. As we did, Nathan turned each one so they were facing the same way. Stealing a look in the crook of his arm – as users do – there was an absence of tracks. His skin was clear and clean, even moisturised. I tried to glimpse at his eyes, but he kept his head low. I noticed the tag in his jeans pocket – Diesel – and the black cap had an embossed logo on the back which I hadn't noticed before – Hugo Boss. Nathan was definitely in the do-gooder's group, but unlike the others, he wasn't chatty or friendly. I didn't think he was here on his own accord.

An enigma which piqued my interest.

I reckoned he was a community service case. Had he done prison time? More likely he had got off. Fraud perhaps, maybe even drunk driving. Was this a way to shed his guilt? He didn't seem like a kiddie-fiddler. Even though I didn't know him he just seemed too *nice* to prey on children. I had to stop myself – I was judging him in a way I didn't want people to judge me. A ballet dancer! No one would have believed that when I was passed out with wet trousers in a shop entrance.

Towards the end of the shift, I watched as Nathan followed Paul to the reception desk and faffed around with papers. He proudly pulled one out and started writing on it, before passing it to Nathan to check and sign. As it passed, I saw the unmistakable purple square with six disjointed horizontal white lines across it, forming an abstract 'E' back-to-back – the ridiculous corporate logo of the National Probation Service. I was captivated. He looked like he wouldn't say boo to a goose, that a stiff wind would knock him over. But something must have snapped in him. Spellbound, I felt the urge to go over to speak to him.

The question was: would he speak to me?

Chapter Five

Our hair was dripping with sea water as we returned from our boat trip exploring the corals. My shirt over my bikini was almost dry to the touch, such was the heat of the sun. A Bikini! At my age. Never did I think I would be wearing a skimpy bikini at forty-five. Yet it feels so natural here in this slice of heaven. Sommy was busy laying out a lunch of rice salad and fresh bread.

"He must have a twin," I commented to Nathan, due to the speed that he would dash about, seemingly being able to be in two places at once.

The food was plentiful, enjoyable and healthy. Over lunch, Pierre animatedly told us about how he grew up with his fisherman father on the south coast of France.

"I saw first-hand the destruction of the fishing industry," he would say, waving his finger with fruit slushing out the corner of his mouth. "What it was doing to the seas. So, I went to the Université d'Aix-Marseille to study marine biology."

Such a cliché, but his accent was so silky, drawing us into his charm and ideologies.

"I, how you say, flunked my course. Too many girls and too much weed," he chuckled as his eyes glazed over. "I worked on my dad's fishing boat as well as doing odd jobs and making money from nothing. Anything to get a bit of money. I left France with every Euro I had ever earned in my back pocket, travelling by train and boat across the world until I finally ended up in Indonesia. Ah, the things I have seen. I worked for charities and hotels, on fishing boats and bars. Anything to keep the adventure going. And here is where I am now. I found a purpose in doing this project of ours. Who knows if I stay or if I go, or even when! One thing is for certain, I have a friend for life." He glanced over at Sommy who was leaning against the side of one of the shacks. He put his hands together and raised them to his forehead.

"Inshallah," he said, proudly.

Pierre's adventure sounded fanciful and wildly exotic as he regaled stories of his travels. Nathan's eyes bulged in awe as spoke. How much of it was true we didn't know, the Frenchman was a good storyteller. He loved the attention and enjoyed the company. Hell, I was enjoying myself too. The sun was on my back, the view was gorgeous and my feet were in the finest, softest sand I could ever have imagined. His enthusiasm was incredibly contagious, both myself and Nathan wanting to hear more. That would be for another time because after lunch Pierre led us into a dusty courtyard where several white domes that we had seen on the seabed were stacked on top of each other. In a corner stood a gas canister, long strips of white metal and an empty plastic chair. Next to the domes were two of the white plastic buckets that he had been so interested in on the boat. Inside were piles of harvested coral, about two to three inches long, covered in clear water. Nathan came over and peered over my shoulder into the bucket.

Pierre and Sommy came over, the latter carrying two chairs, one in each hand. Pierre sat on one of them and pulled a white bucket in between his knees.

"Okay," he said, as the rest of us pulled up a chair. "This is a polyp from the area we visited this morning. Sommy and I took these yesterday before you arrived." He pulled one piece out of the bucket and let the water slide down his arm.

"Coral," he began in teacher mode, "is a living organism, an animal. It is made up of these things, polyps. The hard part is calcium carbonate. The polyp is the outer skeleton, the shell if you like. It cannot survive only like this. It needs algae which live inside. It is the algae that gives the polyp its colour. The algae and the polyp must live in harmony together. The algae takes the sunlight and gives the polyp food. The polyp in return hosts and protects the algae. Ying and yang. If there is not enough sunlight or too much heat, the algae dies leaving a white skeleton." He pointed to the side of one of the huts where a dead white coral carcass lay on the ground. A relic and example of death.

"On the other hand, if there is too much sunlight the algae grows and grows and suffocates the polyp and the polyp dies." He pointed again to the dead skeleton. Pierre was deadly serious. Any joyful tone in his voice had disappeared. "If the conditions are right, then the coral thrives like we have witnessed this morning. It is a big job, saving the planet. 'Warriors' need help," he said, winking at me.

"The internet was slow to arrive here, but we managed to create a website, and, well, here you are! You help pay the bills and of course, accelerate our progress. We are honoured that you are here." He put his hand on his chest and bowed his head. It felt like a mocking gesture. Sommy's face showed that it was genuine. I wasn't sure how much Nathan had paid for us to be there – bed and full board – and I'm sure he wouldn't tell me either.

"So here is what we do. Sommy and I have already welded together these frames. They are coated in non-rust paint." He picked up one of the domes from the top with ease and placed it to the left of his bucket.

"Now, we must be quick as the polyps and algae cannot survive outside of the water for long." He dipped the polyp he was holding into the bucket and pulled it out again. With his other hand, he got a black plastic tie which was in a transparent bag lying next to the chair. He pushed the polyp onto the white frame and fastened it to the iron with the tie.

"Not too tight, we want the polyp to grow but tight enough for it to attach itself. In a couple of weeks, we will cut off the plastic." Pierre's face was a picture of focus and concentration.

"And there we have it. Voila." He pulled another polyp out of the bucket and proceeded to fasten that one too. Sommy knelt and pulled out another one. Nathan followed suit. The three men huddled around the white dome, dipping their hands into the bucket in perfect order.

"That's good Nathan," Pierre commented.

Within a few minutes, Nathan stretched his arms and rubbed the small of his back. Their white dome was covered in little polyps, like caterpillars spaced apart along the horizontal loops that went around the frame. The tiers of potential life. Sommy picked up the frame from the top and staggered quickly down to the water's edge, placing it upside down in the water.

"We will take it later to the coral reef with the others that we will do now."

We sat for what seemed a couple of hours, attaching these twig-like tubes to the base. My back ached from bending over on my chair. Every time we finished a dome Sommy would wander over and give a big toothy grin of approval. Nathan and I would carry the structure to the water's edge and place it inverted into the water. By the time the sun was getting weaker the small bay was covered with about 40 domes, just the white rims visible from the surface. The receding sunlight danced on the ripples. Pierre stood next to me, his hands on his hips and took a deep breath, wrapping his arm around my shoulder. He was so relaxed and laid back that it was probably entirely natural to him. Nathan crept up behind us, the splashing from his feet in the water taking our attention. Pierre turned in surprise, letting his arm drop.

"Beautiful, isn't it? The future. Not only will this help the water, but it'll also help the fish. It will help the salinity; it will help cleanse and oxygenate. It'll mean tourists can come and visit Bali. It is all good. Right, let's celebrate! Who wants a swim?"

Pierre, Nathan and I walked further into the shallow sea and let the warm Indonesian water wash away the sweat and soften our muscles. Work then play. Just like it always was for Pierre, I assumed. As the sun set the three of us splashed around in the water. It was hard to think beyond this adventure.

The future.

I knew I was only here for a couple of weeks but what was going to be next? I didn't have anything to go back to really, yet my future was certain and scary. I had chosen to live with it. That's the right decision, I'm sure of it.

When the sun had long since set, and my belly was full of freshly cooked food, I went to my hammock contemplating what I would do when I got home.

***

I awoke with a start to hear splashing in the distance. I pulled on my t-shirt and walked silently to the frame of the door. The stars were bright and dazzling, the moon a crescent shape just above the horizon. Two figures were coming out of the sea, a white-water cooler in between them, a solid hammock. The outline of the two figures was unmistakably Pierre and Sommy, both struggling under the weight of the box. The dim light from the moon gave a ghostly wonder about the place. Water splashed over the top of the box as they stumbled out of the water. The boat with the two wooden stabilisers bobbed just behind them. They grunted as they walked. I moved my body behind the door frame, my squinted eyes watching them before they disappeared behind the bushes. I heard the thud of the box hitting the ground and an affectionate hand slapping skin on a back. I went back to my hammock, stubbing my toe on my backpack on the way. I stifled a yelp as I lay silently on the thin material and pulled the sides up over my body.

What had they been up to in the middle of the night?

Chapter Six

I didn't see the crate jutting out from under the table. My hands were full as I carried the food parcel to a client. Cans and packets crashed with a crescendo of noise that crackled through the quiet church hall as I fell over. A rush of people came over to me. I felt my cheeks burn and I wished the ground would swallow me up.

My shin tingled; a familiar feeling of a bruise appearing. At least this was an accident. Not like before. A flicker book of the men in my life flashed before me. The bruises were the reason I never trusted men. Beginning with my dad, right from an early age, men took advantage of me. Lied, manipulated, beat, bullied – you mention it I've experienced it. It's why I've never had a 'serious' relationship, and by that, I mean one lasting more than a few months. Even so, I fall in "love" pretty quickly, craving to be worshipped and wanted. Maybe that's not love. Maybe that's desperation needing to be worshipped and wanted. So, I attach myself to men, hoping that it leads to love. The stuff of movies and trashy novels. Of course, a desperate woman means lust to men, not love, and relationships became short-lived. For most, it turns rapidly from lust to annoyance, to smothering, to anger and then finally control. A hand slap here, a lie that he was with his mate and not some other woman there. On one occasion I had handed over my savings so he could pay off a debt and then be truly focussed on me. I never saw him again. Freud would have a field day with me.

Ignoring the offers of hands, I gingerly got back to my feet. Instinctively I looked for Nathan. Don't ask me why. He was checking items off a list, placing packets into another crate, oblivious. Volunteers helped put the spilt packets and boxes back in the crate I had dropped. Paul insisted I sit down in the side room and busied himself with a first aid kit and an ice pack. Grudgingly, I let him fuss over me.

By the time I had left the church Nathan was gone. The skies were already dark despite it being late afternoon. The winter's chill was coming so I hitched up the collar on my coat and headed back to my flat. I thought about him for a while, thinking about how he might have ended up doing community service. But to do that I was judging him – by his looks and his demeanour. I would have hated it if anyone had done the same to me. But I guess that's how we work our way through the world – judging based on a few bits of criteria, filling in the blanks with our own stories, stereotypes and fantasies. I pictured Mike, sitting there conjuring up a narrative based on my looks, my job title, and how spikey I was to him. I thought how he might be spending his evening, sitting alone in a one-bed flat, watching telly, eating a ready-meal for one off his lap, salivating at Susanna Reid and agreeing with everything Piers Morgan said. He might have been sitting in a penthouse with maids for all I knew. With a trophy wife, a butler reading the Daily Mail to him. I tried to shake the labels out of my head. I wanted to be free of judgement when I spoke to Nathan.

When I arrived at the church the next day, I was a bit nervous about what I would say to him, such was the amount of thought I had given to him. He was already there, leaning against a wall right at the back behind the chairs that had been set out for the daily briefing. Mike accosted me as I walked in.

"Alright work buddy!" he said, joyfully. "Feeling better? That was a hell of a clang!"

"Yeah, I'm fine. Thanks." He started chatting to me about the weather, the argument Piers Morgan had had on TV that morning with a 'sodding' Labour MP and how we wondered what today might bring. Paul called for our attention halfway through his monologue and I sat down, conscious that my back was to Nathan.

"Good morning, everyone," he sang. "Glad to see you all again. Jasmine, are you ok?

I nodded.

Mike, would you like to say the morning prayer?" His eyes lit up.

"Yeah sure!" and he gave thanks to the Lord and blessed the clients and the volunteers. I looked around at the other volunteers whom all had their heads bowed for the prayer. I tried to glance behind me at Nathan as I scanned but could only see the black cap perched over his eyes. The finishing 'Amen' caught me out and I had to turn my head quickly. Mike was already eyeballing me like he was making sure I said 'Amen'. Everyone got up and went to their sections.

"So, then Jasmine," he started. "What was it like at that fancy ballet school then?"

I felt my eyebrows furrow and my heart skipped a beat. "Yeah, it was tough. Wasn't the best of times if I'm honest. Do you mind if we don't talk about it? Why don't you tell me about you?"

That gave him his cue to talk about his favourite subject. From where he was positioned, I could look over his shoulder at the sullen figure moving around the metal shelves, pushing a trolley around, filling up the crate on top with items then ticking them off the list he was holding. I nodded and feigned interest in Mike's life story as he droned on. All the while Nathan carried on his work, pushing that trolley around the shelves, putting food into the crate, ticking them off, disappearing behind a large shelf only to emerge with an empty crate and start again. It was the way he moved, how he didn't say a word to anyone else the whole shift, nor make eye contact, that made him so intriguing.

I was desperate to know his story.

Over the course of the shift, I conjured up stories of what might have happened, for him to retreat into his shell. I couldn't believe that he had always been like that. The CPS and NPS did that to people. The police have a way of destroying your confidence, letting you know you are worthless, even before going up before the judge. It takes a long time to get over that. I imagined he had had a decent job before whatever happened to him. He would have kissed goodbye to that. Not many employers like their staff to have criminal records. And his friends and family probably disowned him. Not mothers, mothers never disown. They die but they don't disown. They love you till the end. Just like mine.

Getting arrested is a downward spiral. The first time it happened I was just a teenager. But then it was a slap on the wrist. A couple more times then it started to get serious. I had a criminal record. Almost all the jobs I applied for didn't even reply. Finding a place to live is then impossible. How is it possible to rent somewhere if you don't have a job? And how can you get a job if you don't have an address to put on the application? A snotty bank manager even scoffed in my face when I tried to open a current account. It becomes a vicious circle.

That's when the benefits kick in. Not enough to cover the basics. But then you are in the system – needy and desperate. Warmth comes in different places – drink, bad company, drugs. Once that happens it takes a miracle to get out.

I did it.

But it took a shaking from within. A realisation that I'm better than sharing needles and drinking from discarded beer cans left in a park. To say it was a struggle belittles the process. I had to shun my 'friends' on the street, and stop the drinking myself. Cold turkey is a misnomer. Frozen, painful, bloodbath of a turkey more like. One thing was sure, trying to cold turkey in my bedsit was impossible. The four walls were a prison for my body, my skull a jail for my thoughts. So, two things became my focus: walking and dancing. I walked and walked, not stopping, until my stomach stitched or blisters on my toes became unbearable. Even then I would keep going, determined that the superficial physical pain outweighed the mental pain. I was a female Forrest Gump. Just walking around the capital's streets. I begged for money and food around the posher areas of London, saving my benefits as much as I could. Then I decided to busk by dancing, and that got me better returns – a thin Indian with bloodshot eyes and scratches down her arms performing ballet was a freak act that got attention. With my confidence building, I got in with a few kids and we danced together. I choreographed them and we became quite a busking group. That gave me a purpose and, with the scraps of money over time, I cleaned myself up. Took care of my body and looks, and brought a few clothes, replacing the ones given to me as charity. I started to look quite respectable, so I applied for teaching jobs. Before interviews, I would go to Boots and spray on the perfume tester samples. Rejection after rejection followed when I had to disclose the bit about a criminal record.

Eventually, I got out by starting my own little school. Nothing formal at first but then it grew. I did it. It took time but I managed to break the circle.

With these thoughts in my mind, I couldn't help but think of Nathan. He intrigued me. A curious fish in a different sea. How would it be if I rescued him before the spiral down? Intervene before the vicious circle takes hold. Not many people get out. *The system is the system*, I heard so many times from those that had given up. A helping hand. One less person on the scrapheap. Or maybe I just needed something to do. Or both.

Maybe I could be a hero in his story.

But first I needed to see if he wanted fixing.

Chapter Seven

The gentle humming of an engine – a speedboat engine – woke me. It put-putted to a stop and a rustle of leaves filled the void. I rubbed my eyes and let my brain adjust. Nathan's hammock was empty, the thin blanket was thrown to the end. The sun was high in the sky and the warmth of the air stuck to my skin. I stretched and swung my feet onto the floor, allowing the sand to cover my toes. My mind wandered back to the shadows from the previous night. A dream? It couldn't have been. I mooched out of the hut and saw Pierre and Nathan eating lashings of fruit and eggs.

"Well, good morning to you, fair and gracious Jasmine!" Pierre cried out. "I was starting to worry about you!" Whistling in the distance caught my attention as I stepped out of my hut. Sommy was jauntily walking along the beach, an empty water-cooler swinging from his hand. He waved enthusiastically as he saw me, and I involuntarily waved back.

"What time does he get up?" I inquired as I sat down and helped myself to cut melon and a banana.

"Before the sun rises, as always," replied Pierre, stuffing pineapple into his mouth. "He has been to the market in Amlapura this morning. But today, we move your masterpieces. We move them to the coral reef, to grow and to provide shelter for the fish. It will be a momentous occasion!" He wagged his forefinger in the air for extra dramatic effect.

"I hope you like swimming. We'll carry the frames in the water over to my reef. Anywhere you wish. Place them down on the seabed and over time, the coral will grow. Fish will come and shelter there, and eat their food. You must come back in two years and see for yourself!" He grinned a big smile, pleased with himself. Having dumped the cooler behind a hut, Sommy walked past, shirtless, his flip-flops slapping against cracked heels. He submerged into the sea, next to the rows of domes, their round bottoms sticking up, the gentle waves brushing against them. It was the first time I had seen him in the water.

He grabbed a frame and pulled it seawards, his hands and feet making a frothy wake as he swam out. All eyes were on him.

"He will take them out the furthest. For you, you can put them anywhere you want," Pierre explained.

"Pierre?" I chirped, without really thinking of entirely what I will say next.

"Yes?" Pierre replied.

"You said yesterday, that, well, the algae and the polyps live in unison. If there is too little sunlight the algae can't grow, and the polyp dies. That's not going to happen here, right? But you said if there is too much sunlight, the algae grows until it suffocates. There's tons of sunlight! You can't control the sunlight so how can that happen?"

"Yes! That's right! Good question Jasmine! Haha!" The question delighted the Frenchman. "If you leave the algae to grow, it will do just that. Grow and grow and grow until it covers the animal. The animal will suffocate. But you forget one important aspect here. Fish! The fish eat the algae. And that controls the algae growth."

"That's true. But when you started this project, did you just expect the fish to come? You know it's in the middle of nowhere." Nathan leant forward on the edge of his seat.

"You might think it is the middle of nowhere but in the sea, there are currents which carry fish. They do come naturally. Build it and they will come! Haha! But you are right Jasmine. Everything needs balance. Today, we are making a man-made coral reef. It needs help. But I'll explain... no! *Show* you the help tomorrow. I will show you everything. For today, come on, let's take those beauties out to the sea!" With that Pierre jumped up from his chair and ran into the sea, water splashing high around his legs until his whole body was submerged. He surfaced and called out "come on, the water is lovely!" With that Nathan and I ran into the water and dunked our heads.

The frames were easy to pull from their overnight resting place. The water gave little resistance as we swam one hand pulling water and the other hand dragging the iron domes. The water was warm, clear and clean. We all swam back and forth 8 or 9 times to pick up a frame and drop it on the ocean floor. I followed the coral channel and placed our frames in between the main stretch and a lonely-looking dome which had been plonked a couple of metres away. A bridge between the old and the new, making one connected organism. It was a wonderful experience, swimming in those beautiful waters, with the sun shining in a bright blue sky, knowing that no matter what small difference I was making, it was a difference. This is what dreams are made of. For the rest of the day, we sunbathed and rested on those lovely golden sands.

I thought about Nathan and how he longed to share these memories and experiences with someone. He didn't have anyone, after all his friends and family disowned him. Except for his mum of course. I wished I could share this too, tell my future children the wonders of the world, that mummy created a home for future generations.

I contemplated my decision again and agreed with myself. I'm doing the right thing.

This perfect picture would live and die with me.

***

Early next morning we were back on the long boat, tummy full of fresh fruit, nuts and banana pancakes. Sommy took the aft and deftly paddled the boat out towards lines of red flags bobbing up and down in the distance. Nathan put his hand over the side of the boat letting the rise and fall of the waves dance through his fingers. I did the same, our fingers making trails through the crystal-clear water. The bottom of the sea was dark blue, the occasional fish swam silently up from the depths. Ahead, away from the lines of red flags, a wooden hut loomed on the horizon, floating on the water. On either side of it, there were what looked like wooden railings, extending to the left and right visible just above the surface of the water. Nathan was sitting bolt upright as we journeyed closer to it - it was clear this part of the adventure was unknown to him. I looked around and Pierre, sitting next to Sommy in the back of the boat, had a huge smile on his face, delighted that he had fooled his guests. His long curly hair was blowing in the wind, revealing shades of grey underneath his brown locks.

As we arrived, Sommy steered our boat so it aligned perpendicular to one of the wooden rails. Now it was clear the hut stood adjacent to six giant squares, with wooden planks dividing them up - walkways to and from each compartment. As Pierre and Sommy helped us out of the boat the large contraption rocked as the weight leant to one side. The wood creaked, unused to so much weight on one side.

"Welcome to my nursery!" Pierre called. "In each of these areas I have fish of different sizes. Over there," he pointed to the furthest net, "are the babies. You can just see the net, it has only small holes. Then as you move around, the fish are getting bigger and the net holes are getting bigger. We made it ourselves!"

Nathan and I surveyed the homemade structure, mesmerised by Pierre making his dream a reality. He was breeding fish so that his reef didn't suffocate, and by virtue, increasing the fish stocks he was so worried were depleting.

"Wow," I said, impressed. "All this effort for some fish? It must have taken a lot of time, and money, to do all of this."

"You do not just wake up and become a butterfly," he quoted, a huge, proud smile on his face. "It takes many months and nurturing. People help. Sommy of course, and tourists like you."

"What type of fish are there inside?" asked Nathan, ignoring the remark and reaching down to put his fingers in the water, making gentle splashes to attract the fish.

"It is all grouper fish," Pierre said. "They sit at the bottom of the seabed, so they won't come up. Grouper are important to the corals, they eat the smaller fish. They are very clever: they hide in the sand and then when their prey comes, they jump up. Grouper aren't handsome fish - they have a huge bottom lip, and their mouths are mainly open." He jutted his bottom lip out and moved it up and down, much to the delight of Sommy who laughed hysterically. We couldn't help grinning as Pierre played the clown.

"Now, there are two things you need to know about grouper. Number one: they have very powerful jaws. They don't bite and chew like us humans do. They clamp down and suck very hard. It's how they kill and consume their prey." I wished that I'd been able to transform into a grouper fish when my dad went on one of his rages.

"The second thing to know" he continued, putting two digits in the air, "is that a grouper fish can change from a male into a female." Nathan suddenly lent back. His face whitened. It looked like he was going to faint and fall into the water. I imagined the transwoman coming to the forefront of his mind. That's the thing with shame – always present, just hiding around the corner waiting to shine a light on your past. It can flick on at any given moment and knock the wind off your sails.

"Are you okay, Nathan?" Pierre said, concerned. "Are you seasick?"

"No. No," he sputtered. "I'm okay."

"Yes, that got your attention. Ha!" He said. "All grouper are born male. When they mature, they turn female to favour reproduction. As is natural, the male grouper desperately wants to produce young, so changes."

Now it was my turn to go pale. I kneeled on the wooden planks. My shame.

Pierre continued, "The problem then becomes that there are too many females! So, what happens?" He looked at both of us expecting an answer. We shrugged our shoulders. "Are you sure you're okay? You both look very pale," he said as his face dropped to a look of concern. We both nodded our heads. He took that as a cue to continue.

"Well, if there are not enough males to satisfy the females, they change back! They become a male again! When they are big enough, we open the nets and let them go free. That's what we are going to do now. Come, please help me."

He motioned for us to spread ourselves evenly around the square we were currently standing at. He bent down and grabbed hold with both fists a part of the net, shoulder-width apart. Sommy did the same, and we all followed suit. Pierre counted down from three and we all pulled up the net.

"At the bottom of the net is the pole. When we lift, it disturbs the sand, and fish move about. Hopefully, they move to the outside of the net. I don't know how many fish we have released in the water, but we see them all the time along the reef. The population is growing, and we are all happy. We are seeing all sorts of other fish come. Remember though that the grouper fish is the predator. We have another nursery, exactly the same, about one kilometre in that direction." He pointed out towards the horizon.

"There we are breeding parrotfish. These are beautiful, colourful fish. They eat the algae from the polyps, and the grouper fish eat the parrotfish. I've made a little ecosystem in the sea. All those three things attract other fish, large and small, and it kicks starts the process. Simple, right?!"

Nathan and I nodded.

"Come on, let's go home," he cried. "Oh, wait, I forgot to tell you about the parrotfish. Well, there are two things you need to know. Number one: their beak is very sharp, to get the algae you see. Peck, peck, peck. Don't put your fingers near its mouth. Secondly, guess what? The females turn into males! They transform themselves. Haha! You see, they are both clever!"

Nathan turned his head away, raising his hand to his mouth, and then vomited into the sea.

Pierre chuckled to me, "seasickness huh?"

No, I thought. There was shame again, shining its humiliating light.

Chapter Eight

Nathan was sitting down, hunched over as if he had a pain across his stomach, his elbows on his knees, his knuckles cradling his chin. His cap was still pulled down past his eyes. Paul was blathering on about how many vouchers and food parcels we had handed out the previous day.

"Righty-ho, we're going to mix things up a bit today," he said, in his usually jolly voice. I had no idea where he got his energy from in the mornings. "I want you to all experience the three areas of the foodbank. So, I'd like you to buddy up with someone in a different section and learn the ropes." I sensed this might be my chance to speak to Nathan. I raised my hand.

"I'm happy to do the warehouse."

"Oh, that's great Jasmine. Um, why don't you swap with Nathan, and Nathan can buddy up with Mike." My shoulders sagged whilst Mike gave a two-handed thumbs up.

"Is that okay with you Nathan?" He lifted his head which revealed his eyes. Dark brown and soft. Bags hung under them. He shook his head ever so slightly.

"Oh. Um, right. Damon, you were in assessment, weren't you? You go to collection with Mike, and, um, Jasmine, why don't you buddy up with Nathan." Nathan turned his eyes to me. I gave a smile and he turned back, ever so slowly.

After the prayer, I rushed over to Nathan as he carefully moved his chair to the back of the room.

"Hi I'm Jasmine!" I chirped, a bit too excitedly. I immediately regretted it as I sounded like Mike. He looked at me and nodded his head.

"Nathan," he replied flatly. I followed him over to the shelves stacked high with tins, packets and boxes, where he picked up a white leaflet and handed it to me. On it was a list of food items. He grabbed an empty green crate sitting on the floor and dumped it on a trolley. The metal clanged in anger. He jutted it towards me and stopped.

I looked up at the shelves and down at the piece of paper.

He just watched me under the peak of his cap.

"I'm guessing we pick the food off the shelves and tick them off the list, like down the supermarket?" I said.

"Yes."

"Okay then."

He didn't move.

This was awkward.

Very slowly, he moved his hand up to the top of a shelf and lifted a tin of chopped tomatoes and put it in the empty crate on top of the trolley. He nodded his head to the paper in my hand and I quickly ticked off the first item on the list. Then he pulled the trolley a couple of inches towards him. We shuffled forward, repeating the process with each item. When all the boxes were ticked, we pulled and pushed the trolley to a metal scale. He lifted the box and put it carefully on the scales and noted the figure down on the white piece of paper, carefully folded it and laid it on top of all the food. He then lifted the crate and put it back on the trolley, pulling it to the collection area and placing it in a space on the shelf.

"Is that it?" I said.

"Yeah," he said, shrugging his shoulders. It was like speaking to a teenager.

"Can you say more than one word at a time?" I felt like I had slipped into teacher mode. He looked up mischievously.

"Maybe," he smiled, the first time I had seen any emotion from him.

"Oh good! Well, I look forward to that," I said, grinning back.

I thought I'd give it a try showing my vulnerability first to open him up.

"I'm not one of them you know," nodding over to a well-dressed group sipping tea in a circle. "A do-gooder. I'm one of you." He looked up sharply. "I've used the foodbank before, been out on the street. You know, had it tough."

He looked at me blankly.

"So, you're a do-gooder then?" I pushed. "You know, doing all right. Volunteering out the goodness of your hearts. Giving back."

"No."

"Then what's your story?"

He picked up a piece of white paper and handed it to me. Then lifted a crate and put it on the trolley. He pulled the trolley along the shelves. I followed and we started our procession around the shelves, filling the crate and ticking off the list. As we got to the pasta and rice area, I couldn't take the silence anymore.

"I'm a good listener you know." He looked up momentarily before picking a tin of sardines from the shelves. "You know, we've still got two hours left of the shift. I'm going to keep asking you." He stopped abruptly, looking up in frustration. He was going to say something, maybe tell me off, but swallowed it. Then he just carried on, pulling the trolley back. I tried a different tack.

"I saw your probation papers. I'm guessing community service." I said casually, picking up a six-pack of crisps. He froze where he was, lifted his head slightly, head slanted to the side. It was almost menacing with the black cap hiding his eyes.

"I mean I wasn't spying or anything. Just recognised the paperwork. You were with Paul. I didn't read anything." I paused, waiting for a reaction which didn't come.

"I've done community service before," I said softly. "So, know all about it." He lifted his head higher in surprise.

"I know. To look at me," I said sarcastically. He smiled back. There it was again. A youthful smile on a tired face.

"How long?" he asked a croak in his voice.

"60 hours. You?"

"200."

I whistled. "What did you do? Beat someone up?"

"Yes," he said without emotion.

"Wow! You must have done them up proper! GBH?" I couldn't believe this shell of a man could do someone real damage to get a GBH charge against him. I guess you never know when someone snaps.

"ABH," he said in hardly a whisper

"200 hours for ABH!" I backtracked on the loudness of my voice, feeling his shame. "How many times?"

"First offence," he muttered. Now that took me by surprise. That's a long time for a first offence.

"What else did you do then? Apart from batter someone – rob them, spit at the police?" I noticed a spitefulness in my tone, which I regretted. When he shook his head, my mind automatically went to offences against women – surely he wasn't capable of *that*. Then again, men were capable of anything when the red mist comes. It's often the quiet ones. My mind raced through different scenarios, trying to match a crime with this withdrawn man.

"You didn't … *flash* did you?" I said, cocking my head.

"Stalking," he said like he was chewing dog poo. It took me by surprise. "Oh" was my only response. We stood in silence for a while, his head hung. It added up but it still shocked me. *Don't judge Jasmine*, I said to myself.

"Well, it's time to move on then. You did your crime, do your time, then move on."

"Is that what you did?"

"So, you *can* say a sentence then." He lifted his head and I saw the corners of his mouth lift. "Yeah, I did. Wasn't easy. I slipped back in and out. For years. I've stayed in here over Christmas you know?" He nodded, not looking surprised. I cleared my throat.

"Just got to be strong. Don't let anyone drag you down with them. I did. I got dragged down. Difficult to get back up when you have weight on your feet."

"What did you do?" he asked softly.

"Ah you know, a bit of everything. Drugs, drink, fights, a bit of prostitution." His head shot up, startled.

Shit.

I'd been too honest with him too quickly. It just reeled off my tongue. I shook my head screwing up my face, ashamed of myself. Why did I say that? Maybe I'd been thinking about him too much and thought that we had a familiarity. We'd only just started talking. I wished time would reverse by 30 seconds.

"Um….," he began now trying to make conversation, his eyes looking everywhere except my burning face.

"Look. I'm not proud of it okay? I had to do what I had to do."

"I'm not judging," was his reply, although I knew he was doing exactly that. "I meant, what did you do. To get back on your feet." I felt like a complete idiot. I showed my vulnerability too quickly to connect with him, to show we had a kinship.

He pulled the trolley to distract us from the awkwardness, picking tins off a shelf, as if we were having a conversation about curtains in the supermarket. I appreciated it.

"I… I got lucky. Did what I enjoyed." I said, dumping a bag of rice into the crate. "I used to dance. I was quite good before I … Anyway, I got in with a group of youngsters dancing on the streets and started to teach them routines. At first, they were uneasy, as kids are, particularly with someone who rocked up with their whole life in a rucksack. But then I showed them a few moves, and they loved it. We used to meet up every few days after school in the park and I thought I had a knack for it. Busking brought in some extra cash, so I used my benefits to get a bedsit, clean myself up and buy some clothes. None of the handout crap they give out at the shelter. Clothes that fitted me. The kids helped me out too. One of them was training to be a hairdresser so smartened me up; another was doing a beauty course so did my nails. That's the cool thing about kids: if you help them, they help you. It's amazing what happens when you are motivated. Have a focus."

"What did you do then?" Talking felt easier with Nathan than it did with Mike. Maybe it was because I had exposed myself to him, laid myself out bare. I had nothing to hide. Mike would have taken my information and had a field day. I guess the question was whether Nathan would use it against me.

"Luckily. And I say luckily because you need all the luck you can get. One of the kid's dad took a shine to me. Not like *that*. Was pleased his daughter was doing something productive, and not hanging around on street corners. He had an empty shop that he said I could use, temporarily, for the kids to dance in after school. So, we moved there and after a while, a few more joined and word got out. People started *paying* me to join the club. And I was loving it."

"But?"

"How did you know there was a 'but'?" He just shrugged his shoulders. "Yeah, there was a 'but'. *But* I kept falling in with the wrong guys. Not homeless anymore but boyfriends. Treated me bad. My comfort place was alcohol." He sighed and shook his head.

"Yeah, they took advantage of me, and I went back to the bottle. Cliché. That kind dad chucked me out of the shop sharpish. Then the cycle starts again. That's what I'm saying. Don't let bad people drag you down."

"Are you a bad person then? Will you drag me down?"

"Everyone can change,' I grinned. "104 days sober."

"Congratulations," he said, raising an eyebrow.

"What are we celebrating?" Paul said, surprising me as he snuck up behind us.

"My sobriety! 104 days sober," I said proudly.

"Oh well done you! That's great news! You must be delighted!" and he leant in to hug me. I winked at Nathan as he watched.

"That's how you react to good news," I said brightly. Paul beamed. He theatrically checked his watch. "Nearly the end of the shift! Mike's organising a few of us to go to the pub after if you'd like to join us. Won't be a late one for me!"

"I'm good, thanks," I said, thinking of Mike cornering me all evening. Nathan shook his head.

"Okey dokey, next time, eh?" he chuckled as he went on his way. I thought he might jump up and click his heels as he left.

"A bit insensitive isn't it," Nathan said, a worried look on his face. I furrowed my eyebrows, not understanding. "I mean you just said you were sober, and he asked if you wanted to go to the pub."

"I'm allowed to go to the pub you know! They sell other drinks."

"Yeah but. I don't know. The temptation? Smell? Wouldn't you worry you'd slip back?" I nodded, understanding.

"Got you. Well, I can stand it now. The smell of tequila repulses me. Mind over matter. But to be honest, I rarely drank in pubs. It was usually on the streets."

I felt my phone vibrate loudly in my pocket which took me by surprise. Not often my phone goes, and it's usually switched off. I looked at Nathan sheepishly who comically rolled his eyes. I pulled the ancient phone out of my pocket. It was an unknown number, so I cancelled it and put it back. A few seconds later I felt the vibrate of a message.

Paul was gathering everyone around for the debrief. I followed Nathan to the back of the chairs. It always took a few minutes for people to settle down, so my curiosity about the message got the better of me. I pulled the phone out and a voicemail icon appeared. I accessed it, turning so my ear was away from Paul. A woman spoke softly in my ear.

"Oh hello. I'm looking for a Jasmine Patel. I got your number from social services. I do hope I've got the right number. This is Jennifer from the Happy Valley Retirement Home. I'm sorry to tell you, your father is very ill. You need to come and say your goodbyes. Please call me back as soon ......"
The voice trailed off as I dropped the phone. Nathan's head jolted up. It felt like every molecule of air had been taken out of me. Then I saw Nathan start forward. I felt an arm wrap around my waist as my legs stumbled. A million unpleasant images flew through my head.

After 25 years out of my life, my dad's face was in my mind's eye.

Chapter Nine

That night the air was humid and sticky as I lay in my hammock, struggling to get to sleep. I kept tossing and turning, unable to get into any comfortable position. Images of my dad filled my head, sitting motionless in an airless room, his head tilted involuntarily to one side pointing to the window, staring into space. His body slouched over the tatty brown armchair. I would walk towards him, a bowl of mashed-up cereal in my hand, a cotton bib in the other, ready to go around his neck to catch stray food falling onto his stained white shirt. Pulling up a faded-green chair to feed him, I faced him.

But I could only see Pierre's face.

Lifeless, tilted, his green eyes glassy and looking through me. Somehow, in my subconscious state, I knew that these were not real, facets of sleep, but I couldn't rouse myself back to reality. The corner of his mouth was curled, showing a gap where his teeth used to be. I shook my head to try and make the image disappear, for my dad's face to return, to wake myself up. The image disturbed me. I forced my thoughts to focus on something else – the sand, the corals, the sea, the fresh fruit, the dolphins. But my mind cast itself back to Pierre's face superimposed on Dad's. I shook him by the shoulders, I moved his head, yet Pierre's face remained. I took a spoon and dipped it in the bowl, a tiny amount of liquid balanced on the tip. I moved it to his mouth, using the edge of the spoon to lever his top lip up so I could force the food in. As the spoon went in, Pierre's eyes danced into life. His glint, his boyish sparkle shone. The corners of his mouth turned upwards into an eerie smile. The bowl and the porridge fell to the floor. I covered my eyes and screamed. A scream that made no noise. I grabbed hold of the body with both my hands and shook him violently. Back and forth screaming. The face changed from Dad's to Pierre's and back to Dad's with every shake. Tears streamed from my eyes. I was shouting. I was shouting to him saying *why are you doing this, why did you do this to me,* knowing full well it wasn't his fault. I threw him backwards. Like a puppet, the body resumed its leaning position on the chair. My dad's face returned. I felt guilty yet I wanted someone to blame. No, *needed* someone to blame. Who would do this? Who would make so much suffering, not just for Dad but for me too?

A clattering sound stirred me. Yet it wasn't a sound from my nightmare. I opened my eyes, transported back to my hammock. My mind was still swirling with images. It was dark, my blanket was on the floor and Nathan was lying on his back, his chest gently rising and falling.

I heard another sound.

Splashing.

Confused, I swung my legs around, my feet brushing the soft sand by the bed. The dream was still fresh in my mind, and my cheeks slightly damp, I got up and tiptoed to the door. I saw in the near distance two men walking out of the water carrying a white cooler between them. The unmistakable silhouettes of Pierre and Sommy.

Again.

They moved out of the water, onto the sand and past my hut. My body was deep in the shadows, my eyes peered around. They struggled under the weight of the box and I could hear them moving to the back of the huts, to the area where we were fixing coral onto the dome structures. I heard a thud of the container being dropped to the ground and a slap on the skin – Pierre giving Sommy the customary well done. They both silently went to their own hut where I heard a creak of a hammock and a dull thud of a body lying down. I waited a couple of minutes, grabbed a torch and slunk out of the hut to the courtyard.

The crescent moon and its accompaniment of thousands of stars lit the night sky. I held my torch up, in line with my eyes, like I was a detective in a police drama. I saw the white container sitting with a pile of others, the sand beneath it wet with recently spilt water. I knelt before it, checking behind me. Carefully and slowly I popped the fasteners. It made a click which echoed around the courtyard. I froze, listening out for movement. Satisfied there was none, I slowly lifted the lid, the creaking hinges groaning and peered inside. Water was filled to the top of the container and two objects floated inside. I shone the torch light on the contents. Two brightly coloured fish were lying dormant inside, encapsulated in what looked like a thick bubble. The fish were motionless, their gills breathing in and out extremely slowly. Their mouths were not like any fish I had seen, like a beak pursed together. Their bodies were fat and round.

"Those are Parrotfish."

Pierre's voice from behind frightened the daylights out of me. The lid of the container smashed down making a racket as my torch leapt from my hand. I crawled backwards on my bum, struggling to get onto my feet. Pierre followed me, slowly. I'd been in this position before. Usually, there was a belt in the hand. The moonlight shone in his eyes.

"You're a fraud. You're selling the fish for money, aren't you? You're harvesting. You're just a fisherman. The reef is a by-product," I blurted, not knowing where the words were coming from.

"Come, come, Jasmine," he said in a soft voice. "It's okay, I will explain to you."

I felt the hut wall behind my back. Pierre kept walking toward me, blocking any escape.

"You set this up as a con, didn't you? You're farming the fish for profit. You don't care about the reef, the corals. You're in it for yourself!"

"Mon Dieu. Please," he replied, a gentle pleading in his voice, his palms facing me. He was smiling, a big smile. A knowing smile. I was wrong, I knew it, but I didn't want to give up. "Let me explain."

"Of course, you are. Why else would you grab them in the middle of the night? Why else would you do all of this? That's how you make your money, isn't it? For the good of the world? For the good people of Bali?" I felt my voice rising. The dream I just had was still a real vision in front of me. Through watery eyes, Pierre's face was morphing into my father's.

"You lied to us. You made us believe you were doing it for the future. There is no future for you. There is only the now, putting money in your bank account. You are a selfish idiot who only thinks about yourself. You're just like my father." I noticed

Pierre's eyes narrow ever so slightly as my eyes welled up. He extended his arm toward me. Instinctively, I flinched. In the eerie moonlight, his face was my dad's, just like the dream but somehow, I knew this was real.

"Say something!" I saw the shape of Sommy standing in the courtyard, his face obscured by darkness. Then I saw a pair of bare tanned legs, yellow shorts riding to just above the knee, running over to me. As if sensing other people, Pierre crouched down on his knees and wrapped his arms around me. I seemed to melt into them like a comfort blanket next to my cheek. He was holding me tightly, his hand smoothing my hair, he whispered sounds in my ear, I think in French. Maybe a poem such were the bounces of the words. I couldn't see clearly through the tears and I blinked to try and make the water go away. Every time my eyes momentarily closed, I saw my dad, slumped in that big armchair. Every blink I saw a different part of him: his slippers perched on the end of his wrinkled feet; the ends of a frayed belt hanging limp from the edge of the chair; a dirty white dressing gown covering his torso; his contused hands resting on his lap. The only thought that went through my mind was that will be me. It was inevitable.

The ticking timebomb.

It was a vision that I would want no one to see, nobody to endure.

"Shush, shush, shush."

I sat up, wiped under my eyes with the back of my hand and breathed in deeply, letting the present come back. The reality. When my sobbing subsided, Pierre had his arm around my shoulder and looked deep into me. I could see the shimmer of green in his iris. The wrinkles around his eyes showed his age, and the frown on his forehead crumpled in worry.

"Are you okay? Please, let me explain," he pleaded. "You are confused."

Nathan pulled up a chair and sat, his elbows on his knees. I felt wide awake now, miles away from the nightmare, blinking back tears. Pierre pulled up a chair and sat down, leaving me sitting in the sand. The men looking down at me. Surrounded, I felt like a trapped rabbit.

"You are right in some respects, but you are wrong in many others. I am not trying to hide anything. I will tell you the truth. You are right that I take the fish. I take the fish to sell in the market in Amlapura. Parrotfish and grouper bring in good money. Parrotfish are beautiful creatures, colourful fish that look nice in western fish tanks. But also very tasty, like shellfish."

I rubbed my arms, feeling a chill.

"This is simply a case of supply and demand. I breed the fish and sell them. But believe me when I say this: It is not just for my personal gain. I invest back into the sea. I only take the fish when the supply is plentiful and take a few, making sure there are plenty left to breed. You need to trust me on that. I never take any fish when they are ready for breeding, or when they can give birth."

"So why are you doing it in the middle of the night?" Nathan said.

"Ha! Do you know how difficult it is to catch a fish in the daytime?" There was a condescending note in his voice as he turned to face him. "They are slippery little buggers – I think that is what you say! I refuse to use a line and hook. It is cruel to the fish." He tossed his head back, the curls on his head dancing in the momentum looking back at me.

"When you saw the parrotfish, did you see it was in the middle of a bubble? A parrotfish sleeps at night, so to protect itself and to prevent its smell from reaching predators, it emits mucus and covers itself up. That means it can sleep in peace. That is when the poachers come and snatch them."

"You mean *you* come and snatch them," I retorted. He shrugged his shoulders like a Frenchman.

"I suppose you can see it like that, or you could see that I am carefully selecting the correct fish. You see, a poacher doesn't care whether a parrotfish is pregnant. He doesn't care if the fish is transforming from a male to a female. These two things are important because it affects the general population at a time when it needs it most. A poacher just sees the dollar signs. Now, I know these things. I have watched and researched them. As has Sommy. So, I know if a parrotfish population needs help, or indeed when they are spawning. Would you rather a poacher takes the wrong fish, or I take the right fish?"

"I would rather you didn't take any fish," I replied stiffly.

"Yes, yes you are right. But supply and demand. There is demand and I would rather satisfy that demand with the right fish. Also, the reef is relatively new. If there are too many parrotfish, then they will eat too much algae. If it eats too much algae, then the coral will die. Likewise, if there are too many grouper, which eat the parrotfish, then the algae will thrive. It is impossible to play God and control it all. I keep an eye on what is happening and adjust accordingly."

"And that's how you fund this then," Nathan said, waving his hand around.

"Yes, it helps," he said, turning his shoulders. "The fish I sell help make the nets, to buy the iron and the gas to create the domes, for us to eat and keep my dream alive. Is that such a bad thing?" It was a rhetorical question. "Of course, tourists like you bring much-needed foreign money to Bali too, helping us all." Nathan got up and looked inside the white box.

"So, these poachers. How do you stop them from taking the fish?" I asked

"With great difficulty." His eyes refocused. "It is frowned upon in Bali but difficult to police or stop. My reef brings poachers out here – of course it does, there is starting to be an abundance of fish again. I try to warn them off, I set up traps. But it is a battle I may never win. And of course, it happens at night. So, I trust in my vision and my goal to keep building, building, building. Hopefully, soon there will be enough fish even if the poachers are here. But then they won't be poachers. They will be called fishermen."

"I'm sorry," I said, without even thinking it. "I'm sorry I doubted you."

"Thank you. I try my best. Not only to survive myself but for the seas to survive too. But no man is an island." He nodded an appreciative glance over to Sommy, then to me.

We sat in silence in the dusty courtyard. I had no idea what time it was. The stars were still dazzlingly bright and there was no hint of a sunrise. I drew circles in the sand with my index finger like a scolded child. Pierre sat with his knee raised, his other leg underneath it, his arm swinging like a pendulum over the chair. A few crickets chirped in the near distance.

My mind wandered to the future. Not the future of being back at home in the familiarity of my own four walls and mementoes, but of a future when I am old. I pictured myself in the same chair my dad had occupied, my hair grey and long, a nurse trying to cajole food into my mouth, giving up in frustration when I wouldn't oblige. A stranger, an alien whom I didn't know and wouldn't remember. My whole being completely and utterly dependent on this person. No one to come and hold my hand, to keep me company. It was a future I was determined not to inflict on anyone else. To bring someone into this world knowing what that would be like pained me. It was something I would never want to impart on them, and so they never would. I would live out my life alone.

"Do you ever think about the future, Jasmine?" Pierre's voice made me jump as it cut through the stillness. Nathan glanced up.

"I'm sorry, what," I said, accusingly, as if he was reading my mind.

"The future Jasmine. What lies ahead. For the next generation of people, and the next generation and the next?"

"Kind of," I shrugged.

"The world seems to be in a difficult situation. Droughts, floods, disease, pollution, temperature rises. Tsunamis. The big things. It seems quite irreversible. I often think, why do I bother, huh? Why do I spend my time trying to make things better? The other people in the world are making it worse. I saw giant factories in India with thick black smoke coming out of their chimneys all day and night. Some people tell me it is an uphill battle. Like King Canute, trying to stop the tide, right?"

"Yeah, I guess so."

"So why do we bother? Why do we make the effort? We're all going to die anyway. I'll tell you why I do it. For love."

He paused, letting the word circulate amongst us.

"I do it because I love this place, I love nature, and I love the future generations that are going to enjoy it well after I am dead. There is an Indian proverb: Blessed is he who plants trees under whose shade he will never sit."

"I think I've heard it," I said.

"Love is why I think we do anything," he continued. "It's why we have companionship and it's why I think we evolved to be able to talk to each other. The world is being destroyed, but if we are able to give love and able to receive love, it makes everything more bearable. Do you understand what I am saying?"

"Why do you think you have to receive love? Why can't you just be happy that you are doing a good thing and that you don't want anything in return?" I felt my voice shake as I spoke.

"I believe in Ying and Yang. I believe in the balance of power. You must give to receive." Nathan moved as if to say something. I wasn't sure if it was to add to the conversation or to end it. I felt Pierre's eye drilling into me, waiting for a response. I just shrugged my shoulders. What was my dad giving me, entering my life suddenly, years after he neglected me? Except he never really left me. He was always in my memories. What was I receiving? I received bad news. My destiny was laid out in front of me.

"I can't admit knowing what you are going through," Pierre spoke softly, barely a whisper, interrupting the silence, and my thoughts. "I don't know you. I don't know your past. I can't imagine the choices you will have to make in the future. I have met many, many people. The poorest people in the world, the richest, the loneliest and the popular. I think I am a good judge of character. I can tell if someone has good in their heart, or a heart so damaged they can no longer love. I look at you Jasmine, the first time I saw you and I saw a sad soul. You were smiling but beyond, deep in your eyes, there was sadness. But I also see you have good in your heart. You have space for love – both giving and receiving if you allow it. But something is holding you back. Or someone."

Nathan shifted in his chair.

"If you think you cannot receive love then listen to this. On my second day here in Bali I was walking along a beach, this exact beach, in fact, watching the fishermen hauling in their catch. I spotted a man running in between each boat, picking up discarded fish and throwing them back into the sea. I was intrigued. I followed him. He darted aimlessly amongst the boats, changing directions and moving quickly. I watched him do this for two hours. When the fisherman had gone, he walked up and down the stretch of beach, looking, and when satisfied he went to a nearby café, exhausted. I sat next to him and introduced myself and bought him a Coke. I asked him what he was doing. He replied that he was tossing back the fish that the fisherman didn't want. The rejected ones that were too small or the wrong type. The fish were still alive, so he wanted to put them back in the sea. It was a bizarre thing to do. Amongst thousands and thousands of fish, about to be slaughtered and eaten he was picking up the scraps. When I was on the boats in France, they were 'collateral damage'. Waste that maybe the seagulls would take. I said to him, and I remember so clearly, 'why do you bother? It makes no difference'. His reply has stayed with me to this day, it makes me do what I do." He paused for dramatic effort and, enthralled by the story, I entertained it.

"What did he say?"

Pierre turned his whole body.

"What did you say Sommy?"

"'It made a difference to that fish.'"

Pierre took a breath, his eyes were fiery.

"It was like a lightning bolt. You may think you make only a small difference, but it is a *huge* difference to someone else. That individual fish, no idea who is this alien, has its life saved. The feeling that someone, deep down beyond the conscious, who cares, *genuinely cares*, is nearby to help when they are gasping their last breath. That makes a huge difference. I really believe that."

My eyes welled up as my mind flashed back to the care home.

"The next day I went to the same beach, and when those fishermen brought in their catch, I joined him, and together we went among the boats and threw the unwanted fish back into the sea. Sure, some were already dead, others barely alive. We didn't talk, we just raced along the beach trying to save as many as possible. It was the first time anyone had helped him, anyone who understood what he was doing. He was making a little difference and I increased that by 100%. It was a connection which needed no words. And we've worked together ever since, trying to help every fish grow and multiply." Nathan and I turned to Sommy in unison. He still stood in the courtyard, smiling bashfully.

"You see, 'if you don't like something, change it. If you can't change it, change your attitude'. That's Maya Angelou, a beautiful soul. I love her." I swallowed hard. I can't change my future, but I could certainly change my attitude about it. Live life like there's no tomorrow. Perhaps allow someone in.

"Now," Pierre continued, interrupting my thoughts and bringing the attention back to him. "I go and get some vodka. We celebrate." Nathan glanced at me and shook his head ever so slightly.

"What time is it?" I said.

"Tsk, who cares?" responded Pierre quickly. "What difference does it make? We are in paradise. We are happy, no? Time is precious. Let's not bottle it up and wait for tomorrow. Go with the flow Jasmine. Enjoy it with the right people, right here right now!"

He stood up with a flourish and disappeared. As if on cue, Sommy put a table in between us all and, finally, got a chair himself and joined us. As I sat, stretching my legs, Pierre rushed back, holding three shot glasses between his fingers and distributed them between Nathan, him and me, leaving Sommy out. I looked at him who raised and shook both his palms.

"No drink alcohol, inshallah," he said, a wide smile.

Pierre began filling the little glasses with a thin, long bottle of vodka. Nathan glanced at me, not sure what to do next.

"Best vodka in Indonesia," he said, filling the glasses to the brim. He slammed the bottle down and grabbed a glass, holding it up. The whiff of the alcohol sent an electrical pulse to my brain.

"Salut! To my good friend and inspiration: Sommy," he cried pushing his hand into the middle of the table as we copied him.

"And to new friends," Nathan said, raising his glass higher. They both looked at me, Pierre encouragingly, Nathan apprehensive.

"Oh, and to um, new futures," I said. We all lifted our glasses and the two men downed theirs. Nathan looked at me at the same time as he tilted his head back. When Pierre's head was cocked back, I emptied the contents on the sand over my shoulder. I glanced up at Sommy who had watched me, blankly. We thumped the glasses on the table in unison. Pierre was already refilling the glasses. He sat back on his chair, the front legs lifting off the sand.

"Now Jasmine," he said, a serious look coming across his face, his eyes like steel. "You can tell us about your father."

Chapter Ten

The voicemail had knocked me for six. I stood dumbfounded, looking at the little icon in the corner of the phone.

"Are you okay?" Nathan said, holding my arm. "You look like you've seen a ghost."

I took a deep breath and steadied myself. Everyone at the foodbank was looking at me.

"Yeah, I'm fine. Just got to make a phone call."

I walked out of Nathan's earshot and dialled the number. My heart was racing a million beats to the minute.

A bored voice answered.

"Happy Valley Retirement Home."

"Oh yes hi. I've just had a voicemail from you. It's Jasmine Patel. About my father."

"Hold on." The phone clattered onto a table and a distant voice yelled *I got a Jasmine Patel on the phone. About Mr Patel in room 18. Is that Charmaine?* Pause. I heard her pick up another phone. *Charmaine? Mr Patel's daughter for you.* Then a click. It sounded like the phone had gone dead. I waited a few seconds, and then a click.

"Hello. Mrs Patel?" a deep-voiced woman said.

"Yes. Ms Patel," I corrected.

"Uh-huh, Miss Patel. It's been hard getting hold of you." She sounded annoyed. "It's about your father. He hasn't got long I'm afraid love. You need to come and pay your last respects and sort his affairs." She said it so matter-of-factly like it was the umpteenth time she'd said it that day.

"Um, okay. But the thing is. I haven't seen him for, uh, 25 years." The voice sighed down the phone.

"Well, you're his next-of-kin on his records so I guess you'll get a reunion." Now she sounded annoyed. "Do you know where we are?"

"I'll find it," I huffed as I hung up. As I turned around Nathan was standing behind me.

"Okay?" he asked.

"Yeah, my dad. He's not got long left."

"Jeez," he said. "Sorry."

"Don't be. I haven't seen him for years. I've thought about him though. He always appears in the worst moments. Like he's watching me." I raised my eyes to the ceiling as if he was hiding in the recesses of the church hall. "Taunting even. He had this sneer where his lip would curl up and his eye would half-close like he was eating a lemon. Usually, then his hand would raise."

Nathan rubbed the back of his neck.

"You know what? I always wondered if I would see him again. Over all those years, I always thought what if. What if he contacted me? What would I do? Would I see him? Would I ignore him? And now, it's real."

I scratched the side of my face and closed my eyes.

"What are you going to do?" Nathan asked.

"I don't know. I need to think. Fancy a coke?"

***

The pub was a quiet one. The bar was empty and the barman eagerly awaited us as we approached. Nathan motioned for me to order first.

"Just a Coke please." Nathan raised two fingers indicating the same for him.

"Ice and lemon?"

"Yeah sure," came my non-committal reply. Nathan told me to go and find a table and a few minutes later he came back with two pint glasses and settled them down, the ice clinking against the side.

"You okay?"

"Yeah, but you can stop asking me if I'm okay."

"Okay," he said, that cheeky smile appeared again. He was younger than me, much younger. I was glad he was warming up.

"Shouldn't we give your boyfriend a call, let him know where you are?"

"Nah, it's okay. He's at work." I pictured him in his safe office in his safe job. He didn't know anything about my past.

192

Nathan knew more about me than he did at this point. I hadn't been with him long, but I had fallen into the trap and moved in pretty quickly, considering his flat was 100% nicer than my bedsit. With him, I just wanted to think about the now, definitely not my past. I guess I didn't want to lay myself bare, emotionally anyway when I found someone who might care about me. I didn't fancy him. There was no *The One* about him. Just safety and security. I could settle for that.

I took a sip of the Coke, the ice cubes burning my top lip.

"So," he said. "Do you want to talk about it?"

"You know what? Can we leave it, just for a little while? Let me digest it. I've told you about me – warts and all. Your turn." He blushed and hung his head. "I don't want to know the details. But why? What made you do it?"

"I don't know. It started slowly enough, then it just snowballed."

"How did it start?" I was glad for a bit of distraction to organise my thoughts.

"Bored at work, needed a challenge. A hobby I guess."

"That's a weird hobby," I replied sceptically. "What's wrong with football like most men?" He didn't answer. I felt maybe I was being too mocking, making too much light of his guilt. "Sorry, go on."

"Well, in my job, women were easy pickings. I could pick up one or two a night. Not a problem."

"What was your job? Fireman?" I bit my tongue, not learning from my mistake.

"No city banker."

"You? You were a banker wanker?" I blurted out, leaning back to look at him in full. He looked startled; crestfallen. I could see it though; an arrogance in the eyes, the squared jaw of a privileged schoolboy, the shoulders which could carry a consequence-free life, nice skin. White, middle-class and handsome. I was born having to step up to where he began.

"Yeah, I s'pose so." His eyes stared at the floor of the pub. "Lines of coke, champagne on tap, flashing money around.

It was like a magnet." I understood. It was a parallel to my life but not a similar one.

"It got too easy. Money was coming out of my ears and girls would just lay down in front of me. It wasn't exactly fulfilling."

I snorted at the comment.

"Yeah so, I challenged myself. That's what I called them, a challenge, to see if I could seduce a different type of girl. Any girl. One that maybe wouldn't look twice at a 'banker wanker'. So, I followed one, researched them and changed my appearance so that I became their perfect man. Found out their likes and dislikes so knew what to say to them, and how to act around them. When that worked, I did it again. Then again and again."

"Don't tell me: made them feel special, earned their trust then bedded them and didn't look back? Jesus, that's why I've got trust issues," I huffed, feeling my cheeks redden.

"Pardon?"

"Never mind." I picked up my cold glass of Coke. "You little shit," I whispered into the ice, shaking my head.

"Look, I'm not proud of it."

"How many?" The question shocked him. "How many did you stalk?"

"I don't like that word," he said softly, fingering the condensation on his glass. "But about 50. At least," he said, looking down and away.

"Jesus!" I shouted in surprise. The barman looked over at us.

"Not proud of it until you got caught? Guessing the last one found out and you tried to beat it out of her?" He nodded glumly. I took a deep breath. I needed to stop. I was hardly one to take the high ground, but it was men like him that made me who I was – afraid of letting myself fall in love, only to get hurt.

"Did you ever think about your victims?" Again, he looked up surprised, as if the women he had manipulated weren't victims.

"I didn't hurt them. Except for the last one. I didn't lay a finger on them."

"Physically no. But emotionally? Mentally? You string them along, seduce them, making them feel like the best person in the world and like they had found Mr Right, only for you to dump them from a great height. You lied and manipulated them. Did you even say goodbye, or tell them you were off or did you just leave them waiting?"

His silence indicated the latter.

"Jesus," I said, assuming.

"Look, I'm doing my time okay? I know I've done wrong. I'm sorry and it's never going to happen again. I've learnt my lesson."

"How did you get off? I mean how did you avoid prison?"

"I sold a lot of my things. Got a good lawyer."

I threw my arms up in irritation. "Bloody typical," I said to the wall. "Suspended sentence and community service?"

"Yeah," he replied quietly.

"And the girl?"

"Moved back home up north. I heard she tried to commit suicide."

I shook my head in disbelief.

"She had other, erm, issues going on too."

"You think so? We all do!"

"I'm not responsible for her *other* issues."

"No, but you can contribute to them. A straw breaks the camel's back." I wasn't going to push him on her stuff. This was on him. I took another deep breath, trying to calm myself down. Maybe this was the wrong idea. He was the embodiment of why I hated men. Self-serving, manipulative, privileged. Why did men think they could do that?

"And you. You haven't had a rosy past." I knew where he was going.

"I did what I had to do to survive! Don't bring this on me."

"It's a bit hypocritical don't you think? Chastising me for my wrongdoing…"

"The difference is, Nathan," I spat, emphasising his name. "I didn't choose this. It chose me."

"Really? You didn't have a choice to stop drinking? You didn't have a choice to get a job and get off the streets? You didn't have a choice to…." He trailed off. I wished I hadn't said that word. *Prostitution.* It was a hook for him and he would reel it in.

"No, Nathan I didn't. I had an addiction. A medical condition. I did what I needed to feed that addiction. Like you had a choice to stop stalking women, but you didn't. The buzz, the thrill, the excitement. The only difference was you had a lot of money and I didn't."

"You can't blame me for having money. I worked hard at earning it!"

"You think I didn't work hard? Look at your hands. Look at my hands. These are hands from scrubbing toilets and picking fruit off trees. Do you know how much I would earn a day? £25. You probably earned that in a couple of seconds. You think I liked selling my body? I did it to get money to pull myself out. I know about hard work but when the system isn't on your side, it's bloody difficult. I couldn't afford a fancy lawyer to get me off the hook." I took a swig of the coke, forgetting how cold it was. I let out a gasp. Tears were forming. I didn't want them to come out. "You can't get a bank account, you can't get benefits. Hell, you can't even get a food parcel if you don't have an address." The memory of being turned away at a foodbank by some snotty-nosed little paper-pusher tipped the edge and tears flowed. Nathan went to speak but I waved him off, wiping under my eyes. A silence followed.

"Drugs helped me to forget those things, even for a short while. Just enough to feel…" I struggled for words. "…like the world isn't against you."

"You're right," he mumbled. "You can't compare." The silence hung in the air again. A clink of glasses rattled at the bar. I waited for my heartbeat to return to normal.

"So," I said, breathing in deeply.

"So." He repeated. The silence returned.

"What does your boyfriend do?" he asked, changing the subject.

"Something to do with computers. IT or other."

"Does he know about…"

"No. And it's going to stay that way."

"None of it?"

"None of it. I've got trust issues. And he's a nice man. I don't want to ruin it."

"You don't trust your boyfriend?"

"Not yet. It's still new."

"But you trust me?"

"No. No, I don't. But you brought it out." I felt my cheeks burn.

"Sorry."

"Yeah," I muttered in reply. "What about you? Girlfriend?"

He laughed at the ridiculousness of the thought.

"I don't trust myself. I don't think I want to go near another woman. Not yet anyway. In fact, this is the most normal, honest conversation I've had with a woman since…." He raised his eyes at me. I just noticed he wasn't wearing his cap. "…well, for a long time."

"What about family? Did they help?" I asked.

"Mum did. My sister died a few years back. Car accident."

I was taken aback. Maybe I had rushed to judgement. Actions always lead to actions. "And dad?"

"Left when I was young. Don't know him."

Same as me. Perhaps we were similar. Not so opposite to me as I thought. The same side of life's coin. Just different boats in the same storm. Don't judge a person by his crimes, judge him by his whole being. What circumstances led a person to commit a crime? The crime is usually the last chapter in the story. And for most, it doesn't have a happy ending.

He looked like he had shrunken in half over the last few moments. Vulnerable. I suddenly felt a wave of pity for him. Yes, I had judged him on his crime. The context hadn't occurred to me. He was one of us. Fatherless. A broken boy before he even turned into a man.

"Want to talk about it?" I asked.

"My mum died of a broken heart, just a few weeks ago. My sister: I didn't support her enough. She was going to kill herself. Got hit by a car on the way."

No wonder he was downbeat. And he had to deal with the community service whilst grieving.

I knew a few people who had taken their own life when it just became too unbearable and the destructive voices in their heads were louder than the hopeful ones. I let the silence consume us because there are no words; only presence is necessary. We had nursed our drinks down to the bottom. Wordlessly I got up and ordered two more, leaving Nathan in his thoughts. When I returned, he quickly wiped his eyes, like he was shielding a secret.

"God, that's cold," he said as he took a sip, literally breaking the ice. "So."

"So," I replied.

The silence hung.

"Do you want to talk about your dad now?"

"No," I said, matter-of-factly. "Do you want to talk about your mum?"

"No," he replied.

"Your sister?"

"No."

"*Your* dad?"

He shook his head and took a sip.

"We're both fucked up, aren't we?"

He snorted into his glass. Coke spluttered onto his nose.

"I guess we are. Two peas in a pod."

Chapter Eleven

Pierre's comment took me by surprise. I looked up at him and he was staring at me intently, not even blinking, willing me to talk about my father. Without taking his eyes off me he downed his shot in one go. The smell of the vodka hung in the air around me. Nathan coughed, getting my attention.

"You don't have to Jasmine," he said, softly. Pierre huffed and got up.

"By the sounds of it, you haven't spoken about it. It is like a heavy weight on your shoulders. Sure, you can keep it inside you, Jasmine, let it boil like a pot. Or you can release it. 'If you don't get it off your chest, you'll never be able to breathe'," he quoted. "You will feel better, I promise." I felt Pierre's presence behind me; I instinctively pulled my shawl tighter around my shoulders.

"Do you have a quote for everything Pierre?" Nathan said sternly. "Don't force it. It's up to Jasmine."

"You English, with your stiff upper lip." He clicked his tongue and looked away, swinging his empty shot glass between his fingers as he swaggered around the courtyard. Nathan leaned over the table and squeezed my hand. I mouthed a *thank you*. Then he let go and picked up the shot glass. Shrugging his shoulders he tipped the contents into his mouth, squinting as he swallowed.

"Urgh," he spat. "Are you sure that's the best vodka in Bali?" Pierre still looked solemn, but his eyes twinkled at this weakness.

"The best I can find so far!" He picked up the bottle and began to pour but Nathan covered the glass with his hand. Pierre looked despondent at the rejection. Instead, he refilled his glass, motioning to me if I wanted a top-up. I shook my head and pushed the glass away. Satisfied, Nathan scraped his chair back and called it a night. He squeezed my shoulder as he walked past. Sommy took that as his cue to get up and bid us goodnight too. Pierre and I watched them disappear into the huts. He shifted his chair around to be closer to mine.

"So," he began, a conspiratorial tone in his whispered voice. "What's the deal with you two? Are you lovers? Ex-lovers?"

"Oh no," I interjected before he went any further. "Just friends."

He frowned.

"Hmm, just friends huh?" he said with a wink, air quoting the friends. "I am unsure who has the pent-up lust, you or him." He fingered his glass. That's what I admired about Pierre – he was to the point. No BS or hiding behind niceties.

"You're reading too much into it, looking for something that isn't there." I was sure of it. How could Nathan fancy me? I was severely damaged goods. Even my body was sagging and wrinkling, far away from when I had a decent body to speak of. Nathan hadn't even crossed my mind in that way. Pierre's eyes narrowed.

"Seems odd, doesn't it. You follow him halfway across the world. Not knowing where he will lead you to. How long have you known him?"

"A few months, maybe five," I said casually.

"Ha!" he cried, surprising us both, disturbing the silence in the dark courtyard. He looked bashful as he waited for calm to follow. "Seriously? Five months?" a sparkle in his eyes and a mischievous smile on his lips. He bent over, whispering so quietly I had to lean in too. The smell of vodka came off his breath.

"Five months? And you are in Bali, the dream destination of honeymooners. Romantic huh? You cast a spell on him."

"Or he cast a spell on me," I said defensively, remembering Nathan's past.

"Tsk," he dismissed leaning back. He filled our shot glasses up again.

"To secret love," he said raising his glass upward. I raised mine to meet his. I quivered, the smell overriding my willpower. I could imagine the warmth cascading through me if I put it to my lips.

"To friendship without benefits," I corrected. His lips curled into a big smile, the crow's feet on his eyes tightening together.

"Okay, okay. To friends without benefits," and he tossed his head back as I threw the contents over my shoulder. I swear I heard a rustle of cotton in the hut.

"It gets better the more you drink,' he chuckled. He refilled the glasses.

"So, tell me, Jasmine. What made you follow a stranger to the ends of the earth?" he said, rocking back on his chair, his voice still a whisper.

"Adventure I suppose," I said.

"Nonsense," he spat, alarming me with his disbelief. "Try again."

"Um, I wanted to do something different." He leant forward, interested.

"Go on."

"Life back home was getting kinda boring and I wanted a change."

"Hmmm…" he had his elbows on the table, his fingers interlocked. "Go on."

"Nathan gave me an opportunity and I had nothing else going on so…"

"You ran away."

The words that he used to finish the sentence ran down the length of my spine.

"I've never run away from anything in my life. I didn't run away. Well, I guess I left, but I'm going back."

He lent back.

"Maybe," he replied, indifferently.

"What do you mean?"

"Let's see. Carry on. 'You had nothing else going on'… why? Someone of your age…"

"Well, my dad just died so…."

"Aha," he cried raising his finger. A bird squawked in the distance. He didn't care about the volume of his voice, the vodka gave him confidence. As he lifted his glass, he said, "To your father!" He lifted his shot glass and motioned me to clink his. I did and he downed it. I threw the contents over my shoulder again. I studied him as he refilled his glass, his tanned skin, his long wavy hair, the muscles bulging under his t-shirt. All that was missing was a bong or some rizlas. There must be some in his hut somewhere, I was sure of it. He was so charming, so open, so *whimsical*, I felt I could say anything to him. Perhaps it was because I knew, in a few days, I'd be back at home, far away where he couldn't hurt me.

"So, your father died. Why didn't you go back to what you were doing? Before he died."

"I wasn't doing a lot. I was lost. Look, I battled with alcohol for a while." He looked up suddenly. "I'm 112 days sober," I grinned. He looked at the shot glasses on the table, a look of concern on his face. I picked up the glass and threw the contents over my shoulder, smirking knowingly. He leant back and chuckled.

"You're wasting my good vodka. The best!"

"I'm sorry, I didn't want to be disrespectful to your hospitality."

"Opf, there you go again. You English, bottling up your emotions. You can just talk, tell me honestly, rather than lie." That last word hung in the air. He put the cap back on the bottle and put it down by his feet.

"No, it's okay, go ahead," I protested.

"Come on!" he said. "I'm not going to if you're not." A wave of disappointment came over me, like a comedown from a session.

"Thank you," I mustered.

"Was he a drinker? Your father?"

"Yes," I replied solemnly, remembering the beer cans littering our tiny house. "There was a time when I wanted to watch a movie and pulled out a VHS box from the shelf. You know what a VHS is?" He nodded. "I remember it clearly. It was Free Willy, the movie about the killer whale. I opened it and instead of the VHS tape, there was a bottle of brandy. Empty. He must have forgotten it was there."

"Is that your earliest memory of him?" he said, eyes wide open.

"Oh no. I know exactly what that was. I was seven. I know because there were birthday cards on the windowsill. We didn't have a TV then. And he was banging on the window, really hard, shouting through it for mum to let him in. We tried to ignore him, but I was scared, and I remember mum trying to shush me. Anyway, it went on for ages then it went quiet. We thought he'd gone. Then a brick smashed through the window. It knocked my birthday cards over." I swallowed and could hear crickets chirping as if chattering and gossiping to each other about what they had just heard. "That's definitely my earliest memory."

Pierre shifted his feet in the sand, biting his tongue to keep quiet.

"I also remember on my twelfth birthday, when we had a TV, and Dad came home with a video recorder. It had a big red bow on the top. He was grinning. Proud. My mum told me later he had stolen it. He didn't have a job and was on benefits."

"Benefits?" Pierre asked.

"Yeah, money from the Government. If you are jobless or can't work because of medical issues."

"Aha, I understand. Please…."

"Yeah, so I was so excited as we'd only just got the TV, never mind a video recorder! He had a box full of videos too, all mixed up. Some were violent action films, some romcoms, other children's ones."

"Free Willy."

"Yeah, exactly. Free Willy was in there. So anyway, I wanted to watch one of the kids' films and he said no, he wanted to watch an 'adult' film. So, his temper flares and he hits my mum. I know it's hard because she fell on the floor. Then he points his finger at me and starts yelling. Then he stormed out. I'm crouching down soothing my mum. I mean, this was my twelfth birthday and I'm comforting my mum. I should be celebrating with my friends or watching a film on my new video recorder. Anyway, he comes back when I'm in bed, and I hear shouting and screaming, and I'm scared to come out of my bedroom. I heard the front door slam and crept out into the living room. And that's the next memory I can't shake out of my head. My mum lying face down on the carpet with blood coming out of her head. There's smashed glass everywhere. I guess my memory is sketchy cos I can't remember hearing any glass smash."

"That's understandable," he said, reaching out to my hand. "What happened next?"

"I honestly can't remember. That's when the memory stops."

"I've never been in such a situation. I'm sorry you had to go through that Jasmine. I find it strange, don't you think, that you had an alcoholic father, and yet you also turned to it. You would think you would avoid it. I mean, please, I am not judging you...."

"It's okay. I know, it's weird. I've thought about it often too, believe me. I remember drinking when I was fourteen. I had finished detention at school and was pissed off, so went to the off licence and bought a bottle of cider. The shopkeeper didn't even ask me for my age. It's cheap in the UK, I mean really cheap. £2.99 for two litres and strong stuff. More than that vodka. Anyway, my classmates thought I was cool. And that's when it started. Whenever I got into trouble or felt angry at my dad, I'd just drink a bottle of cider. It was warm, fuzzy, and blurred my memory."

"So, an escapism."

"Yeah, I guess so. If it helps you escape the bad things you drink more, and of course, everything feels warm and cosy," I said.

"Your father then? He stayed. With your mother?"

"For a while, yes. At that time, I'd shout at my mum to leave him. And she kept saying I didn't understand, I was too young. I was coming home drunk too and shouting at her. God, I feel bad. She had it in both ears. I refused to look at him, speak to him. I ignored him like the stroppy teenager I was." The words were spilling out of my mouth, not checking to see if Pierre understood what I was saying.

"When I was older, I was out until late at night, getting into fights. I was arrested four times." Pierre raised his eyebrows. "I would pass out under bridges and on park benches. One time I woke up in the middle of a park and craved a drink. I went around looking for empty beer cans and bottles. I managed to fill up a bottle with other people's dregs. Bit of cider, bit of beer, bit of wine. Anything leftover." Pierre pulled a disgusted face.

"Yeah, I know," I repeated. "I'd do anything for a drink."

"But. But what about the taste?"

"Ha! Couldn't care less. I just needed the hit, as it were. And that wasn't the first time. Now I'm sitting here looking back, sober, yeah, it's disgusting. But you must understand the warmth I felt when the fuzziness came over me. Anything to forget about what's at home."

"Or to stop you from going home," Pierre said, crinkling his forehead.

"If you think that's disgusting, another morning, I found a can almost full. I was buzzing. I drank it and felt slimy bits going down my throat. Slugs. Seriously, didn't stop me. I finished the whole can." Pierre's eyebrows raised high, almost disbelieving. "Believe me or don't believe, I don't care," I said in response. I really didn't care.

I knew it was the truth.

Getting all of this off my chest was cathartic – like a weight was coming off. Why was Pierre the one I was telling all this to? I guessed there would be no consequences or shame to be put back on me, at some time in the future.

"And that was when you were a teenager?" Pierre said, interrupting my thoughts.

"Oh no, that was years later. Yes, going back. It turned out my dad was sleeping with a lot of different women. I doubt he even remembered some of them. But my mum found out when he passed out at one of their houses and the slut called her to pick him up. She was a friend of my mum, and just casually called to let her know. No apology or nothing. Like it was perfectly normal. That was the last straw and she kicked him out. He didn't just say 'cheerio' and walk into the sunset. There were fights and ..." Pierre nodded his head in understanding. "That was that. One day he was there, red in the face and screaming, the next day gone. The next time I heard or saw him was a quarter of a century later."

"Wow," was all Pierre could say. "You've been through a lot."

"You haven't heard the worst of it," I said flippantly. He raised his eyebrows in surprise.

"You are a little box of treasures," he smirked. I looked up and noticed the stars were not shining as brightly as before, and the dark skies were lightening.

"Do you think it's almost morning?" Pierre looked up and stretched his arms out.

"I think it's closer to morning than it is evening. We should go to sleep." He bent down to pick up the vodka bottle. As I stood up, he unscrewed the top and poured the rest on the sand. I was shocked.

"What you doing?!" I said.

"Ah, it's not that good anyway. Happy 113th day sober." I reached over put my arms around his neck and squeezed him tight. I whispered a thank you to him and he wrapped his arm around my waist.

"It's okay," he whispered. "See, sometimes it's good to talk." I pulled back, nodded, and walked back to my hut. I heard quick footsteps and a scrape of sand as I went in, and in the growing light, I saw Nathan's hammock swinging faster than usual.

Chapter Twelve

I got back to my flat when the skies were dark and grim. It was always satisfying putting my key into the lock of a decent place, rather than negotiating the scraggy carpets and stained walls of hostels and bedsits. I rushed in and slammed the door, darting into the bathroom. On my way I saw Chris standing in the kitchen, chopping something fresh.

"Alright, Jas?" he called out as I shut the door.

As I sat on the loo, I contemplated the chat with Nathan. Yeah, he'd been an absolute dick, one of the worst kinds. Treating women like he did. To him, it was just a game, but I felt for those women, psychologically tortured into trusting him, when it was all a lie. A concoction to manipulate them into believing something totally false. It wasn't just stalking. It was the next level up. I assumed stalking was from a distance, not actually playing with your prey.

Can someone change?

They had to. I had, hadn't I? I had pulled myself up from the brink and now I was sitting on a clean toilet in a fancy bathroom, with a floor-to-ceiling towel rail. I mean this was how I imagined a hotel. Everything was neat and tidy, towels fluffy and white, expertly folded up. Little bottles of fragrant-smelling shampoos and conditioner. Chris had brought me a jasmine set from some posh shop down the high street and a candle from Jo Malone for my birthday. I hadn't even heard of that name until I came into his life. That evening when I was in the bath, foamy bubbles right to the brim, I thought this was the life and I didn't want to go back. I hid my emotions inside of me, not wanting to give Chris any rope to not like me. My past could stay away; he didn't need to know.

A wave of enticing smells hit my nostrils as I left the bathroom into the open-plan kitchen/diner. I wrapped my arms around Chris's waist as he sautéed a mixture of carrots, bean sprouts, onions and peppers. A hint of garlic wafted up. Again, I thought how lucky I was. Even something as simple and homely as this was a far cry from what I was used to.

"What you cooking?"

"Veg stir fry with jasmine rice. Especially for you." He turned around and pressed my nose with his fingertip. I reached up and kissed his cheek, and some strands of my black hair swung into his mouth.

"Get away," he warned jokily. "I don't want any long hairs in this." He busied himself with the wooden spoon, stirring the bubbling rice on the stove.

"I've made a Bakewell tart for pudding." That was what I loved about Chris. Just got on and did stuff. Even though he was cooking, the kitchen was spotless, clearing up as he went along. I moseyed over to the sofa slid my shoes off and sat down. An artificial Christmas tree stood by the window, it's twinkly lights danced against its reflection. I stroked the material of a thick cushion.

"Anything exciting happen at the foodbank?"

"No, not really. I met a new guy. Nathan."

"Oh yeah, should I be jealous?" He turned around holding the wooden spoon in the air, the glow of the hood lighting him from behind like a god.

"Ha! No. Not if you keep making me Bakewell tarts from scratch." I twisted my mouth. "Um, something did happen though. Bit of news." It sounded serious when it left my lips.

"Oh," he said, wiping his hands on a dishcloth. He leaned against the counter that separated the kitchen from the living room.

"I had a phone call, out of the blue." I was still deciding in my head how much to tell him, as this was a can of worms I didn't want to spill open.

"Yeah?"

"Yeah. From a retirement home. Apparently, my dad is about to die."

"WHAT!"

"Exactly. I was just as surprised."

"How did they even get your number?"

"I don't know but that's not the point."

"Yeah. Sorry," he mumbled. "I didn't know you knew your dad. I mean you haven't mentioned him before."

Well, I haven't told you anything, I thought to myself as he turned off the hobs and came to sit next to me, putting his hand on my knee.

"I haven't heard from him in, like, twenty years."

"Jeez," he said, running a hand through his thinning hair. "What you going to do?"

"I haven't decided yet. Still digesting it."

"Well, you've got to go and see him."

"Why?" I asked in surprise. He looked even more surprised at my question.

"Cos he's your dad."

He looked so confused, bless him. His mum and dad were still on the scene. Married for 40-odd years, detached house in the suburbs. A well-to-do brother living in the home counties. I hadn't met any of them. I kept making excuses. Didn't want to play happy families. Not yet anyway.

"He gets in touch after all these years, and I just forget he's ignored me most of my life?"

"Look, I get it." He didn't but I let him carry on. "You don't want to regret it. You could ask him questions. Like why? What has he been doing? Did he have any more kids? I mean you could have brothers and sisters you don't know about."

I felt repulsed at the thought of him having another family, sticking around and playing the hero dad. My fingertips dug into the sofa fabric. I might just hit him and finish him off.

"Let me think about it, just for a while. It was only a few hours ago when they called." For all of Nathan's faults at least he hadn't pressured me to go and visit him.

"Yeah, of course. Take your time." As he got up, he kissed me on the forehead.

"Come on, dinner's ready."

"How was your day then?" I said as I sat at the square table as he put down two steaming plates of food. Two glasses of water were already on the table, set perfectly above the silver knife. I swear he used a ruler to set the table.

"Ah, same old, same old. We're making progress on a complicated migration project, should be finished in a couple of weeks." My eyes glazed over. "I'm really proud of you, you know." I glanced up at him at his unexpected compliment.

"Why?" It was rare when people praised me.

"Well, the business is going well and you're doing good things at the foodbank." I inwardly sighed. "It can't be easy getting a phone call out of nowhere like that about your dad. You're handling it well."

"Thanks," was all that I could muster, even though I didn't feel like I was doing anything, let alone well.

"I could come with you if you like." He looked at me hopefully.

"No," I said back, rather too sternly and quickly. Slowly, he placed his knife and fork on the table,

"When are you going to let me in, huh?"

"What do you mean?"

"I mean, you're an enigma. I mean I like you and everything. You're great. Special. I like spending time with you. I mean you moved in pretty quickly, that's got to show for something?" I wondered what he was getting at. "Just let me in. Into your thoughts. You're a world away sometimes. I wonder if it's me.

"It's not you," I said, pushing the food around. "It totally isn't you." His shoulders dropped. I thought he might have considered if I was having an affair or something.

"You know, I was chatting to Liam at work today. He was asking about you. I realised I didn't know anything about you. Except for the basics."

"So why are you with me?" I said, barely above a whisper. It was genuine question. Why would someone like *him* want someone like *me*? He turned his face away in frustration.

"Because I care for you. Because I think you're wonderful and talented and intelligent and driven. Because you're beautiful." I felt myself blush. "And because you've got a good heart."

"Yeah?" I said, rather dismissively. It was the only word that came to my lips. He carried on eating, looking down at his plate.

"But."

"There's always a but," I said as he grimaced.

"But sometimes you're distant. You never speak about what you've done before me. I want to know you. Everything there is."

"Trust me, you don't," I hissed back.

"Let me be the judge of that." I didn't want him to judge me. I'd lose him, that was for sure. "Look, I understand we all have a past. I mean we're no spring chickens. But if we are going to be together, live together, whatever it is, you can tell me."

I couldn't explain it. Chris just wasn't the person I could open my heart to. I didn't want to expose myself, make myself vulnerable, for it to all go south. End before it barely got started.

"Let me think about it," I whispered. He cluttered the cutlery down again, making me jump.

"Okay fine," he said, in a way that wasn't fine. "You've got a lot of thinking to do."

"Chris, give me a break. My dad has just got back in touch after leaving us when I was a kid. Okay?"

"Yeah. Well, that's a start. That's a little bit of information that you've given me." I huffed and took my plate back to the kitchen, still full.

With thoughts flashing through my head, I went to the bedroom and closed the door. The sheets were fresh and clean and made a crinkling sound when I laid down. The door creaked open, and Chris laid down next to me, scooping my head into the crook of his shoulder. He massaged my head and stroked my hair. I moved my arm across his waist and let myself melt into his body. My head rose and fell in rhythm with his breathing as I practised my gratitude: the flat, the feeling of safety, a boyfriend who cared for me, my dance school and the kids, the clean smell, food in the cupboard, a dishwasher. It was all very middle-class. I was in paradise, so much to be thankful for.

It was everything I had dreamed of when I was lying in the gutter looking up at the stars.

Maybe I should put my trust in him. Open up.

Perhaps Chris *was* my future.

Little was I to know that five days later it would all disappear.

Chapter Thirteen

The light was strong when I woke up. My head felt dizzy like I'd had a heavy night on the tiles. I knew I hadn't drunk anything, so maybe it was my brain processing the smell of vodka the night before. Or maybe my nostrils could detect fumes from the alcohol-soaked sand. I rubbed the sleep out of my eyes and dangled my legs over the side of the hammock, looking at the wooden slats of the ceiling.

What time was it?

There were no clocks or watches in this little slice of heaven. The time of the day dictated by the position of the sun and the rumble in our stomachs. I could hear Nathan outside chatting in broken English. He had taken to Sommy and they would steal little chats together. As it happened Sommy was from Thailand, and this fascinated Nathan. Particularly the Tsunami, which had happened when Sommy was just a boy. Jeez, I thought. What he and I were going through at similar ages were light years apart. But the similarities – the scars, the trauma, the loss – he seemed to breeze through it. He was the happiest person I knew.

I shook my head to rid myself of the comparison and swung my legs out of the hammock. Thick grey clouds were overhead. It wasn't as warm as usual; a wind was rustling the tops of the trees. I passed by Nathan's empty hammock into the cool air. Sommy and Nathan were deep in conversation as I approached them. The table had a smattering of fruit, lots of empty skins and half-eaten melon slices. I interrupted them.

"What time is it?"

They both looked up.

"Good morning, Miss Jasmine," Sommy chimed. Nathan stood up and faced me.

"Are you okay?"

"Yeah, yeah, I'm fine. Why?"

"It's past midday, just concerned you know."

"Oh yeah, I'm fine. Jet lag catching up with me. Bloody hell, you should have woken me."

"Nah it's fine. Pierre isn't even up yet. What time did you get to bed?" I noticed his cheeks blush.

"No idea. Couldn't have been that late. The stars were still up," I lied, not knowing why.

"Did you, erm…." He motioned a drinking sign with his hand. "Wasn't sure with the drink out…"

"No, I didn't. Thank you for asking though. 113 days."

"Congrats," he said with a smile. "Have something to eat." I scraped a chair over, sat down and sucked on a juicy watermelon slice. It was heaven.

"GOOD MORRRRRN-ING TUL-AM-BEN!" The war cry shocked us all. Pierre was standing arms raised filling the door frame of his hut, naked from the waist up, a huge smile on his face. Warm and cheeky with that glint in his eye.

"Someone's in a good mood," Nathan commented rather unnecessarily.

"Oui, I am. A storm is coming in and we need a bit of rain. Eh, Sommy?" Sommy nodded his head obediently. "We can't go out onto the water today, too choppy. Is that the English word?" Nathan and I both nodded at the same time. "Instead, I have an idea. We take a day off and visit the monkeys!" He said it with such childish enthusiasm I couldn't help but let a squeal out. Nathan frowned at me.

"What? Monkeys are fun!"

"Monkeys naughty," Sommy said playfully.

"Let's do it! We go in ten minutes," he said as he reached for a banana and slice of cantaloupe before rushing back into his hut. "Bring your swimming things too," he called back.

There was a rush of excitement as we quickly gathered our things and Sommy loaded food and drink into the old Mercedes. Pierre insisted, almost pushed, Nathan into the passenger seat and jumped into the back as I climbed in next to him. It took Sommy three attempts to get the engine going.

"You need to sell more parrotfish," Nathan said. My skin prickled at his words.

"Haha! Right!" Pierre responded, slapping his shoulder from his position behind him, making him jump. Either he ignored the sarky comment or took it in unintended jest. I was starting to think Nathan had a chip on his shoulder, but dismissed it as jetlag – we were still only a few days in.

Eventually, we were on the road, retracing the route we had come from when we first arrived. This time I noticed more of the landscape, perhaps because I was less dazed. The vegetation was much thicker than I had remembered – almost spilling onto the roads – plus so many blind corners and small, stony monuments to the gods. The clouds were still thick in the air and the tops of the trees were swaying. The air was still t-shirt warm, and I hung my arm out of the window catching the breeze. As we swung in and out of bendy roads, a huge volcano loomed in the middle distance. Nathan, in the front seat, tried to aim his phone camera to get a snap.

"Active volcano," Sommy would say, pointing every time we saw it. Coming along the other way were open-windowed buses, full of westerners with bright coloured clothing, young girls with plastic braids and boys with wispy facial hair.

Finally, the road opened. A busy café and shop on one side of the road and a perfectly paved road opposite, streams of tourists with expensive-looking daypacks and beige shorts forming an ant line and disappearing around the corner.

"This is where the tourists come to enter the temple," Pierre chuckled. "We are not tourists."

Sommy carried on, turning down a single dirt road, changing down a gear to handle the steepness of an uphill climb. Tall trees lined the path as the tarmac got more pot-holed and bumpy. Pierre kept knocking into me, appearing to edge closer with each jerk of the car. Beyond the treeline, I could see the ground slide down the sides of the mountain. Ahead a thin grey mud-bricked building appeared on the right-hand side. Sommy squeezed the car into a sloped concrete space right outside, knocking into a yellow bin as he stopped and pulled up the handbrake. Pierre swung open the door, a scooter beeped and swerved, narrowly missing it.

"Oops," he said in response, dancing out. We all got out carefully, slamming the doors shut. A woman sat on a dusty blue chair outside the building next to an ancient Coca-Cola-branded fridge. Sommy walked over to her and handed over a wad of notes whilst Pierre went to the back of the car, opened it, and took out a pile of cotton clothes. He handed them out –a blue one for Nathan, a brown one for Sommy and a striped green and red one for himself. He gave me a pink and a turquoise one.

"Sarongs," he said. "Tie them around your waist. Jasmine, you need to cover your shoulders too." A squawk in the trees got our attention. A rustle of branches high up. Pierre strode over, looking up.

"Come, look," he said as Sommy went to the boot of the car. We walked over to the treeline looking, not sure what at. Suddenly, a monkey, about the length of my arm, jumped down and ran between my legs. He deftly picked up a banana that was laying there. I turned around and saw Sommy, clutching a bunch of bananas, laughing his head off. He handed one to each of us and suddenly there were loads of them all around us. Pierre broke off a piece and put it on his head. A monkey instantly jumped up on his shoulder and sat there chewing the fruit with its tiny hands. Nathan pulled out his phone and took a photo, but a monkey jumped up at him and tried to snatch it.

"Oi!" he shouted. The monkey hissed back at him.

"You should probably put that away for now, when the food is out," Pierre advised, although it had an air of a teacher telling off a pupil. Nathan pocketed the phone and bent down, holding out a piece of banana. A baby monkey ran up, snatched it out of his hand and ran back, snuggling into his mother's fur. She bounded over, screeching at him for more. More and more monkeys came into view, screeching and hollering at us. It was a magical sight albeit slightly scary. I couldn't think if I'd ever been to a zoo, let alone seen wild monkeys in a forest. Sommy tossed the remaining bananas far into the forest and they darted after them disappearing amongst the trees.

"Quick," said Pierre, motioning us across the road and through a white gate, where the shop woman held it open and then slammed it shut when we all were in.

Nathan and I strode into a wide courtyard. I turned back to see Pierre and Sommy staying where they were by the gate, a big smile on their faces. Pierre spun his hand and motioned me to turn around.

A structure appeared to our left, making us stop in our tracks. Two identical triangular pillars stood tall and sentry, like a pyramid cut in half and then moved apart to create a vertical gap down its centre. The outsides of them formed giant steps to the top with each step containing black curling eagle-like heads facing inwards. Intricate carvings dotted every inch of the white pillars. Through the hole, the volcano we had seen from the car was framed perfectly in the centre. It was like a mirror had been placed in the middle – one side reflected from the other. It was a perfection of symmetry. Hypnotised, Nathan and I walked towards it, drawn like a magnet. As we got nearer, as if on cue, the sun peeked out behind a cloud, bathing us and the monument in sunlight. We heard gasps from the tourists next to us and the clicking of cameras. I felt an arm around my waist as I took in the view.

"Beautiful isn't it," Pierre said. "It's called the Gates of Heaven." Nathan turned and I noticed him glance down at Pierre's arm around my waist. I moved forward so it dropped, hoping to get a better look at the view beyond the gates. Pierre continued, "This is supposed to be the oldest temple in Bali."

We walked closer to the gates, being careful not to get in the way of tourists taking photos, noticing steps going down to the valley below.

"There are actually seven temples here. Another one is behind you." Nathan and I turned around quickly, both taking an inward gasp as we saw the other temple, yards from where we were just standing. We hadn't even noticed it when we walked into the complex. In front of us were three sets of steep stairs next to each other, reaching up the mountain to three towering temples with tiered roofs looking proudly down. In-between the stairs, running up their length, were little terraced gardens, adorned with ornate carvings and statues.

We started to climb the stairs, the steepness making it hard work. A monkey jumped down from a tree, hissing at us but Sommy shooed him away. By the time we all got to the top, we were all sweating profusely. We turned to look at the view, even more breath-taking than before – the three sets of stairs rolling down to the courtyard to the Gates of Heaven and the volcano beyond. Tourists formed a queue to get their photo of them standing in between the two pillars. I felt like a God watching them from above.

Pierre sat next to me, brushing my leg as he did. I felt Nathan quickly glimpse at us from the corner of his eye and shuffled away, just a few inches.

"What do you think of the Gates of Heaven?" Pierre said, breaking the silence between us.

"Heavenly," I replied and gave him a wink. He winked back, a big smile on his face.

"Did you say there were seven temples up here?" Nathan asked.

"Yes, they are further up. It will take three, maybe four hours to walk. It is beautiful. Many tourists do not go to visit. But these are the most famous. And in my opinion the most beautiful to look at." I caught Pierre looking at me when he said that.

"Let's get a photo between the gates and then I have another surprise for you. Nathan!" Nathan glanced at him.

"Race you to the bottom!" and he jumped up and ran down the stairs two at a time. Nathan chased after him. Sommy and I looked at each other and rolled our eyes. *Boys*, we seemed to say to each other, and he smiled a large toothy grin in response. At the bottom, they were still panting as Sommy and I reached them.

"Who won?"

"I did of course!" Pierre said flexing his muscles. "The older man won!"

"You had a head start," Nathan protested, bent over and panting. Pierre put a sweaty arm around his shoulders chortling. Nathan swatted him away.

Sommy paid a local to take our photo on Nathan's phone and we all posed in between the gates, the volcano behind us.

Back in the car, Sommy drove us down the mountain and eventually onto flat lands. The single-file roads closed in on us with overhanging trees and close-calls with trucks and cars coming inches away from us in the opposite direction. Pierre grinned like a child whenever a vehicle came too close, and

Nathan squirmed to the middle of the car. The road became a conveyor belt of corrugated-roofed shops, temples and basic houses followed by miles of lush tropical rainforest. Every so often, I glimpsed the imposing volcano growing bigger through gaps in the canopy. The lulling of the car rocking and beeping were making my eyelids heavy. I felt a nudge on my arm.

"Nearly there, Jasmine."

As Pierre said it, a light suddenly filled the car as the trees disappeared to reveal a large expansive lake, the volcano sitting on the opposite bank, seemingly rising from the rippling water. A few birds glided along the water's top, making ripples with their feet as they skimmed the water. It was another majestic, heavenly view. If only the patchy grey clouds had disappeared, then it would be a picture-perfect moment. When Sommy pulled the car over to the side of the road, Pierre threw his door open again. He danced to the water's edge and put his hands on his hips, admiring the view.

"Come on!" he called back. "Last one in is a wet chicken!" and he tore off his top and waded in, making a splash whilst diving in. Nathan and I raced to the water's edge, pulling off our clothes, my bikini underneath. The water was so cool and clear I could've drunk it. I dipped my head under the water and let the water wash over me, cleaning away all the sweat from the day. Pierre swam over to me and grabbed my hands, both of us treading water, the volcano over his shoulder.

"Heaven?" he asked, a huge smile on his face.

"Definitely!" I beamed back.

"Hey, Nathan, come over here!" As Nathan swam towards us, I noticed Sommy still standing by the car, one hand on the bonnet, looking over at us.

"Is Sommy not coming in?"

"Nah, I don't think he wants to get his car seat wet," he grinned. "I have another tour guide fact for you, now we are in the water. Nice, isn't it?"

We both nodded our heads vigorously.

"See that volcano over there? It's active. And right now, well, you are also in the crater of a volcano." He watched our faces drop, delighted. "Don't worry it's not active. But this is part of the same chain of volcanos. Obviously, this is very old." He scooped up water over his face.

"Let me tell you something. 19th June 2011, not many years ago, the surface of the water became covered with green and white dots. The villagers had never seen anything like it. They all became worried because the fish in this lake is their livelihood. Many fish here but if you go over to the other side there are lots of fish farms, just like I have but smaller. They farm *Ikan Mohair*, which, back in France, I know as Mango fish. It is not native here, so the villagers thought maybe it had brought poison or a disease. The next day, the villagers woke up and saw thousands and thousands of fish lying dead on the surface of the water. The fisherman, very superstitious, did not want to eat the fish so left them in the lake. Guess what? The next day all the green and white spots disappeared. Apart from the dead fish, everything was back to normal."

"What caused it?" Nathan asked.

"The villagers, they think it is the gods," his finger reached out from the water and pointed upwards. "They think it was a punishment, for overfishing, for bringing in a foreign fish. So, they prayed, removed the nets and took fewer fish out. They let the native fish population grow back and then left them. They used lines instead of nets. Of course, it worked."

"And do you know the real reason?" I asked.

He tried to shrug whilst treading water. "Who knows. A mystery. Maybe it was algae. Maybe poison. Maybe temperature change. Maybe it was God. Who knows? Many fish died and the villagers immediately changed how they fished. I wished others would follow their example." He tutted and turned to face the volcano, the warm golden rays of the setting sun reflecting off the green rainforest climbing up the sides of the volcano. Dark clouds began to gather at its summit. The air turned a chill and the wind picked up as Nathan swam back to shore. I laid back and kicked up the water, letting the warm water keep out the chilled air. Pierre bobbed up and down next to me.

"Can I ask you something, about last night?"

"Sure," I said, not knowing what else to say.

"It must be hard talking about your father, your past like that. But it is good to do. Did you feel better after?"

I had to admit I did.

"And today, did you feel good?"

"Yes Pierre, it was amazing, I loved every second."

"Good. And did you think about your father at all today? Be honest."

"No, not at all. Why?"

"Well, you gave something to me. Honesty. In return, I wanted to give you something back. Beauty. And you received. Ying and Yang. I wanted to show you that our individual struggles are tiny in comparison to the beauty and size of the world. We are here for a blip in time. We all have our little battles but what is important is perspective. The waves will still crash, the sun will still rise, and the Earth will continue to turn. Us humans have a way to magnify the insignificant. Sent an email you didn't mean to send? Spent too much on a handbag? Think about a little fish. All they worry about is where to find food, breed and not get eaten. Do they even worry? Pah! Imagine the fish telling you it is stressed because it forgot to send an email. Or it felt guilty having eaten two chocolate bars. You would laugh! The beauty that surrounds you will live forever. Those dead fish here in this lake? Wasn't their fault. But it caused a massive change. Your father? Not your fault. But you survived how best you could, fought through it and now look at you. Swimming in paradise. Your father's death could be the massive change that you needed. To let go."

He stopped and looked into the sky.

"'The tiny seed knew that in order to grow it needed to be dropped in the dirt, covered in darkness and struggle to reach the light.'"

He looked at me satisfied.

"That's beautiful. Who said that? Gandhi?"

"No, Jerry Springer." I sniggered and his face creased into laughter.

It must have been the moment, the light or maybe the view, or just paddling in a volcanic lake in heaven, seeing beauty all day but I felt a connection with him. He was sincere and trustworthy like I could tell him anything. Like I'd known him for years. Something I couldn't do with Chris, or even Nathan.

It was a feeling that he wouldn't throw my vulnerability back in my face.

"Pierre," I began. "There's something else about me...."

"Shush," he interrupted. "I don't want to know. All in good time. Let us enjoy the moment, the beauty. Don't upset the Ying and Yang."

He laid back his head in the stirring water, his tight torso rose to the surface. The waves made him bob about. Thick clouds were gathering at a pace and the tops of the trees were being whipped about. I looked over to the shore. Nathan stood looking out at us, his yellow swim shorts flapping in the wind, his hands impatiently on his hips.

"Thank you," I said, in barely a whisper. I caught a glance at Pierre, floating on his back, not a care in the world. His hair sprayed out in the water and his eyes unfocused. I felt I was staring.

Gently, he tilted his head and our eyes met. They seemed to want to say something. Then screwing up his eyes, lying half-submerged and looking up to the sky, he said to himself, "It's going to rain tomorrow."

Chapter Fourteen

The lock was taking the piss, moving around like that, playing a game with me as I struggled to put the key in. A neighbour opened their door, concern on his face.

"Are you okay?"

"Yeah, just grand sweetie," I heard myself slur. *Hello old friend.*

The damn key still wouldn't go in. He came over.

"Here let me help. Jasmine, isn't it?" His voice was kind and sweet. He took my hand and guided it to the lock, letting me slip the key in.

"Oh!" I giggled, like a schoolgirl. "Why, thank you, kind sir." I tried to give him a seductive look, but I could feel my face not doing what my brain was telling it to do. The door opened surprisingly quickly, and I fell in, hitting my head on the carpet. I burst out laughing and stroked the floor.

"Hmmm, I'm home baby," I said, sprawled out.

"Can I help you with anything?" the friendly neighbour said behind me. "A glass of water perhaps?"

"Got anything stronger," I purred, reclining on the floor, propping my body up on my elbow. I must have missed it because my head banged back on the carpet. At least it was soft and cosy. The neighbour darted off and I closed the door with my foot. I crawled to the sofa and managed to get up on it, opened my bag and was delighted when I saw the brandy bottle, like a well-kept surprise that someone was hiding from me. The crackle of the lid was satisfyingly crisp when it gave way, and I took a swig.

God, it felt nice.

Like a familiar friend had returned and we were enjoying old times. I tipped the bottle back and saw that it was empty. That's strange. A couple of seconds ago it was full. Maybe my friend had shared it. I threw it down on the floor and it bounced on the carpet. Hmmm, that was strange too. Whenever I used to throw a bottle, it would smash instantly. I picked it up and threw it down again. Same thing! How bizarre. It just bounced and nestled into the fibres like it was snuggling down for the night. I got up and walked around the flat, opening cupboards, taking things out, and looking for anything to drink.

Good God, Chris was a loser, wasn't he?

Not one drop of alcohol in the whole flat. I tripped over something on the floor and landed back on the carpet. I got on all fours just as the door creaked open. Chris was filling the frame.

"Jesus Jas, what's happened?"

I sat on my bum, cross-legged. I tried to sit up straight and failed, leaning over and back onto the carpet. In another universe that would have been funny. But Chris' face wasn't enjoying the show. He was picking things up off the floor and putting them on the counter. Knives, spoons, forks, pasta, cereal and rice were all over the kitchen floor.

How the hell did they get there? Chris is usually so tidy.

He went behind me and pulled me up from beneath my armpits. My legs wouldn't support my body, like one of those toys you had as a kid where you pushed the button underneath and the clown flopped around. You know, the one without a head. Why did they make that clown without a head? That was stupid. It would give kids nightmares. Chris was talking to me. What was he saying? He was mumbling, not making any sense. Then I realised the voice was feminine. I giggled.

No, that was my voice.

He was dragging me to the bedroom.

Okay, here we go, I thought. Chris was feeling frisky. I started talking dirty to him. Well, my brain was crystal clear in its speech, it was my damn voice that was making some other shit up. I purred on the bed. He was taking my clothes off, my jeans, my knickers. He dumped them on the floor. They made a clumping sound like they were soaking wet. I spread my legs and looked at him seductively. He turned, walked out, and shut the door. Maybe he was going to get himself ready. I heard rustling in the kitchen.

Hmmm, kinky.

He was taking ages. I looked down on the floor and my clothes were gone.

Why is he taking so long?

I got up and put some knickers on. Those damn leg holes. They were moving as I was trying to put my legs in them.

Aha! Beat you.

I put on jeans but they were playing the same game. But I did it. I opened the door and the flat was in darkness. Chris was sleeping on the sofa, a duvet over him. Just his little head poking out.

Hmm. Well, the flat was all nice and tidy. Maybe that's how he got his kicks.

I tried to focus on the digital clock on the microwave. 02:15. Yikes, that must be wrong. Could have sworn it was dinner time a few minutes ago. My shoes were arranged neatly by the front door. I grabbed the bag sitting perpendicular to them and snuck out. I giggled liked I was playing truant. The air outside hit hard.

Bloody hell it was freezing!

A fine mist was blowing over the lampposts. I wished I had put a coat on. A bright light sparkled in the distance. A moth to a bulb. It didn't seem far, but it felt like I was walking for ages. The garden walls kept coming closer and further away from me as I went down the street. Parked cars jumped in front of me. I got to the bright light and stepped in through the door, the warmth engulfing me.

Ah, that was a nice, familiar feeling.

I went to the fridge and scooped up a couple of bottles of cider, a six-pack of Stella (*I've got money now, none of that Tenants stuff for me!*) and a hip-flask-sized bottle of vodka for good luck. I thought of Chris on the sofa and decided he would appreciate a packet of peanuts. The man at the till ran through the items.

"Thank you, brother," I said as he gave me my receipt and I tried to fist-bump him in solidarity. He just looked at me in disgust. Nothing worse than leaving a fist-bump hanging. The cider fizzed as I opened the bottle. The liquid warmed my whole body as I stood out in the cold. I chucked the empty in the bin next to the off-licence and unscrewed the cap of the next one.

Was that...?

I squinted down the road. It looked like Chris, running up the road.

I'd never seen him run.

He looked comical. I giggled at the figure coming toward me. His face was all crumpled.

"What the hell are you doing?" he said looking at the peanuts and Stella on the pavement by my bare feet.

Shit, I forgot to put my shoes on! I remembered grabbing my bag. Must have forgotten to put the shoes on. They were right there! What an idiot.

I looked innocently up at him.

"I got you some peanuts." I smiled sweetly. He bent down in a huff and picked up my stash and grabbed me roughly by the arm, dragging me down the road.

"Oi, what you doing?! Get off me!" He shushed me as my voice echoed in the stillness. I followed him, stomping like a caught schoolchild. He was walking fast, pulling me along. I couldn't take a sip of my cider, despite trying a few times. We got back to the flat and he expertly put the key in the lock and turned it.

Woah, I thought, *he's got superpowers.* Or maybe the lock only obeyed him. Like Aladdin. Or Harry fucking Potter. He slammed the six-pack of Stella down on the counter.

Careful! They're going to explode when I open them. I made a mental note, tapping my finger on the side of my head.

"What are you doing," he said, his face screwing up like he had just stepped in dog poo.

"Making a memory. Why?"

He rolled his eyes. "What the hell happened today, Jas?"

"Ah!" I said, pointing my finger up in the air. I missed, brushing my temple instead. "I had a drink."

"I can see that! How many?"

"Details, details. I don't know. I don't count."

"Yes, you should. I know exactly how many I have."

"Yeah, but you're a goody-two-shoes ain't ya." I tried to swipe his nose and missed, by a couple of metres.

"Seriously Jas. When did you start drinking?"

"Today or….?"

"Today, Jas!" he was getting frustrated. I was quite enjoying it.

"Oh, I don't know. Lunchtime maybe. No. It was before lunch because I had a few before they started to hand out the menus."

"Are you kidding me?" he said to himself, running his hand through his hair and twisting away. He turned back suddenly "Have you had anything to eat?"

"Um…." I looked up to the ceiling putting my finger on my chin, thinking. It was a nice ceiling. All white with no marks. The little light bulbs were sunk into their holes, all cosy like little mice tucked up in bed.

"JAS!" He got my attention back.

"Yeah?"

"Have you had anything to eat?"

"Oh. No. Eating is cheating. This is the strong stuff. Why don't you join me?" I reached over and opened a Stella. The spray caught me by surprise, soaking the counter and the carpet. The liquid erupted over the side of the can.

Bloody memory, where were you?

I tried to suppress a giggle but wasn't successful.

"Bloody hell!" was Chris's reaction, not seeing the funny side. He opened a drawer and threw down dishcloths onto the carpet, stepping on them, creating dark marks when he raised his foot.

"Damn waste." I sighed.

"Fucking hell, Jas. What's wrong with you!"

"HAHA! Where do you want to start Chrissy boy?" I sauntered over to the sofa, remembering to lift another can on my way.

Good old memory. Back to normal.

Chris had the dishcloth out so I cracked open the other can and it fizzed. Chris's head popped up over the counter like a meerkat sensing trouble, seeing what the noise was. He cursed. I couldn't remember him swearing before today.

"How come you're opening another one?" he said, astonished.

"Cos I finished that one," I shrugged.

"Bloody hell Jas. How can you drink so quickly with a body like yours?"

"Practice Chrissy boy, years of practice," I said as I laid back on the sofa feeling like a boss.

It was weird because suddenly there was a bright light. My clothes felt different. I opened my eyes and the flat was full of sunlight. I got up and went to the bathroom. When I came out the flat was pristine. My shoes were tidy by the door and not a smidgen of anything untoward. I thought it might have been a dream but for the thudding in my head.

I could do with a drink, and get my head straight.

I rifled through the cupboards and drawers. Not finding anything I looked in the bins. There they were. Six crumpled cans of Stella and a squashed cider bottle.

Fucker.

And then good old memory came back.

Ding!

I danced, nay, shimmied into the hall, bent down and picked up my bag.

Aha.

They nestled amongst pantyliners, lipstick and chewing gum was a shining hip-flask-shape bottle of vodka. It was like I had found the Holy Grail. I undid the cap and finished the bottle. The bedroom door opened and out popped Chris, his hair dishevelled and bags under his eyes like he'd been out all night. He eyed the bottle in my hand and muttered a *Jesus.*

"I know right! The Holy Grail!"

He glanced at me like I was an idiot, a look of absolute disgust on his face.

"You've got a problem," he said, pointing at me in the eyes.

"Yeah, so?" I said, trying to grab his finger but instead squatted air.

"We need to get it sorted. I'll find an AA meeting nearby or something," he turned back into the bedroom. I called after him.

"Tried that already Chrissy boy." The door shut in my face. "IT'S YOUR FAULT YOU KNOW!" I screamed at the door. I heard movement beyond and it opened slowly. Just a creak.

"My fault you drank like a fish, pissed yourself and passed out. Twice."

"No, not that bit. Yeah, that was my fault. But you, YOU, told me to say, 'I love you' to my dad, and he fucking died didn't he!"

"He died?" His face dropped and the door opened fully.

"Yeah, he died. I told him I loved him, just like you said, and then he died." I pointed my finger in his face, poking his nose, but missed.

"Why didn't you tell me?"

God, I needed a drink.

"Yeah, good old dad." I swung my hips around and headed to the sofa. The vodka was coursing through me now. I could feel it in my belly. Chris followed.

"Died last night. Or whenever it was he died." I tried to count how many days it had been but gave up. Like before, the days just disappeared. Chris knelt on the floor, one knee raised, looking intently at me.

"I'm sorry."

"Oof," I spat. "Are you? What are you sorry about? You told me to tell him, I did, he died. Another man in my life gone when I said those bloody three words." Chris seemed to look through my body. I leaned back on the sofa.

"What do you mean?"

I rolled my eyes.

"Jesus Chris, do I need to spell it out? Yeah, I'm an alcoholic, yeah, I've been in abusive relationships, yeah, I'm a bloody sad case. You want me to leave now?"

"Leave? Why would I want you to leave?"

I sat up in surprise.

"Because that's what usually happens," I said, confused.

"I don't want you to leave! I want you to get better! We need to do it together. You need to help yourself!" I leaned forward and patted him on the cheek. It was a nice gesture ruined by a burp, which made him pull away in disgust. Even I could smell the beer, cider and vodka on my breath. Smelt good. Needed some more.

"Easier said than done Chrissy boy. I tell you what. Pop down to the shops for me and get me some parasecimol...

Parateimol... parasitamol. Some bloody aspirin and we can chat about it huh?" He jumped up in hero mode, ran to the bedroom, threw on jogging bottoms and a t-shirt and was out the door quicker than a flash. He popped his head around the door before it shut.

"You sure you're okay? If I leave?"

"I'm a grown bloody woman Chris!" He nodded and left. I smiled. Naïve young man. I pulled on my shoes, grabbed my bag and walked out of the flat. I saw him running towards the off-licence. I went the other way, swinging my bag against my leg, walking in a zigzag to the supermarket where beer and spirits were cheaper. Much cheaper.

The next time I saw Chris was two days later in the local police station, with the mother of a hangover.

And the realisation my future was out of my hands.

Chapter Fifteen

Heavy rain pitter-pattered on the tiles above me. They sounded thick and juicy, not the pins and needles type in England. From my hammock, I could see bulging grey clouds. A few rolls of thunder rumbled overhead, creating an eerie excitement.

"Well, that's a tropical storm if ever I saw one!" Nathan said, bursting into the hut. His face shone with teenage glee. "Think we're going to be indoors today."

Sommy was crouching under the overhanging roof of a hut cutting into a green coconut. I opened the door and looked up. Large droplets splattered on my face, causing me to crease my face. Another one dropped hard onto my forehead. I made a sprint for Sommy and hid under the eaves next to him. He stuck a black soggy paper straw into the top of a large green coconut and passed it to me. Water dripped onto its smooth skin and snaked down. He shrugged his shoulders at me.

"Will not be long," he said pointing up to the sky. Holding the fruit in both hands I walked out to the courtyard. Rain lashed down on me, soaking the skin on my legs and arms.

No point battling it.

I turned the corner in the direction of the sea to see what a tropical storm looked like over the waves. The first image I saw was Pierre, unmistakeably him, riding the rolling waves on a white surfboard, his legs crouched and his arms outstretched, moving the board to the left and the right with his feet. The sea was a choppy cauldron of white peaks and crests. Seabirds rode the wind, darting head-first into the water looking for fish that dared to rise too far up.

From where I was standing, I could see the water glistening off Pierre's body, his long hair bedraggled, hanging in clumps by his ears. The momentum of his board slowed as he neared the shore and he dived head-first into the water. He resurfaced and shook his head violently, the spray mixing with the mist rising from peaking waves.

"Mr Pierre, he like to surf," Sommy said, surprising me. "He no like when water too calm," he shrugged. "Perfect surfing weather!"

We looked out for a moment watching him slither back onto the board and paddle his arms, moving out to the horizon. Sommy chuckled and left. I leaned against the wall and looked out to sea. He really was a burnt-out hippy. I reckoned he was a similar age to me, well into mid-life, yet he still had the thirst for adventure, youth and danger about him. Unlike me. I thought it was time to wind down. I'd had enough adventure and danger in my life.

Why couldn't *I* be young at heart?

That was a mindset thing, I thought, watching him swim frantically towards the beach with a growing wave chasing behind him.

If he could do it, why not me?

He jumped up on his feet and expertly moved the board, gliding horizontally along the advancing wave. As the board slowed again, he stood up straight, like a meerkat, and spotted me. He raised his hand and waved goofily back at me at the same time as stepping off the board and crashing into the water with both feet first. I watched him swim back to shore, the board trailing behind on a black strap.

"Bonjour!" he trilled as he ran up the beach, surfboard under his arm, the rain lashing down. "What a day huh! Doesn't it make you feel alive?" I nodded silently. He came up close to me, water cascading down his face, off his chin onto his chest. I stood my ground and looked up into his eyes. He held them for what seemed like an eternity. I thought he might have felt my heart beating out of my ribcage.

"Can I join you under there?"

"Yeah, yeah of course," I spluttered. He stepped forward, almost pinning me to the wall, and rested the surfboard upright against the hut. He cocked his head and I reciprocated. A smile crept on our faces. At that point, Nathan stepped around the corner, as surprised as we were. We separated quickly, Pierre stepping back into the rain. I felt my cheeks flush.

"Oh," Nathan said, a look of dismay on his face. "Breakfast is ready. We're eating in your hut Pierre." And he turned and disappeared around the corner. We looked sheepishly at each other, like naughty schoolkids, and I gave a half-hearted shrug.

"Come on," he said. "Let's eat." Leading the way around the corner into the courtyard he looked up to the skies. "It won't last long."

A table was in the centre of the hut scattered with boiled eggs, nuts, pineapple, melon and bananas. Nathan was swinging in Pierre's hammock, his feet dangling underneath, eating a peeled banana, watching the Frenchman intently. Pierre grabbed a towel and wiped himself down, humming to himself. There was tension in the room. I sighed, wrapped my hair up in a towel and took a boiled egg, sat cross-legged on the floor, and peeled it.

"It will stop raining about midday," Pierre said matter-of-factly, sucking on a slice of melon. "Then, what do you want to do?"

"How do you know so exactly?" Nathan questioned, a spiteful tone to his voice.

"Ah, it's a best guess. It's what usually happens." Nathan huffed at his response and swung his legs down and made for the door.

"I'm going to have a rest in my hammock," he said through tight lips as the door swung shut. Even above the noise of the rain on the tiles, we heard the creak of the other door and the slap of metal on wood.

Pierre made eyes at Sommy who quietly got up, piled a few pieces of fruit in his hands, and walked out of the door, using the back of his foot to make sure the door didn't make a noise when it closed.

"Sommy will look after him," Pierre said, picking up a bottle of water from the table, unscrewing the cap and tilting it towards me.

"Happy 114th day sober." He took a big swig from it. "So, tell me. 114 days huh? What happened to make you drink. I mean I can't imagine you've been drinking since you were a teenager until…"

"…a lady of my age?" I finished. He skimmed my eyes, his hair still dishevelled, framing his face.

"That's not what I meant," he said sharply sitting back in his hammock.

"Yeah, you're right. I stopped, and started, and stopped again. "Peppered throughout my life I guess." I felt my eyes glaze off into the distant memories, mostly happy stories with bad endings. He interrupted them.

"So, 114 days ago?"

"Actually, I started drinking before that, when I was 120 days sober – just a few days after I met Nathan." Us alcoholics had a habit of remembering the exact dates of sobriety. "When my father died."

"Your father!" he exclaimed, almost twisting over in his hammock. "Your father?! I didn't realise he was still part of your life."

"He wasn't. I got a phone call, out of the blue. I have no idea how they found me. I mean, *I* wouldn't even know where to find me."

"Ah, the Government knows many things," he said like he was well-versed in conspiracy.

"Anyway, it was from a care home. The woman said his time was almost up, that I was his next-of-kin and I needed to help sort out his affairs. I couldn't believe it, simply couldn't believe it. I had mixed feelings, mainly of not giving a rat's arse about him."

"But…" Pierre said, leaning forward, an air of realisation across his face. "Something must have made you go, huh? Something inside?"

"Not really. I was with someone then, someone steady, who didn't know my past. He said, 'make peace with him'. If you meant 'something inside', that was I curious to see him, to see what he was like, then yes there was."

Pierre nodded thoughtfully. He motioned his hand for me to carry on, still in deep contemplation.

"So, I went to see him. I was really nervous. Like *really* nervous. Next door to the care home was a pub. I wanted something to calm the nerves, you know, before I met him. It had been so long, and I just didn't know what to expect. If he was regretful or still have a hold over me. I mean, he'd be an old man but that could have been worse. I wasn't sure if I was ready for it. I kinda thought I rushed into the decision to see him. Anyway, I sat in the pub for an hour."

"And you drank?"

"No, I didn't. Didn't drink a thing. Not even water or a coke. I just sat there, building up the courage – thinking of all the what-ifs. When the bar staff moved me on, I had a choice: go home or go in."

"'Faith is taking the first step even when you don't see the whole staircase'," he quoted.

"Yes! Exactly. Although I wasn't sure if I was at the top of the staircase preparing myself for a fall."

"I guess you took that hard first step."

"Yeah, I did. Just went in. The nurse took me aside, into a plain little room with crappy paintings of landscapes on it. I don't know why I remember them. She told me he has Alzheimer's and he won't recognise me but told me I should talk to him and sit with him, that it'll comfort him. Give him some dignity for the last part of his life." I paused to wipe my dripping nose with the back of my hand. My skin and hair were still damp from the rain.

"How did you feel, right at that moment?"

"Um, well, I had two competing feelings. One was a relief, that he wasn't going to be drunk or have a go at me. Maybe it was a feeling of safety. The other feeling was, I don't know, anger, I guess. A burden. A burden that I had to comfort him when he never comforted or looked after me. Or my mum. Just left a trail of destruction – emotionally and literally." I pictured my mum's reaction when the brick came through the window: glass everywhere, cowering under her arms to protect herself, running to me and covering me with her body.

"So, she takes me to see him and I recognise him immediately even after the years. But he's this skeleton of a man, lying in a bed with wires and machines attached to him, dribbling from his mouth. I remember the dribble like those crappy paintings on the wall." I stick my index finger against my temple and twist, screwing up my eyes.

"He looks like he's shrunk, his skin is loose around his cheeks. He looks so fragile and weak like he couldn't harm a fly. The nurse talks to me about the situation, telling me what I should do and say but it just goes over my head. I just asked her 'how long has he got?' She just sighs, looks at him and says, don't know, a couple of days maybe. Like a plumber giving an estimate to fix your bathroom."

Pierre forced a grim smile.

"I can't help looking at his eyes. They were open, just staring up at the ceiling. I hoped that he might turn and recognise me. Say 'hey Jasmine, thanks for coming. I'm sorry about screwing up your life." I sit with him and stare. All horrible thoughts. What would happen if I 'accidentally' switched off the plug or smothered his face with a pillow?" The rain on the tiles came into my consciousness, reminding me where I was.

"The nurse came over with a bowl of soup and gave it to me. I was grossed out. I didn't want to feed him. Shoving it in his mouth like a baby. My own dad! The nurses were so busy running around, that I felt like I had no choice. The first mouthful I put in I wanted to shove the whole spoon down his throat. The nurse eventually came to change his catheter and bag and I saw how weak he was. Defenceless. Unable to even piss in a pot. When I went outside it was night. I thought about it, I thought about going to that pub but I thought what's the point. I came back the next day and the next. Just sat next to him, sometimes watching TV, sometimes reading bits of the newspaper out loud. Feeding him. Plumping up the cushions."

"You did a good job Jasmine," Pierre said softly, his eyes wide, "I'm sure he appreciated it."

"Maybe. But the worse thing was when I was sitting there, I kept thinking I was wasting my time. Why should I give him my time, when he hasn't given me a second in the last twenty-odd years? Longer if you think of the time he was around being abusive." That last word made me blub involuntarily, my stomach pulled itself in. Pierre made to get up, but I waved him away, covering my face.

"Please, take your time. This is healing you."

I took a moment.

"Something was just making me stay. Like a magnet. At the end of the third day, as I was leaving, the nurse pulls me into that little room again. God, those paintings were awful. She tells me I'm doing well. I ask her again how long he has got. She just shrugs her shoulders and says maybe he is a fighter.

Ironic.

She says she suspects that he has many of the markers of Alzheimer's, judging from his medical and police records: age obviously but also a history of bad diet, nicotine and alcohol, past head trauma from fights and cognitive impairment from any of the above. His cholesterol was through the roof. Sounds like a sensible assessment based on what I knew of him. All pretty straightforward. But then she sits me down and tells me straight: Alzheimer's has a hereditary component, that children of sufferers have a higher chance of having it. Everything she said applied to me too: nicotine, alcohol, fights, crappy diet. Add in drugs and ..." I stopped, not sure how much to spill out.

"I noticed, on your arms," he said, keeping his steely eyes on me. "We all have pasts." I rubbed my hands down my arms, suddenly feeling a chill.

"Yeah exactly. Maybe that was why I was angry. Of course, I blamed him for all of..." I paused. "That."

"And it's made you who you are today."

"Oh, shut up Pierre you bloody hippy. It's made me a wreck. I've lost half my life. That seed you were going on about, being in the dark and growing. I'm a bad seed. Yeah, I might grow but it's a tainted seed. And it will always grow diseased seeds." The words tumbled out of my mouth. I realised my cheeks were wet.

"But it doesn't mean you will get it."

"No, but there's a chance. No way I want to be passing even a small percentage down. The world's got enough bloody problems."

"Please, carry on. Is that when you started drinking?"

"No, surprisingly, it wasn't. Yeah, I was angry at him. Not only had he made my life a misery, but even when he was gone, he would continue to make my life a misery. Right up until the end. My end. I was furious. I wanted to punch his lights out.

But I didn't drink. I went home to my boyfriend but didn't tell him.

I felt Pierre was about to say something but stopped himself.

"My boyfriend kept telling me to say to him that I love him. 'See how you feel when you say it. What difference would it make, he wouldn't acknowledge it?' I was still seething. But when I saw him, lying in that bed, with a bib on, he looked so weak, I thought it was pointless. He couldn't raise a finger let alone hurt me. I guess it wasn't his fault he had Alzheimer's. So, I just sat next to him and did what I had done the previous days. And the next day too."

"Did you say you loved him?"

"I tried but the words didn't come. I just couldn't muster it up. But then the next day I did. I said it. I said 'I love you' to him when I got up to go when visiting time finished. I wasn't sure what I expected in return. I must have imagined his eyes flickering when I said it."

"And did they?"

"I don't think so. I don't know Pierre. Even my memory of it is sketchy like my mind is playing tricks on what really happened."

Goosebumps prickled my skin. I assumed it was the shivers of the cold damp of the rain.

I took a breath, wondering whether to say the next thing.

"And?" Pierre said as if reading my mind.

I looked at him. His round nose silhouetted on his cheek, the lines creasing around his eyes inviting me to unload.

"I probably imagined it."

"Imagined what?" he said, leaning in, his eyes wide.

"I swear I heard my name. I swear he said it. His lips didn't move but I noticed a tiny movement in his throat. What he called me when I was a little girl. Jazzy."

Words just spilled out like Pierre had cast a magic spell over me. Words I had never said before. He was right, it was healing like a huge weight had risen off my chest.

"That night I didn't sleep," I continued. "My brain was like a void. I couldn't close my eyes. I kept thinking, over and over, did he say it? Did he really say it? If I was his only family after all these years, how miserable was his life? And all the time I was thinking I am going to go through that. I am going to be that person who dribbles uncontrollably. I'm the one that's going to be fed by a stranger. Yes, I know. What if I don't, or what if there's a magical future cure, what if ... I don't want anyone to go through that for me. I don't want anyone to even *see* me like that. That would be unbearable. That's being utterly selfish."

I stopped myself and covered my mouth with my hand, trying to keep a sob inside.

"It's okay. It's okay," whispered Pierre. I sniffed, wiping the tears away with my fingertips.

"The day after I went to the care home, as usual, got there at 10 o'clock when the doors opened. I wanted to see if he was conscious, whether he might say my name again, or if I had imagined it. The nurse took me to that room with the paintings again and told me my dad died overnight. She left to fetch the paperwork and I'm seething again. Like proper angry. I told him I loved him the last time I saw him, maybe he even recognised me, and he goes and dies. He left me again. Just when I thought he was back, he leaves me again. Gone. This time never to return. Except when I start to get the shitty disease he left me, he'll be back inside my head.

"I signed all the paperwork and this time the pub was calling me in, like a warm, cosy fire. I'm there for first orders and the next thing I know it's dark and I'm in my bed and I've pissed myself. I told my boyfriend to get headache pills at the pharmacy and he went off to get them like a good boy. As soon as he had gone, I'm at the supermarket and I downed a bottle of cider. I brought two more and carried them to a park. The next thing I know I'm in a police holding cell. My boyfriend came and got me out again. Same thing. I snuck out, but this time I was back before him. I hid cans around the house like my dad did in the VHS boxes. Now they've got these thin vodka bottles which you can fit into your socks. So, I'm lying on the sofa with a blanket over me, a stash in my socks and down the sofa. Cans in the cistern in the toilet, one even in a cereal box. Long story short, yeah, I drank until he left me. Or to be more precise he chucked me out. He tried to drag me to AA meetings, but I've done them before. Actually, made it worse and made me drink more. I wasn't nice to him. Hit him a few times. Threatened him. I would have left me."

"Where did you go?"

"Shelters, women's refuges. Park benches. I know, makes you sick right?" He just shook his head in disagreement.

"How did you get out of it?"

"Simply just woke up one day under a bridge. It was raining and I was cold, and I just thought, sod this, what am I doing? I'm a middle-aged woman drinking cider from a bottle. I guess I decided I wasn't going to let my dad ruin me again. I knew what my future held now, and I wasn't going to waste time leading up to it sitting under a bridge. That was 114 days ago today."

"Impressive. Well done."

"I don't want congratulations. I was horrible to a lot of people. Upset many more. I wish I could turn back time."

I noticed the rain had eased off on the roof above.

"Let me ask you something," I said, leaning forward. Pierre looked up and gave a non-committal shrug. "You and Sommy have known each other for some time. You spend pretty much your whole lives together. What if you became ill? So ill that you would need to rely on him forever, that he would need to look after you. Stop living his life. And that you wouldn't even recognize him. If you had a choice, would you give him that burden? Would you not want to leave him with the happy memories you have? Go back to France so he doesn't have to suffer?" Pierre stayed silent, thinking. He appeared to choose his next words carefully.

"I think you are making a big assumption. You think you are *giving* him a burden. You think he doesn't *want* to help. But what if he wants to help? What if he wants to take on that burden *because* of all the happy times you have had? I know where you are coming from, I do. But you think you are being selfish because you are forcing that responsibility on someone. I don't think that. Let me turn it around."

He crossed his legs and interlocked his fingers, placing them under his chin.

"If Sommy became ill and ran away, so I wouldn't see him, I would be devastated. I would want to be there for him, doing all those things you did for your father. Would it be a burden? No. It would be a privilege. For all the sacrifices that he made for me, for all the companionship, for all the hard times, I would owe it to him."

"Even though you know that it will be the most difficult time of your life, so helpless."

"Even more so, yes. It will be even more difficult for him. He would be helpless. I would sit with him even if he didn't know I was there. That would be an honour for me. I often think about my father. I used to hate him. Many things, but mainly because he never said, 'I love you'. He never gave me a big hug. He would never ruffle my hair and say I was doing well. It was only when I was travelling, with lots of time to think, did I realise. Not everyone shows love by physical actions or words. I realised that he would go out on that boat at 4 a.m. to get the fish that fed me, his hands calloused because he needed to provide for me. He gave me presents, he gave me money to buy the things I wanted, not because he had to, but because he wanted to. He wanted to make me happy. He would drive me to my friend's house, and, when he should be in bed ready for the early morning, he'd pick me up late at night. He wanted to make sure I was safe, that our home was safe, and that my life was stable. He gave up his life for me. Did I ever say, 'thank you'? Of course not. I was a selfish teenager thinking the world owed me. When I realized this, I called home. I wanted to speak to him, tell him thank you. Thank you for loving me, thank you for being my father. I was too late."

Pierre paused and I noticed his eyes glaze over. He got up and walked around the hut in a circle and settled back. His eyes were moist.

"He had died a few months after I left home. I felt guilty. After everything he did for me, I ran away, hate in my eyes and my mouth. And all he ever did was love me. The only regret I have in my life, the only one, is that I didn't say to him 'thank you'. You see Jasmine, 'hate has caused a lot of problems in the world, but it has not solved one yet'."

He broke off and looked at his hands. I watched him and thought about my dad. Then I thought about myself, and the life I had planned for myself. That night in the police station, I decided I didn't want to allow myself to fall in love or have children, so I didn't inflict my disease on them. It was to be a lonely life, held together with friendship. But what is friendship? Friends come and go, but family stay together. Stability, familiarity, trust.

"So, you asked me," Pierre interrupted. "If I had the choice, would I let Sommy look after me? Or if Sommy got ill, would I look after him? The answer is absolutely yes. I don't care if he doesn't recognize or know me. I will remember always throwing the fish back into the sea and knowing I will make a little difference. And if you think you cannot love for the 'burden' that will come, that there is a condition to loving you and you loving them then that makes me sad. You have it backwards. Love is unconditional. Fact. Love accepts you for who are, regardless of your past, present or future."

I had never spoken to anyone like I had spoken to Pierre about what was going on inside my head, the dilemma I was battling on my own.

"Look. Let me tell you my story?" He straightened his back and stretched his neck. I sat up in my chair, intrigued. I thought I knew his story. His past.

"After I left university and before I started travelling, I had, well, a very similar situation. My wife. She died."

"Your wife?" I sputtered.

"Yes. I married her and she died twelve days later," he said. I gasped.

"Leukaemia. To be precise she had acute myeloid leukaemia. It means that it takes over the body very quickly. She had it when she was young and then it disappeared. I think you say 'remission'. When we met, I didn't know of course. We were young, partying a lot. We took cocaine, fresh from the boat from Algeria."

He sniffed, his eyes a long way away.

"She had the symptoms, but I didn't know. I thought the nosebleeds and the blood in the mouth were from the coke. Pale skin because we didn't eat well. She got a fever but I thought that was the natural part of the seasons. And our lifestyle wasn't particularly healthy. We were always getting ill. But we were young, we thought we were invincible. Anyway, she collapsed one night after a party and I took her to the hospital. They cleaned her up and discovered it through a blood test. I thought it was routine but, well, obviously they had her records. They gave her three months. If we had caught it earlier, she would have lasted longer."

"How long had you been seeing her?" I asked.

"Three years, seven months, twenty-six days and thirteen hours. You asked if I would sit by someone, comfort them, feed them until their last breath? I did it. I did it for nearly three months. We decided we would marry, even if it was the last thing she did."

I covered my mouth in astonishment. Pierre nodded back.

"We put her in a white wedding dress, and I wore a tuxedo. My father thought I was stupid. Only my mother came to her bedside and we had a ceremony. We had a croquembouche specially made and she had a beautiful bouquet of flowers. Even though I knew there was no future for us, I made her feel special: the most important woman in the world. She died a married woman and I became a happy man."

"That's lovely," I said.

"Yeah. Did my wife want me to run away because she would be a burden on me? Would she want me not to see her? Even if she wanted to, I would not let her. Instead of finding the next woman, I chose to be a better husband. For her last twelve days, she wore her wedding dress, and I my tuxedo, and I spoke to her as she became weaker and weaker. I was holding her hand when she died. We buried her and that evening my mother said to me, 'Pierre, if you want to travel, go now. Don't wait. Life is short and cruel. Go now and don't look back'. So, I did. On my mother's advice, I left France and started to travel with the few Euros I had in my pocket. My father disagreed. I think he died with a broken heart. He couldn't protect me."

A silence hung in the air.

"So now," he said, sucking in the air, looking out the window at the fading rain. "That's how I live my life. Like it's my last day because one day it will be."

I stood up and Pierre reciprocated, quickly enveloping ourselves in each other's arms. He hugged me tightly and I sunk into this comforting, warm embrace, wrapping my arms around his waist. We stood there for what seemed like ages.

A rap on the window frame jolted us and we both turned to the noise. It was Nathan, tapping his naked wrist.

"It's midday, and it's still raining."

Chapter Sixteen

Paul bounded up to me as I walked sheepishly into the foodbank for what I thought was my shift. I wasn't sure. It must have been at least a fortnight since I was last there.

"Jasmine! Are you okay? We've been worried sick!"

The volunteers turned to face me. Then I saw Nathan's black cap moving towards me.

"Yeah, yeah I'm fine," I said, bracing myself for Nathan's words.

"Blimey Jasmine, what happened to you?"

He looked me up and down and around my face, spotting cuts and bruises, my clothes ragged. Even I could smell the dirt coming off me. Nathan stepped forward, seemingly wanting to put an arm around me but I stepped back.

Not here.

"My dad died," I said, and everyone gasped, assuming the domino effect that would have. Nathan tilted his head though, thinking, his face pained to say something. But he stayed schtum.

"Sorry I didn't contact you, Paul. I missed my shift."

"Oh, don't you worry about that," Paul said earnestly. "You shouldn't even be here. Why don't you go home and have some rest?" My eyes caught Nathan's. I didn't have a home to go to.

"Thanks, but I thought I'd come here. Take my mind off... things." Paul registered and sighed.

"If you're sure. But don't do anything you don't want to do."

"I'll look after her," Nathan said, stepping forward. I inched over to him, trying to indicate to Paul through my eyes that privacy was needed.

"Oh okay!" he beamed. "Yes, yes. You two have got on well. We're packing up the foodbank Jasmine. Moving everything out so we can get the camp beds out for Christmas." I nodded, knowing full well why that was.

"Okay," I said quietly.

"Nathan will tell you what to do." He slapped him on the back. "Remember, don't overstretch yourself, okay?"

"Yeah, no problem," I said and followed Nathan to the back of the hall.

"We're just putting the crates onto this trolley and moving it to the loading bay. The others are going to put down the beds when we are done because the church becomes a shelter for the homeless over Christmas."

"Yeah, I know." He raised his head in surprise. We moved the trolley around, him pulling and me pushing, neatly piling leftover food on it. We shuffled around in silence for most of the shift. He hardly looked at me the whole time, focusing on the job at hand. I thought he was waiting for me to speak first. So, I did.

"One day sober," I smiled at him.

"Congratulations!" he beamed back. "First day of the rest of your life?" I shrugged my shoulders.

"Depends."

"Sorry about your dad."

I sighed, dropping my shoulders.

"Don't be. I'm not."

"Were you with him, when he passed?"

"No, it was in the night. I spent a few days with him before…"

"Yeah," he said in reply, not needing me to carry on.

"I had a drink. Or two."

"Yeah."

"I broke up with my boyfriend."

"Oh."

"Yeah. It wasn't right."

"Where you living?"

"Right now? Walpole Park, third bench on the right." He looked up in surprise. Then his eyes furrowed.

"Stay at mine. You don't need to pay me or anything. I've got a spare room. And a sofa. I'll sleep on it."

"Yeah?" I said optimistically.

"Of course."

"But you don't know me. I'm one of them." I nodded my head in the direction of the client's entrance.

"So am I," he said with a smirk.

"S'pose so."

"Just till you get on your feet, mind. Don't want you claiming squatter's rights or anything. Or outstaying your welcome." His cheeky grin returned.

"Who do you think I am? A raving alcoholic, ex-homeless ballerina with daddy issues?"

"I wouldn't want to judge." He winked at me this time. If this had been a different world, a sliding doors moment if dad was different and we had had a happy family, my heart would have fluttered. Instead, it beat in gratitude.

"We'll go straight to my place."

"Good idea. Thanks. Really."

"No problem," he said as he pulled the trolley towards him. "Ballerina, eh?"

***

When the shift finished, we meandered through the crowded streets, shoppers bustling past with hands full of glittery carrier bags and boxes. Lame flashing lights hung down from lampposts and stretched across the roads. Christmas trees filled living room windows, garlands adorned front doors. We turned into a small garden as Nathan got out his keys. I looked up at the terraced house as he put it in the lock. I noticed there was only one doorbell.

"Do you own the whole thing?" He looked back over his shoulder, hand frozen mid-turn. He cocked his head, confused.

"Yeah," he said as if there was no other answer.

"You have done well for yourself."

"You should have seen the car I had before I sold it. Bloody loved that thing."

I whistled in appreciation. The other half.

A wave of nausea came over me as we walked in. It was just like Chris' flat: minimalist and spotless. A flight of stairs with thick carpet led up to a landing. The kitchen had bi-folding doors stretching across the width of the house looking out to a neat garden. A glass table with four chairs. The kitchen had designer furnishing and appliances. A Union Jack Smeg fridge stood to the side.

"Wow Nathan, the boy done well."

He looked at me sheepishly, turning on a tap and letting it run whilst pulling out a couple of pint glasses from a cupboard. I walked around the large space.

Jasmine, you've landed on your feet again. Don't bloody ruin it.

"Have a look around if you want to."

I did want to. I walked back to the front door and looked in the lounge. Twin sofas stood mirroring each other, split by a fancy wooden table that looked like it had just been chopped down. The biggest TV I had ever seen was on the facing wall. A bookcase stood empty, save for a few coins and papers. I faced the stairs and took my shoes off to sink my toes into the inviting carpet.

I wasn't disappointed.

It was like stepping on fluffy baby rabbits it was so soft. I crept up the stairs. Two bedrooms fed off the hallway and a snazzy bathroom looked like it hadn't been used it was so clean. A few expensive-looking toiletries bottles stood on the sink. I went into the first bedroom. Empty. Even the bulb didn't have a lampshade on it. All that was in it was an empty floor-to-ceiling bookshelf. I moved to the front of the house and glanced into the other bedroom.

Spotless.

The double bed was crisp with fresh linen, like a hotel room, bedding tight to the corners. A cupboard spanned the room. Frosted, sliding doors hid the contents. I opened it a smidge, trying not to make a noise. I peeked around, seeing the top rail full of expensive-looking suits. The bottom row was full of collared shirts.

It was like he was a different person from the one I knew downstairs.

I thought back to his crime: adapting himself like a chameleon, not just changing his clothes but his looks too. Manipulating. Saying the right things.

The *perfect* things.

My mind flashed to the foodbank: him at the back of the room, me approaching him, my trust issues with men, him being my hero and stepping in. Inviting me back to a swanky house that would impress me.

My stomach dropped.

Was he playing me? Was I one of his challenges? Was it all an act?

And now here I was in his house. I didn't know what he was doing downstairs. He could have locked the doors and was getting ready to… well I didn't know what. My hairs stood on end as my instincts went on red alert.

The fight mode I was so used to on the streets.

I crept out of the room and strained to hear. I heard him padding about, moving, a scrap of metal on metal. I tensed up and intuitively balled my fist. I turned around, looking for something to grab. There was nothing – no stick or hard object.

He's played me. He's set me up in a trap. This house was a front. It was too clean like it hadn't even been lived in.

I tiptoed down the stairs, ready to let hell break loose.

Chapter Seventeen

Pierre sighed and slowly sat down, deliberately making a show of putting on his tatty trainers and doing up each of the laces. Then he lazily got up, walked to the other side of the room, bent down, rustled a plastic bag as if finding it hard to find something, pulled out a bottle of water, slowly twisted off the cap, took a glug, re-screwed the cap, and sauntered to the door. Nathan's eyes followed his moves through the window, rain intermittently splashing onto his head. Pierre opened the door as wide as he could, squeezing out every nanosecond for added drama. With a flourish, he stepped out onto the threshold, looked up at the sky and held his hand out. He blinked as a few drops landed in his eyes.

"Hmmm, maybe your watch is fast," he said, lowering his head to meet Nathan's gaze. They were inches apart. I noticed veins popping out from Nathan's arms, his fists scrunched up. Sommy's body leaned against the frame of the door opposite, his arms crossed, watching.

A silence.

Both men stood facing each other, like a duel, waiting for the other to move first. The rain pitter-pattered gently above me. Pierre suddenly put his finger in the air, making Nathan flinch. Sommy twitched.

"Aha!" Pierre said, a huge grin mockingly appearing on his face. He put his whole index finger in his mouth, sucked it and pulled it out slowly, putting it high up into the air. He kept it upright, his eyes not wavering from Nathan's. As if on cue, the sun broke through the clouds, filling the courtyard with bright light. It seemed like the temperature rose at the same time.

Then the rain stopped.

Just a few stray droplets pinged off the eaves of the hut.

Nathan's face reddened.

"I think your watch needs new batteries," Pierre mocked, unnecessarily, and stepped towards Sommy. Nathan turned in anger and I moved out quickly, grabbing his wrist. He flicked his head back towards me, his eyes narrowed.

"What you doing?" I muttered under my breath.

"What am I doing?" he said incredulously. "What are *you* doing? He spat out that word, glancing down at me. I pulled his wrist to me, dragging him into the hut. When the door shut, I faced him.

"What's going on Nathan? Huh?"

"Why don't you tell me? *Huh?* Or shall I ask lover boy out there?"

"Are you serious Nathan? How *old* are you? Do you know how you sound right now?" I was getting angry. Was Nathan trying to control my feelings? Like a dad to their teenage daughter?

"I'm concerned okay! Pierre seems like the type to lay on the charm to any impressionable tourist. *Look at me! I'm saving the whales whilst surfing in the rain!*"

"How dare you, Nathan," I said, my voice quivering and rising. "What proof do you have eh? What evidence do you have that he's a player? That's your assumption and that's for you to deal with. What if he's a charmer? Who cares? I'm old enough to look after myself thank you very much."

"I want to protect you, Jasmine, I don't want you getting hurt again."

"Again?" I said, shaking my head. "I don't think I need protecting. I've protected myself quite a bit. In fact, I'd say I've got a P-H-bloody-D in protecting myself. I know how to handle it."

"You didn't after your dad died, did you?" Now I felt the familiar red mist rising inside me. "I don't want you falling off the wagon, slipping back, just for some old horny hippy who'll move on to the next tart as soon as you've gone."

I slapped him, hard, right across the face.

"DON'T YOU FUCKING DARE NATHAN!" I screamed, repeatedly punching him on the shoulders. "HOW FUCKING DARE YOU NATHAN! DRAGGING MY DAD INTO THIS! BRINGING UP MY PAST. HOW FUCKING DARE YOU. IS THIS WHY YOU BROUGHT ME HERE? TO CONTROL ME? TO PUT ME ON THE STRAIGHT AND NARROW? WELL GUESS WHAT, I DON'T NEED SAVING, NOT FROM A WOMAN-BEATER LIKE YOU."

The words just spilt out as I pummelled him, my fists landing on his body as he cowered into a ball. I felt strong arms wrap around my waist behind me as I felt my feet leave the floor, kicking the air. Sommy put his body between me and Nathan as I was carried out.

"PUT ME DOWN PIERRE. SO, HELP ME GOD. PUT ME DOWN!"

"Shhh," he cooed. "Take it easy." As I was carried through the courtyard, I could see Sommy comforting Nathan through the window, his arm reaching up around his shoulder. All I could think of was what a wuss he was. A coward. Pierre backed into his hut and dumped me on the floor, and I made a start for the door. Again, his thick arm blocked my way. He put his hands on my shoulders at arm's length and tried to make eye contact.

"Breathe," he said, repeatedly, each time getting softer. I followed his mantra, breathing deeply. Slowly, the red mist descended back inside me.

"Now, what was that about?" he said when I was calm. My cheeks still felt hot.

"He's being an arse," I retorted, looking away. Pierre put his fingers gently on my chin and moved my face back, trying to get me to lock on to his eyes.

"Are you okay?"

"Yeah, yeah, I'm fine," I said, trying pathetically to shake his grip off my chin.

"He says he wants to protect you. From what?"

"From you."

"From moi? Why me?" he said mockingly. I couldn't help but grin. That would have pissed Nathan off.

"He's threatened by you. You're a free spirit. Living life to the full, out here in paradise. Bigger muscles." I ran my fingers along his bicep. He flinched away.

"Maybe we need to be sensitive," he said, cautiously looking out of the window.

"Look, Nathan's past…." I paused to consider whether it was my story to tell. Whether I should let Pierre know, give him an upper hand. "Nathan came from an alpha-male world. He, well…" I paused again to consider my words. "He used to want to control things. Other people. Other women. For his benefit. I guess he wants to control me."

"In other words, suffocate you."

I shrugged my shoulders. "It's just a theory," I said.

"Based on facts and evidence?"

"Yeah, I guess so." I thought back to his story, what he had done to those poor women, manipulating them. The door creaked open. Nathan stood in the frame. Pierre turned his head around.

"Can you give us a minute," he asked Pierre softly, who looked at me. I nodded. Pierre got up slowly and walked closely past him, their shoulders millimetres apart. Nathan didn't seem to notice, his eyes looking shamefacedly on me. When the door shut, Nathan bent down.

"I'm sorry Jasmine. I'm really sorry. That was bang out of order."

"You're telling me, Nathan. What gives you the right to tell me what I should and shouldn't do?" I glared down across at him.

"None. I've got no right. I just want to protect you, from getting hurt."

"There it is again. Why do you feel you need to protect me, huh? And why do you think I'm going to get hurt? Maybe I see it for what it is? What if I want a holiday romance? That's up to me. What, you think I'm going to get loved up and ask him to marry me and tell him to come home with us. And if he says no, I'm going to hit the bottle?"

I could tell he wanted to say something but swallowed the words. Sensible.

"I'm older than you Nathan for God's sake. I've been there and got the t-shirt. I've been down so far I thought I could never get back up. Me falling in love with a 'horny hippy', as you put it, and being rejected on holiday is pretty much on the pink fluffy unicorn side of my life's scale."

He cast a downbeat face, looking at the sand.

"I'm sorry Jasmine," was all he could respond. "I care for you. I just didn't want to see you hurt."

"Well, guess what," I spat. "Now I'm hurt, Nathan. I trusted you. Trusted you with my past. I didn't think you'd drag it up when it got hot in the kitchen. Throw it back in my face." The waters were stirred.

"You can trust me, Jasmine," he begged. "I made a mistake. I saw red."

"I've had enough of men in my life seeing red Nathan and taking it out on me. Sometimes it was violence. If I was lucky, it was words. Apologising after. Guess what? It happens again, and again. From when I was seven, Nathan, from the age of *seven*, that pattern has followed me my whole life."

He crouched in front of me. His head hung in shame.

"I don't need that in my life anymore," I said to myself, stifling a sob. He got up slowly, almost deliberately and muttered another *I'm sorry*. He slunk towards the door. His shoulders hunched.

"You're right," he said, looking back. "You don't need that in your life."

I turned to stare at the wall behind me. It had paint peeling from the ceiling. I was determined not to let him make me cry. Before the door shut, I could feel Pierre come into the hut. Maybe it was the patter of sand, maybe it was a smell, I can't remember. He didn't say anything as he sat behind me.

We sat in silence for the rest of the afternoon.

And that was the last time I saw Nathan.

Until we met again in Bo Hin, Thailand.

Chapter Eighteen

As I approached the kitchen, I stretched my toes, remembering my ballet training. Not wanting to make a single noise I moved them centimetre by centimetre towards him, Nathan's back turned. He was chopping something, making big gestures with his arm. I spotted the knife block and slowly, very slowly, eased one out.

He turned towards the bi-folding doors, scrapping the peelings of the chopping board in his hands, and throwing them into a brown compost bin.

Was he playing me? Was I one of his stalking victims?

He had behaved so perfectly to me, in the foodbank and in the pub. And after my relapse, inviting me to his place.

If this was his place.

All afternoon and on the way here he didn't push or pry. Previously, he had said a couple of wrong things in the pub, but then again, he wouldn't have known about *that*. There would be loads of things he wouldn't be able to access. Maybe that had taken him by surprise. My mind went back to the time I saw the purple Probation Service logo.

Had he planted that?

If he had done his research like he said he had, he would have known that I would recognise the logo, and as such lower my defences. Was his whole story a falsehood, an embellishment of facts to get me to like him? Would I be thrown away like the others? He had made a mistake the last time, he could have made a mistake again. Or was that a lie? Did he invent a story for me to trust him, that he had chinks in his armour? My heart was racing, hammering so hard I thought he might hear. He was humming a tune whilst he was chopping. Jingle bells perhaps? Still on my tiptoes, I moved my feet quickly – a bourrée in my ballet training – the adrenaline pumping through me as I surprised myself I could still do it, the tiny steps making me look and feel like an ACME cartoon moving to a target. I could see the hairs on his arms as I silently reached around and put the knife against his neck.

"DON'T FUCKING MOVE!"

"WHAT ARE YOU DOING JASMINE?"

"SHUT UP. DROP THE KNIFE!" It cluttered down on the surface. I grabbed his wrist and twisted it behind his back.

"OW! YOU'RE HURTING ME! WHAT ARE YOU DOING? Sweat oozed out of his forehead and his arms making my grip slippery.

"SHUT IT"

"THERE'S MONEY UNDER THE BED. TAKE IT. TAKE IT ALL."

"I don't want your money, you idiot. Are you playing me?"

"What? NO! What are you talking about?" I released his arm. He spun around rubbing his wrist. I pointed the knife up to his neck, causing his head to jerk upwards. He put his hands up in defence.

"WHAT ARE YOU DOING JASMINE? His face reddened, his eyebrows furrowed in concern.

"Are you playing me?" I repeated. "Am I one of your 'challenges'?"

"Wha... no, Jasmine. You are not. Put the bloody knife down. You scared the shit out of me."

I lowered the knife, still keeping alert. He lent his hands against the counter, breathing rapidly.

"Jesus Jasmine," he muttered to himself.

"Look, I don't know you. This," I waved the knife around. "YOU could be all an act. Like one of your games. I ain't falling for it."

He relaxed. "You do have trust issues don't you."

He moved to the square glass table and pulled out a chair. My knife followed him as he went. On the work surface, peppers, carrots and green beans sat chopped and ready to cook.

"I was making you dinner,' he said, seeing me eye up the vegetables. "Didn't think that was a crime." I went over and sat down on the chair opposite him, placing the knife on the table in front of me, just in case.

"I don't know you from Adam, Nathan. I guess my mind played tricks on me. Everything you said, my dad, the ....

events of the last few days. I thought I was being taken for a ride."

"No, Jasmine. You haven't. I get it. You've been through a hell of a lot. No hard feelings." He rubbed the back of his neck, shaking his head.

Sorry was all I could muster.

"You know you're lucky I didn't do my kung fu moves on you and break your arm," he said.

"Oh please. You shat yourself." We both laughed out loud.

"Do you mind if I continue making you dinner, without the threat of death?" I picked up the knife, and menacingly pointed it at him, flicking it to the side to make him move. He slid out of the chair with his hands up, mockingly. He continued chopping. He called back.

"I'll take the sofa. You can have my bed."

I fingered the point of the knife, my foot on the chair.

"Was it here?" I asked

"Was what here?"

"When you, erm. That woman."

He stopped and looked around.

"Yes. In the spare room."

"The empty one?"

"Yeah."

"Why didn't you move. Why are you still here? Doesn't it remind you?"

He sighed and turned.

"You know I don't know. I guess I haven't thought of it. The court case, the community service. Not on my list of priorities. The old lady next door, who dobbed me in, moved out so there wasn't any reason to. Not yet anyway."

A silence filled the air.

"We're both fuck-ups, aren't we?" I said, breaking the tension.

Nathan turned back and faced me.

"Suppose we are," he said with half a smile. "At least we know. Some people go their whole lives not realising. And then it's too late to do anything about it."

"Therapy should be on the National Curriculum," I said.

Another silence enveloped us, both lost in our own worlds. Our journey. Our destiny.

"What do you think you'll do, you know when you finish your community service," I asked.

He filled up a saucepan and switched on the electric hob, placed it on there, scooped up the vegetables and plopped them in the water. He wiped his hands on his jeans and looked around.

"Dunno yet. Maybe sell this place, travel."

"Yeah, where to?"

"Somewhere exotic. Bali maybe."

"That sounds nice."

"Yeah, I found this company, or this French bloke actually, that is trying to do things to save the seas."

"Oh, sounds interesting. Noble."

"Yeah, I might go over there for a couple of weeks, see what's what. After that, who knows. Maybe Thailand. Build a school or something."

"Wow. You've gone from a selfish banker wanker prick to saving the world. Quite a transformation."

He blushed.

"Not quite there yet."

"Stepping stones."

"What about you? What are you going to do?" The water in the saucepan bubbled, and a sizzling sound came from the droplets that escaped and landed on the hot plate. We both looked over.

"Dunno yet," I said. "I've still got remnants of a business. Some of the kids might have disappeared cos I haven't shown up for... I don't know how long it's been. Start again I suppose."

"They'll be sympathetic if they knew your dad died."

"They won't be sympathetic if they knew that I went on a bender and ended up in jail," I said quickly. He raised his eyebrows.

"Oh, yeah, you don't know about that bit." I shook my head. "Anyway, need a place to stay and see how it goes. I seem to land on my feet these days." I made a point of looking around the room. A bell sounded and Nathan jumped up, put on oven gloves and took out a baking tray with golden pastries on it. He organised the food on plates and brought them over.

"Thank you," I said.

"No problem," he responded, tucking in. I pushed a stray hair behind my ear.

"No, I mean thank you. For everything." He looked up, his mouth frozen mid-chew.

"Haven't really done much," he said, his mouth full.

"You've done plenty," I said.

We ate the food in silence, in our thoughts. When we finished, I tidied up and put the plates in the kitchen by the sink and sat back down.

"That was yum."

"Ah, simple. I didn't know I would have a guest. Look, this is going to sound crazy. How much have you got, like in savings?" I looked up suddenly, on alert whenever someone mentioned money.

"Why?"

"Just go with me for a second."

"About a grand. Why?" His head jerked back in surprise. I wasn't sure if it was a so-little or so-much.

"This is going to sound crazy...."

"You just said that."

He smiled in irritation. "Let's go to that place in Bali. Together. Have a holiday. Get over all of this. Me with my 'conviction' and everything that went with it. You with your dad and breaking up with your boyfriend and all. Have you ever celebrated your achievements, like your business, getting out of your mess? Being sober?"

"No, never. I've never been on holiday. Never been abroad in fact."

"What?! Serious?"

I nodded my head.

"Here's the deal. You pay for your flight. I'll pay for everything else. Buy the flight so you don't think you're freeloading off me and I'll pay for the accommodation and food and anything else we might need. I'll organise it and you just come along. Time to get away from it all. Recharge the batteries and think about what you might want to do."

I thought about my future. It didn't look rosy.

"Don't be stupid. Why would you do that and why would *I* do that. We barely know each other. Five minutes ago I had a knife to your throat. I've got major trust issues and following a stranger across the world doesn't help that."

"We don't have to do it now. I mean now now. I've still got hours left to complete before I'm free. Plus, I can't leave the country for a few weeks after. Stay here, start your business from where you left off and then tell them you're going on holiday. I'll help you out. I've got nothing else to do. It would be my project to help you establish yourself and set you up."

"I like the word 'project' better than the word 'challenge'."

He smiled awkwardly.

"There's no rush. Why don't we both think about it? We've got ages. We've got Christmas and New Year to go, then we can discuss around Easter time. No pressure."

"I'll think about it. I'm not going to stay here though. I'll find a place in the meantime."

He raised his palms. "That's fine by me."

It was a pipedream, a far-fetched fantasy. Me, sitting on a sandy beach with palm trees and a bright blue sea. A handsome toyboy splashing about in the water, waving at me and admiring my slim body in my new swimsuit. My past erased and my future ignored. It was stuff Hollywood made real, not an alcoholic druggie in West London with a convicted woman-beater. What was I thinking? Was this even happening? It was too fanciful to believe. Yet it seemed to be within reach. Nathan had inspired me and showed me there was a world out there to be had. Celebrate? I've never celebrated anything. The only thing I had done was acknowledge a sobriety milestone.

That wasn't a celebration.

A holiday was laughable. Both had never crossed my mind, let alone the money to make it happen. On the face of it, Nathan had given me an opportunity. Motivation even. And who knew where it might lead? I had time on my hands and so did he. To suss each other out. To see if I could trust him. *Really* trust him. No pressure. I would use my scant savings to get a bedsit and then use Nathan's help to get the business back on its feet. I could get to know him a bit better. Maybe tell him about my disease. No need to decide for a while. I would think about it.

But of course, deep down, I had already decided to go.

Chapter Nineteen

Sommy rushed into the hut, a look of worry on his face, his words tumbling out.

"Mr. Nathan. He gone."

Pierre casually got up, thinking he had just gone off for a sulk. He peeked into Nathan's hut and then raced out, heading to the road. Sommy and I rushed to join him, to see what he was doing. I had a bad feeling.

The streets were still wet from the heavy rain, mud forming by its sides. Pierre urgently spoke to a few locals if they had seen him, a white tourist. They talked quickly, motioning down the road, waving their hands in the direction of the beyond.

"He's gone in a taxi. Nothing we can do," shrugged Pierre as he walked back to us, looking over his shoulder. "He's a big boy. Come."

He beckoned us back to the courtyard.

"Shouldn't we go and find him?"

"Ha! How?" Pierre scoffed. "You want to go around the island? It takes ten hours round trip. Longer with the rains."

"We could try airport," Sommy said, helpfully. Cheerfully even.

"Yeah, we could go to the airport. Talk some sense into him."

"Maybe he doesn't go there," Pierre said. "Maybe he made a detour and he isn't there when we arrive. Even if he is there. And then what? Beg him back? Too many options. No, I think we leave him to do what he wants. We don't control him, he controls his destiny. No?"

I felt uneasy at us leaving him, without even trying, with a black cloud over our heads.

"If anything happens to him, I'll blame you."

Pierre raised his hands in defiance. "Not me. You can't blame me for his actions."

"I can blame you for your inaction. What happened to the fish you threw back in the sea? Isn't Nathan a fish that needs to be thrown back? He could be gasping for air."

He considered this for a moment and looked over at Sommy. Then cocked his head.

"Sommy. What do you think?"

"I think Mr Pierre is right. I also think Ms Jasmine is right."

"Well, that's helpful," I spat.

"Please, wait," Pierre said to me, his palm laid flat. He walked slowly over to the Thai man.

"What do you think is right?"

"I think Mr Nathan is very troubled man," he said softly. "Many conflictions inside his head." He flicked his eyes to me.

"What do you mean?" I asked, innocently.

"Oh, please Jasmine. It's so obvious. He's in love with you," the Frenchman spluttered.

"No, he isn't," I shook my head to get the thought out. "No."

"Why is it such a surprise? Those words he said, only someone with affection will say this."

"Affection maybe. Love no. He knows about me. Everything. What I did. He couldn't possibly love me." I felt disgusted that someone could fall in love with me who knew all the things I had done.

"And yet he does," said Sommy, in perfect English, almost to himself, barely a whisper. He looked at me with a knowing twinkle in his eye.

"Sommy?" catcalled Pierre. "What do you know? What have you two been talking about, huh?" Sommy just smiled his goofy smile, his bristly moustache stretching over his top lip, shaking his head slowly. The attention was suddenly on him.

"Sommy!" I said, playfully.

Pierre joined in. "Come on! Speak up Somchai!"

"Inshallah," he responded quietly.

Part Three

Somchai

For the first time in years, Somchai hadn't slept. His mind was whirring, going back two decades, trying to remember. When Pierre had passed him the phone, the voice on the other end had taken him completely by surprise.

How was it possible? His brother, alive, and with Mr. Nathan in Bo Hin?

Nothing and no one could have survived the effects of that Tsunami. The scene of devastation in his homeland was absolute. That's why he moved on. Away from the desperation and looking for hope.

He met Mr Pierre when he was bumming around in Bali years later – no job and nowhere to live. Even though they didn't speak the same language, he was instantly charmed. Maybe it was his kind eyes. Maybe it was his energy. Maybe it was his spirit that appealed to him. When Mr Pierre couldn't properly say his name 'Somchai' and used 'Sommy' instead, it made him laugh. The first time in a very long time. Probably since before the wave hit the shore.

He had never thought about going back to Thailand. Why? There was nothing there, only trauma and memories. Now he was jolted back to the place because of Mr Nathan. He had had many conversations with him when he stayed in Bali – just the two of them whilst Mr Pierre was busy wooing Ms Jasmine. And Mr Nathan had been so jealous. Somchai didn't ask about his past but something was stopping him from telling her, to let her know what he really thought. It was like he was afraid. Which was stupid. Life was too short to hold things back, especially big things like love.

When Somchai had drawn a rudimentary map of Thailand in the sand and pointed out Bo Hin, never would he have thought Mr Nathan would go there. He hoped that he had opened his heart during his journey and fate had led him to his brother, safe and well. His chest swelled with pride at thought of his brother, Mee Noi, a policeman. Official and respected. Putting bad guys away and restoring law and order. He tried to picture him in a Thai police uniform but could only picture a young teenager in an oversized beret and shirt dangling off his body.

Yes, he felt good. Mr Nathan was okay and he knew his brother was not only alive but a policeman. A boy who was now a man - had turned something as bad as abject tragedy into something good.

Yes, his brother had done the family name proud.

Chapter One

The old Mercedes rattled and spluttered to a stop. Somchai swung the door open whilst leaning over to the passenger side, gathering up plastic bags of supplies and food. He walked quickly into the courtyard, the handles cutting into his hands. Pierre and Jasmine were standing next to each, both facing him, their faces white and concerned.

Has someone died?

Faces raced through his mind.

Maybe they have decided to sack me.

It was about three months since Nathan had disappeared from Bali and since then, Pierre and Jasmine had become lovers. Jasmine had decided to stay and help with their work. He didn't mind, he liked the English lady who looked like she was from India.

Somchai had thought there might be a time when they didn't need him anymore.

Pierre walked gingerly towards him and put an arm around his shoulders, like a father to a son. He towered above him and moved him forward, towards Jasmine.

"Sommy," he began. Somchai held his breath. "We just had a phone call from Nathan. He's in Bo Hin." A mixture of pride and nausea waved over him at the same time.

Mr Nathan had gone to my hometown?

It hadn't occurred to him that Nathan would go there. He felt privileged that he would. Pierre was talking but Somchai wasn't listening. He was picturing Nathan in Bo Hin. He wasn't sure what was still there as he hadn't ever returned – the rescue services never let him. He wondered if the old monastery was still standing – the only landmark of note in the area. Pierre was shaking him on the shoulder, bent down and looking in his eyes.

"Do you understand?" he was saying, slowly and deliberately. Somchai shook his head confused.

"Your brother," he said. "He is alive." Somchai looked up at Pierre's eyes. A moment of wonder and confusion. When his mind computed the word 'brother', his legs buckled under him.

"Not p-p-p-ossible," he managed to say.

"He is going to call," Pierre said, motioning his hand into a telephone. "In about 30 minutes. Your brother." He smiled, a perfect line of white teeth formed against his tanned face, his hand affectionately squeezing Sommy's shoulder.

"My brother?" Somchai repeated confusion all over his face. "Not possible. He dead."

"No Sommy, he's with Nathan. In Bo Hin." Somchai felt his face drain, eyes darting all over the place, trying to figure out the permutations of how he could have survived.

"How?"

"I don't know. We can ask him when he calls."

Jasmine spoke next, softly. "How did Nathan know?"

"We talk long into night," he said. "Talk about my home. My childhood. Bo Hin. The Tsunami. Talk about you."

"Me?" Jasmine said in surprise.

"Yes, he love you very much."

"That's impossible," she said.

"You see? What is more possible? A dead brother alive after many years or man who loves woman? He not know how to talk to you. About his feelings. I not know why. I think he had very bad past relationship. He scared to open his heart." Jasmine looked down on the sandy floor and raked the sand with her toes.

"He very upset when he argue with Ms Jasmine. I think he go back to England. Now Mr Nathan find Bo Hin and later find my brother? Seem impossible. What he knows what he look like? It mistake. No possible."

Somchai shook his head. He had already laid his brother to rest in his mind, grieved, offered thanks and moved on. There wasn't room in his head, or his heart, to open old wounds, only for them to be dashed.

But somewhere deep within him, lurking in some godforsaken corner of his mind, there was a glimmer of hope, a tiny ember of possibility. He only wished it wouldn't be extinguished before it had time to catch.

There was only one way to find out.

In 30 minutes.
Inshallah.

Chapter Two

The phone trilled and Pierre picked it up before the first ring ended.

"Nathan?"

"Yeah, Pierre, it's Nathan. Is Sommy with you?"

"Yes, yes." He passed the ancient phone to Somchai who was standing right beside him, his hands on his hips, looking intently at the receiver. Jasmine stood by with a chair. He hesitated and Pierre shoved it into his hand. Lifting the receiver to his ear, he shifted uncomfortably on his feet.

"Hello?"

"SOMMY! Thank God. Hold on."

"Mr Nathan?"

The next voice on the phone had a Thai voice. It sounded gruff, unconvinced and questioning. It spoke a fast Thai dialect. Somchai spoke rapidly back. Back and forth like a game of ping-pong, trying to find the truths. A song came through the phone, out of tune and gravelly. Then Somchai stumbled backwards, the receiver dropped to the floor. Pierre, ready and waiting, grabbed hold of him as Jasmine expertly shifted the chair underneath him as he fell, his face pale. She reached out and held his shaking hand. Pierre picked up the receiver.

"Nathan?" It was the Thai man on the other end of the phone who responded. He quickly passed it back to Somchai who fumbled to find his ear. He spoke and waited, spoke and waited. Nodding and smiling a sad smile. Pierre had never seen a tear fall from Somchai's eye before and now they were uncontrollable, flowing down his cheeks. Pierre signalled to Somchai they would wait outside and he nodded, squeezing the receiver closer to his ear.

Ten minutes later, the door creaked open and Somchai's face peeked around. Tears stained his cheeks. He looked so youthful. A child in a man's body.

Pierre jumped up out of his chair and embraced him, smothering his slight frame in his big arms.

"Breathe, my friend. Breathe."

"Was it really him?" Jasmine said, eyes alight.

Somchai pulled back and nodded.

"It him."

Pierre put his hands on his shoulders.

"Do you feel good?"

"I feel...," Somchai stuttered. "I feel confused... and happy. In the medical camps, with the big tents, I see television of Thailand. Everything gone. All homes gone. People dead. Dying in cot next to mine."

He sniffed.

"It not possible," he said shaking his head. "How he survived."

"It's a miracle," Pierre said, grasping his hand. He turned to Jasmine.

"When I was in Thailand, I visited the Tsunami Museum. There is a police boat there. It was out at sea guarding the Royal family. About 2 kilometres off-shore." As always, Jasmine was in awe at his travelling stories.

"After the Tsunami, it was two kilometres inland. Those waves man, those waves carried this boat four kilometres, two of them overland. The waves travelled at 500 miles per hour. Do you know what else travels at 500 miles per hour?"

Jasmine shook her head.

"An aeroplane. Those waves moved as quickly as a jumbo jet. It's no surprise the land was flattened and many people died. Sommy was carried inland too until the waves calmed and he could stand up. It took the rescue teams days to reach that area and set up camps. Sommy stayed there for months, trying to find his family, hoping that they were in one of the thousands of tents."

"So many people," Somchai chimed in. "Many children like me, no family. No mother or father." Pierre reached over and squeezed his knee. "I thought they dead. Too many days go past."

"Did you ask him how he survived?"

"He said he climb tree, holding on. When water pass he look for me. Look for mother, father, sister. No find. Sleep in monastery with other people. Keep searching and then give up." He looked down as he stroked the sand with his feet. "I was far away. Water take me far away." Somchai hung his head.

"It's not your fault," Pierre said, putting his arm across his shoulders. Sommy looked up and cocked his head, not believing it.

Silence washed over them.

"Mee Noi policeman now. In Sikao District. He in charge of police!" His back straightened proudly. Pierre's eyes lit up. It seemed an idea was forming.

"So, what happens now?" Jasmine asked. Somchai shrugged his shoulders.

"We talk again tomorrow. Same time."

Pierre looked him up and down and then to Jasmine, a schoolboy grin across his face.

"How about we *see* him tomorrow?"

Somchai looked up, curiously.

"How about we fly today? Now! All of us. Go to Thailand.

His eyes danced; a fire lit within. Jasmine too had a huge beam on her face. Somchai made to protest.

"No excuses Sommy. I pay. We've got enough saved up." He made to go but Somchai leapt forward and wrapped his arms around Pierre's waist, burying his head in his chest.

"Thank you, Mr Pierre," he said, his eyes full of water.

"Only if you are okay with it. With going back."

"I'm ready, *inshallah*," he said.

"Carpe Diem!" Pierre cried out loud, scooping both of them in his arms and to the huts. "Not a moment to lose!"

Chapter Three

The trio had driven to Denpasar airport in the battered Mercedes, screeching around corners and beeping every slow-moving truck in their way. They rushed inside, hoping to get a flight to Thailand as quickly as possible. They would then figure out how to get to Bo Hin once they were on the ground. As luck would have it, a flight to Bangkok's Don Mueang, the city's second airport, was two hours from departure. They rushed to the gate and boarded the plane, settling down in the scratchy seats.

When the plane was airborne, Somchai just gazed out of the window at the sea below, his mind whirring. He thought how peculiar life was. If he hadn't met Mr Pierre, then he wouldn't have met Mr Nathan. If Mr Nathan hadn't gotten jealous of Mr Pierre, then he wouldn't have had the argument. If they hadn't argued, he wouldn't have gone to Bo Hin. If he hadn't gone to Bo Hin, he wouldn't have found his brother. And he wouldn't be flying through the sky going to see him.

As Somchai sometimes did, his mind travelled back over fifteen years to when the Tsunami hit. The day before, he and his older brother had been hawking souvenirs and towels to the white-skinned tourists, as they always did along the beach in Bo Hin during the school holidays. They had woken early that next morning, playing marbles when Mee Noi noticed the sea had disappeared. Then came a distant rumble, then shouts and screams, people yelling to get off the beach. Without thinking, they had just followed everyone else, running like their lives depended on it, not knowing why. In the chaos, they had been separated.

Two paths leading to two separate lives.

When he snuck out of the refugee camp, Somchai had travelled south, through Malaysia and Singapore. He went where the wind took him – jumping on the back of fruit trucks, stowing behind crates, hitchhiking through the jungle – not knowing where he was going or for how long, stealing food as he went. His boyish charm had got him out of many a sticky situation.

Fate kept him moving. On and on.

Until fate led him to a Frenchman.

As the plane descended over the green and browns of his homeland, he thought about Mr Pierre, who had been more than a friend. He had been a father to him. As generous as he was patient, as charming as he was caring. He always treated him like an equal. Except Somchai was younger than him. There was respect for his elders and he would maintain that. Of course, he would never forget his real father. He still held fond memories of him and thought of him often – bringing in the fish to sell at the market, helping him get ready for school, giving affection to his mother.

But that was then, and this is now.

Mr Pierre had taught him English and provided food for his belly.

Mr Pierre had given him purpose and motivation.

Mr Pierre had taught him respect for the ocean.

The ocean which killed his family.

Sometimes you are the trawler. Sometimes you are the fish.

But sometimes, you can be the saviour.

That is life.

Chapter Four

T he sky was a beautiful mix of oranges and reds as they rushed off the plane to the numerous check-in counters in the vast and gleaming departure hall in Bangkok. They split up to find how best to get to either Krabi or Trang airports. It was Somchai who ran the length of the concourse waving for their attention, cutting them off mid-conversation with the airline clerks helping them.

"I found flight. Tonight!" he cried as they hurriedly followed him to the check-in desk. Somchai chatted quickly in Thai whilst the attendant rattled away on her keyboard, staring intently at the screen. Her lips were painted a bright red and she wore a little navy hat on top of a tight bun. Somchai turned to the expectant couple.

"Flight in 30 minutes. Just after midnight." he beamed. "To Krang."

The woman swivelled in her chair and got up, reaching over to a printer that had spat out some paper. She glanced over it, turned it around and slid it across the counter. Somchai pushed it over to Pierre as he reached into his pocket and pulled out a wad of cash. Jasmine stared at the form, the squiggles of Thai writing and the English words underneath. She fingered it, turning it slightly.

"Sommy," she said pointing at the top of the page. "Is that the right date?" He looked at it and spoke rapidly to the woman. She rolled her eyes in frustration, took the paper back gently and tapped furiously on the keyboard. She scanned her screen, shaking her head. She spoke back to Somchai, who crumpled his shoulders.

"That flight was for midnight, the next day," he said, pointing at the discarded paper. "No more seats on next midnight flight." Pierre threw his arms up in frustration as Jasmine turned away. Somchai spoke again as she tapped her keyboard. She turned the screen towards him and pointed.

"Tomorrow 6 a.m., next flight. To Krabi." He translated.

"That's good!" Pierre exclaimed. "Let's take it." He handed over the cash to Somchai who carried on the conversation.

"No point going into the city for a hotel. Nasty place. Looks like we're sleeping on a bench tonight," he said, glancing at Jasmine to make sure that was alright.

"Oh, I've had worse," she said, looking up at the high ceiling and warm lights.

***

As the plane taxied to the stand in Krang, Somchai looked out of the window at his homeland. Thailand was just like Bali, only flatter. No volcanos or mountains – just land and sky punctuated by swaying palm trees. They ran down the steps of the plane across the tarmac, a heat haze rising in the distance as the temperature rose. The single, squat terminal had little security for a regional airport, and it being an internal flight, they breezed through and into an idling minibus taxi waiting for fares. It ambled through the rural streets, the driver in no hurry despite protests from Somchai, talking urgently and quickly. The roads were just like Bali too, only smoother. It wasn't long before the gentle humming of the engine sent Jasmine to sleep on Pierre's shoulder as the trees and power lines trundled past.

The taxi pulled into an open space on the side of the road. A burnt-out shell of a building, or two buildings, stood derelict. An eerie feeling suggested it wasn't long ago that a fire took place. Somchai's thoughts returned to 2004: homes, businesses, lives destroyed, changed forever. They all surveyed the scene, staring out of the window before he tapped the driver on the shoulder and motioned him to turn down a single-file road. It led to a glorious view of the sea before turning inwards. An opening appeared: On one side a giant brick wall loomed across the area, on the other shacks selling food and fruit and to the side, a bushy tree stood tall – a smattering of locals crouched in its shade. Wide-eyed, Somchai pointed to the brick wall.

"Monastery. Very old." He was amazed it was still standing.

Somchai slid open the minibus door and stepped out. Hot air rushed in, overpowering the aircon. Pierre and Jasmine followed, looking around like they had stepped onto an alien planet. The men under the tree watched their every move.

The minibus drove off, kicking up dust in its wake.

"Do you know them? I mean, do you recognise them from ...," Jasmine said, looking over to the group.

"No, I don't think," Somchai replied.

"Are you sure you want to do this?"

"Sure," Somchai said nodding his head determinedly.

"They might know where your brother is?"

They walked over to the men. They started chattering to him in Thai, wildly gesticulating with their arms.

"No. They say he come now and again. To collect money," Somchai said, his shoulders sagging. A look of despondency etched all over his face.

"Oh man," sighed Pierre as he turned his head towards the monastery. He flicked it back quickly, tugging his ear.

"What about Nathan? Do they know where he is?" Somchai talked quickly and they all pointed to the monastery in unison.

Pierre was off, dragging Sommy and Jasmine by their hands before they had time to think.

Ignoring the humidity, they jogged around the stone wall until the beach opened in front of them. They slowed to take it in, walking towards the sea as if magnetically drawn to it. Somchai turned to look back at the monastery, seeing the big V-shaped hole in the wall. He stopped in his tracks, causing the other two to turn. They all looked up at it in wonder – a relic from the formidable force of the Tsunami. Pierre was the first to climb the rubble at its base, gently running his fingers along the edge as he walked through. The other two followed. The courtyard within was quiet. Then a bell rang inside, cracking the peace. A rumble of footsteps followed. Children ran out, of all different shapes and sizes, some with missing limbs, some hobbling on one leg balanced with a wooden stick under their supporting arm.

"No way," Jasmine said out loud. As if on cue, an average-height white man with a crew-cut haircut, tanned wearing a dirty t-shirt and shorts came out, a child under each arm, playfully struggling to escape, closely followed by a pear-shaped white woman with scraggy shoulder-length brown hair, tanned wearing a dirty pink vest top and shorts.

"NATHAN!" squealed Jasmine at the top of her voice, causing all the children to freeze in their tracks and look at her. She waved her arm high above her head. Nathan carefully placed the children down on the ground and walked tentatively towards her and they gently hugged. Pierre patted him on the back whilst they were in their embrace. Sommy beamed at them all as children started to gather around their legs. Nathan released himself from her grip and put both his hands on Somchai's shoulders. Then he hugged him like a bear, pinning the poor man's arms to his side. The other woman approached them and put out her arm toward Jasmine.

"Hi, I'm Rachel," she said. "I've heard all about you." Jasmine cautiously took her hand, cocking her head, hoping not *all* about her. She looked at Pierre.

"You must be Pierre," she said, slightly less enthusiastically, extending her arm towards him.

"Why are you British so formal?" he said as he grabbed her into a big hug. "We are all friends here, right?" Rachel squirmed out of the hug and looked at Somchai.

"Nice to meet you," she said, offering her hand which Somchai gently shook. She squinted her eyes as if to make them blurry. "Yeah, I can see it. The eyes. The moustache. Perhaps even the cheeks. How long has it been?"

"Sixteen years." It was Nathan that answered.

"You know where he is?" Somchai asked tentatively.

"He'll be here later. He said he was coming here to phone you. For some reason, he wanted to do it with me."

"The villagers, he say he ask for money. Is he bad man?" he said softly. Nathan glanced at Rachel, a tell-tale sign that the others took to mean 'yes'.

"Look, a couple of days ago something bad happened. Did you see the burnt-out buildings? Well, he's an angry man Sommy. He's been through a lot. He has done a lot of bad things yes, to the villagers. To Rachel. To me." He let it hang in the air.

"I am sorry for my brother's actions," he said, bowing his head and clasping his hands together. Rachel shook her head in disbelief, sucking her teeth. Nathan glanced at her and narrowed his eyes.

"It's true. It's not you who should be apologising Sommy. Since he spoke to you, he has mellowed. I thought maybe you two talking would help him. I think *seeing* you will make a huge difference. Sometimes all of us need a spark to start the process of healing, of being a better person." He quickly glanced his eyes to Jasmine and back.

"Can we get a drink?" Rachel interjected, an annoyance in her voice.

"Yeah, I'm famished," Jasmine replied, easing the pressure. "Let's catch up whilst we wait."

They all walked back around the stone wall to the shacks. The shopkeeper brought out six cold Coke bottles with the tops off. He conversed with Somchai in Thai and led him to sit under the Bili tree, the sun now high in the sky. A Thai couple slunk around the corner, not much older than them, their heads drooped low. Somchai raised his eyes at them, dropped his Coke bottle on the floor and the brown liquid glugged out. He leapt up and ran over to them, skidding to a halt in front of them. He spoke and then the woman wrapped her arms around his neck. The man too enclosed them with a hug. Somchai brought them to the group, together with the Pais he had been speaking to. Rachel shifted uncomfortably, looking away, as they got closer. Somchai introduced Pierre and Jasmine to them.

"She my friends. From before Tsunami. I thought she dead too," he said beaming, like a kid who had just found a forgotten stash of chocolate. Pierre stood and greeted them by bowing his head, clasping his hands and putting his nose on his thumb, all in one swift movement. Jasmine copied and the couple returned the greeting. They turned to Somchai and chitchatted with him. Occasionally she would rub his arm and stroke his cheek like she had to touch him to make sure he was real. The shopkeeper stood nearby, listening in. They were talking fast, recounting the lost years. Their faces suddenly turned sour, as did his. The westerners just watched the exchange, sipping their cokes, in silence. Suddenly, the woman started waving her arms, her voice getting louder and angrier, tears forming in her eyes. He husband put a consolidatory arm around her shoulder as she spoke, eventually breaking down. Somchai stood there watching, mouth agape.

An engine hummed in the near distance, taking their attention. Nathan turned his head to the sound. A police car rode around the corner, the lights extinguished on its roof, a badge adorned its side, Thai writing above and below it. Everyone watched it in silence, and everyone stood up, as it idled next to the group. The door swung open and Mee Noi stepped out. Jasmine and Pierre were wide-eyed. Rachel took a step back behind Nathan. Somchai stood stock still staring at the man exiting the car.

Energy fizzed through his veins.

Could it be?

His brother.

Mee Noi stared back, leaning against the open car door like it was a scene in the Wild West – a stand-off, who would blink first. It was Somchai's eyes that filled with water. Mee Noi took a tentative step forward and they stood facing each other, staring into each other's eyes, as if looking for answers right in their soul.

They were the same height. They had the same buzz-cut hairstyle. Their skin was the same shade of dark brown. The length of their moustaches was the same.

Side-by-side, it was unmistakable.

Sixteen years apart, they were so similar, yet so different.

"It's like the Gates of Heaven," Jasmine whispered to Nathan.

"Two peas in a pod," he grinned as he finished his Coke.

Mee Noi's face crumpled. His eyes pinched closed as if feeling a pain deep within. His body started to shudder and Somchai reached out and embraced him.

A warm, comforting hug that released a spirit into the air.

One which had waited sixteen years to escape.

As if in response, the palm trees shook, the birds sang, and the heat warmed their skin.

Epilogue

J ess struggled to get into Starbucks, her back pushing the heavy door open, pulling a bulky buggy behind her. The sky was overcast and grey, threatening a drizzle. She sighed and took a quick look around the crowded café. Rachel was waving frantically at her, an arm high in the air. Jess smiled and wearily pushed the buggy through the maze of chairs, bags and other prams. Rachel stood up, her glowing arms ready and waiting for a huge hug. They squeezed each other tightly.

"My god you are so tanned!" Jess said excitedly, looking Rachel up and down. "You look fabulous! And so healthy! What did you eat?!" Rachel laughed and blushed at the compliment.

"Pretty much fresh fruit all day every day," she said, patting her stomach. "And you look great too!"

"Oh, shut up Rach, I know when you're lying."

Rachel couldn't stop beaming at seeing her friend. She'd arrived back the previous day and, after calling her mum and dad, the next person on the list was Jess who wanted to meet up immediately to hear about all her tales.

"Let me get a drink and you can tell me all about your backpacking adventures!" She grabbed a purse out of the bottom of the buggy and flicked her straight blonde hair as she got up. "You want anything babe?"

"Yeah, please. Whatever you're having."

She peered into the buggy at the sleeping baby, who didn't look so much like a baby anymore.

"God, she has grown so much!" she said as Jess disappeared to join the queue. Rachel couldn't believe the size of Natty. Had she been away that long?

Almost a year.

She thought about everything that she'd done: the travelling, the towns and cities, the beaches, Nathan, the kids in the monastery, the fire, and then meeting Pierre and Jasmine. Especially Jasmine, who grew to be like a big sister. The long talks around the fire, just the two of them, woman to woman.

Now in London, Rachel felt she'd completely changed. A different person. When she arrived back, she expected to see things to have changed too. But the only different things were the betting shop had closed and a Tesco Express had opened on the corner. Even Jess looked the same. Life just carried on.

Jess came back, placed her mug on the table and checked in on Natalie, who was sound asleep.

"I can't believe how big Natty is," she said, as Jess settled herself.

"I know! She's a little terror now. Crawling around, opening cupboards, putting everything in her mouth. I swear she's going to say her first word. Any time now." Rachel imagined the baby crawling around Jess' mum's flat.

"Right. So, tell me all about it. And I mean all the bits you wouldn't tell your mum." Rachel leaned back, mug in her hands.

"I don't know where to start really."

"How about this: Did you meet anyone?" Jess said, her eyes alight.

"Oh, we're starting there are we?!" Rachel said as they both giggled. "Actually, yes I did." Jess squealed in excitement, a bit of gossip on the horizon.

"Yes! A bit of hunky holiday romance. Tell me, tell me."

Something ran through Rachel's head.

"Hold on a minute. Did *you* meet someone?" Jess' pale skin went a bright red.

"Yes! Alright, yes! I wanted to hear about you first."

"That's brilliant Jess! I'm really pleased! No, you first!"

"Oh, okay then. Yeah, he's great, he has a three-year-old. I met him at a kid's meet-up group for single parents. Which is basically real-life Tinder." She smiled what seemed like a desperate smile.

"Doesn't matter Jess! What his name, what does he do?"

"His name is Mo and he's a TV producer."

"How exciting!"

"Yeah, and mum and Jim like him too." She bent over in a conspiratorial whisper. "I think he might..." she looked left and right, "move in." Rachel squealed with delight.

"Oh Jess, I'm so happy for you!" She got up and reached across the table and hugged her. Jess wriggled free.

"Okay, okay, enough about me. Tell me, tell me. How did you meet?" She picked up her mug and took a sip. Rachel noticed her fingernails were perfectly filed and coloured. Her skin radiated. She was genuinely pleased. Rachel took a deep breath.

"Well, I was in Thailand, on a bus heading south. We stopped at a shop in the middle of nowhere and in the middle of the night. Long story short, the bus went off without me." Jess gasped, covering her mouth.

"Yeah, I know. The owners of the shop took pity on me and let me sleep at their place. The next day I walked into town and there was this big monastery. It was damaged because of the Tsunami. Anyway, there were loads of kids in there, disabled, you know legs and arms missing." Jess gasped again, her hand still at her mouth.

"And this English guy was playing with them."

"Tall, dark and handsome?" Jess finished for her.

"Yeah, something like that. So, he sees me and comes over and introduces himself. Confident but not arrogant. I stayed with him in this hut on the beach. Hammock and everything."

"Oh yeah?"

"Not like that! I had the hammock. He slept on the sand."

Jess raised one eyebrow.

"Whatever!" Rachel said. "He was the perfect gentleman."

"Sounds idyllic!"

"Yeah, it was. Anyway," Rachel paused. She'd thought about how she might tell Jess. "Over time, I realised I knew him."

Jess' eyes grew bigger.

"Someone famous?"

"No," she replied, her face dropping. She looked down at her mug and raised her eyes. "Someone you know."

"Me?" she said, starting backwards.

"Yeah. That stalker guy you told me about. Nathan is his name. I thought I recognised him but didn't click. Then I worked it out." Jess's eyes narrowed, disbelieving.

"That's a hell of a story Rach. And a massive coincidence."

"Yeah, I know. I kinda thought it was a sign," Rachel said as she looked up to the ceiling.

"You and your God's plan. Like he has laid out some path for you."

"Yeah, well. I did say to him 'Jess said to say you're a wanker'." She burst out laughing.

"You didn't!"

"I did. And his face dropped like I punched him in the stomach." Jess giggled, until it subsided, shaking her head. She looked up suddenly.

"Wait. It's not him, is it? The person you fell for?"

Rachel nodded her head silently.

"For God's sake, Rach."

Rachel looked up suddenly.

"Of all the people in the whole world, the billions of people, you fell for the bloody stalker. And woman beater to add!"

"He's changed Jess. You should see him. He really has changed."

"Can a leopard really change his spots," she said as a statement, one eyebrow cocked, disbelieving.

Rachel thought back to Mee Noi, the transformation he had made when his brother came back into his life. His anger had vanished like a raindrop into the ocean.

"Yes," she replied softly. "If I have learnt anything on the trip, it was that people can change Jess. Really change. Not just Nathan, but other people too." Her eyes glazed over as she thought of Jasmine, Sommy, Mee Noi, Pierre and Nathan – what they had all gone through and become.

"Me too," she said as she wrapped her fingers around her mug. "There was a group of people who, through coincidence, fate, love or God, whatever you want to call it, we all came together in this place in the middle of nowhere. We had all gone through something traumatic, life-changing. There was this woman called Jasmine. Jesus, you think my life was bad. The things she'd gone through. And will go through. It's surprising she still carries on. She didn't want to love anyone, for fear of rejection, for fear of fear itself. But she fell in love. Head over heels. She won't be alone. I mean, we got on so well. And

Sommy and his brother. They survived the Tsunami. Survived it when so many people died – their friends and family. They hadn't seen each other for sixteen years. They both thought the other was dead. And Nathan brought them together. And Pierre, this Frenchman who started some project in Bali to try to bring coral and fish back to the sea – well his wife died of leukaemia."

Jess looked dumbstruck as the words spilled out – all these names and stories. Rachel would have to fill her in on the details another time. For now, this bit was important.

"He has changed Jess. I mean I didn't know him like you did. But there is no way the man I met was the person you described. He did his time. When Jasmine met him, she said he was a shell of a man. Wouldn't say boo to a goose. Boy, he regrets it. And now he helps others and is such a lovely man. Confident, happy, shining. Genuine.

"Do you honestly believe he's changed?"

"Yeah, I do."

"It's your life Rach, I want you to be happy. Be careful that's all. You were probably caught up in it all. Holiday romance you know. Palm trees, sandy beaches…"

"…I know what you think," Rachel interrupted. "It wasn't a holiday. It was bigger than that. It's such a cliché, but I found myself. And he found me."

Jess rolled her eyes picking up her mug. Rachel glanced to Natty, sleeping in her pram as she thought back to the wonderful kids at the orphanage, smiling and laughing without a care in the world.

"I think I might want one, you know. Eventually." Rachel ran her hands over her belly, over the scar. She had told Nathan everything, how she was so excited to have the baby despite the circumstances and then the stillbirth. He listened and told her everything would be alright. She believed him.

Jess sighed.

"Rach. That's great. I'm happy for you," she said flatly. "So, what happened then. Did he leave you? Did you leave him in paradise?"

"No," she said. "We came back together."

"What? He's here?" she said, turning around, and looking around the café.

"Not here, here. I didn't bring him. I wasn't sure you'd want to see him. Not yet anyway."

Jess shrugged her shoulders and wrapped her hands around her coffee mug.

"Look, I'm sceptical, right? I'm only hearing the potted, romantic version, and it all sounds wonderful and lovely. Everything happened so quickly with... stuff. You took off pretty much after the funeral. Just looking out for you, babe."

"I know. I really appreciate it. It might not be forever, but for now, I'm in a good place. Much better than where I was. And so is he. No one knows what's going to happen and I'm not expecting you to roll over and like him. Just give him a second chance."

Jess stared blankly at Rachel. Eventually, she shrugged her shoulders and sighed, shaking her head.

"It's your life babe. I'm here for you. Glad to have you back." She raised her coffee mug to chink.

It *was* good to be back. The familiarity and order of home, the love of her parents and Jess' friendship. Back in Thailand, it had been a bit awkward with Jasmine and Nathan but that had sorted itself out. In her opinion, Jasmine was too old for him anyway and Pierre was a much better match – a lot freer and flowing than he could ever be. Besides, Jasmine and Rachel just clicked, talking long and deep into the evening. She had never met someone who had been through so much and she had been so open with her story, and her many struggles, that it was entirely natural for her to reciprocate. Speaking out loud about her lost baby, Rachel felt baptised, as if talking washed away her guilt and made sense of everything. Like a weight off her chest.

Pierre, Sommy, Mee Noi and Nathan rebuilt the shop and cafe, although the Pais never looked at Rachel again. When it was restocked and ready to open, Nathan felt it was time to move on. And so had Rachel. Pierre and Jasmine went back to Bali to continue their eco-project whilst Sommy stayed with his brother in Bo Hin – his childhood home – and worked with Anurak in the orphanage.

Rachel and Nathan continued south to Malaysia and eventually into the clean, gleaming streets of Singapore. Wherever they went, they felt like strangers in someone else's country.

Traveller's fatigue, Rachel remembered.

It was time for them to go home.

As they flew over the snow-capped Himalayas, Rachel laid her head on Nathan's shoulder. He was flicking through photos on his phone. Instinctively, he stopped at the picture of a beautiful temple in Bali. Pierre, Sommy, Jasmine and Nathan were standing in front of a stunning volcano, framed between two giant, triangular stone gates. The one he showed Mee Noi.

"Check it out," Rachel said, in half a daze. "A widow, an orphan and a foreigner." She pointed at each of the figures in the photo.

Nathan looked up in confusion.

"You know, the fable."

Nathan shook his head.

"In the Bible? About looking after those in need."

"Don't know it."

"They go to the Gates of Heaven for redemption. And then the locals take them in. It shows love conquers everything, regardless of who you are, as long as you have faith."

Nathan puffed his cheeks out.

"Well, there's a coincidence. That temple is called The Gates of Heaven."

"No way! It's a sign, Nathan. God's Will!"

There was a silence between them. It was Nathan who spoke. Quietly.

"Do you think we've been redeemed?"

Rachel instinctively put her hand on her stomach and thought of the Pais.

"I don't know. How do we tell?"

Nathan took her hand in his and faced her.

"I don't know either. Pierre would say, it is within us. We are the only ones to judge our actions."

"Maybe it's when we've done something good. Like turned it around. Helped others, not just ourselves."

"I guess we only know when we've done it," Nathan said. "How we feel inside. I'm glad we are going home. I liked meeting Pierre, Jasmine and Sommy. Hearing their stories. I'll remember them forever."

"And me, I hope!"

"Of course, and you!" Nathan said as Rachel nestled her head in the crook of his neck.

"Maybe travelling isn't about visiting countries and going to that beach or this temple. It's meeting people along the way, who are different and understanding them. Which helps us understand ourselves."

"Maybe," Nathan said. "Maybe, we need that journey to find our purpose. For example, I want to help others. Not some rich CEO get even richer but those that need a lift or a hand to realise their potential. I think I can do it."

"I think you can. And I'll help you. Together."

"Inshallah," Nathan said softly.

"Eh?" Rachel said, screwing up her face.

"Inshallah. Sommy said it all the time. It's Arabic, for 'if Allah wills it'."

Rachel raised her eyebrows as Nathan turned and stared out of the airplane window, fluffy white clouds gliding by.

She squeezed his hand tightly.

God's Will.

Author's Note

Life is precious.

Most of us are still trying to figure that out, and it's not easy. With our daily demands, social media and our need to be busy we often forget it. Mental health awareness is growing strongly but we aren't anywhere near where we need to be. The illusion of money and success trumps the vulnerability and connection we crave.

During the first wave of the lockdown, I volunteered at a foodbank, where I met many people affected by a collapse of income and felt helpless in the face of Government restrictions and rules. I witnessed food literally going from hand to mouth as those people brave enough to step forward had a meal for the next few days. Covid didn't discriminate. It could have affected anyone in a myriad of different ways.

Whilst there, I was stunned at the number of volunteers who had been in that same position and were now giving back. They had been there and knew of the vital work charities and support groups do. And now was a time to give back. Many of the people whom I spoke to had fascinating stories far away from my sheltered life. My character, Jasmine, is an assembly of those people and I thank them for their honesty, kind hearts and vulnerability to speak as freely as they did.

All of Jasmine's tales are true.

One such volunteer made a big impact on me. He had been an addict, in and out of jail and liked to drink. He looked the part too – scratches on his arm, tattoos, shaved head and missing teeth. Someone whom I would cross the street on a dark night to avoid. Yet he was charming, warm and a realist. He had done bad and was now making amends. He was in a steady relationship with a woman who helped addicts, went on courses to learn new skills and had a job. One day he walked in with new trainers – for the first time he had bought his own pair. The excitement in his voice and face was palpable.

Less than a year later he was dead from a suspected heart attack, aged 35.

One can't help thinking that we are born into circumstance and fate then points its finger at you. A lost job, an erroneous decision, getting involved with the wrong type of people, a mistake. One sliding door moment can change everything. We never know where it might take us until it's too late.

Yet there is a shared commonality that we all have. We are all human. We all share this rock hurtling through the universe. No one is better or worse than the other. Circumstances have shaped who we are. We are all dealing with different things and those different things are harder for some than others.

And here's the crux — you'll never truly know what is harder for some than others.

You only live once.

And so does everyone else.

Be kind.

Dominic Wong
October 2022

Acknowledgements

I would like to thank the wonderful people who bought my first novel – The Opposite Sides of a Coin. Thank you for investing the time and energy to read it and provide such amazing feedback. I am truly grateful for your kind words and appreciate the efforts to raise awareness among others – whether that was through an Amazon review, a tweet or a recommendation. As an independent author, I thrive on reviews and people sharing my work.

Thank you to my friends and family who helped me shape the themes, characters and finesse the flow of this novel, providing ample enthusiasm and encouragement to keep going. I am indebted, again, to Sue Thomas for providing insights and considered feedback on early drafts, Allison Ray for detailed notes which improved so many aspects of this story, as well as my writing, and Julie Shaw and Vicki Willingham for final checks.

The inspiration for this novel came from the wonderful people I met at the foodbank during the lockdown. Without their honesty, Jasmine would not have existed and a big hole would still be gaping in the formation of the narrative. Thank you.

In between home-schooling, the foodbank and house-husbandry chores, I managed to write the first draft in six weeks. When I get the desire to write, I find it difficult to stop! Special thanks, therefore, goes to my wife, Erin Wong, who allowed me the freedom to close the door on an evening and get writing. My children continue to amaze, and inspire, me. Their creativity and resourcefulness know no bounds. Watching them grow up to be young men is a joy and I'm privileged to be such an active part of their lives.

Thank you to my mum and dad for their continued, unconditional love – whatever happens, whatever life brings, I know they've got my back.

About the Author

Dominic Wong is a multi-award-winning marketeer in the theme park and visitor attractions industry. He was the first marketing director at Warner Bros. Studio Tour London – The Making of Harry Potter, as well as Warner Bros. Studio Tour Hollywood and Warner Bros. World Abu Dhabi.

He has created and launched his own innovative tourism products, including a comedy dining theatre production, and advises several high-profile attractions with their marketing strategies across the globe.

He lives by the sea in Bournemouth, on the south coast of England, with his wife, two sons and energetic cocker spaniel.

The Same Sides of a Coin is his second novel.

www.DominicWongBooks.co.uk

Look out for the next exciting novel by Dominic Wong.

The Day I Tickled a Hedgehog

A caper about a bank robber with amnesia.

When Terry Higham wakes up in hospital sporting a thumping headache, he can't remember how he got there. Or who he is. Or how a holdall full of cash ended up at the bottom of his garden. Perhaps his daughter, Laira, and that nice detective can help him piece it all together.

After solving a stalking case, Detective Constable Josh Nicholson is fast-tracked up the echelons. Desperate to prove his worth, he takes on an impossible case: Renowned bank robber Terry Higham has just brought in a bag full of money but doesn't know a thing about it. Despite his superiors warning him to stay away, he's determined to solve it - even if it drives him mad.

"The premise is really, really good, original and belongs somewhere in the market."

Literary Agent

Be the first to know when the novel is released by joining the mailing list at DominicWongBooks.co.uk

Printed in Great Britain
by Amazon

20358006R00180